MIMI

MIMI

LUCY ELLMANN

BLOOMSBURY CIRCUS
LONDON · NEW DELHI · NEW YORK · SYDNEY

First published in Great Britain 2013

Copyright © 2013 by Lucy Ellmann

The moral right of the author has been asserted

No part of this book may be used or reproduced in any manner
whatsoever without written permission from the Publisher except in the
case of brief quotations embodied in critical articles or reviews

Every reasonable effort has been made to trace copyright holders of material
reproduced in this book, but if any have been inadvertently overlooked the
publishers would be glad to hear from them. For legal purposes the list of permission
acknowledgements on pages 340–1 constitute an extension of the copyright page

Bloomsbury Circus is an imprint of Bloomsbury Publishing Plc
50 Bedford Square
London
WC1B 3DP

www.bloomsbury.com

Bloomsbury Publishing, London, Berlin, New York and Sydney
A CIP catalogue record for this book is available from the British Library

ISBN 978 1 4088 3356 8

10 9 8 7 6 5 4 3 2 1

Typeset by Hewer Text UK Ltd, Edinburgh
Printed and bound in Great Britain by CPI Group (UK) Ltd, Croydon CR0 4YY

They work; but don't you think they overdo it?. . . And am I never to have a change of air, because the bees don't?

Charles Dickens, *Our Mutual Friend*

PRÉLUDE

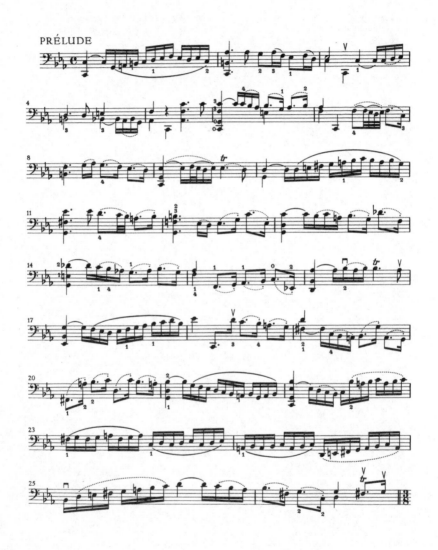

CHRISTMAS EVE, 2010

SO I WAS walking down Madison Avenue reading an article about some Italian reporter who claimed Philip Roth had said something mean about Obama. The guy had interviewed a whole lot of famous writers and they'd all said mean things about Obama and unanimously praised Berlusconi. But it was all BALONEY. The Italian reporter was probably just some louse in the pay of Berlusconi, one of the worst guys in the world.

It was at this point that I slipped on the ice at the corner of Madison and 36th, thereby transplanting myself in an instant from the realm of the lofty, vertical and intellectual to that of the lowly and prostrate. I blame the sun in my eyes. I slalomed for half a block, trying to grab hold of fire hydrants, golden poles and other injurious ironmongery, along with the recoiling calves of fellow pedestrians, my well-iced ass drawing me ever closer to the Christmas Eve traffic, that herd of the hopeless hurling themselves toward family get-togethers or finally giving in on the purchase of some exorbitant toy.

The Good News, I thought as I slid, was that there was now not the slightest chance of my backsliding *instead* into a half-hearted reconciliation with Gertrude, whom I had only just managed to discard—since even she would have to concede that I was now in no condition to present myself at the mass rally of the faithful currently stringing popcorn and glueing sequins on felt at Gertrude's Connecticut country cottage, in the annual effort to assuage her sense of having somehow missed out on something during her lonely if lavish childhood.

Deluded, our first year together, by the elation of conquest, I had actually helped with the decorations, standing at some personal peril on an antique stepladder to wrestle with garlands, or "garland" (as Gertrude perversely called them), miles of coiled strands of once-living foliage dotted with little white lights and big red velvet bows. These we distributed all over Gertrude's mansion (or "cottage") in carefully stage-managed fashion, leaving no architectural feature or Picasso print unemphasized. Receiving in return my very own gunky Christmas stocking made of organic hemp hessian adorned with locally carded wool gently shorn from the happiest of pedigree sheep, then dyed in such deep shades of carcinogenic crimson that your hands come out all pink and stinky when you delve in to get at the presents.

My solution to Gertrude's Xmas Xtravaganzas in the ensuing wearisome years was to put myself in charge of Eggnog production, turning it into a great art and making the stuff so goddam strong I could usually achieve a nauseous stupor before Gertrude noticed what was going on, entitling me to private porch time—where, if necessary, a guy can vomit into the bushes—a ritual marred only by the guests who followed me out there, and Gertrude's invariable questions concerning:

1. The number of mixing bowls used.
2. The number of days the whole alchemical procedure entailed.
3. The proliferation of abandoned egg whites.

For, to throw away spare egg whites would have shaken her already precarious handle on domesticity and Rombaueresque frugality. No holding her back on the Tiffany party-bags though, was there?—those pale blue offerings (otherwise known as guilt trips), bestowed on every blasted gadfly and flibbertigibbet she invited, and blindly accepted by them in conjunction with, but complete contradiction of, the egg-white omelettes and meringues.

Irma Rombauer was in fact responsible for my own Eggnog recipe, but I'd cranked it up a notch. Good old Irma, who had the whole nation swinging behind her there for a while, dressing up in checked aprons to open a million cans of mushroom soup, hash, canned *oysters* even! (Was nothing fresh in 1950?) There they were, saving those leftovers, planning Luncheons, making their One Minute Frosting, Ice Box Cookies, and Milk Toast for the recovering invalid (*did* they recover? on *that*?). Without Irma, none of us would have known what a vol-au-vent was, nor seen our mothers stuff old chicken scraps into one. And what about the dangers of undercooking… well, just about anything? King Spock and Queen Irma, our native pair of know-it-alls, who made a fortune telling everybody how to do it the easy way, from bedwetting to borscht.

Thus, by zigzagging horizontally down Madison Avenue I had saved myself many psychological and physiological torments in the wilds of Connecticut. The Bad News was that I was still on my ass in the gathering gloom, and in Manhattan a man without an upright position hasn't got a chance. Any minute now I'd freeze permanently to the sidewalk where the Jews and Muslims would find me Christmas morning—Cause of Death: sprained ankle. But I was underestimating New York. Of course there was a wacko broad ready to yank me up before checking if I'd broken anything.

"Ya can't sit there all day, buddy, looking up people's skirts," she declared.

"I was beginning to think that myself," I replied, as a firm, untrained hand inserted itself under each armpit from behind.

Once standing (gingerly) on one foot, I was able to inspect my savior—a plump middle-aged gal with brown eyes, and brown curls poking out of her Eskimo hood, her entire torso encased in one of those full-length puffy white numbers that imitate (or *are*?) bedding—before she plunged into the river of yellow cabs, apparently in order to hail me one. At 4:30, Christmas Eve! 3:30 *maybe*, 7:30 sure. But 4:30? "Ya gotta be kiddin', pal!" Time for all good Yemeni taxi-drivers to be home with their fretful families. Sometimes Manhattan goes parochial on you, not cosmopolitan at all but subject to strange suburban rites. The mask slips and you see … AMERICA lurking below, what you came to New York to get away from! So it was handy to have a fine example of a Manhattan madwoman on my side, ready to wade into Madison Avenue until a cab either stopped or ran her over, complete with her bags of touching Christmas treats: chocolate éclairs no doubt, or profiteroles maybe, to be consumed later in solitary squalor under the glare of her pet spider and the bare bulb needed to keep the thing alive.

It worked! Soon ensconced in the fetid folds of a taxicab and distracted by pain (acute), shock (temporary), hypothermia (imaginary), hypochondria (just the usual), and rudeness (innate), I failed to thank the woman. But the sight of her out the back window abruptly erased the sad sack impression I'd formed at first. With her circular face surrounded by fake fur, her pink cheeks radiant (in fact kind of *sweaty*) from her exertions on my behalf, and a slight smile forming on her lips, she now looked more like something Gertrude would cover with glitter and stick on top of the tree.

CHRISTMAS DAY

EQUIPPED WITH MY diagnosis (as I thought, sprained ankle), bandages, ice packs, a pretty premature physiotherapy advice sheet, and the few shreds of dignity that had survived all the doctor-as-patient jokes in the Emergency Ward, I slunk around my apartment like Smokey the Bear, weakened, depleted, a-prowlin' and a-growlin' and a-sniffin' the air. That I, Harrison Hanafan, an eminent New York plastic surgeon with a drawer full of affidavits from admiring patients attesting to my ingenuity and aesthetic awareness, should find myself floundering, CRAWLING ON THE GROUND! I was one of *them* now, the hapless, helpless, needy greedy unwell.

It suddenly seemed clear that I would never ascend Everest, or abseil down the Empire State Building, or fly to the moon—not soon anyway. I'd never be asked to pitch for the Yankees, never carry a bride across a threshold (unless quite a diminutive bride and a very straightforward threshold), I'd probably never be the President of the United States and/or a matador, might never manage to possess a fully equipped toolbox, or conquer athlete's foot once and for all, and my castration complex. Hell, I didn't even have the guts to order my usual Szechuan dishes from the take-out! My whole being was now focused on avoiding discomfort.

Half the man I was, I stuck close to home, further injuring myself, in a cruel cycle of fate, one incapacity leaving you peculiarly susceptible to others. Standing on a low shelf in my closet on my one good foot, in search of my sickbed hat (which has seen me through many a minor cold), I fell, wrenching my shoulder and incurring a cascade of shoeboxes upon my bare head. Having never cooked before (unless Eggnog and microwaving count), I incautiously boiled a baking potato, burnt my tongue tasting the half-raw result, then tried to purée the potato and mangled my thumb in the blender I'd never used before, necessitating a splint of my own devising. A Christmas repast worthy of Scrooge himself! With one functioning hand, one serviceable foot, aching shoulder, and burnt tongue, I called my big sister, Bee, in England.

"I boiled a baking potato, Bee."

"How's the foot?"

"Elevated. So is my thumb. And I'm wearing my sickbed hat. I look like some kind of crazed hitchhiker."

"This would never have happened if you rode a bike, Harry."

Cycling was Bee's solution to everything, and she was the business: Lycra, latex, Playtex (who knows?), helmet, water bottle, pump, puncture-repair kit, banana, raisins, energy bar, GPS, the whole deal.

"Oh, come on," I said. "Those guys don't last long in New York. They bus a new bunch in every day to make up for the ones that got flattened because they rode on the wrong side of the street and never used their lights. Anyway, it's *snowing* outside, Bee! Heavily."

"Where's Gertrude? Hasn't she turned the whole place into a sanatorium yet?"

"We broke up."

"*When?!*"

"A few weeks ago. But I've been working on it for some time."

"You *dumped* her?" she asked, struggling to picture my long-awaited rebellion.

"Dumped her, yes."

"Wow. Great!"

"And now she wants to Talk About It. She wants to review all the 'misunderstandings'. Ingratitude has been mentioned. Don't you hate break-up lingo? At first, it's all so merry: copping a feel, cutting me off a slice, perch and twirl, baby, bumping uglies, my main squeeze. Then all changes to: I'm dumping you. She's history. Creep. Slut. Asshole. Slimeball."

"Hey, does this mean *I* can call her an asshole now?" Bee asked sweetly. Bee had always been repulsed by Gertrude. And Bee was always right.

On hearing of my crippledom, Gertrude had indeed offered to desert her Connecticut crowd and come take care of me. But the fact that Claude, her son by parthenogenesis, had probably mastered English primarily in order to object to Gertrude's perpetually proffered nipples made her offer to come "nurse" me somewhat unenticing. There was actually nothing she could say that would have induced me to see her again voluntarily: in my head was a list about a mile long of things that woman did that bugged me.

REASON NO. 1: She's like a slug in your bed.

REASON NO. 2: Those teeth! It's like opening a freezer: you're blinded and chilled at the same time. Nobody ever jokes around with Gertrude for fear of eliciting that smile.

REASON NO. 3: That menagerie of hers. She's got pets climbing on the counters, hauling themselves up curtains, throwing their weight against closed doors, cantering across the walls, hibernating in the toilet, hanging upside down from clothes rails—and that's just the *goldfish*, desperate to escape their dank tank. Just think of the STINK that emanates from a whole nuthouse on the Upper East Side stuffed with cats, dogs, birds, reptiles, marsupials, amphibians (and their accompanying microbes), all of whom would gladly eat *each other* if left alone for a single moment. (Probably had an iguana in there too somewhere, inching his way towards my neck with savage claws.) One maid was employed solely as zoo-keeper, mopping the vomit and shoveling up a vast variety of turds. It was like a SAFARI, just going over there for lunch. I had to bring my own food, my own paper plates!

REASON NO. 4: Her fake hips. You might see her from behind, as I did, sauntering up 42nd Street, and think she had magnificent womanly hips, but you'd be wrong. Check her out from the side, bud: there's nothing there!

REASON NO. 5: Embroidery. There ain't world enough nor time to embroider cushions, honey, especially ineptly. Gertrude adorns handkerchiefs with mottoes, sews garish flowers on pillowcases, and issues plaques to commemorate joyous American holidays and baby names. The worst was a heart-shaped pincushion she made me sporting the date of our first encounter—the fact that this occurred on *September 11th* (2005), didn't deter her from celebrating it, but it did give me an excuse to hide the obscenity from public view. She also darns, and batiks without irony.

REASON NO. 6: She balls my socks, though I repeatedly *begged* her not to. Give the woman a sock and she'll stretch and twist it within an inch of its life. Her sock balls gave me the heebie-jeebies.

REASON NO. 7: Gertrude as a mother. Poor Claude (her latest pet) would have been called *Sweet Pea* if I hadn't intervened. But even I couldn't save him from the maniacal breast-feeding. A fine 8 lb. baby at birth, but Gertrude was so worried he'd starve to death, she emergency-crocheted a sort of harness that positioned the kid firmly against her chest, and this she wore, nonstop, for months. Okay, I too spend most of my days staring at the breasts of rich Manhattanites, but that baby-bra seemed detrimental to Claude's cognitive development. My opinion counted for nothing though—Gertrude was an expert on parenthood: she'd read an article in *Vogue*.

REASON NO. 8: Gertrude's perforated eardrum, caused (in her opinion) by *me*, all because I phoned her one day when she was getting out of the shower and she ran to answer the phone with a Q-tip in her ear. Was it my fault she'd arranged a doggy play-date that day and the place was awash with even more hairy hounds than usual tearing from room to room? (I bet there was a chinchilla involved somehow too—those little guys get around!) So Gertrude fell, the Q-tip perforated her eardrum, and *I'm* in the doghouse, even though I rushed to her aid and got her the best ENT guy in the business! Okay, it was painful, but that doesn't entitle her to warn everyone who'll listen: "Anybody dumb enough to be Harrison's girlfriend shouldn't use Q-tips." It is not up to Gertrude to dissuade people from sleeping with me, nor from removing ear wax.

The final straw, REASON NO. 9: Her job as an arts administrator. Gertrude's one of those rich women who suddenly decides she needs a job, so she steals one off somebody who really does need a job. Once installed high up in the New York arts hierarchy, she proceeded to exert unwarranted power over the lives and work of people she never undertook to comprehend. A staunch proponent of the caprice, Gertrude saw to it that handsome librettists had it made, while other, less "fabulous", writers, musicians, composers, artists, and film makers had their progress slowed or halted—especially if they were female and no fun to flirt with. The woman sought power, and executed it, with philistine zeal.

So why did I ever suggest to my sister, a sculptor, that Gertrude might be able to help her? It was I who invited Bee up to Connecticut for one of our painful weekends. Bee had never been before and had never wanted to go, but came this once, to sleep an uncomfortable night in a pre-Revolution four-poster and endure the sight of Gertrude knee-deep in the ivy grove. Gertrude would always jump straight into a billowy dress as soon as we arrived and go get some grass stains on it to prove how in tune with nature she was. The whole place was maintained by a fleet of full-time gardeners but Gertrude always made a big show of wandering dreamily through the dawn to fetch me something "real" for breakfast, usually coming back with one malformed carrot she'd picked up somewhere. She wouldn't have known where her fruit trees were if you asked her, and wouldn't have been caught *dead* feeling for an egg under one of her prize hens. But she could talk burdock, dandelion, and lovage soup at you all day if you let her.

By the time Bee asked that evening about the possibility of any grants or public projects she could apply for, Gertrude had spent an ecstatic afternoon among the ferns and the fairies, and answered in full Marie Antoinette dairymaid mode: "But why do you need a grant, Bridget? Why not just live more simply? You could grow vegetables... Who needs fancy stores when you can grow your own asparagus? That grows really well, once you get it started, which only takes about five years. And flowers from the garden are just as good as florists flowers."

"I don't think buying flowers' is Bee's major concern, Gertrude."

"We have everything we need here, don't we, Harrison?" she went on.

"Huh?"

"Olallieberries, juniper berries, jicama, fiddlehead ferns..." (I think she might even have mentioned those chickens, the hypocrite.)

"Bee doesn't own any land, Gertrude."

"But even in an apartment, you could have a window box!" she told Bee delightedly.

Pushed near the limit of endurance, Bee replied, "How self-sufficient am I supposed to get with a window box?"

"In Queens?" I added.

"Oh, herbs grow really well in window boxes," Gertrude assured us, and there followed an endless monologue on every herb Gertrude had ever grown, every wild flower she'd ever picked, watercress this and water mint that, and the infinite culinary uses to which they had been, or could have been, or should have been, put—except in dishes containing fish of course, for Gertrude had never really cared for fish... "I can eat a little tuna sometimes, if it's cooked just right, but they so often overcook it! You wouldn't dare overdo a steak in a good restaurant but there seems to be no consensus on how to cook tuna. It's a real gamble."

Was she being deliberately obtuse, or just plain dumb? I could never be sure.

REASON NO. 48: Gertrude's efforts as a conversationalist (which at first I took as a sign of insecurity). Everything you say is just an excuse for Gertrude to issue some rambling amplification, meditation, or digression of her own. Mention coffee and she'll give you a rundown of every cup she ever drank, and where. Her favorite conversational gambit is the foods she hates, and there are a million of them. But so what if Gertrude doesn't like pot roast? (Who *likes* it?!) She also insists on reducing every topic to the most banal level: if somebody brings up Rembrandt, Gertrude will start jabbering on about some hat she once had that resembled Rembrandt's in a self-portrait but she lent it to somebody who never returned it and therefore will never lend anything to anyone again or not a hat anyway... and other goofy ruminations *totally unconnected to Rembrandt*. She has no idea what conversation *is*, the give-and-take of it. She never listens to anyone else, in fact seems to think she's doing everybody a favor by holding the floor. I tentatively suggested to her once, in private, that she should give no more than two opinions at a time before waiting to see if someone else had anything to add. But she never tried it—she probably never even heard me *say* it, she was too busy trying to find a way to interrupt me.

REASON NO. 49: Insecure, my ass! The woman has the ego of a colossus.

Later that night, you could have seen the berserk figure of my sister Bee running pell-mell from the house, screaming, "You idiot! You idiot!"—like Beethoven when some prince he was counting on suggested he might make do with two bassoons instead of three for a rehearsal of *Fidelio*. I think what finally flipped Bee over the edge was Gertrude's bright idea that she should work smaller, do stuff in clay, use "inexpensive materials", or maybe give up sculpture altogether and get a DOG. Gertrude's answer to everything is for people to become more like *Gertrude*: a nincompoop with a pumpkin patch who can speak coherently only about coffee and cat food. (REASON NO. 81.)

So Bee took up some dopey residency in England, and I, through superhuman efforts, finally extracted myself from Gertrude's clutches, and thus was all alone on Christmas Day, FREE AT LAST—to rearrange my CDs and DVDs. Not alphabetically, that's for zhlubs. My CDs I effortfully shelved by composer, performer, and ensemble: solos, duets, trios, quartets, quintets, sextets, septets, octets, small chamber groups, orchestras, jazz and... Bluegrass (my weak spot—not so much the yodeling as that "high lonesome sound"). Dewey wouldn't have liked my system, but Dewey wasn't *there*. The movies I did by era: the 1920s, the '30s, the '40s, the '50s, the '60s, the '70s, etc., each decade (after the '40s) more redolent of cinematic decline. I never got to watch these movies when Gertrude was around. She was always jumping up and rushing around the room for no reason, or talking all the way through. So, examining them now was like retrieving a treasure trove. I turned out to have a whole bunch of Bette Davis movies! I decided I would revive my psyche, post-Gertrude, by watching Bette Davis—*her* weirdness would be *my* therapy.

But first I had to organize my cartoon collection, this time alphabetically: Alvin and the Chipmunks, Betty Boop, Bugs Bunny, Crusader Rabbit, Donald Duck, the Flintstones, Fritz the Cat, Goofy, Heckle and Jeckle, Hercules, Huckleberry Hound, the Jetsons, Mickey Mouse, Mighty Mouse, Mr Magoo, Penelope Pitstop, Pingu, Popeye, Porky Pig, Road Runner, Rocky and Bullwinkle, Screwball Squirrel, the Simpsons, Sylvester and Tweetie Pie, Tom and Jerry, Tom Terrific and Mighty Manfred the Wonder Dog, Top Cat, Wally Gator, Woody Woodpecker, and Yogi Bear. Well, what of it? What's a plastic surgeon *supposed* to do after a hard day's work realigning human flesh, if not chill out to scenes of imaginary animals getting punched, stretched, bounced up and down, steamrollered, blown to smithereens, and reborn good as new? Brutal, I know, but optimistic! Claude and I had bonded over episodes of *Yogi Bear*, and had watched Olive Oyl deliberate over which size roller skates to rent about a million times: "I usually take a three but an eight feels sooo gooood!"

Hidden among all the DVDs I found some old Ant and Bee books (being about the same size): *Ant and Bee and the Rainbow*, and *One, Two, Three with Ant and Bee*. Now *there* was a true nut: Angela Banner. Puts ol' Bette in the shade! Pondering the perversity of these little books, I realized I'd always sort of associated my sister Bee with Angela Banner's Bee—not his authoritarian side exactly, but because he seems older, wiser, and more on the ball than Ant. Bee's the sensible one, almost parental, the one who holds everything together while Ant gets himself into scrapes. Bee knows what *time* it is, for instance, when to go to bed... Bee's always telling Ant what to do, and he's always *right*.

But when I called up *my* Bee to fill her in on this ancient confusion of mine, she objected to the comparison: I'd forgotten how much she hated being compared to a bee. She deflected all my well-meant attempts to flatter her by praising Bee, and cited as evidence of his dopeyness: *Around the World with Ant and Bee*.

"What about that madcap hunt for Bee's lost umbrella?" she asked. "*That's* not sensible, it's insane! At *Bee's* insistence, they travel the world asking people if they've seen his stupid umbrella. Big surprise, nobody's seen a microscopic umbrella belonging to a bee."

"But Bee's *mobile*. That's the great thing about him!" I pleaded. "Ant just hitches a ride on Bee's back when they go to the store, then manages to drop all the groceries on the way home. One little tart, two little apples—"

"Yeah, yeah. Six little eggs... Look, Harry, I'm kind of in the middle of something here..."

"And then, and then," I babbled, finding new relevance in *Ant and Bee* the more it irritated Bee, "after dropping all that stuff, Ant falls too and hits his head and has to stay home for three weeks—he's a shut-in like me! Doctor's orders."

"Ew, I always *hated* their doctor. He's two hundred times their size, and *human*, and makes house calls to *insects*? He really freaked me out."

"Freaked *you* out?"I said. "What about *me*? You're the one who was always reading those books to me! You showed no mercy. I think we both permanently depressed ourselves reading those things. How'd we get hold of them anyway? Nobody else in America was reading *Ant and Bee*. They're so. . . English! Hey, you want me to send them to you?"

"What would I do with them here? I've got England right outside the window."

Poor Ant, poor Bee. I'd have to give them to Claude instead. But first I had to read them myself—to remind me of the olden days. Also, I felt a certain affinity with Ant right now, as a fellow shut-in. But when *he's* sick in bed, he receives get-well parcels from everyone in England, and Kind Dog. Where were my parcels? Bee and I always wanted to know what was in these parcels of Ant's, especially the biggest one, labeled, "Do not open until Ant is better," which turns out to contain two wind-up tin motorboats, the SS *ANT* and the SS *BEE*. Ant and Bee launch them immediately. We longed for similar boats! But it was the *labels* that really got me. I found some at the dime store one day and labeled every piece of furniture in the house, forgetting to take them off before my dad came home and realized what a corny goofball he had for a son.

My study of Ant and Bee was interrupted by Gertrude, who called to ask what I was doing.

"Nothing," I said warily. "What are *you* doing?"

"Oh, trying to source some cucumbers for the punch,"she replied. "But all the markets are out of cucumbers! Can you imagine? I don't know what else to make. Well, *que sera sera*." (This was really about Eggnog, because my absence had forced her to rustle up a substitute beverage: "punch". It sounded godawful.)

REASON NO. 224: Gertrude's philosophy of *que sera sera*. Gertrude likes to come across all scatterbrained and laid-back, like she was just some simple goose girl who leaves things to chance. Like hell. I never saw a person take fewer chances. She doesn't even take a chance on her kind of sun cream being available in the Hamptons, but packs the car with thirty gallons of the stuff. She never took a chance on *me* either (my loyalty or love); instead, imprisoned me in bookings, duties, organizations, and five-year plans. The box at the Met, wines that won't mature for a decade, the pigs of Piedmont already scouring the land for truffles in anticipation of our next autumn trip... And her putrid musical ventures, those kooky salons and soirées she put on, where the tanned and the toned tried to talk learnedly about Schubert or Mozart or Dohnányi. I once heard a whole bunch of them discussing who knew Dohnányi best—*none* of them knew Dohnányi at all! A few may have *glimpsed* him coming down a shady path at some music camp. Much was made of that shady path. As for Schubert, it was his *death* they liked best. They acted like he only wrote that stuff so we could think about syphilis the whole time it's being played. NO MORE! No more entanglements at Tanglewood, no more glimmers of hope at Glimmerglass.

ALLEMANDE

NEW YEAR'S EVE

WHEN I WASN'T playing Schubert impromptus on the piano (without the pedals), I listened to my box-set of *La Bohème* again and again, as a kind of cardiovascular workout (a reminder of that dimly remembered thing: romance). So now I had a sore ankle and a sore spot for Mimì, a real hankering for the flower-girl to come warm her little cold hands at my artificial log fire, which couldn't be much worse than Rodolfo's fire (all *he* had was paper!)...But what was I thinking?! Not another bohemian! I'd barely rid myself of the last one yet: Gertrude's phone calls had gone down, post-break-up, to two or three a day, as opposed to six or more, but it still wasn't the decisive split I'd had in mind. And now she wanted Explanations. To be kind, I didn't give her any.

"Is it somebody else?"she asked. "You've found somebody else!"

"I found my senses, Gertrude."

Some of her bewilderment was understandable. Nobody usually ends an affair in this town without snagging a replacement first.

The fact that I hadn't indulged in the conventional two-timing stage was an indication of just how intolerable Gertrude *was*. I'd ditched her for her own deficiencies, not because I was cunt-struck on somebody else.

Gertrude was like one of those boa constrictors, those *beautiful creatures* people in Florida keep as pets until the thing gets too big and uncontrollable—whereupon they let it loose outside to terrorize the neighborhood, until some jerk finally comes along and shoots it. The snake was set up for a fall from the start! You take a wild animal into your home and then blame it for being wild. It was Gertrude's *nature*, for chrissake, to be obnoxious, and my mistake to have had anything to do with her, no matter how appealingly she sauntered up 42nd Street. I CHOSE the woman, I ushered her into my building and made what I considered a suave pass at her in the elevator, the actions of a supposedly grown man. And she could still slither into my life and undermine me, even from the snowbound wastes of Connecticut.

"Did I say something wrong? Did I do something horrible?" (Yes, and yes.) "Didn't I try to please you? I took you into my home, my *family*, Harrison. I gave you everything...!"

"I'm no family man, Gertrude. I told you that from the beginning."

And yet, my biggest regret in breaking up with her was the loss of Claude. I would really miss that kid, and I'd worry about him too, stuck over there all alone with Gertrude (and the army of au pairs). But what could I do? He wasn't my son—Gertrude was already pregnant when I met her, having had herself artificially inseminated on a whim, some months before. When we broke up, I thought of asking for visiting rights but didn't, for fear that she'd use my fondness for Claude as some sort of weapon.

I once asked him, "How was the playground today?"and he answered, "Homoerotic." What a guy! And what a vocabulary— Gertrude must've read *Webster's* to him when he was still in the womb.

The sprained ankle had given me an unforeseen vacation from work, and after some initial shock at the extent of my solitude and spare time, I discovered: my apartment! Always scooting between New York and Long Island and Gertrude's various approximations of bohemia in Manhattan, Connecticut, and Hilton Head, I never had time to enjoy it, and it's a great apartment! Neither bohemian nor po-mo metro minimalist chic: my place was "modern" in about 1920. It's a converted penthouse loft at the top of the CENTURY FABRIC DESIGN CO. building in the Garment District (36th, between 7th and 8th), a business long defunct but still proudly commemorated in gold lettering over the front entrance. It's now mixed-use, with about a million mysterious enterprises going on below me: hats, buttons, hooks, eyes, feathers, SM gear, rubber nurse uniforms, transgender lingerie, godknowswhat. I sometimes study the brass-framed list of my fellow inhabitants while waiting for the elevator, trying to imagine what the hell they're all up to in there:

FEATHER FLAUNT
THE QUICK-FIX COMPANY
COUTURE CUTEY
BARRY'S BRAS
JEEPERS & CO.
MATERNITY PANTS

FIFI FUN
CHOCOLATEX
BUSKYDELL CORP.
SNAPPY ZIPPER...

Living in the Garment District is very convenient—you never have to wash a shirt, just go down and buy a new one at Ramin's! I work across town, right by the Morgan Library, so daily pass all of female fashion, from underwear to eveningwear. I'm a block away from the General Post Office too, where on tax day a guy runs up and down the steps dressed as an Excedrin, passing out free samples to late filers.

The elevator doesn't reach my floor—you have to walk up the last flight on foot (sprained ankle or not). But because I'm on the top, it's very quiet: I can play the piano whenever I want, and don't have to listen to other people's idiotic choice of music. I don't own the roof terrace, but nobody ever comes up there so it's effectively mine. Gertrude had hopes of turning the whole place into an urban farm, but my main use for it is as a lookout post for terrorist attacks and more benign types of fireworks. It's also a bracing spot for the first cup of coffee of the day, while staring at the ancient faded ad for boots on a building opposite—

LOOKS WELL
FEELS WELL
WEARS WELL

—which pretty much sums up how I feel about my apartment! Another sign further on, "BAAR & BEARD'S" (ladies' scarves), reminds me to shave.

The best thing about my apartment is that there are no dingy areas. Dinginess is the source of all human misery. There's a skylight over the front door, and windows on three sides of the building. Light *fills* the place, coming in from all angles, drifting through internal doors and windows, over diagonally cut white breezeblock walls, and bouncing off the high ceilings. It's airy in my eyrie! Some of the woodwork is dark mahogany, but most of the doors are filled with old frosted glass. And, next to the French doors that open out onto the roof, there's just one huge window that stretches the length of the living room, a slanted wall of glass. The coziest thing in the world is to sit under this window at twilight when it's raining heavily outside and the water patters on the glass, forming a steady sheet of drips through which you glimpse the twinkling lights of a million other windows and the bridge (a guy's always got to have an escape route in sight).

So now, a martini to the left of me, fire to the right of me, piano in stasis before me, and all of Manhattan in motion behind me, I sat in torpor, my foot on its footstool, my head in its fool's cap, and a pad of foolscap on my lap in case I wanted to jot down anything melancholy. This activity was not new: my List of Melancholy Things pre-dated my break-up *and* the sprained ankle. It's my life's work.

LIST OF MELANCHOLY

- Liszt himself—such bombast, and for what?
- Mimì, a torn and tender woman
- being alone on New Year's Eve
- forced marriages among five-year-olds
- master's degrees in highway lighting

- the rushed minimal morning walks of a million Manhattan mutts
- puppetry
- pep talks
- the Great Auk
- shrimp-eating contests
- unpredictable air fares
- pregnant women pushing strollers uphill like Sisyphus—just stop *breeding*, why don't you?
- the existence of Walmart
- Superman T-shirts
- Bach's solo cello suites, especially No. 5; also, 2 and 4... aw, throw them all in (they all exhibit "exquisite melancholy")

My kitchen is triangular, which turns out to be the perfect shape for a kitchen to be: everything's visible and within reach. There's even a little table and chair in there for eating sandwiches in a hurry. My kitchen's equipped with every gadget known to man, gifts from grateful patients and patient girlfriends, or worry-warts like Bee (who sprang a juicer on me some years back when she noticed the only Vitamin C I was getting was from the celery in my Bloody Marys). I've got technology up the wazoo in there: a milk-frother from a cappuccino-lover who'd hurriedly assumed, on the basis of a few nights together, that we'd be sharing breakfast more often than we ever did. A lemon-zester, from a patient who claimed it was symbolic of her new zest in life since the rejuvenation job I'd done on her. An egg-boiler (for one egg at a time), a panic-buy of my own when I realized I'd reached maturity without knowing how to boil an egg (but *had* I reached maturity? And how would *eggs* help me if I had?). And an olive-pitter

I mistakenly thought necessary for making martinis. A bread-maker, that had continued kneading its dough long after the girl who gave it to me walked out for good. An electric nutmeg-grater that must have cost more than a lifetime's supply of nutmegs (this, from a woman much taken with my Eggnog and our Eggnog snog out on Gertrude's porch one Christmas). And its rival, Gertrude's five-hundred-buck coffee machine that took up half my counter space and looked like it would be of more use printing revolutionary pamphlets. I also had a big fancy stove with six burners and an inbuilt griddle I never used, microwave, fridge, automatic ice-producing freezer full of gin, vodka, and an ancient carton of sherbet (which somehow always got forgotten at the sight of the gin), dishwasher, prehensile-mangling blender, my mother's long-retired Revere Ware pots, and the weighty tortilla pan I purchased at a medical conference in Bilbao, under the influence of an attractive anesthesiologist and too much Rioja. All the conveniences of modern life were there! (*And* I'd even read the manuals.) And crackers—a guy can't have too many crackers.

But I went in the kitchen on New Year's Eve and thought, how the hell do I just heat something up in here? And my appliances stared back at me, seething with resentment and hope. USE ME! CHOOSE ME! ABUSE ME! TAKE ME! SHAKE ME! BAKE ME! AT LEAST PLUG ME IN, YOU DOPE! It was scary in there! I cautiously backed out and, with the assistance of an old cane (bought long ago in a moment of self-deception, for the purpose of hill-walking), hauled ass down to the diner on the corner and got me a nice big bowl of matzo ball soup. You can survive a New York winter as long as you know where to go for soup.

Revelers were trying to revel outside in the snow. I watched them rush past the windows, and felt another pang of New Year's exasperation about my lovelessness: no kiss at midnight for me. No Mimì either. But it was a fairly abstract concern, since Gertrude had ruined me for other women. Love now seemed ridiculous and Wagnerian to me, like the Bugs Bunny cartoon when he dresses up as Brunhilda and Elmer Fudd falls instantly in love, bellowing, "Bwoonhiwlda, you're so wuvvawy!" and Bugs sings, "Yes, I know it. I can't help it!"—Wagner *and* all of human sentiment, mocked in one cartoon. Wagner deserved it. NO CHAIR, not even a box at the Met, equips you for such interminable spectatorship.

Fortified by soup, I inched my way through the snowy wastes. For fear of being knocked over by the movers and shakers, I turned down a dark alley, feeling like an Antarctic explorer who'd had to leave his sled team behind to eat each other. "I may be some time." The snow was a foot deep in places; I tackled each glacier as it arose. It was peaceful in the alley, an ideal spot for the unloved. Heaps of trash and tinsel peeked out from under snowbanks, and I came upon a ten-foot-high Styrofoam Santa who stood with his face against a brick wall, as if he'd just slipped out of some bar for a pee. Poor old Santa—his day was done, adoration time over. I stumbled on toward the North Pole (represented by the lights at the end of the alley) until I heard a voice. Not Santa's luckily, but a muffled *miaow*. A cat, out in weather like this?

"Ain't a fit night out for man nor beast!" I said to him, and the cat miaowed louder. A W. C. Fields fan! I headed in his direction, as unthreateningly as possible, to see if the cat needed any help. The miaowing seemed to be coming from behind a snow-covered mound of trash, and it became more frantic the closer I got. I scraped the snow away and, under a pile of crumpled bikes and lost umbrellas, finally saw a small form moving around. I put out my hand to pat him, and he obligingly tried to reach it but was prevented by a bunch of spokes. Maybe he'd gone under the bikes for shelter in a blizzard, and they'd shifted under the weight of the snow, barring his exit. Anyway, what might have seemed a safe sleeping spot before the snowstorm had become a potential tomb. It was freezing out there! He couldn't survive the night.

Luckily, Pick-up Sticks was my ancient rainy-day specialty. I'd honed my skills by making Bee play it again and again when we were kids. (A talent that had proved handy in surgery too.) So I now carefully removed one knot of metal at a time, trying to prevent the whole structure collapsing onto the cat, who continued to cry out to me as I worked: he was a friendly little guy. When I finally got him out and placed him gently on a thin patch of snow, he limped right over to me and rubbed himself against my legs. A limp?! That did it. I couldn't leave a fellow crip out in the cold. I'd search for his owners some other time—for now, he was coming home with me. And when I picked him up he clung to my shoulder like a baby, but weighed so little I had to keep checking he was still there beneath my thick glove.

Back in the apartment, I put him in a sink full of warm soapy water to raise his core body temperature (and clean him off), an ordeal he tolerated pretty well, for a cat. What emerged was a handsome young fellow, with black, white and reddish fur.

"What's black and white and red all over?" I asked him. No answer. "A newspaper. Get with it, man!"

In the kitchen I found him some milk and an old ham sandwich, which he politely ate. So easy to please! Then he investigated my whole place, every nook and cranny, undaunted by his limp. He was particularly taken with the scalloped window seat below the slanted window in the living room, instantly recognizing it as the longest cat bed in the world. He jumped up and paused to stand there on his back legs, front paws on the window sill, looking out at New York.

I was about to lay down some newspapers in a closet, for him to use as a temporary cat-box, when I remembered an extremely bijou tray of 100% organic Irish peat-bog mulch, or some such thing, that Gertrude had lugged over at some point and dumped on my terrace intending me to grow tarragon or lemon thyme in it, maybe sorrel. Thanks to the gaudy phosphorescent swirls and curlicues around its rim, I was able to find it in the dark and brought it in. Bubbles, as I now called him since his bubble bath, instantly recognized the true purpose of Gertrude's agricultural gift and scrabbled energetically in the dirt. He was clearly not feral. He was sophisticated, trusting, and accustomed to human contact and the demands of domesticity. But so *thin*—he must have been faring for himself on the streets of Manhattan for some time. And now he was sitting on my lap, licking my finger, and looking up at me with love. I hadn't felt this good in years! Gertrude rarely licked me, and never liked me. Hell, she'd hardly even noticed me.

I checked his legs for any sign of a wound that might cause the limp, but nothing seemed amiss. He'd probably sprained an ankle, or the feline equivalent (my veterinary knowledge was scanty), but at least he didn't seem uncomfortable. He luxuriated in the warmth and companionship offered, and stretched out on his back to have his stomach rubbed. This cat really knew how to live!

At midnight, we went out on the roof terrace together. I held Bubbles to my chest so he wouldn't get lost out there in the dark, and we watched the faraway fireworks that seemed to mark his arrival.

NEW YEAR'S DAY, 2011

FOR HYGIENIC REASONS, I set up a bed for Bubbles on the window seat he liked so much in the living room, and left him there when I went to bed, but he soon nosed his way into my room. The door slowly opened a crack and then he peered in, looking comically astonished at first to find me lying there. Then with great self-satisfaction he joined me on the bed. He filled almost as much surface area as Gertrude ever had, but was a lot more fun to have around. He slept more soundly too! When we got up in the morning, he moved to a sunny spot on the window seat, while I went out to get cat food. He wolfed it down while I drank my coffee. I hadn't felt this heroic since childhood!

Childhood is a largely dishonorable business and I remember very little of it (this is what *Bee* is for). My early years were notable for one vaguely heroic act on my part (among a lot of unheroic ones), an act so mythologized, sentimentalized, eulogized, and fetishized by my family that it eventually had to be *catheterized* to restore some sense of scale.

Now it seems nothing compared to the heroism of an ant. Imagine being born an ant and having to uncurl yourself in some musty, dusty, rustly nest, realizing there's no time to lose, your life of running around starts NOW, and a whole realm of unexplained duty awaits you.

I uncurled myself in the twin towns of Virtue and Chewing Gum, incorporating just about all the dualism a body can stand. Chewing Gum came first, established in 1880 by a gum manufacturer lured there by the mighty Chevron River, which suited his methods for dispersing the toxic by-products of the gum-making process. The gum was so good, a Bible town grew up right alongside: half the town chewed, the other half chewed your ear off.

My infancy was cozy, cozy to the point of being oppressive. I was a sitting *duck* in that high chair, with Bee stealing my food and poking me in the eye all the time with her Barbie dolls (even the tits on those things are sharp!). Mom cleaning all around me—back and forth with the vacuum cleaner, the mop, the dusting, the polishing, the folding, the ironing, the instant wash-a-rama of every plate and spoon we touched, the militaristic straightening of the eagle ornaments that hung on every wall, as if the nation depended on the surveillance work of these bas-relief birds. A million naps undertaken listening to Mom talk to some doofus on the phone while I pondered dust motes. (Phones and vacuum cleaners still fill me with melancholy, even in their dormant states.)

But my mother loved me! I know everybody thinks he was a cute baby, but I have it *in writing*—a letter my mom wrote to my teacher once, when I was in some kind of trouble at school (as was my custom):

Harrison was such a delightful
baby. He would totter over to you,
arms outstretched, always smiling.
He was the sort of child someone
might try to steal! And better than
a puppy at cheering you up. He was
so trusting, he had no idea there was
anything sad or bad in the world.
Give him a wooden spoon and a
cardboard box and he'd be happy
as a clam banging on that box all day.
He also liked making piles of stuff...

I gave you the facts, man—I was once a cheerful dimpled baby who pleased his mother.

This cozy setup of ours was punctuated by the precise arrivals and departures of my father, the great unknowing, unknowable American dad. Out he'd go every morning, with his old briefcase echoing the angularity of his suit on his slightly pudgy 1960s body; and later return, giving off a whiff of car smell from the jalopy his parents had given him when they got themselves a new Chevy. Armed with these accoutrements, our father displayed an obtuseness which at best amounted to kindly indifference—No hard feelings, kids, I just don't give a damn what goes on here all day—compounded by his determined obliviousness of his wife's concerns, chief among them being ME, a distinction that often elicited his fears for my masculinity.

My admiration of *him* was unassailable, since he was in charge of a vehicle. Mom, a pedestrian and bus-user, earned my contempt. I liked to rile her in the grocery store: success was when I got her to yell, entitling me to sympathetic looks from strangers and apologetic candy from Mom.

The first vehicle I ever revered was my little red truck, the envy of the neighborhood, a miniature pickup truck with real headlights, red upholstery, horn, a dashboard covered with knobs and dials, and, under the chassis, the hidden source of propulsion: pedals. I drove that truck everywhere, couldn't be parted from it. And one morning, at about the age of three, I drove it across the street and straight into the nice green Chevron River that surged so appealingly past our house. The truck floated fine and I held on for a wild ride, carried for miles clinging to the steering wheel, giggling and wiggling my toes out behind me in the water. People who saw me go by held their hands to their mouths or started running along the bank, hollering. I paid no attention. I was on my way in the world, and there can be no better feeling. I was happy as a clam in fact, until a boatload of cops fished me out, and left my beautiful red truck to spin away downriver (instilling in me my first real doubts about cops).

But WHY was I forced to use my truck as a boat, when there was a big old canoe sitting in our garage? The canoe had been hanging in the rafters since before I was born, left there by the previous owners of our house when they moved to Wyoming. But every time Bee and I asked if we could get the canoe down and try it out, Dad claimed the people who owned it might come back for it some day. *Nobody* ever comes back from *Wyoming*! They're stuck there, moaning, "Why? Why?" No, they were never coming back for their stupid canoe. Our parents were just lazy stinkers.

They were the least adventurous people I ever knew! In my whole entire childhood we only left Virtue and Chewing Gum once, apart from trips to the farmers' market just outside of town, where Mom bought stuff for bottling. Talk about corny! She was always pickling something—'maters, cukes, watermelon rind—for what good it did anybody. But one day, for reasons never specified, we all bundled into the hot car and drove through flat, hot plains and hazy, underpopulated towns, where other families mysteriously chose to live, past HoJos and blueberry stands and pet zoos and picnic spots, never stopping, despite our pleas and threats from the back ("I need to go to the bathroom!" "I'm gonna throw up!").

When you're a kid, you don't really know if you're going to *survive* boredom. It feels life-threatening. Bee and I played I Spy and Ghost, but there were long stretches when she just stared out the window at her imaginary stallion, Hollenius, who was apparently galloping beside our car the whole way. I was left to glare at the brown semicircle of my mom's head, just visible over the front seat, or else chortle my way through my joke book, with which I tormented my family for years. "What's yellow and goes up and down? A banana in an elevator!. . . What did the mayonnaise say when somebody left the fridge door open? Shut the door, I'm dressing!. . . What did one wall say to the other wall? Meetcha at the corner!. . . What trembles at the bottom of the sea?. . . Aw, forget it." (A nervous wreck.) And then, a minute later, "What's black and white and red all over?"

The only relief came when Dad thrilled us, and horrified Mom, by taking his hands off the wheel at 50 mph to demonstrate to me how big a salmon is. I was just beginning to grasp the fact that he and I were allies of some kind: MEN. Mom and Bee were there to be outstripped. Dad and I had developed a habit of guffawing at anything Mom or Bee said (when I remembered to). Our confederacy had solidified over many months of touring the drug-stores and movie houses of Virtue and Chewing Gum where Mom had been on dates before she met Dad. He was curiously fixated on these historic locales. The rage and power of the man! And yet he had a fine tenor voice—and could yodel. He yodeled his way through "Sparkling Brown Eyes" for us now, with Bee and me chiming in from the back seat as his echo.

> *There's a ramshackle shack*
> *. . . (There's a ramshackle shack)*
> *Down in ol' Caroline,*
> *That's calling me back*
> *. . . (That's calling me back)*
> *To that ol' gal o' mine.*

He followed this up, as usual, with:

> *Just a song at twilight*
> *When the lights are low*
> *And the evening shadows*
> *Softly come and go.*
> *Though your heart be weary,*
> *Sad the day and long,*
> *Still to us at twilight*
> *Comes love's old sweet song.*

And "The Brown and the Yellow Ale", which made Bee and me snicker, due to our scatological interpretation of its meaning:

He asked was the woman with me my daughter
O the brown and the yellow ale!
And I said she was my married wife.
O love of my heart!

He asked would I lend her for an hour and a day
O the brown and the yellow ale!
And I said I would do anything that was fair.
O love of my heart!

By the time we stopped at a motel, I was comatose in a corner, having seen nothing out of the window but the tops of pine trees for hours. It was twilight and I stood unsteadily in the tree-lined parking lot beside the road, feeling smug about the people still stuck in their cars, driving by. *We* had somewhere to stay, and it wasn't the usual kind of motel either, some U-shaped, two-story, paint-peeling number surrounding a bug-blocked pool. No, this was a real log cabin by a lake, with a fireplace! Bee and I went nuts when we saw it. That night we slept on camp beds with eiderdowns and feather pillows, perched on a balcony above the main room. She and I always spoke of that place later as the epitome of COZINESS. We were cozy in our beds that night, peering down through the wooden banister rails at our parents talking quietly by the fire. The illusion of contentment was profound.

The next day, there were pancakes at a nearby diner, and foot-dangling on the jetty. The lake was darker than we'd thought the night before, and full of yuck-muck lurking in the murk. Bee and I insisted on swimming in it anyway though, and this was when Mom forced us to make one of the most peculiar decisions of our lives:

since we hadn't brought any bathing suits she wanted us to choose whether we swam in our undershirts or our under*pants*—so as to save one dry item of underwear for the ride home. How do parents think this sort of stuff up? They all worry far too much about you catching cold.

I chose to swim in my underpants; Bee chose her undershirt. I always thought she made the wrong decision. The sight of her bare ass in the water embarrassed me. I felt kind of sorry for her. But we soon forgot about this sartorial conundrum (although I'm *still* thinking about it!), as we attempted to make it to the raft in the middle of the pond without getting sucked down into its muddy depths by leeches, or something worse. We were all too aware of the slimy black fish that must live in that slimy black pond.

Then it was back in the car for the long drive home, with goosebumps (despite the change into dry duds) and Baba Yaga stories, another of Bee's bad choices. Baba Yaga gave me the creeps, with her peroxide-yellow hair, her mangy old cat, and that house on chicken feet. Baba Yaga flies cumbersomely on a pestle (god only knows what she did with the mortar) and all I could think about was her torpedoing toward me, top speed, with those mile-long bazongas of hers, dugs she had to spread out on a clothes line to dry! And her saggy-baggy arms, and legs so dimpled her thighs were striated with *folds* (horrific details of bodily decay I must have observed at Virtue Gum Factory summer picnics, where middle-aged women tended to let loose with shorts and sleeveless tops, to mind-boggling effect). But what about those claw-like hands, and the arthritic jaws, with which Baba Yaga would munch me if she got the chance? No good could come of those old teeth and old teats. Baba Yaga eats like a *man,* like she OWNS the place, and spits the bones out into the dark gelatinous lake...

When we reached our street, Dad woke us up by saying, as always, "And so they turned the corner to find the smoldering remains of what was once 39 Cranberry Avenue," which never failed to amuse us. But it wasn't smoldering yet.

MARTIN LUTHER KING JR. DAY

MY "CAT FOUND" NOTICES had been up for two weeks now without any response. Bubbles was safely mine. I briefly considered issuing some "GIRLFRIEND DUMPED" signs as well, to see if anyone rose to the challenge of taking over Gertrude's role. But Bubbles had already done that, proving himself a superior companion on almost every front (no *sex* was on offer—but sex with Gertrude wasn't a grievous loss). He wasn't clingy or demanding, like some people I could mention. He just liked to be near me. He loved me! In fact he was the most even-tempered and well-adjusted personality I'd ever known, sure of himself, but never arrogant in that standoffish feline way, and always affectionate. He had great concentration abilities too, and would stare for twenty minutes at a time at a pigeon on the roof, or a spider on the floor. Liked watching baseball too! Bubbles was clearly a very intelligent cat. Also a big investigator: he'd check out any open door or closet, but he was polite about it and didn't knock things over—he wasn't searching for food or anything, just having a good look around. And musical! There was nothing he liked better than lying atop the piano licking himself while I played Schubert.

The vet checked Bubbles out and found nothing wrong with him besides emaciation, which was diminishing. His teeth were good, and the limp had vanished. The vet gave him a few vaccinations and recommended a diet of Fancy Feast cat food (the Classic variety, not the grilled kind or the stuff with gravy), because it's just meat, instead of all the buckwheat and pumpkin seeds and barbecue flavor Manhattanites think their cats need. "Cats were made to eat meat," he said with unexpected vehemence. "This is all they need, nutritionally." A real cat-food zealot. Nuts, but I liked him: he wanted the best for Bubbles.

The only other thing he could tell me was that Bubbles was female, not male. I was surprised. But in the end, what's the difference, with a *cat*? We're all so hooked on these dichotomies: male/female, human/animal, right/wrong. We *act* like they're opposites but they're not really, just part of the same spectrum. You neuter a cat and that's the end of it, just as Virtue neutered Chewing Gum and Minneapolis neutered St. Paul. Bubbles had already been spayed, so all I had to do was adjust with grace to his/her new gender. (As far as I knew, he/she didn't give a damn about *mine*.)

I added "gender changes" and "dualism" to my List of Melancholy, along with "*Ant and Bee* books". Also, "shaving." It occurred to me that shaving gives men an airtight excuse for vanity and self-obsession—otherwise we'd be obliterated by hair! During my convalescence, I'd had time for several ornate additions to my list. The entry on "bathrobes" had numbered subdivisions:

WHY I HATE BATHROBES

1. The belt never stays tied.

2. Often an old Kleenex in the pocket.

3. They're always too hot.

4. And frequently tartan.

5. Remind me of slippers.

6. Or of men lounging around in Sears catalogs. Next page: a billion socks.

7. Reminiscent of oddly formal occasions in childhood— Christmas and sleepovers—when pj's are for some reason deemed *not enough.*

I was clearly not ready to go back to work: I hadn't regressed enough yet. I couldn't face anyone else's pain but my own, *especially* the patients'. You have to gear up for that, crank the old smile into place. Nor did I feel like leaving Bubbles. So it was fortunate I was my own boss: my time off was up to me. I kept my partners notified of my progress and in return was sent get-well cards and hot-water bottles from the nurses, and a bunch of flowers weekly—leaving me free to whirl the whorl of hair on my left wrist, examine my collection of clutch pencils, accidentally unravel a whole sweater Gertrude had knitted me (just by pulling on one annoying thread), and look up cheerleading websites, which turned out to be all about *bulimia*, not ponytails and candied thighs. What boors women are, always thinking about their stomachs!

The next item for my List of Melancholy was "bulldozers": the fact that I'd never yet driven one and now probably never would.

Come on, you get in that windowed rookery and start manoeuvering those gears, turning the thing 360 degrees, lifting and lowering the scoop! The verticals and horizontals, the bare molded flanks, the mammoth treads, the shiny joints and pistons, the giant nuts and bolts, and all the greases needed to make those monsters go! So goddam male it breaks your heart! The sheer weight of it, its steadiness under duress, the power, the know-how—the determination in its makers to build *the machine you need,* whatever the consequences. Its pliant usefulness, as those arms lift beseechingly aloft!... All I've ever wanted, all *anyone* really wants, is to get inside a bulldozer and make it do its stuff.

Then I realized I should add Berlioz to my list, or rather, listening in early life to too much Berlioz, or what I took to be Berlioz. I *ruined* myself with that guy. My parents must have fallen prey to a Record of the Month deal at some point, so we were burdened with an over-abundance of Berlioz and Buxtehude records. I dutifully listened to them all, convinced that I was a budding composer. My parents were strict about bedtime (6:00 on schoolnights) so, after grappling with some grim roundel of grilled ham topped with a slice of pineapple (an early example of "tower food" and my least favorite meal), I'd be lying there with the summer sun still streaking in over my bed, waging my desperate nightly battle with "Berlioz." My task was to put an *end* to the symphonic strains I couldn't get out of my head, by coming up with a final chord or coda so crushing and climactic it would quell an entire orchestra and blast old Berlioz into outer space where he belonged.

"DA-DAAA" was never enough. "Dadada-dadada-dong-deeeee-dadoooooo!" No. "Bam-bam BANG, ba-ba-badaaaaah vroom zissshtee ta!" "Dumpety, dumpety, ra-ra-ra-tatarata-tatatat-tee, RA-CHUNG!!" "Tum-tum-tum-tum-tee-dee-TEE-TEE-wham-PAH!" Every time I thought I had him beat, Berlioz would sneak back in with a distant harp or piccolo, and my toils would begin again. A guy could spontaneously combust, *combust* I tell you, doing this stuff! You have to *build* to one of those climaxes, you can't just stick one on at the end of something (maybe Berlioz had the same problem). I suffered aural apoplexies of this nature every night until I discovered James Bond movies: it was only by superimposing Bond tunes over the Berlioz that I finally managed to get some shut-eye.

These torments, and my dad's insistence that Bee and I each play an instrument, were the only exposure I got to music apart from the arrival of the Virtue and Chewing Gum Philharmonic in the school gym, one afternoon a year. We all had to file in, sit down, shut up, keep still, and listen to the concert. If the teachers saw a foot tapping, or your head rocking a bit to the music, you were out. Most of my early Beethoven moments were therefore gleaned from the corridor outside. The real point of this cultural event wasn't the music but the military exercise of making us (and the orchestra) assemble and disassemble. It didn't help me much with Berlioz.

Another of my neurotic insomnia strategies was Tongue Bandit. In this game, my tongue was a bandit on the run from a posse of lawmen. The bandit has to scramble along the cliff face of my teeth, looking for a foothold or a gap he could squeeze through. But the rocks are slippery and it's hard to find purchase (unless I'd just lost a baby tooth). The lynch mob's closing in, so sometimes the desperado has to make a sudden leap for freedom. This got me through many a bout of sleeplessness or boredom at home and at school until Gus, the class pest, noticed something weird going on in my mouth one day and yelled out in the middle of Geography class, "Hey, Harrison's about to puke!"

When I was older, bedtime moved from 6:00 to 7:30, but by then I could climb out of my window at night, slip the six feet to the ground below, and go commune with animals in the woods, or try to. I had a tracker's book of scat, paw prints, and animal silhouettes, which I hoped would help me locate some entity that wanted to be befriended. But these excursions too were often destroyed by Gus, who'd turn up with a frog he'd just disemboweled, or a squirrel he'd skinned. (Gus's real name was Fergus but he'd stripped the Fer off that too). He considered himself a rugged outdoorsman, and hunted *me* down, to lecture me to death on Churchill and World War II (Gus's favorite war), or serenade me on his stupid guitar.

Gus was an addict of fright. He was the kind of kid who was always snapping your underpants as you went past his desk, or plotting vengeance against the teachers who of course hated him (everybody did!). But he was a good source of maniac stories, which we were all crazy for—though for quite a while I didn't even know what a "maniac" *was*. I had the idea it was something like a *midget*, probably because of the maniac story in which a maniac manages to hang on to some honeymooners' car door for miles and miles, after they refused to give him a ride. I figured only a midget could survive a journey like that, hanging on to a door handle. This confusion kind of wrecked *The Wizard of Oz* for me, and might never have been cleared up if Bee hadn't called *Dad* a maniac one day.

"But he's six feet tall!" I said.

"What's that got to do with it?"

She'd called him a maniac because of the canoeing lessons. Dad had finally caved on the canoe front—he didn't get the big old canoe down from the garage but he bought us a cheap inflatable one, a mild act of benevolence he followed up with a lot of denunciation of Bee's attempts to use it. When verbal scorn failed, he bopped her on the head with the plastic oar one day, and kicked the canoe so hard it shot out into the middle of the river with the tearful Bee inside it. She drifted quickly out of sight downstream, and had to walk home for miles with the deflated canoe under her arm.

My real friend at school was Pete, the sweetest guy I ever knew. Pete was in love with death: whatever game we played, he had to be the dying cowboy, the dying spaceman, the dying cop or robber. He loved to be carried, twitching, off a battlefield. He was also an expert on *melancholy*. Everything got Pete down: flightless birds, dying daffodils, the ultimate futility of the patches my mother sewed on the elbows of my jacket... Over the years Pete pointed out to me the inherent sadness of stale bread, old newspapers, nipples, empty envelopes, house plants, shuffleboard, "Greensleeves," goose migration, dry tufted grass "like old man hair," the color pink, babies, lambs, puppies and kittens (the fact that they all grow up), knitwear, unused fireplaces, and my mother's tomatoes all lined up for bottling (Pete had chanced upon the little-known staring-at-the-produce stage of the preserving process). The world was a cornucopia of melancholy for Pete!

I still fret about my scuzzy Mr. Potatohead, which I traded one day for Pete's trusty stopwatch. Does everyone agonize over the unfair swaps of yesteryear?

But now, safe in adulthood, I no longer needed Tongue Bandit because I could watch Bette Davis movies all day! And pat Bubs. Whenever my lap was available, Bubbles would claim it, and it was available to him (her) most of the time, since I was still trying to keep my foot elevated. Bubbles proved a much better moviegoer than Gertrude ever was: Bubbles could *concentrate*.

So there I was on Martin Luther King Day, sitting around in shorts and a T-shirt (due to my antipathy to bathrobes) watching *Now, Voyager*, with Bubbles draped across my legs enjoying a cat nap that had been preceded by an extravagantly long patting and purring session. This had ended in sound slumber only when I let my hand lie still on her. She liked that. Leaving me free to *give myself* to Bette. But for once I was transfixed not by Bette Davis's eyes, like two rogue planets trying to found their own solar system, but by her *eyebrows*. In the first scene Bette—severely depressed, nearing thirty, still living at home with her mother—spends all her time carving ivory boxes and secretly smoking. As a result, apparently, her eyebrows when she first appears are hairier than Claude Rains's—and *his* are all over the place! It must have been so long since anyone in Hollywood had seen a real pair of unplucked female eyebrows, the make-up artists (precursors to my own profession) panicked and slapped two walruses on her face. Dr. Jaquith (Claude Rains) comes in mumbling something about pipe-smoking. Forget the *pipe*, man, get a load of those *brows*!

It was at this point that my cleaner, Deedee, barged into the apartment, my cleaner who had specifically requested long ago that I should never be around when she came to clean. Or, if I had to be home, I was to let her know ahead of time so that she could wear *pants*—she always wore pants, it seemed, when men were present, to prevent any sexual overtures. I was never at home in the daytime, I assured her, though privately I had felt a little aggrieved. The woman was at least sixty years old, and not top on the list of people I might wish to ravish. Also, I spend my life trying to *help* women, not violate them. But for five years I had duly made sure I wasn't home on Deedee's cleaning days, and left her monthly check on the hall table. The mix-up today had occurred because she'd been off on vacation for a few weeks over Christmas; in the meantime I'd wallowed for so long in sickness, sloth and solitude I'd appropriated my own apartment and clean forgotten about my cleaner!

But here she was, wearing a spotty, dotty dress (not unlike Bette's mid-breakdown) and I, barely clothed at all! Apologies, apologies. I stood up and tried to make my way to the bedroom. But at the sight of my limp, Deedee rushed to my aid, and supported me all the way back to bed. She even tucked me in and brought me a sandwich, her own lunch, straight from the deli. I almost couldn't swallow it, so touched was I by the ministrations of this near-stranger after all those weeks alone. I wasn't used to compassion—that stuff's for laymen! To top it off, she admired Bubbles, who cheerfully followed Deedee around, until the vacuuming began.

At some point in the morning, Deedee brought me my mail. She must have thought I couldn't make it to the hall table or something, where I'd dumped it (out of apathy, not incapacity). So I felt I had to open it. The first envelope was from old *Gus,* for chrissake. What did *he* want with me? I thought I'd successfully freed myself of his sinister influence decades ago. Wasn't warping my whole childhood enough for him? But there's no telling what bug will crawl out of the woodwork these days, with the internet-spurred fervor for reuniting. (Word to the wise: there's a reason why you lost touch, guys. You hate each other!) How had Gus even gotten hold of my address? In the letter, he informed me that he'd just been let off for stabbing his ex-girlfriend's mother when she tried to stop him seeing her daughter: the usual kind of scrape he got himself into. His acquittal parties were a regular feature of our high school years. Now he had some proposition for me he wanted to discuss. "Wanna meet?" he asked. NO.

Next in the pile, as if magically drawn to me by my sickbed descent into the past, was a letter from Chevron High, our old high school in Virtue and Chewing Gum. Now and then they'd do a mass mailing to see which of us had died, and I would normally have thrown it straight in the trash. Why should I satisfy their ghoulish curiosity? But under Deedee's kindly supervision I felt compelled to open it, and inside was a surprisingly cordial, obsequious, even gratifying letter from the new principal, asking if I'd come give the graduation speech that summer. Having never met me, this fellow managed to regard me as a credit to the school, and was sure the students graduating in June, 2011 would be fascinated to hear what I had to say. Chevron would pay my way and put me up at the Chewing Gum Plaza Hotel...

The thing is, speech making *is* my Everest—it had been an insurmountable difficulty to me throughout life. I'd had trouble giving the shortest of talks at a million medical shindigs. Even intimate, casual clinic meetings to discuss diagnoses, prognoses and lawsuits amongst "friends" could undo me. I'd rather talk to strangers! I displayed all the usual symptoms of stage fright: cold sweats, hot sweats, trembling, nausea, shortness of breath, abdominal cramps, coughing fits, hiccups, stuttering, fidgeting, corpsing, inexplicably rushing, forgetting what I was supposed to say altogether, and bouts of slapstick: I once dropped a whole cup of coffee on the person next to me as I got up to speak (about scalding marks). And what I always wondered was WHY—why must the show go on? Why is there never any getting out of the SHOW?

Also, I hated that place. I'd been fleeing Chevron High all my life, and now they wanted me back? And if so—why hadn't they asked me *before*? Did the School Board wearily consult a list of old alumni each year, debating which corny goofball could be cajoled into returning? I couldn't even picture the old codger they'd rustled up for my own graduation. All I knew was, I only had six hours left to lose my virginity before I finished high school, and his speech was taking up one of them! The whole ceremony was just a big inter-ruption of my quest to get laid. Everything was an interruption! The only sage advice I wanted from that old geezer was how to get laid and *quick*.

Why didn't they ask Gus instead? Nothing like an ex-con for speechifying. What did they expect me to talk *about*? I'm a surgeon, a manual laborer. No Churchill! Did they want me to rhapsodize on the benefits of getting your double chin rescinded and artificial dimples installed? Or maybe just testify to the great moral prin-ciples instilled in us at Chevron High during those four joyless years? All I mastered was Math and masturbation (sometimes simultaneously), and that it sucks to have zits. ("Talk about that!" my colleagues would cry. "Drum up some acne work for us.")

I must have been delirious from watching *Now, Voyager* too many times, because Dr. Jaquith's advice to Bette *post*-breakdown, as she's boarding the boat, came back to me now: "Be open, take part, be curious, unbend!" If Bette could take on *South America*, maybe I could return (briefly) to Virtue and Chewing Gum. This was the sort of guy Chevron had made me—lazy, scared, shy, indecisive… but also susceptible to sycophancy and old movies. So I wrote back saying I'd do the damn speech—and had my mechanical pencil ever turned up, the one stolen from my locker in 1978? I sealed the envelope and let Deedee mail it when she left—and *then* I got the heebie-jeebies, with the jitters, with the sweating, with the hiccups. I had just volunteered for the surest form of vexation: senseless, vapid, unpaid public humiliation. What was I thinking? This was no South American cruise, with Claude Rains just a phone call away!

But I could call Bee. Bee would help me. Bee always had an answer and she was usually right—except for that time she made me dress up like Little Lord Fauntleroy and drag her through the hot streets of Virtue and Chewing Gum, while *she* sat in splendor on our little red wagon: our contribution to the Fourth of July parade. Bee was Fauntleroy's mother, I was the truth-telling, charity-giving goofball. We really killed that day—killed a lot of patriotism anyway.

"Why would you want to talk to those bozos?" was Bee's first question, once I got hold of her.

She was in a bad mood. Her Canterbury patrons had pulled the plug on one of her Coziness Sculptures. Bee, the least "cozy" character I ever came across, had started making these emblems of domestic calm and peace she called Coziness Sculptures some time back: they consisted of assemblages of found or bought materials which she housed in tamper-proof Perspex boxes and displayed in public spaces, to work as subliminal mood-enhancers for passers-by, "a salve for anxiety and despair." She'd discovered that the English populace was in particular need of cheering up, and as soon as she got to Canterbury, had made it her mission to comfort them. So it was a blow to be told her efforts were not deemed worthwhile.

The latest (rejected) Coziness Sculpture was a peaceful fireside scene involving a comfy armchair, a glass of wine, foxed leather-bound book lying open on an antique table, small Persian carpet on the floor; everything suffused in a warm, soft yellowish light supplied partly by the (pretend) fire and partly by an art deco lamp on the table. But her patrons (through their representative, some guy Bee couldn't stand) were quibbling about the cost. They wanted her to use a *paperback* or no book at all, a junk-shop table covered by a fake lace tablecloth, a cheap ugly armchair, a mat painted to *look* like a Persian carpet, and no lamp—she was supposed to light the whole scene with hideous low-energy bulbs. In Bee's opinion, no "coziness" would result.

"I saved them money on the fireplace!" she said, referring to some sort of clever hidden flickering-light effect she'd been work-ing on, suggestive of a log fire just out of sight. "The whole *point* was to have a nice old copy of *Our Mutual Friend* lying open at my favorite bit, when Eugene knocks Mr Boffin's recommendation of bees as role models." And she ran to get the passage so she could read it to me over the phone (when was she going to deal with *my* problems?). "'I object on principle, as a two-footed creature,'" recited Bee, on her return, "'to being constantly referred to insects and four-footed creatures. I object to being required to model my proceedings according to the proceedings of the bee.'"

"I know, it's great," I agreed (thinking of Bette's scary mother in *Now, Voyager* who mockingly remarks, "Are we getting into botany, Doctor? Are we *flowers*?").

"This is the bit I really like...," Bee continued. "'Conceding for a moment that there is any analogy between a bee and a man in pantaloons (which I deny), and that it is settled that a man is to learn from the bee (which I also deny), the question still remains, what is he to learn?... They work; but don't you think they overdo it?... And are human labourers to have no holidays, because of the bees?... And am I never to have a change of air, because the bees don't?' The guy's a genius!" Bee said. "The only good thing about being here is that Dickens spent a lot of time in Kent."

"I'll beat him from top to bottomus," I said, trying to cheer her up with our old Bert Lahr game.

"Who, Dickens?"

"No, your hippopotamus of a *patron*," I said. "They commissioned you, right? And now they're making trouble about it."

"Yeah, I know. If you don't like my peaches, don't shake my tree! ... But their minion's more like a crocodile."

"I'd add him to the woodpile!"

"Or maybe a gnu."

"I'd show 'im the ol' one-two!"

"Canterbury's such a dump."

"I'd give it a big red lump!"

"Did I ever tell you about the water?"

"I'd take it to the slaughter!"

"No, Harry, listen! It's full of white stuff. It leaves white rings on all your glassware. *Scum* forms on the top of my tea that looks like tectonic plates!"

"Try a cup."

Bee finally attended to my dilemma and came up with an idea: look in the phonebook, maybe I could find an evening class in public speaking or something. This was quite a concession on her part, since I'd driven her nuts as a teenager by reading phonebooks for pleasure (sometimes out loud!). But once again she was right. There were millions of people in the Yellow Pages who claimed to be experts in public speaking, after-dinner talks, wedding speeches, PowerPoint pontification and corporate presentations: a whole hierarchy of coaches, consultants, professors, presentation maestri and mentors, trainers, gurus, shamans, and lamas were gathered there, all pretty eager to present themselves if nothing else. But I finally settled on a guy called M. Z. Fortune, because he held seminars in New York (everybody likes a "seminar") and had a sideline teaching firemen how to give presentations. (What did they give speeches about? Dalmatian care? Maybe they were much in demand at arsonists' conferences.) I'd always had a soft spot for firemen (and their *vehicles*). Firemen seemed much superior to cops. Firemen are noble—and so tidy! All they do is rescue cats and people, comfort them, and establish order out of chaos. They make *nice*. Even without the 9/11 massacre, you can't beat firemen for heroism. I think I now felt that even being *indirectly* connected to firemen might somehow help me with my speech, so I emailed this M. Z. Fortune for an appointment.

Then I sat down to play the piano. Lately I'd been playing Smetana, Ligeti and Scriabin, but now I tried Pierre-Laurent Aimard's "Collage-Montage," a piece that reminded me maybe too much of *Gertrude*: it's a medley of explosions, confusions, disagreements, rifts, sulks, and slammed doors, all of which Aimard (like Berlioz!) seems to have a terrible time bringing to an *end* (just as I did with Gertrude). I worked my way toward the finish now with all due vigor and determination.

Fortune soon replied. We arranged to meet for lunch at Kelley & Ping (my choice) on Groundhog Day, which was only a couple of weeks away. He suggested I read his book in the meantime, *The People's Guide to Presentations*, and bring it to the restaurant so he'd recognize me. I was in deep now: reading a self-help manual? Dickens, I imagined, it was not.

Actually, Bee doesn't *always* know everything in the Ant and Bee books. In *Ant and Bee and the Rainbow*, it's *Bee* who gets all bent out of shape... He can't keep up with Ant in this one at all. They agree on how to paint the old tire to look (a bit) like a rainbow ("So Ant and Bee happily began to paint the rubber tyre with the colour called... RED", etc.), but it soon emerges that Ant's got a better color sense than Bee. Ant paints his ping-pong bat VIOLET, while Bee paints his a hideous BROWN! A brown bat hardly compares with a violet one, but nobody says anything.

I learned most of what I know about mixing colors from this book. But you have to feel sorry for Angela Banner. The woman never saw sunshine in her life! England had continuous cloud cover, according to Bee. No wonder Banner knew nothing about color—you've got to go to the French Riviera like Matisse, or just *be Italian*. The lack of sun explains the melancholy muted light in all Ant and Bee books—and why Ant and Bee have to create their own rainbow in the first place, painting that tire they find half-buried in the unreal earth.

COURANTE

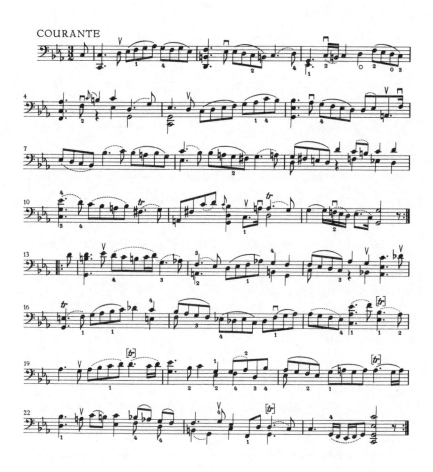

GROUNDHOG DAY

LIST OF MELANCHOLY

– the pigeon couple on the parapet outside, one dying, the other standing helplessly by
– continuous cloud cover
– the penny-pinching English, who wouldn't give Bee her art deco lamp
– artist-in-residence posts
– phonebooks
– the word, "churlish"—Bee had giggled when I said it might be churlish of me to refuse Chevron High's invitation
– people who attempt to dissuade other people from using words like "churlish"
– balloon animals
– self-conscious ten-year-olds
– accordions

- crapholes of the famous (Bee had given me a coffee-table book
  for Christmas)
- whale eyes, cow eyes, elephant eyes
- Velcro
- returning to work after a period of intense inactivity

Living in New York you cannot fail to notice millions of people heading godknowswhere, and this cannot fail to fill you with melancholy. They eat, they sleep, they shit, they stink, they speak. Some speak only to *themselves*, and I was getting like that too. It was time to go back to work.

The girls in the office made a big fuss of me and my limp and my cane, and cooed over all my other assorted ailments too—I spared them the burned tongue but owned up to the sore thumb. Cheryl, our trainee nurse, said just thinking about my thumb injury made her feel faint. Some nurse! (In her defense, her professionalism was compromised by infatuation: she had a wholly unrequited crush on me.) Soon it felt like I hadn't been away for a month at all, like I hadn't been away for a *moment*. The receptionists, Jean and Cathy, saw me as a welcome depository for all the office gossip they'd been stewing over alone, and kept rushing into my office every ten minutes with a new ice pack and tidbit of news, keen to get me up to speed on my colleagues' every bout of public drunkenness, their displays of impatience, the sniping, the griping, the fits of crying, the secretiveness... One intern had seen about ten patients in a row with his fly open, but it seemed to have been a genuine mistake, not a sign of some poignant aberration. Jean told me which patients had croaked, either before or after treatment; Cathy, that a sweet doorman had died in my absence, shot dead near his home trying to stop a fight; a fund had been set up for his wife and kids. Some workman had slipped on the newly waxed floor by the elevator, surfed on his stomach down the hallway and broken his nose, but he'd been offered a free nose-job to stop him suing.

All the stuff of office life. If it weren't for the adoring Cheryl though, I might never have heard about the antics of Jed Stockton, MD, a preppy junior doctor who'd not only participated in a weekend of tag-teaming with a bunch of fellow med students, but filmed the whole episode on his cell phone, and was now offering to show it around the office to anyone who'd look. I asked Stockton to come into my office—but *not* in order to check out his directorial debut.

"How you doing, Harrison?"

"Who was the girl involved, Jed, may I ask?"

"You heard, huh?" He seemed pretty pleased with himself. "She's a nurse. You know what they're like. She doesn't mind, she likes it! We're always going over to her place when there's nothing else happening. She's keen. Well, you know, keen on *me*, and if she wants me, she's got to put up with my crowd. That's the deal."

"Refer to the manual, Jed," I suggested, when he finally shut up. "This isn't how doctors are supposed to behave." He seemed truly perplexed: never had his camera work been received with so little enthusiasm. "Jed, I'm afraid you'll have to take your questionable bedside manner elsewhere. I'm letting you go."

Sure, there were plenty of ties hung on the doorknob when I was a med student, the stuff you do to prove you're a red-blooded American male. And cadaver fun of course—finding body parts in your bed or your beer. But we did draw the line at gang rape. I even got over my little propofol habit pretty fast—I didn't need Michael Jackson to *die* of it to know I had to stop (or did he die of plastic surgery?): I got tired of waking up not knowing who or where I was (and I was priapic enough, I felt, without any help from "milk of amnesia"). Martinis, Bloody Marys and sleep became my chosen forms of oblivion from then on.

None of us was particularly focused on chivalry at the time. Until Rosemary, my first love, my policy had been to dump (or be dumped) before anything got too serious (a strategy, come to think of it, that I immediately resumed, *post*-Rosemary). Three weeks was my standard contract, two months tops, sooner if there was any sign of sexual waning in either party. I developed a fine technique for keeping women at bay: always imply there's something much more important than them going on, even if it's just gloating over your mechanical pencils or attending yet another HMO meeting. What matters is that you *Keep the Supremacy.*

I had no trouble finding women (everybody likes a doctor), and I don't think I ever hurt anyone—though I feel some chagrin over the girl I dropped because her *mother* got cancer (after I'd badgered the kid for months to go out with me and screwed her silly several times). A real operator.

But everything changed when I met Rosemary. She had the most beautiful curvy shape but didn't know it: the girls all hated their bodies according to the requirements of our era (self-doubt from which my profession has infinitely benefited). Rosemary came over one night for a party my roommates were throwing and she never left. We talked and walked and ate and slept with each other for the next three years. This was the first time the whole male–female combo made sense to me. Sex had a purpose at last: pleasing Rosemary! I relished her softness, her smoothness, her curves, her verticals and horizontals. She made sense of New York for me, *its* verticals and horizontals, its highs and lows. Everything suddenly became sensual, the heat on the street, birds, shade, rain, reflections, strange liquors: for some reason, Rosemary and I took to ordering side-cars (the first to do so since the 1940s).

The essence of a thing runs through it: tomato leaves smell of tomato, coriander seeds smell of cilantro. Every mouse smells of mouse, every house of house. What I loved about Rosemary was her smell—not a *rosemary* smell, though that would have been apt. No, she was no plant, she was my honey. And yet—those EGGS of hers! Rosemary had an obsession with eggs, real or fake, eggs of all shapes and sizes: ceramic eggs, china eggs, glass eggs, marble, wooden, paper, plastic, gold or silver eggs, eggs with scenic views inside, tiny eggs, enormous eggs, eggs that wouldn't open, eggs that wouldn't shut, furry eggs, flowery eggs, feathery eggs, eggs in glass cases, voodoo eggs, comical eggs with flashing lights and steam coming out, a big cloth egg she liked to take to *bed* with her, egg earrings, egg mobiles, egg-shaped place mats, egg-shaped egg timers! She collected every picture of an egg she could find. She even had a large ornamental egg covered in opals and rubies, and I *tolerated* it. But, really, what is the point of a jewel-encrusted egg?

My first patient on Groundhog Day was an egg-shaped woman. Or maybe she was groundhog-shaped. She was some kind of egg and groundhog hybrid, so fat it was impossible to detect any expression in her face.

"My little boy's about to start school," she told me, "and I'm worried he'll be bullied."

"Why would that be?"

"Because I'm fat," she said flatly.

She *was* fat, but her reasoning seemed thin. I sensed there was more to this maternal concern than met the eye and, sure enough, when I examined her, I found badly healed burn scars that must have been causing her great discomfort. She'd put on all this weight *since* the burning incident, so the stretched skin was pulling at the scars and irritating them. After she got dressed, I sat her down and asked about the scarring. Without much hesitation, as if *bursting* to admit it all, as if all that fat was just layer on layer of smothered trauma and protest, she told me the ghastly thing that had happened to her. She'd been married to a guy who continually raped her, sometimes at gunpoint. When she became pregnant, he flipped completely and doused her with kerosene while she slept, setting the bed alight. Nice guy. Her little boy was born unharmed, but she was badly burned. And when she started divorce proceedings against her husband, the lawyer tried to rape her too!

So the whole thing about the kid, her anticipation of his being bullied, was really a side issue—the woman was sick of being mistreated *herself*. She needed a full-time shrink! Not my field. My training only equipped me to alleviate her physical symptoms. In recognition of what she'd been through, I offered to fix her scars for free. (My colleagues would grouse about it, but so what? I too could be compassionate.) But she didn't care about the scars, she said, she was only interested in protecting her boy from ostracism. Reluctantly, I then suggested a gastric band (not something I could do but I could find a friend who would, and I'd gladly pay)—but she objected to this too.

"There isn't time. He starts kindergarten in March."

Lipo was what she wanted and lipo was what she insisted on getting. This too was outside my province. My patients are rich, and the rich are rarely fat these days. The *poor* are fat, and the middle classes are the ones you see jogging everywhere: the thinwardly mobile. But I gave her the name of a lipo guy and told her to come back afterward and we'd see to those scars. She said she'd think about it. Then, with the assistance of my cane (which Cheryl found so sexy), I limped out to the foyer with the woman to prevent any chance of her being bullied, mistreated or ostracized on her way out.

I'd forgotten the dreariness of our waiting room, despite our marketing advisor Andy's extensive efforts to de-medicalize it. What we needed to establish, he'd informed us before the revamp, was a calm, clean, *cozy* atmosphere, so that as soon as they stepped inside the door, our prospective clients would get the feeling that plastic surgery's no big deal. "It's not like buying a house, or a car!" he said. "You've got to make it. . . fun. It could all be fun!" So the place had been done up to look like a kind of luxury holistic therapy center or relaxation and meditation spa, with minor elective procedures on offer—rather than the sadomasochistic, money-grubbing, life-endangering torture chamber it really was. Under Andy's direction, an interior decor consultant installed thick creamy carpets to break any shaky patient's fall (and muffle the whimpers), and indirect lighting that glowed kindly on post-operative abnormalities (as kindly as energy-saving bulbs *can* glow). We were also advised to position fresh flowers everywhere to mask the smell of piss and pus and disinfectant. Casual attire was the agreed look; no suits, no ties, no white coats, just a loose shirt and jeans, even a baseball cap. We all looked like we were on vacation, or still children! In fact, everything was done to alleviate fear *except* sparing people painful, invasive surgery. We even had classical music piped into the waiting room so the old trouts could listen to the "Trout Quintet."

Today it was "Heiliger Dankgesang" though, the piece Beethoven wrote in response to a terrifying illness of his own (one of *my* choices), but the irony was lost on this crowd. Even if they'd wanted to, nobody could've heard the violins over the incredible din being produced by one family—various children, parents and a grandma. The main source of boisterousness was a little girl of about two and a half, who was racing around the room talking to herself. One of her arms was in a cast, but it didn't stop her being feverishly active. The adults seemed united in trying to ignore her—but why didn't one of them take this itchy kid out to a playground or something? They couldn't *all* need cosmetic surgery.

The child was in a world of her own and her restlessness was troubling. It was *maniacal*. I watched as she approached the decorative column in the middle of the waiting room that our designer had persuaded us looked "Grecian" (though it seemed straight out of *Star Trek*—when they beam themselves onto some planet that *looks* beatific but proves to be an illusion, really just hot rocks and craters). The kid was no aesthete: she embraced this stupid plaster pillar passionately and started humping, grinding her hips against it in mock-ecstasy. She was doing a very professional-looking pole dance in our waiting room! She knew all the moves.

Somehow, I didn't think this was the kind of "fun" Andy had in mind.

The child kept looking behind her for approval—not from everybody, just her *dad*—she was looking his way the whole time she pumped and twirled. I caught the guy's eye and could see it all immediately: he had made this tiny kid watch porn and act it out for him at home. He was the one who'd taught her this stuff. He looked guilty as hell, pretending not to notice what she was up to. You could tell this wasn't his customary stance, since the kid seemed so surprised by his indifference to her porno efforts. She was obviously used to getting more of a rise out of him than this. And what was with the broken arm? Had he done that to her too perhaps, when she refused to play the game?

The next time I caught his eye, he'd governed his shame and stared back at me with defiance. I retreated to my office, shaking. I tried to calm myself by thinking of Bubbles. What was she doing right now? Probably sleeping on the window seat in the sun, dreaming of the bad old days with Styrofoam Santa, incarcerated in her bike igloo. I had tried to make up for all that by keeping her warm and well fed ever since, giving her a life of coziness and Fancy Feast (a life I kind of envied right now).

My reverie was interrupted by Cheryl bringing in my next patient, the pole-dancer's *mother*, who sat down and didn't say anything. This happens a lot. Patients seem to expect me to point out to *them* what their particular eyesore is: they've worried about it so much that, by the time they come see someone, they think it's obvious (even if it's penile dysfunction!).

"Well, what can I do for you today?" I prodded.

She shrugged.

"Is there something specific you came to see me about?"

"Well, look at them!"

"Um, at. . . what?" I asked.

She indicated her breasts. I waited. It really wasn't my job to preemptively decide what the patient's particular area of self-doubt was. Finally, she gathered herself and said, "They're too big. My husband said so." (Of course they're too big for *him*, lady—the guy likes little girls!)

I dutifully did some measurements of her small, symmetrical breasts, as if studying the problem from a medical point of view, then announced authoritatively, "Your breasts are *not* too large. They're perfectly in proportion to your body. Now, if they were causing you back pain, or—"

"My husband wants me to get something done," she replied dully.

"No ethical practitioner would advise surgery under these circumstances," I told her. This wasn't strictly true. I did unnecessary boob-jobs all the time! Changing already acceptable breasts into breasts that were equally acceptable, but slightly different, was my forte. Nonetheless, I tried to weed out the ones who were just doing it because they hated themselves.

Now she seemed on the verge of tears, and gestured dismissively at her chest. "But I can't. . . keep. . . looking at these things!" I offered her a Kleenex and let her cry. With that husband, she was entitled to it. Then she asked again, "But couldn't you do something?"

I stuck to my guns about the surgery but finally asked, "Have you considered therapy?" Adding, "For your *husband*."

She looked blank. "Oh, he doesn't have time for that. . . " (Don't be so sure, you dope—he has time to train his own kid to be a geisha girl!)

I told her I'd need to consult one of my colleagues about her case, and got her to go back to the waiting room. The truth was, most of my colleagues would happily take on this breast reduction. Hell, they'd do a female circumcision on their own mothers if they were paid enough. Bit heavy on the scalpels, light on the scruples, I sometimes felt. I didn't consult any of them. I went straight to the receptionists' private office instead and told Cathy to call the cops. Cheryl got all excited.

"Why? *Why?!*"

"Don't ask," I told her, feeling that if I went into the whole thing right then, I might throw up. "Just get them over here and keep that family in the waiting room until they come."

I limped back to my office, wishing I had a bucket of cold water to pour over my head. Boy, great to be back! But my next patient made me feel better—a young woman in a miniskirt and spaghetti-strap top, who strode in and started joking around.

"Nice office," she remarked. "See you're keeping the flower thing going in here."

"Flowers!?"

I swiveled my chair around and found that somebody (Cheryl?) had shoved a whole basin-load of tiger lilies on the window sill behind me. I hadn't even noticed before, but now the perfumed stink of them was dizzying. I turned back to the girl with a look of perplexity and she laughed. But what could her problem be, I wondered. She looked confident enough, though I thought she must be cold. Why do women have to display so much bare flesh these days, as if advertising constant sexual availability?

"When I was a kid," I told her, "we dressed *up* to go to the doctor. Now it's like everybody's off to the beach—in midwinter!"

"You sound like my dad. I do have a coat, you know."

"And a very healthy metabolism, I guess."

"What about you? You're wearing sneakers! Call yourself a doctor in that getup?"

"You win." I liked her. Sassy patients are the best. "Anyway, what can I do for you today?"

She slowly pulled up a portion of her minuscule top, to reveal a long straight scar cut diagonally across her middle. How could a girl this savvy and sophisticated have gotten herself knifed?

"Yeah," she said, in response to my questioning look. "My very dumped boyfriend did it to me."

"Why? I mean, how did it happen?"

"I stayed out too late, or didn't fold his newspaper right. I don't even remember. The guy was impossible. The trouble is, I can't wear half my clothes anymore. I can't let people see this! So I, uh, wondered if there's something you could do about it. Can you hide it or something?"

What *is* it with women? Pole dancing at two, and by twenty they're running around half-naked getting *stabbed*. And now, she was at a great social disadvantage, since more and more surface area has to be provided, blemish-free, for public view. Even the midriff, always a tricky area, is now subject to scrutiny. It took all the plastic surgeons of Manhattan to keep up with the midriff demand:

muffin-top lipos were selling like hot cakes, and this poor kid's
social life might dry up if I didn't disguise her scar.

Cheryl burst in as planned.

"Cheryl," I said sternly. "Don't just barge in when I'm with a
patient." What a ham. This was a well-rehearsed routine of ours,
designed to make the patient feel more important. Except, this
time it was for real: the police had arrived. So I booked Miss Back
Talk in for a pre-surgery checkup and joined the cops, who looked
none too thrilled by their nebulous task. They were already skep-
tical about finding any evidence, and probably despised me for
making them fill out forms. But they took a statement from me at
least, and talked briefly to the dad in an empty consulting room. He
gave me the gimlet eye as he left with them for further questioning at the station, with his family trailing along behind. I wondered
if anything would come of it. But so what if they couldn't prove
anything? At least the guy had had a scare.

As a result of my firing Jed, calling in the cops, and using a cane,
Cheryl's crush had now taken on a note of *fawning*. I teased her
a bit, saying, "Ah well, Cheryl, not everything can be cured with
a nip and a tuck, you know. Sometimes we have to call in the
big guns." Then, in a cloud of glory, left for my lunch with M. Z.
Fortune, my corpsing advisor. I'd never been so thrilled to escape
the office.

In the taxi, my thoughts drifted back to Rosemary. I hadn't
known what I was doing. I ignored all the bad omens, persever-
ing against the odds (and the *eggs*) in service to my hare-like lust,
blithely copping a feel in front of the German Expressionist paintings she took me to see, or horsing around under hailstorms at

the beach in Montauk, where Rosemary's troubled parents had a summer place. I'd been impressed that Rosemary played the cello, until I realized she wasn't just out of tune but couldn't count to save her life. The poor girl had no sense of rhythm at all! She could sort of disguise her difficulties when playing Bach solo cello suites, since she was on her own with them (though she played them like exercises—no sign of any exquisite melancholy). But you have to be able to count if you want to play Beethoven and Brahms cello sonatas: I would try to accompany her on the piano but she'd always come in too early or too late and then bust out crying.

She had no notion of time. Very late for assignations too. In the end, I suspect the late and the punctual will never really hit it off. Opposites attract, sure, and couples sometimes compensate for each other's deficiencies, but a few similarities come in handy too. The tidy and the messy just grate on each other's nerves until one of them *dies*. You need at least some agreement on vital issues, like a shared interest in wine, and how much of it to drink a night, or beach versus museum vacations, or what time to go to bed. And punctuality. (I also insist that my girlfriends share my nostalgia for the labels on Epicure cans, those polished, inedible-looking fruits set against a black background: exquisite melancholy! The images may look unappetizing, but Epicure cans have seen humanity through many tough times.)

Rosemary's mom was an alcoholic; it was the DAD I was fascinated by. For a man whose wife spent half the year in the Betty Ford Clinic, he seemed remarkably affable, and very welcoming towards *me*. In response, I exhausted myself trying to show him what a good guy I was. I worked hard as a start-up surgeon more for Rosemary's father's benefit than my own or Rosemary's. I tried to please her; I tried to please him. Somehow it wasn't *enough* to impress a girl, I wanted to impress a man too! Then, just when I had her dad where I wanted him, coming at me with the cigars and the bonhomie, Rosemary with her usual lack of timing turned against me (maybe that was *why* she turned against me?). I knew something was up when I was relegated to a position lower than an egg.

But it was the loss of that family that really hurt. Even the mom had an appealing side, or so I told myself. I was all ready to start cashing in on security, stability, fidelity, coziness, a place in this family (a place in Montauk too), a million fried-clam dinners, my wines chosen for me by a real connoisseur, a whole plausible future of efficient Thanksgivings and Christmases in the bosom of a family whose traumas seemed less excruciating than my own... and it was all snatched away. Kaput! No more clams and climaxes, no more canoodling in the dunes with my colleen, or meditative strolls on the beach with the sozzled ma. No zone of *warmth*...

These ruminations were forcibly interrupted when the cab in front of mine stopped so suddenly we rammed right into it. The drivers jumped out to wrangle. I was irritably extracting myself and my coat and hat and briefcase from the back when someone came up behind me and stole my cane! I turned around and saw a broad running up Broadway, waving my cane in the air, yelling something like, "You bastard, you come back here!" at some guy disappearing into the crowds of Union Square. I lumbered after her, making slow progress due to the wintry terrain and my faulty ankle. But she wasn't that fast herself. I caught up, and then she turned on me!

"Are you following me?" she asked.

"Well, yes! Yes, I am."

"What the hell for?" She sure was steamed about something.

"That," I said, pointing at the cane in her hand.

She looked at the thing as if seeing it for the first time, and without ado dropped it on the ground, leaving me to make a clumsy dash for it before it rolled into unscooped poop.

"Jeez," I couldn't help remarking.

"What's with the limp?" she asked.

"The limp's why I need the cane!"

We looked fiercely at each other for a second—and then we recognized each other. She was wearing a different kind of coat, a gray one this time, and no Eskimo hood, but it was the gal who saved my ass on Christmas Eve.

"It's you!" she observed.

"Hey, you saved my life on Christmas Eve!" I said. And remembering that I had never thanked her, I started babbling, "I guess I really should have thanked you... but I had no way of getting in touch."

"It was nothing," she said. "I mean, what I *did* was nothing, not that your life is nothing... " She was blushing, quite becomingly. We started walking to our respective cabs. "That was John, my ex," she said, nodding back toward Union Square. "His mother wears army boots."

So, not a crackpot in the Gertrude sense maybe, but a crackpot nonetheless. I thought this might be all the explanation I needed, we could say our friendly farewells and scoot. But she was determined to fill me in on why she'd sprung from her taxi like that when she caught sight of this John character on the street—leading to our collision. It was all John's fault too that she'd run off with my cane.

"You realize you almost caused whiplash in the guy you just saved a month ago?" I asked mildly.

"I had to get hold of him."

"Still gone on him, huh?" Though she wasn't my type, I kind of liked the look of her: strong bone structure, nice lips, tender brown eyes, and a mop of brown curls peeking out of her hat. A curious mixture of the erratic and erotic. She stopped dead. I was scared she was going to hit me!

"GONE ON HIM? You gotta be kidding. The guy's a criminal! He stole my quilt."

"Your... uh, what?"

Our drivers had settled their differences and were now honking at *us*. But before ducking into her taxi, the crazy dame shook my hand, with a notably firm grip, and said, "I'm Mimi."

"I'm just *me*," I clowned.

And she was gone, whisked away down Broadway in a cloud of snow and steam. I exhaled my own cloud. As kids, Bee and I pretended to be sophisticates smoking cigarettes in weather like this, waving our twigs around as if brandishing cigarette holders. (Who uses cigarette holders anymore? Who even smokes?) I watched the steam rise from my mouth and suddenly had a sensation of utter happiness.

> *There was an old soldier*
> *Who had a wooden leg,*
> *Had no tobacky*
> *But tobacky he could beg.*

There was a little duck
And he had a wooden leg,
Cutest little duck
That ever laid an egg!

The skin on his tummy
Was as tight as a drum:
Every time he took a step,
A rum-a-dum-dum!

Despite the car crash, I was right on time when I got to Kelley &
Ping, and bounded up the steps, my bad ankle temporarily *cured*,
perhaps by the cold. I went to the counter and got a big bowl of duck
and noodle soup, and sat down at a little wooden table to await M. Z.
Fortune, whose book I had obediently bought and attempted to read.
It sure wasn't Dickens, but it wasn't as turgid as Hobbes either, or an
electrical appliance manual. In fact it was pretty snappy, with touches
of humor, and covered every kind of oral presentation, from small,
difficult business meetings to weddings and after-dinner speeches. It
was all laid out for you, clearly and succinctly—the style of delivery
the author recommended for a *speech*. But the more I'd read about
manipulating the audience with your tone of voice or timbre ("as
lumberjacks would say"), and swaying people with your authority
and your credibility, your jokes and your anecdotes, your charm
and charisma (just being a doctor apparently wasn't going to swing
it), the more I quailed. To impress an audience, I had to project a
friendly, folksy (but not *too* folksy), brave, down-to-earth, and expres-
sive demeanor (rather than just my usual nauseous one), and make

expert use of "benchmarking", "hooks", "nutshell endings", and "limited-opportunity windows". What's more, according to M. Z. Fortune, a speech should break down into chunks, with no more than three ideas per chunk, and no more than three chunks per speech. Nine ideas? I didn't have *one*!

"Every speech, like every dog, has its head, middle, and tail." Where was the *rest* of the dog, I wondered—and what do you do if your dog of a speech lifts its back leg in the middle of your peroration? Another piece of M. Z. Fortune wisdom was, "Take fresh breaths whenever opportunity allows." This was something I felt I'd been doing all my life without being told. After reading his book, I dreamt my speech was a *hot dog* that I had to eat in three bites: chomp, swallow, breathe, chomp, swallow, breathe, chomp, swallow, breathe—I thought I was going to choke! (When I told Bee this, she said she'd seen me eat a hot dog in *two* bites.)

M. Z. Fortune would have his hands full getting a speech out of *me*. But before I had a chance to look around for him, *Mimi* appeared again! My shadow, my familiar, my very own New York nut-job, clutching her own bowl of soup on a tray. Who was following whom? And without asking, she sat down at my table and started ripping her clothes off, her coat anyway, which she dumped on the only other available chair. Where was old *Fortune* going to sit?

"What'd you get?" was her only remark, as she peered into my soup.

"Duck and noodle."

"Oh, I got duck."

"Well, that's great," I said. "But, uh, actually, I'm meeting someone..."

"So'm I," she answered, unfazed. "A client."

What was she, a *hooker*? She seemed too sweaty to be a hooker—she kept mopping her brow.

"So, as I was saying, John—" she began, as if our conversation on Broadway had never been interrupted by separate cabs and a total change of location.

"What?"

"The guy who stole my quilt. We were only *together* a few weeks! And then when we call it quits, he asks for the keys to my apartment, like he just wants to pick up his stuff, and then he makes off with Aunt Phoebe's quilt. Some lover-boy!"

"I thought it was *your* quilt."

"She gave it to me."

"Ah, hmmm, family heirloom..." The chick was demonic, even by Manhattan standards. A Baba Yaga from the Bronx who could supernaturally command Christmas Eve traffic, steal canes, threaten lover-boys, and turn up wherever I went! I needed a quiet life...

"And when I called him up about it, he said he'd SOLD it! Can you believe that?"

"Sold it? To whom?" I asked, actually sort of astonished that such depravity could revolve around bedcovers.

"The museum of annoying folksiness. You know, uptown."

"They bought your blanket?"

"It's not a *blanket*, it's a *quilt*. Slave art. Slave labor! You know how hard it is to make one of those things?"

"Uh, no. Not really."

"It's hard work. Very intensive. *Subversive* too," she went on, "turning old bits of crap into something fancy. Rags and rage, that's what quilts are made of!" To emphasize the point, Mimi bit a peapod in half that she'd found in her soup.

"Sounds like a new name for the Sanitation Department," I ventured. "Rags and Rage. You know, those 3 a.m. guys."

"It was the last one she made before she went berserk!"

"Who went berserk?"

"My Aunt Phoebe. From all that stitching and bitching. That's what did it. See, she belonged to this quilting bee." Mimi ate some more soup. "They sold her down the river. Called the cops when she started putting cat shit in the quilt stuffing. The creeps had her locked up!" (Bellevue. So it ran in the family.)

"Not very comforting though, is it, a comforter full of cat shit?" I remarked.

"It's not a 'comforter'! Anyway, Aunt Phoebe had finished *my* quilt before she hit her cat shit phase."

"Well, that's all pretty, pretty amazing, but I, uh, have to. . . " I suddenly remembered I was supposed to display M. Z. Fortune's book prominently on the table so he'd find me. I fished around in my briefcase and then attempted to position *The People's Guide to Presentations* against the wall between our two bowls. Mimi immediately snatched it and started flicking through it in a bored sort of way and getting soup on it!

"Hey!" I protested.

"Okay title. Not sure about the cover. Good story?"

"Could you just put that back over here like a good girl, so the guy I'm meeting will see it when he comes in?"

"What guy? Oh, the *guy*."

"And no, there's no 'story.'"

"Subplot then, if it hasn't got room for a *whole* plot?"

"No subplot either," I said, increasingly concerned about how I would handle M. Z. Fortune's arrival. Move to another table, I guess.

"You seem to like this book a lot, huh?" she continued.

"It's okay. A bit too much jargon," I said, lowering my voice in case M. Z. Fortune was in the vicinity.

Taking this as an invitation for a conspiratorial confab, Mimi leaned forward and whispered, "Yeah? Like what?"

"Well, things like 'hooks' and 'benchmarks' and 'limited-opportunity windows,'" I feebly replied. "To tell you the truth, I don't really know what he's talking about."

"Hmmm. Must be some good bits though," she said.

"Yeah, well, it's funny when he tells you not to jingle your keys and your change in your pockets as you speak, and you're not supposed to give a speech while unconsciously covering your groin with your hands. That's the fig-leaf position. It distracts the audience, apparently."

"So you want to give a speech, huh?"

"I don't *want* to, I *have* to. At my old school. They asked me to do the graduation speech this year."

"What's it going to be about?"

Thinking up something on the spot, I answered, "'How I Hated School.'"

"You're going back to your old school to talk about how you hated school?!"

"Yup."

"Great! I hated school too," she declared, and absent-mindedly pocketed the book.

"Hey! You're not going to steal that too, are you?" I asked. "First my cane, now—"

"I can't steal it. It's mine."

"What!?"

She leaned forward again and whispered, "I wrote it," before turning a deep pink once more. "So I guess you're my client!"

"Huh?" Wait a minute. *This* was the person I'd enlisted to help me calm down about giving a speech? This whirling dervish? With the blushes, with the blankets, with the boyfriends. . .

"You're Harrison Hanafan, right?"

"You're M. Z. Fortune?"

Why I'd assumed M. Z. Fortune was a man I don't know, but I had. I even had a firm image of him in my head, and he didn't look anything like Mimi (didn't have her bone structure).

"That's not my real name, ya know," she was saying. "I took it for professional reasons. The *M*'s real though: that's for Mimi."

"What's the *Z* for?" I asked, trying to recover my equanimity. "Zsa Zsa?"

"Nada. Business people just expect to see a middle initial. It makes 'em feel safe."

"Well, how about the Fortune?"

"Yeah, that's what *I* say! 'Fortune' is there to help me *make* one. You know, like Johnny Cash. Or Neil Diamond, and Goldie Hawn. Goldman Sachs. State your claim in your name, that's my motto. It doesn't hurt to remind people you want money!"

"I've met some pretty destitute Goldbergs in my time," I argued. "And Adrienne Rich isn't rich... I don't think."

"Bet she wants to be though," Mimi said, chomping on a piece of duck. "Anyway, can't hurt."

I noodled around in my noodles, wondering what I was getting myself into. Yet, at the same time, I had a feeling this Mimi person would make a fine public-speaking coach: *she* was so weird and unpredictable, she'd make giving a speech seem a breeze!

"Maybe you should aim higher," I told her, "call yourself Fort Knox, or Priceless Gems. Cadillac Chevrolet... Unmarked Fifties..."

"Yeah, I like that one. President Unmarked Fifties, ladies and gentlemen."

"But what about *my* name? Too much alliteration, right? And no outright begging."

"What, Harrison Hanafan? I *love* your name! That's why I agreed to meet you! I don't usually teach people privately. My work's mostly seminars." She added with a tinge of gloom, "I help businessmen."

"Tough crowd?"

"You wanna live in New York, you gotta do something for assholes," she said.

I nodded. "My work's pretty reliant on assholes too."

Then Mimi grabbed my arm and said, "Hey, do me a favor, will ya? It wouldn't take very long..."

I didn't know what to say. This woman had after all saved me from an inglorious fate on Christmas Eve. I owed her! *And* I liked the feel of her hand on my arm.

"See, I've gotta find my quilt," she pleaded, "at the museum, and I don't want to go alone!"

Ingratitude was not mentioned (this wasn't Gertrude I was dealing with) but without much further coaxing I canceled my appointments and soon we were in a taxi (the first we ever shared), and there was something about the pull of the meal and the wheels and the woman, or maybe just the combo of taxi upholstery and afternoon off, that made it feel like a DATE. You hit that taxi interior, tucked into your own cozy little nest back there, and it's Pavlovian: a kiss seemed imminent.

But we'd already reached the museum. First we trailed through the Tinware Room.

"I guess I should've been saving up my tinfoil," I said to Mimi. "I'd probably have enough for a sundial by now. Or a commemorative tea set."

"Or a magic, healing nose," she said, studying some fine Mexican examples of legs, arms and organs cut out of flat pieces of tin.

The Weathercock Room was full of long-immobilized, formerly revolving emblems in wood and metal—some political, some ironic, some abstract, some figurative, some painfully fragmentary and weatherworn.

"Look at that mermaid!" Mimi called out, dragging me over to a *double entendre* weather vane from Nantucket, that featured a demure clothed lady on one side and a bare-breasted mermaid on the other. Mimi had instantly detected the best thing in the room.

"You can just imagine a crowd of sexually frustrated whalers standing below, hoping the wind will turn."

The Painted Furniture Rooms I *liked*, because the black or green or red chairs, decorated with little paintings of fruit, flowers, tall ships, birds' nests, horses frolicking, and a lot of miniature Jefferson Monticellos, reminded me of Epicure can labels.

"Do you like Epicure cans?" I ventured to ask Mimi, but got no answer. She'd already charged into the Old Washboard Room, which appeared to be a chilling tribute to housework. Propped up like gravestones stood dozens of riveted slabs—on which a million graying cotton shirts must once have been energetically rubbed, slapped, and squeezed. It gave me the heebie-jeebies.

"Boy, how wouldja like to have to do *that* every day?" Mimi exclaimed.

"Mimi, I don't even grate my own cheese," I said. "Or, not without some kind of calamity."

The Rag Rug Room was next, and to my horror Mimi wanted to walk on them.

"Uh, I don't think you should take your shoes off—"

"But it's the greatest *thing*, walking in bare feet on rag rugs. They don't *look* that nice, but they feel sooo gooooood. . . "A guard approached, and steered us sternly into the Washington D. C. Handmade Souvenir Room. There we saw about a billion White Houses made out of stamps and bottle tops, Lincoln Memorials done in popsicle sticks, and pencil holders adorned with brutish impressions of Capitol Hill.

"There seem to be no depths to which patriotism won't aspire," I mused, but Mimi seemed oddly enchanted by a group portrait of Abe Lincoln, Teddy Roosevelt, and what looked like Barry Goldwater, painted on a thimble. I felt strangely humbled by her ability to appreciate its well-meant shabbiness.

The Moccasin and Tomahawk Rooms were kept reverentially dark, out of respect for genocide. We almost tripped over each other trying to get out of there into the Slave Doll Room, which was full of rotten-looking dolls, literally rotting away before our eyes. One display case was stuffed full of antique doll limbs.

"I don't know about dolls," I said. "They kind of give me the creeps."

"Me too," Mimi said, to my relief.

"But why do girls like them?"

"They need somebody who can't fight back."

"Is that why they like riding horses too?"

"Nah, that's just about power and speed. Nothing can stop you when you're on a horse."

"My sister had an imaginary one."

"So did I! Clark Gable."

"Hers was Hollenius."

We took a spin around the Spinning Wheel Room.

"Okay, I can see that these things were state-of-the-art technology at some point," I said. "But do they have to be turned into totemic objects and plopped in the window of every cake shop in New York? 'Here's your popover, sir—need anything *spun* with that?'"

Mimi smiled. "The idea of women spinning from dawn to dusk gives people an appetite."

"The *customers* should have to spin a few yards of yarn before they get their food."

"Or knit something."

"Oh, no knitting, please!" I shuddered, thinking of Gertrude's woolen creations.

On to the Butter Press and Butter Churn Room: it really stank in there. Just as much as you'd expect, only more so. What was happening to me? I used to be a reasonably useful member of society. Just that morning, I'd performed several creditable functions and now here I was, examining butter molds!

At last we reached the Quilt Room, a darkened, spotlit *cathedral* to quilts. Some were laid invitingly on fake beds (well roped off—to deter itinerant sleepers), others hung from the ceiling, or against the walls; and each was individually lit and labeled as if it were a quattrocento masterpiece. I trudged around, unimpressed, but Mimi seemed to be in her element, zigzagging all over the place to look at each one. She obviously knew a lot about these things, even without reading the labels—when she did read them, they only seemed to incense her.

"Look at this one!" she fumed. "'Stitched with love'! Quilts are stitched with *loathing*. That's what's good about 'em!"

"You're sticking with your 'rags and rage' theory, huh?" I just couldn't see the rebelliousness of bedspreads. Nor could I be convinced that they were significant works of art. After (reluctantly) studying an ornate quilted tableau of historic events, I said to Mimi, "It's not Leonardo though, is it?"

"Yes it is!" she replied.

"It's not Van Go—"

"Yes it is."

And, standing before a red-and-black Amish number, "It ain't Rothko."

Mimi had had about enough of this. "Look at that Crazy Quilt," she said, drawing me over to a jazzy-looking blast of color. "*That's* abstract, that's modern. . ." I did like "Crazy Quilts" a bit better than the rest of these bedspreads. They were like Cubist collages, and at least tried to break up the monotony of all that obsessive repetition. But chintzy or minimalist, innovative or traditional, revolutionary or docile, slavish or self-indulgent, quilts *all* seemed a little crazy to me. Why waste so much time sewing cloth together, for chrissake? Stitch, stitch, stitch! It's got to be a major cause of arthritis. I wasn't too happy about the thought of all those Bellevue cases either, armed with needles, every loop a noose in their minds for some worthless jilter, some Casanova, cad, scoundrel, some nebbish, some nudnik, some no-goodnik who done 'em wrong. All this taut, fraught cloth—no wonder we have castration complexes!

"What *is* it with women and cloth?" I murmured. "Do they have to pull the threads so *tight*?"

"Thrift," answered Mimi. "Women are always broke."

"That doesn't explain the pillow fights."

I was deep in unhappy contemplation of an ancient quilt dominated by a goofy central rose design made up of at least one million zillion petals—sheesh!—when I heard a commotion going on in some dark corner of the room.

"Step back from the quilt, ma'am," said the same guard who'd shown us out of the Rag Rug Room. I went over and there was Mimi standing *behind* the museum rope, clinging onto a truly beautiful quilt. Her aunt's, I assumed. The design was abstract and geometrical, with a pattern of thin diamonds of intense color, set against a black background (not wholly unlike the colors of Epicure cans!).

The Firefly Quilt
Circa 1960
The Bronx

The brighter diamond shapes seemed to twinkle on and off like fireflies. But that didn't excuse Mimi's attempt to tear it off the wall! The quilt wouldn't budge, but Mimi fell awkwardly over the rope—and into my arms.

"Thanks!" she said, looking up at me, her face glistening madly. Still, there was something luscious about her in that pose.

We were now escorted down into the bowels of the museum, in order to be reprimanded. As we waited for the elevator, Mimi whispered, "I need you to do something for me."

"Huh?! What now?" I asked, a little ungraciously.

"Just act like you're my lawyer."

"Like I'm... what?! I'm a *doctor*, Mimi, not a lawyer. Doctors are better than lawyers. Lawyers take your money and don't even give you an ointment."

"You won't have to say much," she coaxed. "Don't forget you owe me. Madison Avenue, Christmas Eve..."

"What, were you busy or something? Did I hold you up? I already said thank you!"

"Think of it as your first lesson in public speaking."

"Public *sneaking*, you mean."

After a few walkie-talkie confabs, the guard delivered us into the care of a long-legged arts-and-crafts PhD student, who led us disdainfully through corridors stacked full of folksy clutter: piles of old newspapers, scary bassinets, bashed enamelware, rusty pots and pans... probably a few crapholes of the famous too.

"Whewee!" I said under my breath. "Time for a garage sale."

"Focus!" ordered Mimi.

"*You* focus!"

Any minute now I was going to start laughing. To steady myself, I told myself this was my big 007 moment. The glamorous PhD student's *froideur* somehow seemed to demand James Bond suavity in return. But first Mimi and I had to sit in what looked like a couple of old baskets, in a dingy waiting area outside the Director's office, where one plucky little plant was perversely striving to survive. I was beginning to think it might be a *faux* plant made by nineteenth-century craftsmen in Arkansas, as light relief in between wrestling those hopeless basket chairs into being—when we were ushered in to see the Director. I was all ready for Donald Pleasence, complete with the white cat clawing its way up his lapel (you can tell Donald doesn't like that cat—his suit's been ruined by it). But I was wrong again: *another* gender switch! The Director was a woman. Is EVERYBODY a woman these days? They sure get around.

This one, I immediately detected, was a Manhattan art-world person in the Gertrude tradition. In fact I might even have met her at one of Gertrude's Dohnányi parties. The woman had never whittled anything in her life and clearly had no time for us because *we'd* never whittled anything either. After a few unpleasant pleasantries, Leggy whispered something in her ear—but before the Director started interrogating us, Mimi took charge.

"We've come for the Firefly Quilt," she announced to my surprise.

"Yes, I see," the Director replied. "Would you prefer a slide of it, or do you need a digital reproduction?" She really was not on the ball.

"Reproduction?!" Mimi turned red with fury. I thought I'd better intervene.

"Excuse me," I said.

"And you are. . . ?"

"Hanafan. Harrison Hanafan. Ms. Fortune's attorney." The Director seemed to soften, either awed by my shaky Bond act, or by the idea of lawyers. "We would like to discuss your recent acquisition of the Firefly Quilt," I continued.

"I believe we acquired the Firefly only about a week ago," she proudly began. "It's a fine example of quilt-making of the period, with finer materials than is customary. It shows an astonishing awareness of quilting traditions, Amish and Ohio influences in particular—"

"Madam," I broke in. "We are not concerned right now with the item's place in history. We have a more urgent purpose: to restore it to its rightful owner. The article in question was never knowingly sold by my client, to whom it belonged. It is stolen property. Did you establish the quilt's provenance before you bought it, may I ask?"

Flustered, the Director replied, "Well. . . the man said his aunt made it! Quilt provenances are notoriously difficult to. . . I think he said her name was Sophia—"

"It's Phoebe, and she was *my* aunt," Mimi broke in. "Not *his*!"

"I can assure you," said the Director to me, as if she only wanted to deal directly with Bond, "we bought the quilt from the bona fide owner. I have the paperwork here... somewhere... " She now glanced anxiously at Leggy, and began to shift piles of papers around on a desk that was beyond folksy: it was chaos! Leggy raised a leggy eyebrow and went over to assist her, but you could tell they were never going to come up with any document relating to the quilt; not fast anyway.

I barged in. "What you've got there, madam, is a hot quilt."

The Director and Leggy looked at each other, then stepped outside the room to confer. This was a moment of great danger for us—because of the temptation to *guffaw*. Mimi and I studiously avoided eye contact. The two women came back, with an offer.

"We have decided that in fairness, subject of course to official clearance... we should consider selling you the quilt," said the Director stiffly, fearful of admitting (to a lawyer) any failure in the museum's procedures. "We will only require you to meet the price the museum paid for it." Success!

"How much?" asked Mimi, suspiciously.

"Twenty-five," answered Leggy.

"Twenty-five dollars?! Trust John to sell it for—"

"Twenty-five thousand dollars," Leggy corrected, the eyebrow rising ominously again before she and the Director shared a classic Laurel and Hardy nod of mutual approbation.

Next thing I knew, we were in the museum shop, where a reddened Mimi bought ten bucks' worth of postcards, her mouth a tiny dot of fury. To cool us both down, I took her to MoMA to see Matisse: to MoMA with MiMI! She studied one of his odalisques for some time before saying, "Was that Sherlock Holmes you were trying for in there?"

"Sherlock Holmes!? I'm wounded. That, Mimi, was my best James Bond impression! I thought I'd never get a chance to use it."

Then we did crack up.

We went back to her place in Grove Street afterwards, to her cramped kitchen with its view of a brick wall opposite. Mimi fixed us huge Scotch and sodas and we sat at her bashed-up kitchen table, talking shyly about things. I think profiteroles came up, and their (debatable) relation to vol-au-vents. After a while she said she had to go have a shower, and left me sitting there all alone, making whirly patterns on the table with my wet glass. When I got tired of that, I wandered around the apartment, a funky little place with an unexpected sunken living room that must have seemed the hottest thing in about 1964. The bedroom was surprisingly spacious. It seemed dark and calm in there. Hours passed, or so it felt. "Mimi?" I called out, but she couldn't hear me over the sound of running water. I went back to the kitchen and poured myself another whiskey and wandered with it into the bathroom.

There was Mimi, in a towel, reaching up for something, one breast exposed. She looked just like Delacroix's Liberty leading the people! A brave, sturdy dame with freedom on the brain—bayonet rifle in one hand (or, in Mimi's case, a damp towel), French flag in the other (comb), a load of dead supporters or enemies at her heels (pile of discarded clothing), and one big foot peeking out like the Statue of Liberty's (minus the questionable sandal). If I didn't shave, I could have been the Abe Lincoln lookalike, standing protectively by with a gun my own (glass of whiskey). There was none of the fragility of Gertrude about this gal. Nor were those the delicate flower-sewing hands of Puccini's Mimì. This Mimi was no vulnerable waif or stray, no flower-girl. In fact, she wasn't my type.

It was really that *bathroom* of hers I first fell in love with! The one thing my apartment lacked, a great old-fashioned New York bathroom with white hexagonal floor tiles, squared black towel rails, black-and-white tiling around the walls, a white china toilet-paper recess, and that great wide square sink with its mammoth X-shaped faucets. Mimi had it all!

She'd now gone into the bedroom, and I thought I heard her say, "Why don't you kiss me?" This request seemed highly unlikely, so I went back into the kitchen, but there were too many circles in there. A few fireflies too. So I went to join Mimi instead, walked right up to her in her towel in her dark bedroom and her miasma of mayhem, and suddenly thought, I must kiss this woman before one of us *dies*.

Our four lips met, like the four corners of the earth, the four elements, a foregone conclusion. I didn't see stars but there were skyscrapers and my mother's raspberry jam and bulldozers and dachshunds. Some Matisse odalisques too, and cops, news flashes of politicians and flood victims, a quilt or two, Schubert, a Grecian pillar... and Gertrude. Yes, some lingering guilt toward Gertrude tried to throw me—misplaced, an error, a reflex, a shield against the unknown, the last refuge of the unadventurous. I pushed it aside. I think I saw tall pines waving against an evening sky, baskets, some chair I used to own: I ricocheted off all these obstacles in search of Mimi. Her towel slipped down, which distracted me, and

I suddenly wondered if I might have jumped the gun, forced myself on her, offended in some way. Maybe she hadn't suggested kissing at all, only said something like, "Where's the Kleenex?"

She smiled though, that smile that always got me, and all my hesitancy dissolved: I wanted to kiss her whole being, every kooky thing she'd ever done, every thought in her crazy head. I had to be near that womanly softness of her, to hell with the exact qualities of her body that I was overtrained in noticing. Jumping hurdles of my own prejudices—too tall, too big, too old, too bold?—I kissed her hot temple, her hot temper, her neck, her hair, her warmth, her alienness. I wanted to know her everything. I ran my thumb down her unfamiliar belly until she moaned.

A kiss is a big step, an opening, an honesty, a transgression. There's something *equal* about it, this mutual penetration, a relaxation (if only temporary) of self-love. Forget dualism—in the midst of a kiss you're neither male nor female, yin nor yang. You're not yourself! I only paused to ask, "You don't embroider, do you?" before Ant and Bee painted the tire the color called RED, and we went to bed.

VALENTINE'S DAY

"WHY DO YOU look at my hands?"

"Because they charm me," I answered, kissing them, and it was true. I was now an advocate of Mimi's large hands and strong feet, and the well-rounded calves that sloped dramatically down to her unsprainable ankles. Mimi's feet seemed HEROIC to me, the kind of feet Liberty would *need* to man those barricades. *A mighty woman with a torch, whose flame was the imprisoned lightning.*

Mimi *was* heroic: heroic in the grocery store sniffing out the bargains, heroic on the subway pushing her way onto crowded trains, heroic when eating, when drinking, when sleeping, when laughing, just heroic all the time! Heroic in her beliefs, her angers and upsets, heroic when she dropped to her knees and took my cock in her mouth, heroic when I turned her to fuck her standing up, heroic coming and coming under the ceiling fan in her wide square bedroom. Heroic lying spoon-style behind me afterwards, calling me darling.

Is this not love?

When you first get together with someone, you hammer out a cosmos—through moments of discord as well as contentment. It's your Big Bang period. From then on, the way you interact has been established. Things evolve, sure, you can refine it. But the major accommodations have been made and met, parameters set, no-go zones delineated, and you'll pause before disturbing these balances and tilting the whole thing off course.

Mimi turned out to have a lot to say, but not in Gertrude's meandering megalomaniacal manner. Mimi had firm views, clear enemies, and battles to fight. None of it seemed aimed directly at *me*. It was exhilarating to watch, and had a strange erotic charge. Mimi was brash, she was brazen, I wasn't even sure she was completely *civilized*. And sometimes she'd lash out at me too, like a cornered animal: I was communing with nature at last.

"Where there's life, we can rail!" she declared one morning out on the roof, with the wind in her hair.

"Okay, but don't lean on the railing."

Mimi on power suits: "Power suits don't work. Power works."

Mimi on jobs: "Work's bad for you. It drives everybody nuts in the end! That's why I went freelance. If I wanna stay in bed, I stay there."

This wasn't exactly true—despite her fantasy of flexibility, Mimi always seemed to have to email somebody or Xerox something, frustrating all my endeavors to keep my own workload down to a minimum in order to be with her!

Mimi on parenthood: "You share your genetic defects with somebody, and then they get your crappy furniture when you die? Some deal." We were in total agreement on procreation: its unnecessariness.

Mimi on male bonuses: "They earn five times what women do, and still expect you to chip in for dinner!"

Mimi on sports: "What good's an Olympian to *me*?"

Mimi on guys on the subway who spread their legs and their newspapers far and wide: "We all paid the price of a ticket. And I like opening my legs too!" This she then demonstrated to me, in the most beguiling way.

Mimi on the Hadron Collider (which she insisted on calling the Hard-on Collider): "Who needs a big machine to re-create the chaos at the beginning of the universe? Chaos we got!"

"How about a Tippi Hedren Collider instead then?" I suggested. "You just throw birds at her until she flips."

Mimi on the guy who claimed to have started an extramarital affair with a complete stranger, involuntarily, while sleepwalking as a result of taking an antidepressant: "Yeah, sure."

Mimi on a beer company promotion prize of a whole "caveman" weekend for five guys—free beer, video games, sports channels, and room service: "Five drunks in a cheap hotel."

Mimi on breast cancer campaigns: "Them and their pink ribbons. It's sexual harassment! They never let you forget your breasts are a liability."

Mimi on bras: "Tit prisons. Who decided tits have to be this stiff and high anyway? The UN?"

"But without bras," I argued, "I'd have even more boob-jobs to do and I'm sick of them!"

"I didn't know men could get sick of breasts."

"Not of breasts maybe, but of altering them in accordance with their owner's latest caprice, or her husband's."

Mimi was pretty suspicious of my profession. We battled it out one day over Yankee bean soup and borscht at B & H Dairy on 2nd Avenue (even when you're in love, you still need soup!). I was admiring her lips, and made the mistake of saying they were beautiful.

"They're just my lips. Don't separate 'em off and compare them to other lips. You're not at work now, buddy."

"Well, shut up and kiss me then!"

She did, then resumed her rant. "Who decides what's beautiful anyway? It's all a matter of opinion, right?"

"Well, according to my partner Henry, beauty was decided *for* us by evolution. Hairiness in men, for instance, hairlessness in women. Sexual characteristics got exaggerated over time, since the people most universally recognized as desirable were the most likely to find mates. Youthfulness is another widely accepted beauty trait, because it implies fertility. Evolution decided it, and we just help it along."

"That's bullshit," declared Mimi.

"Look, Mimi. Imagine nature is the tailor, as a teacher of mine put it, and we're the invisible menders when the suit gets a bit worn out."

"Hmmm."

"Honey, it's just a job."

"Hmmm."

Those "hmmms" of hers.

"Some people really need help, Mimi, or their lives would be ruined! I had a woman in once who'd grown a *horn* on her forehead!

Just an excess of keratin, easily removed—but in the Middle Ages she would have been dragged from town to town as an emblem of cuckoldry or something!"

"Or burnt as a witch," said Mimi, taking a big bite of challah bread. "But come on, Harrison—most people's lives aren't *in danger* if they don't have a nose-job."

"All I know is, a lot of middle-aged women come to me complaining they feel invisible."

"But being invisible's great!" Mimi said. "You can do whatever you want and nobody notices."

"I have this sudden twitch in my neck."

"That's 'cause you're talkin' through your hat!"

I quickly changed the subject to Haydn. "You know how Haydn was taught to play the drum? When he was three years old, they hung a drum on a hunchback's back and Haydn walked behind him with his drumsticks, tapping away. Later, he got the full drum kit with high hat and cymbal, requiring six hunchbacks and a midget who played the kazoo."

Mimi almost spat her borscht everywhere, something it's important not to do in such a small space. At B & H, you try to avoid any sudden movements, so as not to upset lethal quantities of hot soup. I moved on from midgets to a confession of my midget–maniac problem in childhood. Mimi had had similar mix-ups: she'd thought cirrus clouds were serious, and for a long time, to her mother's shame, called water "agooya", ravioli "ravaloli" and beef bouillon "Beef William."

"Did you know they've just invented a way of manufacturing sperm artificially?" I asked next, just to get a rise out of her.

"Isn't there enough of it around already?"

"Yeah, the thing would be to *de*-invent it," I said. "Everybody talks about recycling and hybrid cars but they never think seriously about overpopulation! If we could just stop having babies, we wouldn't need all these apocalypse scenarios." (Another bugbear of Mimi's.)

"But what would Hollywood do, without the end of the world?" she mused. "They aren't happy unless people are looting and drowning every place. And then a guy gets into his SUV and somehow saves the day, or at least his own stupid skin."

Mimi on Cormac McCarthy: "He writes about cowboys and the apocalypse. Enough said."

Mimi on Branwell Brontë: "Who cares?"

She got mad about a million different things! But she could be easily charmed too.

Mimi on generosity: "Some people are so generous it breaks your heart. Pavarotti's generous. And that guy who had to land his plane in the Hudson. When they were all standing in the cold out on the wings, he gave his shirt to one of the freezing passengers. The shirt off his back! *You're* generous too. You're generous with your cock."

Forget the soup, cancel my appointments! Taxi!

Bubbles and Mimi had formed an instant rapport—almost as if they knew each other already. There was occasional competition between Bubbles and me over who got to sleep on top of Mimi. But most of the time our *ménage à trois* worked very well. When we all woke up entangled together on Valentine's Day, I started telling Mimi about the way my parents had incarcerated me in my bed as a kid, thereby putting me off bedtime for life (until now). She found my Berlioz problem funny so, getting bolder, I stood up to declaim, "It was in fact during those sleepless nights that I, like Edison, came up with my best stuff." Then I gave her some examples of my youthful "inventions" (so far unpatented):

1. Every sidewalk a conveyor belt.
2. Every basement a swimming pool.
3. Every attic a planetarium.

Mimi had invented the same stuff herself. Still, I had more!

4. Aquarium bathtub: translucent sides so you could have real fish in there—octopuses, sharks, baby alligators, whatever you want (Bee always wanted sea horses).
5. The Tornado Room-Tidier: a machine you place in the middle of your room and it spins faster and faster, blowing all your toys and clothes and shit into the corners and under the bed. Instant appearance of order.
6. The Yuck-Suck Machine: this consists of a pump, a disposable "reservoir" (plastic baggie), and a tube going down your sleeve, ending in a discreet nozzle. When you're presented with unfamiliar food at a friend's house (like Beef William, for instance), the Yuck-Suck secretly siphons it all up. Particularly good on cabbage and gravy.
7. The Nickel-Stick Shooter: this contraption divides your Kraft Karamel Nickel Stick into individual pieces, OR shoots them at your friends in a mild, harmless way your mother can't

object to—your mother who, by banning you from all toy-gun ownership, even water pistols, has relegated you to a life of insecurity and social ostracism.

"The musings of a kid who felt trapped in his bed, in his room, in his family, in his town, in his universe," I said in summation, before noticing I was much too far away from Mimi and rejoining her on the bed. "I was imprisoned at *school* too. Locked in the play-pen: a sort of solitary confinement for hardened class scapegoats. I had to eat my lunch in there all on my own!. . . Unless Bee came."

"Bee got into trouble too?" asked Mimi, reaching over to stroke my thigh.

"No, she just came to keep me company. She never got caught for anything. But she was a bit of an outlaw too. It was Bee who taught me how to squirt toothpaste at people from the top floor of the library. They thought it was bird shit. That was great! Later, she became the town's only graffiti artist."

I grabbed Mimi and forced her to bestraddle me so I could caress her hips and stomach and look up at her breasts while we talked. "Happy Valentine's Day, Mimi."

"Happy Valentine's Day," she returned, and bent to kiss me.

Possessiveness suddenly struck me as the sexiest thing in the world. I held her tight. "Be mine," I said, and meant it.

She *was* mine.

"Tell me you love me."

"I love you," she murmured. I already knew it. The girl was crazy about me!

Mimi wasn't crazy about Valentine's Day though: she considered it only a shadow of its former glory, a fake and faded version of ancient fertility rites or something. "The only reminder of its real purpose is all the vulvas," she told me.

"Huh?"

"Yeah, all the pink valentine hearts. Those aren't *hearts*, Harrison. *You're* a doctor. Hearts don't look like that, vulvas do! *Open* vulvas. They're all a throwback to prehistoric vulva worship, that's what those heart shapes are."

"HUH?"

"Prehistory. You know, before the Bronze Age."

"Before the Bronze Age? Before the Bronze Age, missy, there was nothing. Nada. Zilch. Niente."

"Before the Bronze Age, *mister*," Mimi said, "we had two hundred thousand years of peace, music, dance, arts, agriculture, and goddess worship!"

"... Any cuckoo clocks?"

"People still act like the whole human race cracked out of an egg about five thousand years ago," Mimi said, getting up and putting on her purple kimono. "They totally forget about prehistory."

"I'm getting the feeling prehistory's your favorite bit of history."

"Sure," she said, brushing her hair.

"But you can't just pick and choose the bit of history you like best, can you?" I asked her.

She turned on me. "Why not? *Men* have!"

"Well..."

"I always knew there was something fishy going on, the way history's taught in school. And then I realized: they leave out the first two hundred thousand years, and they leave out *women*! All they care about is male history, patriarchy—but that's only been going maybe five thousand years. Five thousand years of teenage boy hissy fits, with sulks in between. What a mess."

"Well, that's an interesting perspective on the whole of Western Civ—"

"Everything was going swell, you know. Matriarchy worked! Then men took over metalworking and used it to make more and more powerful weapons... And then they domesticated the horse..."

"Gotta domesticate that horse!"

"Yup. It's not *horses'* fault, but from then on it was just rape, rape, rape, war, war, war, colonizing everybody and wrecking stuff. Everything became about men and their death wish. They colonized *us* too! We don't even know what women *are* anymore, they've been suppressed for so long!"

I liked this dirty talk. I went over to colonize *her*, and we ended up back in bed, where she started to tell me about "pockets of matriarchy," which at first I took to be a euphemism for vulvas—I was exploring *her* pocket of matriarchy as we spoke. But no, "pockets of matriarchy" turned out to be islands and other isolated, peripheral places in ancient Europe, where vestiges of prehistoric, female-centered cultures survived a bit longer than elsewhere, with remnants still apparently detectable now. Places like Malta, Sicily, Sardinia, Orkney, Ireland...

"Yeah? That's nice," I said, not fully concentrating (my head under the blankets, my tongue seeking out *her* peripheral spots).

"There are still signs of it," Mimi said, "um... in folklore and customs, and ceramics... mmmm, Harrison... And there are these big bulbous Venus sculptures... in Malta and places... And vulvas, paintings and... Oh!"

"Any quilting?" I asked, mounting her.

"No... But... ahhh... cave paintings... Women did all the cave paintings, Harrison..." And then there was no more talk for a while.

"Pockets of matriarchy, huh?" I said later, getting dressed. "Sounds like pussy to me. No, not *you*, Bubbles!" And I grabbed Bubbles, holding her belly up like a babe in arms. She loved that. Some tickling was involved.

"Matriarchy's a much more natural way to organize things," said Mimi dreamily from the bed. "Without mothers no mammal would survive. *Meerkats* are matriarchal."

"You want me to be a meerkat?!"

"Bubbles is a mere cat."

"Well, I'm sure there's a lot to be said for the Stone Age, Mimi, but all I know is, I wouldn't want to have been born before Bach. And ASPIRIN."

When we eventually went out, the streets of New York were full of vulvas, just as Mimi had predicted: vulvas in every window, vulvas painted on the buses, vulva-shaped balloons outside restaurants, dogs with flashing vulvas on their collars, taxis sporting ads for vulva-related events. And every corny heart shape made me horny again for Mimi. I would never tire of this feisty gal.

We walked the High Line all the way down to the Village, so Mimi could pick up a few things from her apartment, then on to Washington Square to sit on a park bench. Things seemed a little less capitalistic and warlike there than in the rest of New York, if only for the moment. Some buskers were taking turns playing a baby grand they'd somehow wheeled into the square, and a bunch of students were standing stock-still in the middle of a path, never flinching, for reasons unexplained (a very strict form of Simon Says?). Washington Square was our new spot—we were middle-aged after all, and liked looking at dogs! (From *afar* that is—neither of us wanted to own one.)

"So, if women handled everything in the Stone Age," I began, "and men took over in the Bronze Age—"

"Iron Age," she corrected.

"Then what Age are we in now? I guess it must be the Nuclear Age..."

"Nah, the Diet Age," Mimi decided, as a huge, fluffy, perfectly white Samoyed puppy rode by in a small shopping cart. "All anybody wants to conquer now is their stomach."

Next, a basset hound lumbered valiantly by. How do they manage to walk at all? Four marvelous black standard poodles came the other way—curly-haired and not overly trimmed: true urbanites.

"I think it's the Front Age," I grumbled, "with all the boob-jobs I have to do."

"This is BIG, Harry. It's just like *Rear Window*!" Bee exclaimed when I called her later to tell her about Mimi. "You know, when Jimmy Stewart can't decide about Grace Kelly—"

"*Nobody* can decide about Grace Kelly."

"And Thelma Ritter says a man and a woman should come together like a couple of taxis on Broadway: WHAM!"

"Yep. WHAM!"

"Well, I knew something was up." Bee always knew when I fell in love with somebody, because I'd forget to call her. But we *had* to talk on Valentine's Day, no matter what. Bee and I had a thing about official public holidays and how stupid they are—especially since Nixon changed all the dates around (what a nerd). But we made an exception for Valentine's Day, because Bee had claimed it as her own, *reclaimed* it from all the marketers, greeting card companies, restaurants, and anonymous stalkers. Bee wanted to get Valentine's Day back to the friendly affair it was in childhood—when you'd send cards to everyone in your class, stuffing them into a communal cardboard mailbox, and chosen pupils got to do the deliveries— back when Valentine's Day was *fun*. So over the last twenty years, Bee had turned Valentine's Day into her own personal art project, and every year sent out hundreds of valentines that were really little works of art. She used a lot of found materials. One year, just a bus ticket (she must have saved them up for decades) with the message, "Come up and see me some time, Valentine!" Another year, all you got was a stick of Virtue gum: "Stick with me, Valentine." Or a little packet of cloves: "I clove to you." One of my favorites was a wilted petunia stuck on paper inscribed with the pun, "Bee-mine." This year, she'd sent out tea bags, with a note saying, "For you to keep or steep, Valentine." Given the recent shooting in Tucson by a guy inflamed by right-wing propaganda, I told Bee the note should have said, "Some Tea Party this is!" But that wasn't Bee's style. Her valentines were sweet and quirky, not bitingly satirical.

She wanted to return to the subject of Mimi, and when I told her that at a crucial stage in our courtship I took Mimi to see some

Matisse, Bee said, "Well, of course! The guy's an aphrodisiac. All pattern, light, and color. The artist of the middle-aged—"

"The Middle Ages? I don't think so."

"The *middle-aged*. I don't mean he got mellow or soft or something. I just mean he's got the *preoccupations* of the middle-aged, like plants, warmth, comfort... Why else does everybody get obsessed with cooking and gardening in middle age? And art. All the stuff you're too busy to appreciate when you're young. *Luxe, calme et volupté.* You finally know what really matters in life. Nature. Love. Food. Flowers. Sex..."

"Sex! Those goldfish? Come off it!"

"The odalisques, Harry, the odalisques! All those half-dressed women, lounging around taking it easy. Stretching their arms up over their heads. Those women are sex on wheels! And this is what you realize in *middle age*, that life is about *pleasure*, that's what it's for."

"Jeez, all I get are people worried about their jowls!"

I tried out Mimi's valentine-vulva theory on her: Bee said she'd keep it in mind for next year's valentine. "It'll be a doozy!" she declared. Bee was thrilled I'd finally found someone I could laugh with. "But *Mimi*? Isn't it a bit like dating Tosca, or Violetta, or some other doomed damsel of stage and screen? She doesn't run around in a nightgown, does she, looking all hollow-eyed?"

"No sign of any nightgown yet," I said proudly. "Though she does have a kimono..."

"Ah, Madame Butterfly then!"

"Sorry Bee, gotta go. Call waiting."

"Aw."

Sometimes Bee did anything to keep me on the phone. She was lonely over there, I guess. I didn't ask her about *her* sex life— Bee's amorous activities since her disastrous marriage to Hunter had been pretty minimal or, like her valentines, ephemeral: none of her men seemed to last more than a couple of weeks.

When she met Hunter, she was a few years out of art school and, like most art graduates, doing art in her spare time while *waitressing*. It's amazing how many women stick with waitressing as a career, women probably as talented as my sister, women yearning to paint or dance or act, but nobody'll let them (or pay them) so they're stuck carrying plates, announcing specials, and getting goosed the rest of their days. But Bee must have been pretty desperate to think marrying a cop was the answer! The marriage reeked of self-delusion from the start. She gave up art completely to be with that jerk and live on Staten Island within yelling range of his entire family. The time had come to either get serious about art or run for the hills. She ran. There was nothing I could do about it; those were my propofol days, followed by my Rosemary days. None of us knew what we were doing, we were in our *twenties* for godsake. And Bee didn't seem to want anything to do with me anyway, which I interpreted as a sign that she was deeply in love, so I left her to it. Rosemary and I only went out to Bee's place once, for a barbecue with all the family. Hunter was in charge of the food.

"Who wants a hot dog?" he kept asking. "Nobody?"

Yes, NOBODY. Hunter's nephew was there, this tiny little kid just starting to talk. I asked him what he wanted to be when he grew up and the kid said he wanted to be a *girl*. So Hunter whirled around from his manly post at the grill and said he'd break the

kid's leg, which his whole family seemed to find remarkably funny.
Apart from the nephew, who started crying. Rosemary and I left
as soon as we could—left Hunter to his hot dogs, and Bee to her
blinkers. I never saw the creep again. A few weeks after the barbecue, Bee called me up and admitted Hunter had been hitting her
for months, under the approving gaze of his barbaric relatives—
while I'd attributed her strange muteness to love. But *why*, when
my work at the ER brought me into daily contact with women
with that same blank look, who'd all been beaten to a pulp by guys
like Hunter? And she was still *defending* him (those women did too):
"He has a tough job," Bee told me over the phone. It was only the
incident with the nephew that had brought her to her senses.

I took the day off and rushed over to Staten Island to help her
get out of there before Hunter got back from his "tough job"
pushing papers. After that, she seemed to sit for weeks at my little
kitchen table, telling me things he'd done that I still can't bear to
think about, like the time he picked her up by her heels and threw
her against a wall. I wanted to *kill* the asshole, but Bee wouldn't
even report him. Cops don't like accusations against cops, she
said—my big strong sister who was now scared of going outside,
scared of crowds of people and big spaces and loud noises. I had
to content myself with the fact that she was safe at least, since the
jerk never showed any interest in hunting her down, content to
despise her from afar I guess.

For the first few months she was quiet, too quiet. But then she
started up with the Bach solo violin partitas that got her through
adolescence, and the more three-dimensional they became, the
better I knew Bee was. Soon she was sculpting clay monsters. Then

she started making these very artful arrangements of junk. They filled my whole apartment (a smaller place than I have now). I never knew why she did those things, but I bought a few pieces off her anyway, just to cheer her up, and eventually she was able to get a studio in Queens, where she could live and do art. And once she was there, she got to work proving all her old teachers and her dissatisfied father and her asshole of a husband WRONG, WRONG, WRONG about Bee.

Within a year she had her first solo show in a one-room gallery in New Jersey somewhere: round, flattened disks of fired clay that formed paths all over the floor. They looked like individual pieces of dried-up desert soil, about a foot wide, cracking around the edges, and people were supposed to take their shoes off and *walk* on them. The show got closed down pretty fast for safety reasons— big outbreak of athlete's foot, sprained ankles, who knows? But I think of those crazy cowpats now like Beethoven's "Heiliger Dankgesang": Bee's stepping-stones out of the abyss.

I hung up on her reluctantly, but I really did have another call, and thought it might be Mimi. It wasn't. It was Gertrude, probably phoning to find out if I was wearing my days-of-the-week socks on the right day. Even though she called less now, she still had a knack of calling at just the wrong time. Lately I'd managed to avoid a lot of these Gertrusions by being at Mimi's, or being *in flagrante delicto* and not answering, but she'd caught me off-guard this time. What was she after?

I tried to be kind, and was able to listen to her news of Claude with genuine interest. He was starting kindergarten, but Gertrude wasn't worried about his being ostracized. She was more concerned about how to get him straight from there into Yale. She'd already bought a duplex in New Haven in anticipation.

"But what if he ends up wanting to go to Columbia?" I asked.

So then she finally came out with it (the real reason for calling): "I really just wanted to say Happy Valentine's Day, Harrison!"

Oh, jeez.

"Happy Valentine's Day, Gertrude," I replied.

Talk about damsels in distress!

Later on, Mimi and I shunned all the pink-menued restaurants to eat at home. She was starting to make good use of my kitchen, and that night cooked me her specialty: Amatriciana, a matriarchal dish, she claimed, made from guanciale, chili and tomatoes, or "love-apples." Tomatoes are an aphrodisiac. (My mother never said!)

I hadn't gotten Mimi a Valentine's Day present. "I'd give you the moon," I told her apologetically. But it turned out she already owned it.

Mimi on the moon landing: "Women were in tune with the moon from the start. Menstruation's a lunar cycle. Prehistoric women invented the first calendar, a *lunar* calendar with thirteen months. You *have* to understand the moon if you're gonna *farm*, or fish. Or follow the tides and stuff. Then men turned the moon into a *bad* thing, trashing the lunar calendars, and adding all that *leap year* crap. The lunar calendar is much more exact: there really are thirteen months in a year! They even turned the number thirteen into an unlucky number! And then they go bouncing around on the moon itself? Get off! That place belongs to us!"

"Don't go to the moon, Mimi."

As Mimi stirred her sauce, which, despite her disdain for corniness looked like a pretty classic Valentine's Day dish to me—rich, red, and velvety—I started telling her about Bee and her English patrons, and how she never wanted to go to England in the first place.

"What does Bee stand for anyway?" Mimi asked.

"Bee? Bridget."

"Ah ha, ancient goddess of springs and waters."

"A goddess? My sister? Well, what about Harrison then?" I asked winningly. "What does *that* mean?"

"Patrilineal, sorry. Doesn't mean anything except Harry's son. Retrograde."

"Tell that to Harrison Ford!"

We ate in the dining room, looking out at the sparkling lights of other Valentine's Day celebrations in a million other apartments, then went into the living room with another bottle of wine. Mimi sat on the window seat patting Bubbles's head in a way I vaguely envied, while I played Scarlatti on the piano. During a melancholic Scarlattian pause, Mimi suddenly said, "Why don't you help her?" My thoughts raced involuntarily to *Gertrude*, whose phone call had left a shadow over my evening, but Mimi wasn't interested in Gertrude. She must mean Bubbles.

"Bubbles?" I asked. "What's wrong with her?"

"No. Bee," she said firmly. "Why don't you give her some money?"

"Huh?!"

"She's a struggling artist," Mimi went on. "You've got some spare cash, I take it. Why don't you help her out?"

The idea had never really occurred to me—Bee was my big sister, after all, always one step ahead of me in the world. Sure, I'd buy lunch, or a sculpture now and then (and put it straight into storage), but that was about it.

"I guess I thought she might find it... sort of patronizing," I mumbled feebly. "Bee's *older* than me. It might, uh, change the dynamic."

"Aw, she'll get over it," said Mimi.

And then she did come pat my head, as I'd wanted her to, and soon I had her on my lap, in my power, with my hand in her pussy, exploring her, imploring her, *possessing* her, making her go limp in my arms.

PRESIDENTS' DAY

MIMI ON THE MALE conspiracy to deny, betray, and confuse women: Mimi had an unsettling theory that men routinely deny women what they want. "They're always criticizing what women do, what they eat, what they read," she felt, "and depriving them of sex!" This sometimes influenced her take on movies.

Mimi on Now, Voyager: "The thing is, underneath the dowdy dress and the fat suit, she's all raring to go. She doesn't want to carve ivory boxes, she wants sex! She's thought about it a lot, and she's all for it."

Mimi on Deception: "Bette's just trying to be with the man she loves, and all she gets are these two guys *angry* at her the whole time. *They* get to decide her fate. If they'd only let Bette choose."

"Then what? A *ménage à trois?*"

"Nah, she wants the cellist. Claude's a stop-gap."

Mimi on Ryan's Daughter: "All that sea and space and sky, and *still* no room for female sexuality. Sarah Miles can't get laid without being called a whore and having her hair shorn off!"

Mimi on Niagara: "She only kills Joseph Cotten because he's getting in the way of her finding sex. He's not fucking her. This is *Marilyn Monroe* we're talking about! She doesn't have to put up with that."

Mimi was wary of me too, just waiting for signs that *I* wanted to deprive her. Like every woman I ever had, Mimi'd washed up battered on my shore, after enduring a collection of guys who neglected, cheated, bored, or irritated her, or *stole* from her, and she was highly sensitive to any sign of rejection. The first time I fell asleep without making love, she lambasted me the next day.

"Don't stop fucking me," she warned. "There are consequences to not fucking: less kissing, less touching, less talking, less naked-ness, less intimacy, less sharing of the bathroom, less perfume, less lipstick, less—"

Bubbles, always eager to defuse tension with playful antics, now leapt onto a high shelf but lost her footing. She fell, bringing down a whole bunch of box files with her. I checked Bubbles over for injuries, while privately applauding her diversionary tactics, because Mimi was thoroughly distracted by the task of gathering papers that had fallen out of the box files. She thereby came across my most recent list of inventions. Yes, I'd never stopped inventing stuff.

"What's this?" she asked.

So I read them out to her, giving fuller elucidation when necessary:

1. Music Pills: on the move and need some Rachmaninov pronto? Need your Beethoven fix? Forget the iPod. *Swallow* a sonata or

two. Mozart lozenges, Schubert inhalers, and Shostakovich skin pads also available. Baroque music pills to put under the tongue after breakfast (when they always play baroque music on the radio).

2. The Soap-Cope: a soap dish that actually works. No more soap left sinking into its own slime. (*How* it would work, I didn't yet know.)

3. The G-Spot Spotter: when the duties of manhood seem too onerous. . .

4. And its cousin, The Locator: this handy electronic screen maps where you leave all registered items around the house, throughout the day: watch, keys, cell, wallet, glasses, testicles, crackers, love letters, dog, cat, umbrella, cane, pastrami on rye, whatever you want to keep track of. Useful for quick exits.

"I know, I know," I said, bashfully folding the piece of paper and stuffing it back in the box. "Men's capacity to goof off knows no bounds."

But instead of being disgusted with me and my silly inventions, Mimi was delighted! "I didn't know you were still inventing things," she said. "Invent some more!" She was tolerant of my List of Melancholy, but seemed to *love* my inventions.

So what had started out as a spat over *my* demoralizing *her*, ended with *her* encouraging *me*. All was not lost, in other words. This was something I had to tell myself occasionally, for I had old wounds too. Not just the scars of half a decade of incompatibility with Gertrude, but reverberations of mystification from an assortment of disappointed girlfriends, some of whom took their revenge by knocking me pitilessly (one even derided my choice of salad once—so I like arugula, what of it?). As a result, I had a deep fear of anything going wrong between Mimi and me, and tended to panic if we disagreed on anything. If she even went quiet, ghosts of Gertrude's week-long sulks sprang to mind. I wasn't really used to having arguments, or even discussions: with Gertrude, you never got a word in edgewise, and hardly ever wanted to.

La Bohème, I found, is a comfort to all lovers who think they've messed things up: it's full of worrying upsets and separations, but Rodolfo and Mimì love each other (I'm not so sure about Marcello and Musetta) and all is forgiven at the end. Puccini proves to you that this is the stuff that counts. Or, so it seemed at dusk on a rainy day, sitting canoe-style on the couch, with Mimi's head nestled against my chest and water streaking down the windowpanes outside, as we listened to *La Bohème*. Puccini has to get everything in, in a very short space of time—anger, pain and passion, hope and desire—and he does it! Of course the story is tragic, but that day, with Mimi close at hand, it no longer seemed to be about death, only *love*. And sex. (Maybe you have to be in love to realize it.)

Mimi on La Bohème: "It's a multiple orgasm in musical form!"

It was quite a contrast to going to see *La Bohème* with Gertrude in our box at the Met (Zeffirelli or no Zeffirelli). *Then* I couldn't wait for Mimì to kick the bucket! The last scene was excruciating: she keeps reviving! *I* died a million times (or fell asleep anyway), only to find, again and again, that Mimì was still going strong. In Gertrude's company, the whole opera struck me as goofy, phoney, pointless, and confused, a dumb duel between male high jinks and feminine melodrama: too many starving-student pranks (tricking the landlord, evading the bar bill) versus all that guff about bonnets and muffs. But now, with my Mimì in my arms, it *did me in* when Mimì gets her muff! Puccini's one composer who knows how to end something: "*Mimì! Mimì!*"

Rodolfo would have given Mimì everything he had (if he'd had anything)—and I wouldn't deprive my Mimi of anything either if I could help it, certainly not my body. She didn't need to worry about that. How I *loved* to seek her out beneath her pubic bone, her mantel, her lintel, her window sill, her fire place. Blood and bone, blood and bone, that's what women are!

Mimi was perimenopausal, hence the blushing, the sweating, the sudden showering, a mood swing here and there, and much flinging off of clothing (then having to put it all back on again a few seconds later). She often had to fling *me* off as well, unfortunately, when she got too hot. About once an hour, she would pull away from me in bed, or rush out on the roof to cool off, or start searching her purse for her forest of paper fans from Chinatown.

Mimi on fans: "It's cheap, lightweight, handy technology, and it works! All thanks to the wind-chill factor."

"Which my dad always said doesn't really exist," I told her. "He always objected when weather forecasters mentioned wind-chill factor."

"No wind-chill factor?! That's a goddam lie. How come fans work then?"

"Well, he'd say they don't, that the energy you expend fanning yourself *counteracts* any cooling effect you think you're getting. I know, he was a very tedious kind of guy. He said electric fans don't work either. They're self-defeating machines because the motor's heating up the room: the fan gives an *illusion* of cooling the air, but doesn't actually lower the temperature of the room."

"You're making me feel hot," she mumbled.

"That was his take on electric fans. But I think he was just too stingy to buy us one."

"On his advice, birds wouldn't fly: it uses up too much energy!" fumed Mimi. She was getting steamed over my dad's controversial wind-chill-factor-theory repudiation. And how cute she was when she tried to sound scientific. "Wind, or the breeze from a fan, maybe doesn't lower the temperature. But see, it blows your *surface* heat off ya, so at least for a minute or two there's nothing *between* you and the colder air around you. . . So you *feel colder*!" she concluded triumphantly. "Anyway, the wind-chill factor exists, and your father's nuts."

"I know."

"Thousands of years of people fanning themselves can't be wrong!"

"Yep."

"Where is this guy? I'd like to talk to him."

"Long gone," I answered. "A real deadbeat dad. He abandoned us. Well, I was in college when he skedaddled, but my mom was left to fend for herself—and fend off the guys from the bank too, who wanted to repossess the house. All she ate were grilled cheese sandwiches for years, before I was able to help her out a bit."

"Well, what was his game? What was he so messed up about?"

"We never knew! Just a card-carrying jackass."

I loved the thought of Mimi telling my dad what was what. The only thing better than that was the fact that she would never have to meet the guy (if she had, she probably would've killed him in about five minutes).

What I began to notice about Mimi's hot flashes was that they were often preceded by a *cold* spell: she'd move closer to any source of warmth, or gather blankets about her. Almost immediately, an anxious, flustered period ensued, during which she'd try various methods of cooling down, in a vain attempt to avert the hot flash that was on its way. It was kind of fascinating to watch! To get a feel for how severe the symptoms really were, I had (much to Mimi's amusement) a special little notebook devoted to the subject:

MIMI'S HOT FLASHES

TIME	SUSPECTED CAUSE
7:33	metabolic surge on waking
8:10	reaction to coffee (hot liquid and/or caffeine effect?)
9:26	physical activity: sartorial (getting dressed)
10:04	emotional charge (concern about being late to work)
10:53	social interaction (talking to grocery cashier—*mean guy*)
11:12	change of environment (entering warm building)
11:25	phys. activity: sartorial (taking coat off)
12:38	phys. activity: sartorial (putting coat on to go out)
1:16	phys. activity: sartorial (taking coat off at crowded diner)
2:20	change of environment (warm taxicab)
2:41	no known cause (sitting still *outside*, in Wash. Sq., watching dogs)
3:39	emotional charge (some slight embarrassment)
4:47	sexual arousal (kissing me)

5:16	phys. activity (walking fast)
5:52	reaction to red wine (alcohol)
6:38	emotional charge (defending prehistoric society's lack of a work ethic—"They worked when they pleased. Probably about three or four hours a day, tops! It's much healthier. And there was plenty of time for fun.")
7:24	phys. activity: sartorial (put coat on too soon in preparation for leaving bar, then got detained)
8:40	sexual arousal (proximity to lustful man: *me*)

She was pretty sick of these hot flashes, and I could see why, as I watched her rush from rooftop to radiator all day long. But she also firmly disapproved of the medicalization of natural female functions, and refused to see the menopause as another kind of Curse. Instead, she suspected the Change marked a new source of power—if only she could tap the energy her body was expending on getting hot and cold all the time (particulary during seminars!).

Mimi had to hold a seminar at a place near Columbia one day, and we met up afterwards at a joint called La Mirage. We ate their apple turnovers, but we weren't happy with La Mirage. It should have been called Le Barrage (of Bullshit), it had been so effortfully filled with conversation pieces. You could barely get to your table to start the conversation! Your way would be barred by a floor lamp consisting of some mannequin legs in fishnet stockings, topped with a red lacy lampshade that was supposed to look like a corset from a New Orleans bordello, *circa* 1905. What is pleasing about seeing half a woman's torso light a room? For no particular reason (this was no cordon bleu hangout) there were also a lot of big ugly shiny plaster figures of fat French chefs, complete with stripy shirts and berets, which made you want to get a sledgehammer and pound and pound them. A fake, purely ornamental version of the High Wheeler bicycle was used to hold flowerpots containing artificial plants. Perhaps worst of all, staring straight at us was a six-foot-high teddy-bear, the purpose of which was simply to look stupid. And a large tree took up all the space in the middle of the room, growing straight out of the floor. Fake, fake, fake, fake.

All of this made *me* mad and Mimi hot—she was fanning herself energetically, I assumed out of exasperation with the decor. She then remarked, "You know, thar's gold in them thar hills."

The Wild West accent was a bit of a surprise. "What hills, Maw?" I asked.

"Hot flashes! Somebody could make a fortune."

"M. Z. Fortune by any chance?"

"Me?! I don't know how to invent anything. I was thinking... *you*. Niche market! Think of the billions of women—they all reach the menopause eventually, and they need help! For about five or ten years, each!"

"Well, what about HRT?" I suggested. This was something I'd been meaning to broach with her.

"That just delays the symptoms! You still have them in the end. And anyway, hot flashes aren't a disease. You shouldn't have to take pills. Who wants to mess up their hormones and get cancer? Going through the menopause is kind of interesting, and not having to worry about pregnancy anymore is great! It's not that the Change is so bad, it's just... strange."

"Not as strange as that stuffed bear," I pointed out, gesturing at our dazed companion.

"What I really hate about it is having to *explain* the menopause to every damn fool I meet, whenever I get hot and sweaty. It's embarrassing! Do you realize what it's like in a seminar when I turn purple?! I feel like I'm about to *explode* about twenty times a day. Hey! Maybe it's the *menopause* that's responsible for global warming..."

"Well, what about cooling pads and stuff?" I feebly offered.

"Who wants a bright blue pad on your face in the middle of a meeting, or at a party? Or in *bed*? No, what women need is something inexpensive but reliable, harmless, inconspicuous, with no side effects, something you could just *hold* maybe, or grab when you need it."

"Well, Mimi, you know, my inventions have pretty well all stalled at the planning stage," I said, remembering my father's contempt for our little endeavors, the constructions Bee and I made out of spare bits of stuff left hanging around the garage: *we* called them inventions, he called them a waste of wood and old nails. "I don't even feel the need for the Locator now, you're so good at finding things for me!" I told her. Mimi had an uncanny ability to find stuff for me in my apartment: missing socks, keys, combs, books, pencils, movies, music, ice cubes, cocktail shaker. "How do you do it anyway?" I asked her.

And she replied, "I eat it, then vomit it up when you ask for it"—a vicious mockery of my amazement about her magical traits, but maybe not so far from the truth. Women *are* demonic. Baba Yagas all! When I mentioned this Baba Yaga resemblance though, we were back in prehistory.

Mimi exclaimed happily, "Oh, Baba Yaga? She waxes and wanes like the moon. She's got connections with seasons, harvests and decay, see, life and death, summer and winter, hot and cold. She's both! Hey, come to think of it, she must be menopausal! The goddess of hot flashes! Baba Yaga's got it all... And that house on chicken feet—"

"Oh no, not the house on chicken feet!" I pleaded, but she showed no mercy.

"Her house turns in a complete circle, Harrison, because *she's* cyclical, like the seasons and the tides. Everything's cyclical..." she concluded, twirling the whorl of hair on my wrist with her finger, before attempting to wolf-whistle in appreciation of Baba Yaga. Nothing came out though. Forty-eight years old and the woman couldn't whistle! A sort of tornado would sometimes gather in her mouth and she'd puff out her cheeks, pucker her lips, and say, "Hey, listen! I almost got it!" But she never had. She wasn't even close.

So that night, once I was drunk enough, I decided to teach Mimi to whistle. "Make your mouth like an ocarina," I said, and when that didn't work, "Okay, like the fipple of a recorder."

"Fipple!? Not nipple?"

"Fipple. The part just above the bulb at the top of a recorder. Now breathe in and out. Stop blowing!"

She kept heaving great gusts, with no sign of an audible note forming—all wind, no whistle.

"Forget your teeth!" I commanded. "Your mouth's not open enough. You have a beautiful mouth. Don't purse your lips like that... You make whistling noises in your sleep, so do it now!" (I was not the most patient of teachers.)

"I can never sleep with you again," she answered, but she kept working on it, me demonstrating, Mimi copying. It went on for hours! At one point, I told her she owed me twenty-five bucks for the lesson. She didn't reply, just kept effortfully inhaling and exhaling. And finally—she got it! One note soared, loud and clear and very, *very* high. I tried to get her to do a scale next, but she just stuck with her one note, like someone on a high wire who might fall off if you broke her concentration.

She was so pleased with her new ability to whistle that, later that night, when we were going to bed, she nearly cried with gratitude.

"That'll be *fifty* bucks, in that case," I told her.

She really loved me for getting that whistle out of her. I didn't realize then, but that was really the beginning of Mimi trusting me. After that, she blossomed. She became more loving, more relaxed, more outspoken! Nobody had ever given Mimi enough of his time. Nobody ever did *anything* for Mimi. Her friends and family all wanted a piece of her, wanted her to listen to *their* problems and do stuff for them. The endless phone calls to her mom in the Bronx (whom I hadn't yet met), that took Mimi away from me!

True love is a FACT: it makes every reunion good, and separations troubling. Mimi would start to doubt me when we were apart, so I learned to egg up my demonstrations of devotion when we were together—who did it hurt? I suddenly had someone I couldn't do enough for, that I would do *anything* for. Mimi shat, Mimi pissed, Mimi farted in her sleep and had hot flashes and zoned out during some of my best jokes—and I didn't mind any of it! My beautiful lunging goddess who yelled in orgasm, to her own surprise.

Real love is *ferocious*. It will carry you along like a river and serve you for LIFE, if you're loved in return. It will succor you. You will have your truest friend, someone to share your wine and your birthday with, your apartment, your music, your politics, your trash, your heating, your wallpaper, your bathroom and all your secrets (or the more interesting ones anyway), your mind, your body, your sleeping and waking self, your dreams (if she'll listen), your blender, your bills and taxes and taxis and movies, your skepticism, your optimism also, your complex coffee machine, the childhood experiences that fucked you up good, and all the joy and crumminess of life.

It works! Sexual partnership. It's not compulsory, it's not involuntary or inevitable, it's not painful or difficult or confining or monotonous either—don't put up with it if it is! It's the bee's knees. *And* you're no longer solely responsible for the success or failure of your cocktail parties.

DAYLIGHT SAVING TIME

TO MY GREAT joy, Mimi let me sit in on a few of her seminars for firemen. I proudly watched her spruce up their talks on salary scales and training plans into gems of piquancy, humor, and historical relevance (no *pre*history though, I noticed—that she saved for *me*). In return, I made Mimi endure an entire Friday evening with my partner, Henry, one of the original co-founders of the practice, and the twenty-ninth-best earlobe man in the business. He and I had had our differences—we once had a fistfight in a bar over medical ethics (I was in favor of them). But I now tentatively regarded him as a harmless roué and buffoon. All he could talk about was women and female beauty. The guy sure loved his job! It gave him a chance to look at women all day, and to credit himself with making them more beautiful, though that was a pretty dubious boast. His wife didn't seem to mind his locker-room chatter about all the beautiful women he'd ever seen or helped, or the ones he couldn't help because they sadly hadn't asked for help—but Mimi got a bellyful that night, and finally suggested Henry check out a few other things women might have done besides being beautiful.

"But what?" he chortled. "Where are the female composers and artists, the female scientists and philosophers?"

"They're around, they're just ignored!" Mimi replied.

"Oh no," Henry cried, with a boisterousness I thought ill-advised. "You're not one of those feminists, are you?"

"You're not one of those misogynists, are you?" she replied.

He glanced my way, pityingly, and I could have clobbered him, given him a good punch on that double chin of his (formed from years of looking down on people) that no surgeon had yet been able to correct. He revved up the charm. "Tell me, my dear, what do you have against us poor men? We really try our best, you know—"

Without a pause, Mimi replied, "War, racism, injustice, destruction, tyranny, feudalism, monarchies, mercenaries, pirates, despots, the slave trade, the Ku Klux Klan, global warming, capitalism, corrupt bankers, wife-beating, the Freemasons, monotheism, radioactive waste, ugly architecture, animal extinctions, toga parties, pubic hair removal, sniper rifles that can shoot people a mile away, and failure to do the dishes."

"Ah, war," mused Henry, caressing his double chin protectively, as if sensing it was in some kind of danger. "But isn't that a small price to pay for getting things *done*?"

Mimi yelped. "*Women* are the ones who get stuff done! Not least, raising children. Do you know how much work it takes to get a single person up and running, from birth to adulthood? And then to have to watch them get raped, exploited... killed! Every person men murder is some poor woman's child!" She was magnificent.

"Oh, my dear, I see you take the *little* view. Are *you* a mother?"

I stood up. "When you're goofy, Henry, you're goofy," I told him. "But when you're idiotic and goofy, it's offensive." And I swept Mimi out of there before he could think up a riposte.

When we got outside, she flung herself at me, kissing me passionately in the cold night air. "You're a hero!" she claimed.

"Hey, maybe I should have made you meet Henry sooner!" I joked.

We kept kissing along the street as we walked back to my apartment.

"'People don't do this in New York,'" I said, quoting Bette Davis in *Deception* (when she and Paul Henreid embrace all the way back to *her* apartment).

"But *we* do," murmured Mimi, with just the right intonation: she even got my movie references! What a doll.

A little further on, she erupted. "What is *with* that guy?"

"Henry?"

"He seems to think he's some kind of woman-worshipper. Goes on and on about women all evening, like he's really into us or something. But the truth is, he spends his whole life callously *comparing* women's looks. That's all he does! He's like the President of Female Attractiveness or something! I bet he keeps a chart."

"I think I saw it floating around the office. They take bets."

"He talked about beauty all goddam night! It's so... annoying! And insulting. 'Cause, either he thinks *I'm* beautiful, and therefore the subject of female beauty must be endlessly fascinating to me, which it ain't, or he *doesn't* think I'm beautiful, and thinks I oughta try harder, which I won't. But just who does he think he is? Does he really think we're here to please *him*?! That doofus?"

A small "SHADDAP!" came from an upper window.

"It's... a sort of hobby with him," was all I could offer as an explanation.

"That guy," she resumed, "makes millions persuading women they'll be more fuckworthy after he's sliced off some bit of them or added something. But EVERYBODY's fuckworthy! We'd all fuck anybody in an *emergency*..."

"TAKE IT SOME PLACE ELSE, LADY!"

Mimi was not so easily silenced. "WE'RE ALL FUCKWORTHY!" she yelled back. I hurried her away before something fell on our heads, but after a few blocks we slowed down and she said more soberly, "All this pressure on women to be beautiful. It's just plain mean."

"I know. And because of it, men have to spend their whole lives *reassuring* women that they're beautiful!"

"Yeah, life is tough all over," she laughed.

"*You're* beautiful, Mimi."

"So are you, and let that be the end of it!"

I was intrigued by Mimi's complete lack of faith in the value of plastic surgery. I was beginning to agree with her. Some "specialism" this was, working with a prick like Henry all day, and poking around remodelling healthy tissue for a living. What good was it? But then I remembered my successes, the sad sacks who had really needed my help.

"The trouble is," I said to Mimi as we tottered, entwined, towards home, "people are always trying to surpass each other in the youth and beauty stakes."

"Nobody surpasses anybody," said Mimi firmly. "We all die in the end."

I loved that gal. I would give anything to be with her forever, give *her* anything. So later, sitting on the window seat together, drinking martinis (much better than the ones at Henry's bar), I gave her my biggest secret, something I hadn't told anyone since drunken days in my twenties: the real reason why I'd gone into plastic surgery. The fire.

We all love a hero, bad boys made good, ogres with a heart of gold, righteous spies (007), triumphant sportsmen, politicians unexpectedly proven honest, brave, sincere and humane, teenagers who jump off the Golden Gate Bridge and survive, composers "on the verge of international fame." Every *war* produces its ersatz heroes, a whole new jerk circle of the gallant and the good. But if you want real heroes, you need look no further than *beetles*, the most successful species on earth. Want to rise and prosper? Get yourself a hard undercarriage, enclosable wings, and a carapace.

Apart from my father's claim to have gone over Niagara Falls in a barrel (something I *believed* for a while, even though I knew him to be a guy who had a hard time just getting out of Virtue and Chewing Gum), ours was not a family that displayed a lot of heroism. Our ancestors kept violent ends to a minimum. We had an uncle who could take his glass eye out at the dinner table. Some other ancient figurehead could only talk by holding an electrode to his throat (following cancer treatment), and there was a distant cousin who made balloon animals. But we hardly ever saw those guys. My dad must have alienated them like everyone else in the world, accused them of stealing a spoon or something. We were the classic American nuclear family, enacting our own private annihilation, with a dad who could not be figured out, and a mom whose bottled-up woe, like her tomatoes, we consumed daily.

All the neighbors were hypochondriacs, but one day Mom blew their angina, fainting fits, uterine prolapses, dandruff, and cyst scares right out of the water by coming down with a real disease: scoliosis. She had to have a metal rod inserted in her spine and spend a year in a cast.

I sat with her in the hospital after her operation, doing cross-word puzzles and handing her the back-scratcher Dad had bought her—a long stick with a tiny hand carved on the end of it (a maniac's hand!), with which she could get at itches inside the cast. Then Dad and I would drive home, picking up a few hot dogs on the way. These he chased down with some highballs in the den, and a lot of yelling. Bee had reached puberty, and the guy couldn't stand it: the makeup, the phone calls, the hair-curling, the hair-straightening, the clothes, the colored pantyhose (for some unknown reason, he felt all pantyhose should be black), her cleavage, her bralessness, her "sloth," her selfishness, her ingratitude, her incorrigibility. . . Everything *about* Bee irked him. And then she had the nerve to get involved with Cliff—how dare she kiss boys while her mother was sick in the hospital? When Dad came home from work one day to find Bee and Cliff making out in the dark in the living room, with *Lord of the Flies* on TV, he flipped.

"Take a chill pill," Bee told him after he'd banished Cliff and ordered her to her room. She slammed the door and played her Laura Nyro records really loud.

Mom eventually returned, in a body cast that stretched from her neck to her ass, like the most unflattering girdle, and lay helpless on her high Victorian bed for months, eating ice cream and homemade strawberry compote. She *had* to eat it: if she gained or lost five pounds she'd have to go back to the hospital to get a new cast put on. She'd worked out exactly how much ice cream she had to eat to retain her original plumpitude. Bee's services were now required, not just cooking and cleaning but helping Mom in unimaginable ways in the bathroom—while all I had to do was try to prevent anyone at school finding out what was going on. I was embarrassed by this mom in her carapace, and my drunken dad, always exploding. I was eleven: embarrassment was a guiding force!

Mom was almost ready to have the cast removed when Dad stomped in one day, announcing he'd quit his job at the gum company. Goodbye, golden pension. Mom cried, and Bee huddled over the phone in the den, talking to Cliff. I just hid in my bed. *O the brown and the yellow ale*—the shit and piss of family life! When I got to sleep, I dreamed about the balletic wrists of river weeds, waving goodbye all day and night to the river as it passes over them. On the surface of the Chevron, stuff sometimes got jammed up, but underneath there was constant flow, miles and miles and miles of it. Water is so determined.

I was dreaming about the guys, Gus, Chester, me, and Pete, wandering along the riverbank searching for older boys, hoping to cadge a cigarette—a favorite activity at the time. We didn't just smoke them, we used them to singe holes in Styrofoam cups— pretty sophisticated, huh?—creating melted Styrofoam dot-to-dots that spelled out our names, or dirty words, or porno diagrams. But in my dream we couldn't find any boys with cigarettes. Instead, we heard something approaching us through the bushes—a maniac? No, a lion! He made a terrible rumbling sound as he sprang into the tree above our heads. The other guys fled along the bank, but I thought I'd be safer in the river, and dove down deep. I knew I was safe down there and somehow managed to breathe for a while underwater, before I woke up, choking. I couldn't see a thing, not even my night-light, because the room was full of smoke! I scrambled to the door, but when I opened it something huge and angry lunged at me: more smoke, combined with ferocious heat. I had to face it though, to get to the rest of my family. Once I was in the hall, through the smoke I could see the glow of a blazing fire in the kitchen.

Of the four elements, only two seem threatening: those two sworn enemies, fire and water. Water can engulf you, *quickly*, drown you; and fire is a LION, indifferent and uncontrollable. There's no negotiating with it, no telling where it wants to go or what it will do. Fire is a realm unto itself, unearthly, ornery, and ignorant as hell. Fire has no idea you're in its way, it can't see you (not that it would *care*). You and your slippers and your mother and the roof are all equally palatable, and fire will burn right through you in its brainless effort to survive. But it's *not* alive, has no will, no stake in whether it burns or not. It has nothing to gain, no progeny to look out for, no pension to protect, no interests, no plans, no needs, no worries. It feels no hope, no pain, and no despair. Fire *isn't* maddened, it only seems so. It's more like a virus. But it's hard to believe it's not out to get you, hard not to sense its rampant joy in its own finite life, and its triumph over earth and air and water, by coming into being at all. Hard to believe, in the midst of it, that a fire doesn't get *off* on itself, sadistically. And—it's not a great thing to meet in your hallway.

TV and comic strips had provided me with all the exclamations necessary for a rich and full life: Ahoy there! Timber! Geronimo! Eureka! Kerpow! Kerplunk! AK AK AK! AIEEEE! Boom! Hey, watch it, buster! Arrgh! Boing! Hiyo, Silver! Kiss my ass! Why I oughta...And FIRE! I duly yelled "Fire!" again and again, but my family wasn't buying it. They must not have watched the same TV shows. Maybe no one had actually cried "Fire!" for a hundred years, for all I knew, and it was the equivalent of yelling "Blackguard!" "Brigand!" and "Gadzooks!" (Even in the middle of a disaster, I was worried about being a corny goofball.)

Giving up on that idea, I banged desperately on Bee's door. She sleepily opened it, making the fire in the kitchen brighten and a cloud of smoke rush at us. We ran the other way, towards Mom and Dad's room—where we KNOCKED, we were so well trained! There was no response, so we defied taboo and entered. Drugged to help her sleep inside her itchy cast, Mom was sound asleep in the center of that tall bed of hers (the bed Bee and I always secretly coveted and jumped on when nobody was around). Dad wasn't there, so Bee and I just started tugging at Mom to wake her up. Smoke was coming in, so Bee kicked the door shut with her foot, making windows burst elsewhere in the house. This sound was what finally woke Mom, who started to scream. We screamed too, when we realized she wasn't capable of doing anything for us! She couldn't even get off the bed without help. Working from both sides, Bee and I had to slide our panic-stricken mother out of bed and drag her over towards the window. She didn't seem able to move.

Bee jumped down onto the lawn below, and braced herself to break Mom's fall (we'd been trained to be very respectful of that expensive plaster cast). I got Mom onto the window ledge. She sat down okay, but when I tried to swivel her around so her feet were sticking out the window, she said she wasn't going.

"Come on, Mom, it's not that far down. You'll be okay."

But it wasn't fear of the drop, or hurting herself. It was a stubborn, deranged refusal to leave the house she'd tended for so long.

"I love this house!" she cried. Okay, she'd spent half her life fixing the place up, keeping it shipshape, but now it was time to disembark. "I can't leave!" she yelled. "I love this house!"

This was hysterical behavior. I knew from TV and the movies that when women get hysterical you have to slap 'em! But I didn't dare slap my *mom*, so I just kept prodding at her, nudging her further and further out the window. She was so upset, she barely noticed what I was doing, and finally Bee grabbed hold of one of Mom's feet and tugged. Mom was still wailing, "I love this house!" when she wobbled a bit, overbalanced, and fell, landing on Bee. Making me the last to leave the sinking ship, a role honored in song and story: I reached the ground a HERO.

Or so my dad said, when we got far enough from the house to be able to speak over the roar. For some reason, Dad had been outside when the fire started, so he ran to a neighbor's house to call the Fire Department. Then he'd watched helplessly from afar—it was too hot to get near the house, and the neighbors forced him to wait and let the firemen handle it—they were professionals, they would know best how to get us out. So now he just kept clapping me on the back, while Mom peered at the smoke pawing at her dream house, and started to keen. She sounded like a very tired hyena.

Not everything is lost in a fire. The firemen threw all our furniture out onto the front lawn and doused it with water and foam, so later we found whole drawers of intact, if damp, stuff: clothes and board games and Christmas ornaments, books, papers, schoolwork and prehistoric family heirlooms nobody wanted. I didn't care, I just watched the firemen, whose heroism I now connected with my own. It was a thrill just to be up so late! But nobody could send me to bed: no bed!

Later, it was decided that the fire had started in the kitchen and was therefore somehow Mom's fault—she'd recently resumed a few of her kitchen duties. Women are the bearers of fire, after all. They're always fooling with it: ironing things and boiling things and baking things and burning things. But the actual cause didn't matter anyway, except to the fire inspectors—the insurance company paid for a whole new house to be built. Mom insisted on the new one being exactly like the old one, right down to the tricky window catches, the one and only bathroom, the thin walls, cramped bedrooms, lack of porch, and every other inconvenient detail. The only outright changes she allowed were a few more closets, a slightly bigger fridge, and insulation in the attic so that *I* could have it as my teen-age lair, in tribute to my bravery and strength of mind in an emergency (Bee's bravery went wholly unrewarded).

While the new house was built, we all got to live in one room in a motel—not a log cabin this time, just a dump where we ate hot dogs every night, and Mom resented the maid service for depriving her of her usual housework routine. We slept in two big double beds, Mom and Bee in one, Dad and me in the other. For six months! No sign of Cliff *now* (his parents had zipped him off to a prep school, just to get him away from Bee, or so she said). Dad never spoke, just drove us over once in a while to see how things were shaping up with the charred remains of what was once 39 Cranberry Avenue.

My standing at school went up briefly, when news spread of my heroism. Until then my popularity had largely depended on the free samples of gum my father loaded me up with for "product-testing" purposes. He was trying to turn America into a nation of ruminants (I guess it worked!). I was supposed to get kids' responses to the jingles while they ate the gum: *Catch the Chattanooga CHEW-CHEW, all the way to Virtue!* Or, *It's bad to be glum! Try Virtue Gum!* And if you think I wasn't regularly beaten up by kids chanting, *Every monkey in the zoo knows I love Virtue!* you're nuts. Did my dad want to get me KILLED?

Pete and I became engrossed in firemen and especially fire *engines*, studying them intently, from the Button & Blake sixteen-man hand-pumper of 1857, to the "Type 7" double-tank combination engine of 1911. Also the Firecracker, an old engine with a hydraulic platform that had a telescopic upper boom capable of reaching seventy-five feet! That sort of stuff killed us. We loved every aspect of firefighting: the siphons, the stowage, the hooks and the ladders, the pumps, the hose reels, fire poles, foam, dousing techniques, tenders, the different divisions, uniforms, fire stations, and old photographs of fire crews all lined up in front of their apparatus. We even liked the "inevitable crowd of onlookers" who gather at every fire as if it's their civic duty to gloat. (This is how Cary Grant manages to steal the pickup truck in *North by Northwest*—everybody's looking the other way, staring at the exploding tanker. People can't resist a fire!) Pete and I had a problem with the Dalmatians though: we felt they could be asked to do a bit more, at least attend fires and pull a hose or something.

Mom redecorated our new house with a whole new bunch of knickknacks to be dusted, and Bee got fat, conspicuously *un*-heroic, wearing an old coat all day and night, smoking dope, and tearing her hair out. The manic playing of Bach partitas on the violin shook the house, and her graffiti sideline shook the town. Nobody in Virtue and Chewing Gum suspected a girl was behind all the Day-Glo BH's all over the place, but they should have, the letters looked so much like bulbous female breasts and buttocks.

There were complaints in the local paper, the *Daily Virtue*, about the town being terrorized (or *territorized*) by this *BH* character, and about a million janitors scrubbed away at the emblems with ineffectual brushes and corrosives, while Bee sat in the woods, glowering. I told her it's bad to be glum, try Virtue gum—and she swatted me like a fly for about five years.

"And that's how I got into plastic surgery," I explained to Mimi, who by now was lying on her stomach on the window seat, looking up at me, with Bubbles nestled in the small of her back. "I started out as a burns specialist, treating kids who'd disfigured themselves with fireworks, and firemen caught in back-flashes, or girls who'd had acid thrown at them by spurned lovers, and plenty of car-crash victims. Then I moved into facial-trauma cases: beatings and knifings. From there it was but a small step to reconstructive surgery after mastectomies. But the practice just kept going upmarket, everybody trying to make their pile... and now all I get are women who want to give their husbands new tits for Christmas! Women who want to be babes, and men who want the Berlusconi makeover, so they can *date* babes. I know it's all nonsense, but I don't know what to do about it... " But by then Mimi had dislodged Bubs and was holding my head against her soft, warm, original-edition belly.

THE IDES OF MARCH

MIMI WAS STILL asleep in my bed when Gertrude called.

"What's the matter?" I asked gruffly. "It's kind of early."

"Japan."

"What?"

"This is a major disaster, Harrison!"

"The earthquake, you mean." It was four days since the tsunami.

"No! My dividends! Japanese shares have plunged. I invested heavily in the Far East."

"Gertrude, the bodies are still washing up on the shore! How do you think the *Japanese* would feel about your money worries?"

"They're worried about the effects on the economy too," she answered.

"Oh yeah? Who? The people searching for their relatives, or the radioactive workers in the nuclear plant?" All I could think about were the pictures of Japanese rescue workers pausing to pray before searching debris for the bodies of strangers.

"Well, I heard that people in Tokyo are a bit nervous about after-shocks, but people south of there aren't worried... The Japanese have no capacity for empathy, Harrison. It's not part of their culture. They don't care about people they don't know."

"No, Gertrude, YOU don't care about people you don't know. YOU have no capacity for empathy!" I hung up. The woman was a menace. She'd probably *caused* the earthquake and tsunami! I should have known, when she ruined *Paris* for me, turning the whole place into one big shopping mall for herself. (REASON NO. 894: Anyone who can wreck Paris can wreck the world.)

I needed a drink, or drugs! I needed to let off steam... But Mimi was still asleep, and I tried not to mention Gertrude too much anyway. Also, Mimi wasn't really up on the News (she'd made a decision years before not to follow current events, since they were unbearable, and she had exhausted herself trying to think up solutions). She was made aware of major stuff like the earthquake in Japan by going to diners where people would talk about it, and bars that had unignorable TV screens that gave you devastating head-lines in between football games.

But Bee and I had an agreement that, whenever the world was threatened by a nuclear accident, we had to TALK. So I had someone to go berserk with now. I got her during her lunch—she was eating a grilled cheese sandwich (like Mom), something she'd personally introduced into England. I gave her the latest on Gertrude's atroci-ties (which now seemed to me inextricably linked to those of the nuclear industry.)

"Who gave nuclear energy adherents the right to make the

world uninhabitable? They should all be indicted for crimes against humanity," I said. "And that includes Gertrude!"

"They're all such liars, that's what gets me," said Bee. "The nuclear industry attracts the biggest liars in the world. It's just about money. The BBC too! All they talk about is the Japanese *economy*. They've already forgotten the dead. It's so... churlish!" (Ah ha! Bee had been converted to the word "churlish." That comforted me somewhat.)

"Bee, how could I have been with that creep for five years?"

She laughed. "You weren't really *with* her. You were... kind of out of it for a while there, Harry."

"Aw, shit."

"Hey, I saved a woman's life!" said Bee.

My sister, whom I remembered a shivering wreck in my kitchen, was now a rescuer of women! She'd been walking behind some couple in Canterbury, and heard the man haranguing the woman. So Bee walked faster, trying to get close enough to deflate the guy a bit, or at least embarrass him into silence. Then the couple stopped in a doorway, and Bee had to walk past. But when she got to the corner, she saw that the guy had pulled a knife and was shoving it in the woman's face. So Bee ran back screaming at him and the man took off. By then the woman's throat had been slashed, and she crumpled to the ground. Great place, Canterbury. I'd assumed England was pretty safe!

Bee tied something around the woman's neck and tried to phone for an ambulance but got put through to Liverpool for some reason, hundreds of miles away. Then some other woman who'd seen what happened offered to take them to a hospital in Ashford, only about fifteen miles away (the Canterbury hospital had no real ER). They finally got the injured woman there and she'd been stitched up and was going to be all right.

"But I was scared the whole way that she'd hemorrhage or something," Bee told me. "I wished you were there! What good's a doctor in the family, if he's miles away in an emergency?"

"Bee, can't you just stay in your studio and make your Coziness Sculptures?"

"Oh, I'm not doing them at the moment. I got sick of all the quibbling about money. I've started something new. I'm out on my bike most days, doing research."

"What are you researching? Daffodils? Thatched roofs? Knife crime?"

"Heartache. I'm collecting inscriptions from tombstones, mostly war graves. There were so many people killed in England in war after war, you'd think there'd be nothing left of this little country. There isn't *much*, actually. The weird thing is, they always mention the guy's role in the Army, as if the real tragedy isn't that he died, but that they lost a *sapper*, whatever that is, or a gunner, or a pilot."

"I think it's a guy who digs trenches."

To get to these graves, Bee cycled. She would cycle to the train station in Canterbury, the one called the *West* Station, although it was further east than the *East* Station ("as if the whole town revolved on its axis at some point," she said), cycle straight onto the train, sit there for a few short stops, then cycle off at some country station, riding right along the platform, out the gate, and onto the road, never getting off her bike for a moment. It was usually a short spin from the station to the churchyard, which she could see from the train by checking for a steeple. (Bee seemed innocently proud of the simplicity of these little journeys of hers.) And there in some old graveyard she'd note down inscriptions like:

WE ARE PARTED ERIC DEAR
FOR JUST A LITTLE WHILE.
AGED TWENTY.

Or,

A NOBLE BRAVE BOY AND SON.
GREATLY BELOVED.
AGED SEVENTEEN.

"Seventeen!" Bee said to me. "It's unbearable."

"Just don't get yourself killed, Bee, on that bike of yours. I don't want to have to come over and bury *you* in one of those graveyards: 'SADLY MISSED. DOPE GOT HERSELF RUN OVER. AGED FIFTY-THREE.' "

The memorial that bugged Bee the most though was right around the corner from her house. It wasn't a war grave but an ugly obelisk commemorating a whole load of Christian martyrs who'd been burned at the stake on that very spot in about 1550. Their Canterbury martyrdom must remind Bee of her *own*, I suggested. But it wasn't so much the way they died, or why, that irked Bee—it was the way they were commemorated on the monument. Most of the martyrs were named in full, but two were referred to only as "Bradbridge's widow" and "Wilson's wife."

"It's so... patronizing," Bee said. "You go to all the trouble of getting yourself *burned at the stake*, and they can't even bother to remember your name?"

"Bit of a wasted effort, you feel?"

"It reminds me of Dad! *Of course* I wore that old coat all the time! Because he made me feel like crap."

"I don't really see the connection—"

"Men patronizing women, that's the connection!... Always making me feel like I wasn't the daughter he wanted... But I was the daughter he *made* me," she said, starting to sound tearful. She was right about him: to me he'd voiced his revulsion, not just for her coat, but for her retreat to Maine to live on a commune with a bunch of hippies and wild dogs, a lifestyle choice designed to drive him bananas. Also, her decision to go to art school, which he refused to pay for—while *I* compliantly took his dough, got the fancy education, and became a doctor not handy in an emergency.

"Bee."

"You're not going to defend him, are you?" she said.

"No. I was going to commend *you*, for saving that woman's life. I think they should make you Queen Bee."

"I'd rather be a dame."

"Well, you *are* abroad."

An old joke, but she fell for it, which was a relief: there's nothing worse than hearing your sister cry three thousand miles away.

"Bee, I, uh, I told Mimi about the fire." Bee was surprised, since we never usually mentioned it to anybody. "I still have one question though. Where *was* Dad that night? What was he doing *outside*? I never figured that out—"

"Harry..." she said in an odd tone.

"*What?*"

"Don't you know?"

"Know what?"

"Dad started the fire."

"Dad...? Oh, come off it!"

"No. Harry. He tried to kill us that night. Tried to kill us all! The guy was a maniac! Mom protected him, she took the blame. But that's why she was never the same after the fire. She wasn't just mourning the house, she was regretting the whole marriage!"

"She should have left him," I mumbled.

"Mom believed you stick with your husband, Harry, even if he turns out to be a gargoyle drooling rainwater off the Chrysler Building."

After we hung up, I headed into the sunny dining room where Mimi (awake at last!) was holding a jar of Cheryl's *please-date-me* marmalade up to the light, marveling at it as if it was Roman glass or something! I couldn't stand the stuff. It might *look* pretty, but it came at a price: Cheryl kept loading me up with preserves in the expectation of romantic results. I can't be bought that easily!

"How can you not want this marmalade?" Mimi asked.

"Mmmh?"

"Just look at the sun coming through it," she said, as she turned the jar this way and that, admiring its amber color and the bits of orange rind floating in the clear jelly, which, to me, looked like tadpoles suffocating in swamp water.

"Jams are seriously undervalued," Mimi went on. "Just like quilts, and cooking. Because *women* did them."

"Hmnh." I looked around vaguely for the *New York Times*.

"When in fact they're some of the best things in the world!" she said happily, putting the marmalade down among its fellows, in order to wrestle a coffee capsule into Gertrude's high-tech coffee machine.

"What?" I really couldn't remember what she'd been talking about.

"Jam, Harrison."

"Ham?!"

"Jam! I'm talking homemade jam here, *women's* work. Part of a whole world of unpaid work women do... Probably a remnant of matriarchy and prehistoric, nonmonetary work, when people just chipped in and did what was needed... Hey, you're not listening!"

"Yes I am."

"You didn't hear a thing!" she said, and suddenly took up a boxing pose, as if she was going to give me the ol' one-two. I went over to her and took her hands, her strong hands that I loved.

"It's just... something Bee just told me over the phone."

"Bee?! Well... what?"

I sighed. "That the fire... wasn't accidental. It was my dad."

"He started it?" She didn't sound too surprised.

"Yeah."

She lifted her hand to my cheek, and kissed me on the neck.

"Did you already guess?!" I asked her, astounded.

"Well, it did sound a bit fishy," she said.

We sat at the table in silence for a while, surrounded by frog spawn.

"I still don't know *why* though," I mumbled.

"Because he lost his job maybe? The pension and everything. You think he was worried about money?"

"Aw, he didn't lose his job. That was a big lie. He was just in a bad mood. No, he stuck with that dumb gum job till the day he left town for good. Bee thinks he was sick of having a sick wife... A pubescent daughter too. He hated Bee as she got older... Fathers are the worst!" I said, thinking of the pole-dancer's dad.

THE FIRST DAY OF SPRING

IT WAS SPRING at last, the sky a creamy blue, tweety-birds a-tweeting, lords and ladies leaping. In Central Park anyway, on every bench, against every tree, couples were frantically entwined. It was like *Watteau* in there! One sunny day, and out come the flirtatious looks and the mandolins.

"What a cliché," Mimi witheringly observed. "Just because it's spring doesn't mean you have to mate!"

I was about to concur, the first impulse of the lover, when I remembered that all of my own romances, the more major ones at least, had begun in the spring (including *this* one)—how biological can you get? And yet we soon we succumbed to some canoodling of our own, along with everybody else.

"Let's try to knock this thing into shape," she declared abruptly.

"Knock *what* into shape?" I asked eagerly, looking around for a more discreet hidy-hole.

"Your speech, Harrison, your speech."

"My what?... Oh." We had already covered many types of oral presentation, I fondly recalled, devoting ourselves daily to questions of expressiveness, responsiveness, fairness, intimacy, inclusivity, rhythm and repetition... I'd totally forgotten about my *speech*. Who could think about Chevron High in the midst of this?! Why taint love with worry? But now it seemed it was School Time again.

"Ya do remember my book, right?" she asked. "So, what's your Speech Objective?" We wandered aimlessly through a sunless sinless clearing, devoid of couplings. I tried to remember what I could of Mimi's book. I knew it mentioned something about Speech Objectives—but what?

"My Objective," I said boldly, "is to survive."

"Hmmm, maybe we'll work on the Objective later," Mimi conceded. "Now, how about content? If you could talk about anything you wanted, what would it be?"

"Melancholy?"

"Nah. Not for a graduation speech, Harrison!"

"Why not?"

"You really need to be thinking more in terms of a pep talk, ya jerk. Give 'em something rousing, something a little jazzy! What else you got?"

"Crapholes of the famous?"

She'd seen the book, but NO.

"What about your job, you wanna talk about that?"

No, I wasn't going to talk about my stupid job. Things had recently reached a new low at the office. The police had dropped the charges against the pole-dancer's father, on the grounds that they'd found no evidence. No evidence, my ass. What was the pole dance she did if not "evidence"? When I objected to their decision, reminding them about the broken arm, which alone was a classic sign of violent abuse, the cops said that, according to the girl's mother, the kid fell down in the playground. So they believed the cowed mom, not me. But I'd looked into the guy's soul, and it wasn't pretty in there.

What's more, the fat woman with the burn scars, who'd wanted to protect her son from bullying, had now undergone the liposuction she demanded, and *died* from post-op complications. So now the boy didn't have a fat mom—he had no mom at all! And I'd attended a group scold-fest about freebies for nothing (in needless preparation for fixing those scars of hers), a whole hour of being lambasted for letting the side down and making my colleagues look bad, just because I did the occasional charity procedure.

"Nope, don't want to talk about that," I told Mimi.

"Oh." She looked at me inquiringly. "Okay. Well, what happened to your 'How I Hated School' idea?"

"Okay, I'll do that."

"But you've got to narrow it down, Harrison."

"Aw shucks."

We walked on through dim-lit glades. And then I had it.

"Sex camp!" I declared, scaring a squirrel.

"Sex... what?" Mimi asked.

"Sex camp. It's an old idea of Pete's, a pal of mine in Virtue and Chewing Gum. We decided it was cruel to force teenagers to go to school. Nobody can concentrate at that age! They should all be having sex all day long, until their hormones settle down enough to study."

"So you'd send them to some kind of concentration camp where they have to have sex all the time?"

"A *nice* camp! Where they have *consensual* sex. With *each other*, by the way, not dirty old men or something. Look around you, babe!" I said, gesturing at some horny youngsters we'd just passed. "Those kids don't need high school, they need sex camp."

"So, how long would they go for?"

"As long as it takes. Months. A few years maybe. Maybe more!"

"Hmmm, I just don't think you'd get many parents to agree to their kid leaving home as soon as they hit puberty and going to a sex camp, however 'nice' it was."

"I was thinking more around the age of fifteen or sixteen. And it would be totally voluntary! You don't *have* to go. If you're happy living with your stupid folks and going to school, stay there. But if you'd rather get laid, this is the camp for you!"

"And they just have sex? All day?"

"Sex is what the teenage body's *made* for, not dribbling basket-balls. Sex is all they're good for! Nobody learns anything in high school. They're too busy suppressing their sex drive. Most teen-agers spend the whole time stoned, listening to crappy music, playing computer games, and turning into self-obsessed nut-jobs. By the time they're old enough to wield any power, they're too apathetic and depleted to *use* it. They're ruined by all those years of sexual deprivation. High school's such a waste of youthful energy, which should theoretically be a useful global resource. These kids should be out saving people from floods and famine, building pyramids, starting revolutions, and having sex!"

I could tell Mimi was getting to like the idea—she was a firm opponent, after all, of sexual deprivation. "So you'd give them a few other tasks as well, at this camp of yours, besides sex? A pyramid to build or something?"

"Oh, I guess so. If they were in the mood. And a bit of first-aid training maybe, carpentry, cooking, that sort of thing. Nothing too taxing."

"How about contraception?"

"Yeah, get them straight on *that* first of all."

"I think they should learn handyman skills, and. . . and farming. And teach them about the tides, Harrison! Nobody understands that stuff. And what about art, music, dancing. . . ?"

"All a fine complement to sex," I agreed.

"And pottery? And then there's weaving, and quilting!"

"Uh, yeah, I *guess* so. . . "

"Sounds like matriarchy to me!"

We walked on, arm in arm, Mimi dreaming of matriarchy, and me mourning my past. All I did as a teenager was stare at my *zits* for four years, surrounded by beautiful unreachable girls that drove me nuts! I was stuck for a whole year sharing a bench in chemistry with Arnie, a seating arrangement we attributed to the fact we both had zits. One day the chemistry teacher, Mr. Zomboni—where do teachers get those names?—brought in this big bottle of hydrochloric acid and warned everybody it could cause severe burns. So Arnie turns to me and says, "You think it would work on zits?" That's how much we hated ourselves.

We had no idea why we wanted the girls, or what we wanted from them. Most of our interpretations of womanhood were based on movies like *Psycho* (we'd moved on a little by then from maniac stories). We had developed a taste for the doomed and the damned, nice worn-down women ripe for the picking (this was the only type of girl we could imagine putting up with us!). Despite my awareness of Bee's painful struggles to get dates, I was heavily influenced by people like Gus and Chester, who convinced us that girls had no real interest in sex and only put up with it as the result of a dreary system of bribes, lures, tricks, and entreaties. On my allowance, that meant no action at all: I was never going to come up with the corsages, fake pearls, and ice-cream sundaes necessary to make any headway towards getting some head.

We wasted *years* puzzling over girls and their labyrinthine mysteries (some cyclical, some conical!), combined with the widespread supposition that everybody was *gay*: we vastly underestimated the heterosexual impulse. (For all his bellowing about homosexuality, Gus was famed for his falsetto and butt-wiggling imitations of girls.) Chester with his big chest was our puberty mascot. We watched *him*, to see what would befall *us* next, not just biologically but emotionally. The perplexities of his love affairs! Chester finally tried to simplify it all for us by dividing girls into nuts or sluts. Nobody liked or trusted Chester, but we had a grudging respect for his encyclopedic understanding of the opposite sex, due primarily to his long-term molestation of his own sister, now *dead*: she'd drowned by accident, swimming in the Chevron (not strictly his fault, but somehow it shamed us all).

Adolescence is such a dead end, you put up with all this depravity because you think there's no escape. There was a period when we were trying to deduce how big a bush the girls had, using their *eyebrows* as a gauge. The hairier the brows, the hairier the bush, we arbitrarily decided, and the hairier the bush, the more we scorned the girl! (Bette Davis's eyebrows in *Now, Voyager* would have terrified us!) And what gets me now is how beautiful they all were, even the ones we were *sure* were ugly. We had our pick of a bunch of sixteen-year-old *dolls* and all we could do was mock them, number them according to our manly, mutually agreed bombshell-appeal score sheet, and plan mass outrages against them (never carried out). Our ignorance made us hate them; we blamed them for our own ineptitude. Oh, we were a pretty discriminating bunch all right, questioning every flaw and keeping a sharp eye out for bow legs, knock-knees, thick ankles, flat chests or alternatively, huge, unruly melons, stupid hairdos, mannerisms, and accumulations of fat in what we considered the wrong places. Now, after years as a cosmetic surgeon, all I wanted to do was look upon women with their flaws *intact*. Rounded, dented, dimpled, flabby thighs, what of it? THEY'RE FEMALE LEGS, RIGHT?

The need for sex camp was clear—how else do you turn these fickle lads, these horny heathens, into valued members of society? Something Gus never achieved. Gus's only solution to high-school dissatisfactions was to fantasize *at length* about a school massacre: Mrs. Benkowsky, the history teacher, begging for her life, Mrs. Hamnavoe breathing her last among her algebra books, Mr. Zomboni (chemistry) exiting fatally through a third-floor window, and old Mr. Leigh Hampton (woodwork)—best not to go into what Gus had planned for him, but various saws were going to come in handy. And then, the hundreds of girls caught in the cross-fire, or machine-gunned on purpose, hiding under library tables or dying in full view with their skirts conveniently hitched up or torn off. "Yeah, yeah," we told him, bored stiff, but still he continued, picturing the river of blood in the parking lot and having to thread his way through the bodies for a defiant stand-off on the roof of the gym. . .

I had to listen to this stuff! I was stuck with these guys: it was either them, or sitting around with Pete and his doldrums, his melancholy, his complaints about the low avocado quotient in his avocado salad. I shunned him, I shunned everybody, and risked even the accusations of homosexuality in my Herculean, Evel Knievel efforts to manoeuver my way through those corridors—throwing myself into books and music, and eventually launching myself over the heads of my contemporaries like they were so many empty barrels to vault.

Despite my recalcitrance as a student *now*, Mimi was determined to help me, so from that day on, we would often head over to the Village, eat some meatballs at The Little Owl and then go back to Mimi's place to study famous speeches. According to her, Obama's were models of hooks, inclusivity, anecdotes, limited-opportunity windows and whatnot. We looked at his inaugural, which was fine, but Kennedy's is more memorable: "ask not. . . ask what. . . ask not. . . but what. . ."

"It's the repetition," Mimi informed me (she was very keen on repetition), "that gives the audience a chance to catch up. It's comforting, and it helps emphasize stuff. Repetition can hide a lot of inconsistencies too. Of course, you can overdo it and sound like a feeb!"

"Thanks for the warning."

"Martin Luther King's a *genius* with repetition."

"You mean the 'I have a dream' stuff."

"Not just that. There's one bit where he keeps saying, 'Now is the time... Now is the time...' Under all the gentility, he's impatient. That's what comes through."

"Now is the time to kiss," I ventured, and she concurred.

"Hey, wait, I've got a tape of it," she cried, and ran out of the room.

"Of what?" I called after her.

"Of all these speeches."

"I was scared you'd say that."

We had one whole tutorial just on old Gus's favorite, Winston Churchill, whose 1940 speech about fighting on the beaches had everything, according to Mimi: honesty, rhetoric, rhyme, passion *and* repetition. To me, it read like a lesson in military history, and suffered from purplish prose. But you can get away with a lot in wartime. Mimi pointed out that it's when he quits reciting past events and changes into the future tense that the rockets really start to fly. She also liked it when he lowers his voice for the most famous bit.

"See, he holds back, and back, and back, only rising on the 'never,' in 'we shall *never* surrender,'" she said, and played me the section several times, in which he talks about fighting in the fields, and in the streets, fighting on the hills and dales, with growing strength and confidence...

"We shall fight with commas," I joked (on the page, I felt Churchill could have done with a few more periods).

"The audience provides the punctuation, if you say it right," Mimi assured me. "That speech had them all yelling and weeping at the time. It's dramatic stuff!"

I was touched by Mimi's efforts. She really didn't want to fail me as my presentation coach, and even though I couldn't concentrate very well right now (just like a teenager in the first throes of lust!), and had managed to *forget* how scared I was of the whole faraway occasion, I appreciated her interest in instilling in me the rudiments of speechmaking success—and her apparent conviction that it would work.

Next, we read what Mandela said at his trial, a five-hour oration in which he coolly outlined the four forms of violence open to protestors, after law and democracy have failed them: sabotage, guerrilla warfare, terrorism, and open revolution.

"Ya see?" said Mimi. "*He* uses repetition too."

But it was the ending that got me: his declaration that he's willing to die if necessary, to achieve freedom and democracy.

"Now, there's a guy who knows how to end something!" I commented.

Then we did Khrushchev's denunciation of Stalin in 1956: Comrades! Comrades! What Mimi liked best about this one was the reference to Lenin's *wife*. In the middle of the speech, Khrushchev quotes a letter from Lenin to Stalin, showing Lenin already knew what a scumbag Stalin was in 1923—because he was obnoxious to Mrs. Lenin on the phone. For Mimi (and maybe even for Khrushchev), this told you all you needed to know about Stalin. I took a liking to Khrushchev—but his speech was so long!

Old Russian joke: Is it possible to wrap an elephant in newspaper? Yes, if Khrushchev gave a speech the day before.

Long speeches reminded me of Gertrude. There's a reason why conversation exists. It's *unnatural* for one person (Gertrude) to hold the floor for ten hours! But Mimi said the whole trick of public speaking was in creating the illusion that it *is* sort of a conversation.

Gaddafi's rambling speeches outdistanced even Khrushchev's. Some of them could go on all day and night! But Mimi was lenient: we looked at one that was a mere four hours, and we really just skimmed it, paying particular attention to the ways in which the technique of repetition can go *wrong*.

"The guy's trying to hang onto power by boring everybody to death," Mimi said. "Like, giving a never-ending speech will somehow save him."

"Yeah, who does he think he is? Scheherazade?"

It now occurred to Mimi that it might take *me* about four hours to explain my sex camp idea: unlike those guys, I'd only have about twenty minutes to get my message across at the graduation ceremony. "Not all audiences have the patience of Gaddafi's crowd," she warned. Aw, phooey, back to the ol' drawing board! Now I had no topic, no skills, and I was no Churchill.

"I'm no Churchill," I said to Mimi.

"Yes, you are," Mimi said, with a confidence I found absurd, even from my loving speech coach. To make up for it all, she came out with me afterwards to buy a state-of-the-art toolkit.

"Why do you need it?" was her only question.

"I don't know. I just always felt it was something I should have."

FULL MOON, MAY 17TH

MIMI WAS STANDING on the roof terrace one morning, looking down at a debate going on below between three cops, some trash collectors, several construction workers, and a mailman or two. She suddenly turned to me and asked, "Why is it men need a uniform for every occasion?"

"To remind them what they're supposed to be doing."

"Yeah, they don't multitask."

"Nope, we're very single-minded. It's written into our DNA: men hunted, while women did *everything else*."

She leaned over the railing and yelled down at the fracas (I hoped inaudibly), "WHY DON'T YOU ALL JUST GO HOME AND PLEASURE YOUR WOMEN?" Then she sat down next to me and elaborated on her theory that nature is based on female pleasure.

"Females are more *capable* of sexual pleasure than males," she proclaimed. "They have more erogenous tissue. The clitoris is actually bigger than the penis, ya know. And the vagina isn't just a tube or something, for releasing babies and receiving sperm. It's a sperm sorting station! The vagina decides *everything*. See, if the male doesn't please the female, his sperm's less likely to be seen by the vagina as suitable fathering material. That's why it's up to the male to *please* the female. It ain't just about banging beaver all the time."

"Unless you're a beaver," I said, kissing her palm. But she retrieved it soon after, so that she could pound the arm of her chair for emphasis.

"This is why prostitution sucks. It's the exact opposite of what should be happening. Female pleasure is what matters, *biologically*. This is why *courtship* exists in nature!" Mimi said. (She pronounced it "naytcha," which I loved.) "And foreplay. Otherwise, it would just be rape, rape, rape all summer long. But it isn't! Rape isn't common in nature. Most male animals go to a hell of a lot of trouble to *please* the female. Male birds have the best feathers. Hey, you better tell Henry: it's the *male* birds that have to put on the beauty show."

"Yes, the show must go on!"

"So ya see, Harrison, the penis is a pleasuring tool designed for *female* pleasure, not male. The female orgasm is the important one, the male orgasm's no big deal."

"I'm sorry to hear that."

"The future of the species depends much more on the female orgasm. That's just the way it is. Even female fruit flies expect to be given a good time!"

"Are we fruit flies?" I asked, remembering Eugene Wrayburn's objections to being equated to a bee.

"This is what we're made for, that's all. But fidelity—that's a side issue. Sometimes you have to share! As long as males are serving female pleasure, that's what counts. Of course, if men freak women out by being unfaithful, that isn't going to increase female pleasure either. It all has to be weighed up." Mimi's rhetorical momentum was building towards some sort of climax of its own. She was glorious!

"In nature, male animals are all out there courting females, protecting females, feeding females, and giving them orgasms. Only *people* have given this whole happy system up and turned sex into something just for *men* to enjoy."

"I do," I admitted.

"We've got it all ass-backward!" she exclaimed, contradictorily fondling me at the same time. "Men are off the beam! They've ignored female sexuality for centuries and deprived women of *billions of orgasms* they should have had!"

"Get your ass in there then!" I ordered, dragging her back to bed, where I matched my thrusts to the drilling and hammering going on outside. She went *crazy* for it. There were at least three more female orgasms in the world that day (but who's counting?), and it was my avowed intention to make up for those centuries of omission whenever I could.

By Mimi's prehistoric reckoning, we'd now been together four full moons (moons, or lunar months, were the only thing she considered worth marking). By *my* calculations, we'd been together *five*, having been in synch, on some metaphysical plane or other, ever since we first met: we'd made it through Christmas, New Year's, Martin Luther King Jr. Day, Groundhog Day, Valentine's Day, Presidents' Day, a non-Leap

Year, the Ides of March, St. Patrick's Day, Easter, the British Royal Wedding, World Asthma Day and Mother's Day.

We were way past my usual three-week cut-off point, as well as the tricky two-month juncture. And still there wasn't a sign of any waning (*except* the moon's). What was mine was hers, and hers mine: by osmosis we had become happy occupants of each other's apartments, happy as long as we were *together* there. Mimi was fascinated by the showroom opposite my place, full of cardboard boxes; I was fond of The Little Owl, the pretty restaurant on her corner. So what if you sometimes run out of socks? I was working on getting much more relaxed about sock issues.

I had the day off, Mimi didn't: she had some photocopying to do before a seminar she was giving that afternoon. I played her the *Appassionata* while she got ready to go. But I really didn't want her to leave, and suddenly became much *less* relaxed. Maybe it was Beethoven's fault—he's good at raising your anxiety level (not all classical music is as soothing as Gertrude's musical pals made out). The thought of Mimi alone on the streets of New York with her big bags of photocopying began to unnerve me. I usually tried to keep a lid on my protectiveness and jealousy but, you know, in between their crackpot ideas and their huffs and their puffs (and their muffs), their bold declarations that they have the right to go where they please, their tirades, their tantrums, their intransigence (I sound like my *father*), not to mention their "incorrigibility" (his favorite putdown), plus all the hot flashes, PMT, PND and VPL, women are VULNERABLE out there—and it makes a man feel vulnerable too, if he's in love with one. But when I mentioned to Mimi I was worried about her going out alone, she said it was the dog shit that worried *her*.

Mimi on dog shit: "Anybody allowed to shit wherever they want obviously *owns* the place!"

All I could do was tug at her skirt hem like a puppy myself, and race ahead of her into the bedroom, where I flung myself naked across the bed as further enticement for her to stay. I just wanted to *roll in my sweet baby's arms* all day! No dice. She left, promising bagels on her return.

So I lay on the bed watching Bubbles dream, her paws and muzzle twitching heroically as she ran wild somewhere, hunting, eating, or escaping something. I was wondering dozily if there was a Big *Sleep* after the Big Bang—the universe sure seems to like its shut-eye (even plants slumber: it's amazing we all have to be *out of it* half our lives, it seems such a waste of time and resources!)—when I heard a knock on the front door. Maybe Mimi had relented, and/or forgotten her keys. I threw on her kimono (just in case five *builders* were out there instead, wanting to get access to the roof) and headed for the door. I was fond of this kimono. It bore no resemblance in my opinion to a bathrobe. It was too silky, too exotic, too erotic, and too *short* to be a bathrobe, and had an elaborate floral design on it instead of the classic bathrobe's trad plaid. So I cheerfully opened the front door, *flung* it open in fact, flung wide my arms *and* my kimono to receive Mimi—but it wasn't Mimi, it was Gertrude. If only the Japanese had shown more empathy when constructing their kimono! I primly wrapped the flimsy thing around me, and let her in: one cannot stand on too much ceremony with old flames. *She* wasn't wearing all that much either, just some thin shapeless vintage hippy number—for which she'd probably coughed up about a thousand bucks.

"Hello, Harrison!" she sniggered.

"Hello, Gertrude. How's it going?"

"Fine, fine," she said as she stomped in, proprietorially throwing her coat down on the hall chair. She was peering this way and that, no doubt trying to see if there was a new woman around—I still hadn't actually told her about Mimi, but I knew she suspected something was going on. Without a word, she headed for the kitchen.

"Uh, what do you want, Gertrude?"

"I came for my coffee machine," she said. "I need it."

"The coffee machine? Uh-huh."

She didn't need that coffee machine! She had a million of 'em. Was she genuinely fearful that my new woman, if I had one, might perform perversities on her percolator? I just wanted to get her out of there before Mimi came back. In aid of this, I helped Gertrude pack the stupid machine (and its manual) in its various boxes, and gathered up all the stray unused coffee capsules lying around. This wasn't easy, since for modesty's sake I had to hold the kimono together with one hand, and shove the capsules toward Gertrude with the other, one at a time. She milked the situation for all it was worth, taking her time and chatting about Claude while we worked, saying how well he was doing at kindergarten, how happy he was at home...Like hell he was. I didn't believe a word of it. The kid must be going out of his mind! But he had his own ingenious methods of distancing himself from Gertrude. Sure enough, with the help of his nanny, Claude had just embarked on a huge new art project (which Gertrude, being pushy, was keen to support): he was painting a mural in the outside hallway. Get that? The *outside* hallway. Between this absorbing task and school, he probably only had to encounter Gertrude at suppertime. I felt a pang of remorse though, when she told me the subject of the mural: Yogi Bear. He was obviously missing me! This reinforced my fury with her, since it was her decision I shouldn't visit the poor guy, or have him visit me.

But then I saw her frail back from behind, as she carried her enormous coffee machine out of the kitchen, and a wave of magnanimity came over me. I felt like a louse. I was the happy one after all, I had love, while Gertrude had nothing but her culinary contraptions and a kid she'd never understand. And that *zoo*, of course. Though never wholly convinced by her ardor for animals, I wanted to be affable, so I lamely told Gertrude I had a cat. She instantly threw down all the coffee paraphernalia and started that act she always puts on with pets, as if she alone is capable of bridging the species barrier. The transition from snoopy to soppy was surreal.

"Oh, can I *see* it?" she squealed. "Where *is* it?" ("It"?!)

Bubbles was probably still asleep in the bedroom, blissfully unaware of what was coming her way, but when I called her she trotted into the living room with her usual politeness, and rubbed against my leg.

"Uh, Bubs, this is. . . Gertrude," I said reluctantly.

Bubbles recoiled from Gertrude's hand. If I were a cat, I wouldn't want to be scratched by those pointy claws either. Hell, I wouldn't want to be touched by Gertrude, *whatever* I was! She sure knew how to wreck my day. She timed her Gertrusions so well. But she couldn't have found a *good* moment to come over to my apartment, because there was never going to be one. Now she was chasing poor Bubbles around the room. They were over by the window, where Gertrude was making hissing, supposedly kissing, sounds at her, calling her Bubs—a name only Mimi and I were allowed to use! Bubbles slid underneath the window seat and stayed there, clever cat. Undaunted, Gertrude hitched up that dopey diaphanous dress, squatted down, and started to paw pointlessly in Bubbles's direction.

"Here, Pussy, here, Pussy!" she cried.

I was now worried that Bubbles might get stuck between the wall and the radiator, so felt I had to intervene. At first, I attempted to work *around* Gertrude, scrupulously avoiding any physical contact with her. But she wouldn't budge from her spot in front of the radiator. The only way for me to get at Bubbles was to lean over Gertrude from behind (as if we were back doing it doggy-style, as in days of yore!). Gertrude kept inanely trying to help. "Here, Pussy," she squealed.

"*I'll* deal with the pussy, Gertrude," I said sternly, groping around on both sides of her. "If you'd just move a little to the right..."

"But Harrison, it's so big, I think it's stuck!" Gertrude giggled, squirming under my weight as I felt my way blindly toward Bubbles.

"Yes, it's getting bigger and bigger," I admitted: Bubbles had lost all her initial scrawniness and was now turning into a fine matronly cat (I'd have to start cutting back on the Fancy Feast). But why was I calling her "it"? She'd been "he" for a while, then "she", never "it"! The only explanation was that I wasn't myself, thanks to the aggravations of being with Gertrude again, and being with her *in a kimono*. And now I was getting down and dirty with her on the floor! I couldn't take any more of this. "C'mon!" I said in sudden exasperation and, clutching the woman around the middle, I yanked her bodily up from the floor, meaning to deposit her a few feet away. I realized too late that the silkiness of the kimono, combined with a Pavlovian reaction to my close proximity to this familiar body, was rousing base instincts in me. Gertrude interpreted this as a come-on!

"Oh, Harrison, I've missed you so," she murmured delightedly.

For godsake, didn't she know no m.o., no intentionality, no Plan of Action, can be attributed to that organ? Plenty of rhymes, maybe, but no reason. It goes up, it goes down. Big deal. *It doesn't know what's going on!* Having high hopes of me now, Gertrude somehow wound her snakelike arms around my legs. My only chance of escape lay in making a dash for the bedroom; but it was no good, she held fast and *floored* me! (She's stronger than she looks.) I fell flat on my face. She flipped me over, and now she was all over me, slithering and sliding, muttering all kinds of indecencies, and *undulating* like there was no tomorrow.

I grabbed hold of a piano leg to use as leverage, but she wasn't going to let me go. I seem to remember *biting* the piano leg at one point, in my efforts to avoid a fate worse than death. Who knows what outrage would have been perpetrated in another second or two, if a whole bunch of soft round objects hadn't started raining down on us from above. I got biffed by one in the face and looked up. . . and there was *Mimi*, clutching a bag of bagels. How long had she been there??

Gertrude jumped off me and ran towards the front door, the coward. But Mimi kept pelting her with bagels (the perfect matriarchal missile: soft and round, with that vaginal hole), until Gertrude got angry and retaliated with coffee capsules.

CAT FIGHT!!!

Mimì! Mimì!

I phoned again and again but she wasn't answering. This filled me with irritation. Come on, girl, what do you take me for? Do you really think I'd be banging that bore while you were out buying bagels? BOY, that made me mad!

And I thought she loved me! Just the day before, we'd sat canoe-style on the couch, Mimi in my arms, me nuzzling her brown curls—the epitome of coziness and peace! For Mimi, I'd run down ten flights of stairs, hoping to beat the elevator, but she was too fast for me, and gone by the time I got there. For Mimi, I'd stood barefoot on 36th Street *in a kimono*, enduring the whistles of work-men! For Mimi, I'd suffered the slings and arrows and outrageous misfortune of Gertrude, who passed me out there on the street a few minutes later, her arms full of her priceless coffee machine.

"You look ridiculous, Harrison," she'd said in triumph.

"I *am* ridiculous," I'd replied, before plodding back upstairs to my disheveled apartment and discomfited cat.

"Well, Bubs, how about some coffee and bagels?"

Instead of the *Appassionata*, I played the *Tempest* for the next few hours. Both pieces are for the heartbroken, but the *Tempest* is full of blood and flood and fire... *This* is what rejection does to you: you lose all resistance to crass ideas about music! And the more I played it, the more I took the whole débâcle out on Mimi. *Your feet's too big*! Women are always complaining about the size of *men's* feet, but

Mimi's! Sure, they might be useful when manning barricades, but this was *Manhattan* in a period of relative calm!

Absence, combined with guilt and shame, made Mimi seem alien, not my *mate* but some kind of interloper who didn't suit me after all. I had never worried about her physical peculiarities when she was by my side, kissing me and sassing me around; but in retrospect, she had her flaws. Was it really necessary to be so plump? I knew I was dating a middle-aged woman, I'd *accepted* that, but those bulges under her bra straps at the back—this was new territory for me. For Delacroix, it wasn't a problem. Liberty's wearing loose-fitting clothing, sans bra. But in an age of more or less universal bra use, a man can indulge only so much *bulge* before starting to wonder if he doesn't deserve better. Female flesh is supposed to be smooth and soft and curvy, not all furrowed, dented, and squeezed, like a ball of rubber bands. In fact, Delacroix could *keep* his feisty flat-footed weirdsmobile for all I cared!

Going out with Mimi now seemed a mockery of what I did for a living—and she'd have been the first to admit it! She was none too kind about my sorry profession. The point was, how was I supposed to turn up at plastic surgery conventions with *Mimi* on my arm? All the other guys used their women as *ads* for their talents with Botox or the scalpel; the women were works-in-progress. Henry always brought his patients, convinced that they were proof of his beautifying skills. Aw, screw him too, *and* his beauty addiction.

And then I thought of that night on the street, after Henry drove us nuts, how Mimi called me a hero, and kissed me... and the *Tempest* gradually subsided. I just wanted Mimi back! So what, if I was trained to disapprove of some of her physical flaws? What's a love affair without a little ugliness? You need some counterpart to heady joy or you'd conk out! It gave love *gravitas*, like in *Ant and Bee and the Rainbow*, when you get that scary cross-section of the old buried tire. The top half, above-ground, can be laboriously painted to look (a bit) like a fake rainbow, but the other half's stuck in the cracked earth, lonely and unreachable, with stones sticking painfully into its sides: a *memento mori*. "We all die in the end."

My next move was to go howl like a hound-dog outside Mimi's building, also pound on the door and ring the bell, but Mimi wasn't there or wasn't answering. *Mimì! Mimì!*

So I went home and called my sister, who found the whole thing funny!

"You said what?!"

"I said I'd deal with the pussy... or something like that. Aw jeez. I don't know what I said, but it wasn't good."

"Gertrude must have been pleased with herself after."

"She did look pretty happy."

"Just give Mimi a little time. She'll get over it."

Gertrude phoned later to apologize.

"Yeah, well, thanks to your little cameo appearance there, Gertrude," I said unforgivingly, "my girlfriend isn't speaking to me. And we were planning to get *married*." (I'd just decided.)

"Married!?"

So then I had to comfort Gertrude!

Despite Cheryl's vain hope that I was newly available, only Bubbles helped fill the gap left by Mimi. Bubbles was the better purrer, but I ached for Mimi. Rodolfo's cry of *Mimì! Mimì!* went through my head a million times a day—though, when I got home from work I swallowed rom-coms by the dozen, not Puccini. *Sleepless in Seattle* made me cry! My List of Melancholy, which had lain dormant for a while, began to spiral out of control.

LIST OF MELANCHOLY

- the "Ready" bell on microwaves
- beeps of all types
- truck-reversing sirens and recorded messages
- car alarms
- alarm clocks
- xylophones
- glockenspiels
- this pain in my temple!
- Roman centurion sandals
- Kentucky-fried-chicken-kickers, and the chickens they kick
- barn dances
- my mother's raspberry jam (no longer available)
- upholstery, especially those *buttons* that hold it all together
- Dick Cheney
- data fraud
- adultery
- Boy Scouts
- Girl Scouts
- linoleum
- women all over the world, stretching their arms up over their heads
- Mimi's flattened straw hat

That straw hat of hers turned up in my bedroom closet (a Mimi minefield), and I remembered Mimi admiring it, saying, "Look at the work that went into this, Harrison! So intricate! Look how it's woven. See how rounded it is at the top? That's an art!"—a remark that entangled *me*, wove *me*, and entitled me to make a grab—for Mimi, not the hat. The hat was caught in the fray and got crushed.

Intimately examining it now, sitting on the floor of my closet, I had an idea—EUREKA!—a solution to my present predicament that went well beyond the usual roses, chocolates, or chocolate roses, of other two-timing bastards. In my capacity as Mimi's attorney I gave the museum of annoying folksiness a call, and offered to buy the Firefly Quilt back from them after all. Humble Pie was consumed. After some toing and froing with the director and her aloof assistants, a price was settled on. It had gone up (practically double) and, given that I'd never spent that much on household decor before, it took some strength of purpose to blow it on a blanket. But I was by then too pleased with my cunning plan to backtrack. They said I could pick the thing up on Monday.

I filled the time by getting all sentimental over my notes on Mimi's hot flashes, and then—in direct defiance of my arse of an arsonist dad and his disparagement of my early inventions—I got to work inventing the hot flash remedy: Meno-Balls™! I made quick progress during my lonely nights without Mimi, and soon the Meno-Balls™ had progressed from being a whim to a fully formed concept. I'd need a little development help from technicians, chemists, engineers, chemical engineers, and chemical-engineering technicians, before I could patent it—making the things *cold* was the problem. But I had one little breakthrough all on my own: Space Shuttle tiles. These I thought might offer just the right kind of heat resistance necessary for the cold version of the Meno-Balls™, allowing them to retain their low temperature despite the influence of the woman's own body heat.

The Meno-Balls™ were based on letting dualism work *for* us for once, not against us. They would consist of two separate "balls," or flattened disks, one red, one blue, or one square, one round (the exact distinction didn't matter, as long as the woman could quickly differentiate between them in a hot flash emergency). They would be lightweight, rounded, compact, and easily held in the palm of the hand. The woman could keep them in her pockets, on her desk, or under her pillow; one to heat her up, one to cool her down. Perhaps she'd have one in a left-hand pocket, the other in the right, so that she could grab them surreptitiously to offset whichever unpleasant sensation (heat or cold) was currently impending, without anyone else having to know (thus avoiding all the questions that so aggravated Mimi).

By gripping the ball, she activates the mechanism that heats the ball up or cools it down. It may have been a case of Inventor's Euphoria Syndrome (a condition I just made up) but I had a hunch that simply knowing these devices were readily available would alleviate many of the symptoms. No more panting, sweating, blushing, nausea, or palpitations with Meno-Balls™! I could hear the jingles already: *Feeling hot or feeling cold, now in silver and in gold. . . Meno-Balls!* and *Don't you cry, Don't be shy, This is why: Meno-Balls!*

The main thing was that the balls would be harmless and non-invasive, with no side effects whatsoever, thereby complying with Mimi's insistence that the menopause is not a disease. They might even have other applications. Handy for hikers and fishermen, or children with fevers, people stuck in snowdrifts or in the subway in August, who knows? All I really cared about though, was pleasing Mimi.

But I needed a better name. Meno wasn't great—*women*-o would make more sense. And Balls was *all wrong*: it seemed to imply penis envy. They weren't necessarily going to be *balls* anyway: they could be just about any shape, as long as they were rounded, palm-sized, pleasant and easy to hold, with no sharp edges, and unobtrusive in a pocket. I thought of calling them Pockets of Matriarchy™, but that was too long and convoluted: who wants to go to the drugstore and ask for *Pockets of Matriarchy*™? Even if the woman lived in an actual pocket of matriarchy herself, like Malta, it would still be a mouthful! In the end I fixed on Pocket Change™, a pun I felt I could just about bear.

At the office I was facing a backlog of my least favorite customers: MEN, with their penile dysfunction and Berlusconi revamps: nose-jobs, eye-jobs, facelifts, hair transplants, collagen, Botox, even boob-jobs. *I* blamed Berlusconi; my colleagues *loved* him, and followed his surgical schedule with great attention, since whenever Berlusconi got his eyelids done, our patients wanted theirs done too—not to look younger, I was beginning to think, just to look like Berlusconi!

I didn't see the point in fixing men up. Sure, I could turn a guy's crow's feet into hummingbird talons, but there's no getting rid of his *deep soul ache*, is there? They were on their own with their erections too—not my problem, man. Take Viagra, or get a hobby, baseball cards, Lego, Bridge, mechanical pencils, just leave me out of it.

We don't all have to be Casanova, you know, or even Berlusconi. I had enough trouble with my own cock.

You think it's easy being in charge of a penis? It's a full-time job! This is how you first learn responsibility, as a boy. You have to keep this vulnerable piece of wandery flesh from getting *squashed*. Every bout of roughhousing is a threat—this is why these games must be practiced again and again! That's all sport is for: the honing of prick-protection skills. The thing's just *hanging off you*, in constant danger of injury or excision. If it's true everybody wants a piece of you, this is probably the piece. Dogs are at just the right level to snatch it in one gulp. Chairs, desks, tables, car doors, and doorknobs all seem designed to gouge it. A hundred times a day you have to check on the darn thing, not just to guide it when peeing, but to execute many little sartorial adjustments.

The only way to handle such a responsibility is to make your cock THE CORE OF YOUR BEING, so that you never forget about it, *ever*. You make a pet of it, give it a name, fondle, pat, and feed it, even try to *train* it—though it's like training a stick insect. Every time you take a piss you attempt to discipline it. Hell, just whipping the thing out *in time* takes practice. And in winter, you teach it to write dirty words in the snow.

Your dick has a nocturnal existence of its own that you can't take responsibility for, but both its conscious and unconscious eruptions demand study and assessment, its spasms and jisms dutifully graded from the humdrum to the rum-a-dum-dum. You are your penis's protector and advocate, its 24-hour carer, its slave and its supervisor, its bodyguard and its biggest fan. When necessary, your fist provides the services of a concubine. You learn your prick's needs, its desires, and how to encase it in comfort behind a million historic fastenings, from gentle buttons to the more perilous zipper (that might at any time turn on the item it's supposed to guard). Behind these flaps, your cock is left to nestle cozily in its jockeys or its jockstrap, or its *leopardskin posing pouch* (I speak as I find). Through barriers of cloth, and mind control, you attempt to restrain it, and only let it loose when you've checked the coast is clear.

But do you really trust your old play-pal there an inch? The thing's an enigma! It's not just the snap decisions to quadruple in size. Any minute now it'll go down and STAY DOWN, and your whole life will be over—you'll become one of those guys who give blowjobs, gratis, at gas stations. You're plagued by fears of plague too, the possibility that your cock might be too cocky some day and bring home a disease, come over all cankerous, unappealing to mouths and cunts alike. *Or* that you'll just get prostate trouble like all the other poor zhlubs and that'll be the end of you. For this is the most important relationship of your life, and not to be trifled with! You clear space for your cock, make room in society for your cock. Cocks demand territory (ask any dog).

ALL YOU REALLY WANT IS FOR THE WHOLE WORLD TO BE NICE TO YOUR COCK.

Playground joke of my youth: This guy has such a big dick he has to wind it around his neck like a tie. He goes to the theater one night and his date keeps playing with his tie (as women always do). Suddenly, the lights come up and the manager comes out on stage and says, "Could the gentleman in the third row please stop throwing ice cream onto the stage?"

We killed ourselves over that one.

Being in love means you're *not* in sole charge of your prick anymore—someone else is looking out for it too! And I was pretty pissed at having lost my little assistant. Surely Mimi would be drawn back to me by the miraculous magnetic pull of my cock? Apparently not.

But Quilt Day at last arrived. The money had gone through in daily installments of $10,000, and Leggy finally called me to announce that the Firefly Quilt was ready for collection. I had a drink on the way, just to gather my faculties, then moseyed on over to the museum, where I was coldly handed a big brown-paper parcel tied up with string—a lot like the ones Ant receives from the whole of England and Kind Dog, when he's sick in bed, except mine was labeled "Harrison Hanafan", not "Ant", and had cost me $48,000. And for something that cost me $48,000, it sure wasn't very well wrapped! Maybe Leggy had wrenched it peevishly off the wall at the last possible minute.

I was planning to rush straight over to Mimi's and lay it at her feet. If she wasn't there, I'd use my keys and (in *reverse* of that klep- tomaniac scuzzball, John) leave the quilt there as a love offering, my own act of vulva-worship. But the absolute necessity of getting this operation right made me nervous. I was trembling, dizzy, I was nauseous: I was having a hot flash! (It felt almost as bad as giving a speech.) So I took that old quilt to a place in the Village I knew called Milady's, where the Bloody Marys are perfect—and pint-sized. The quilt and I had a couple of them, toasting Aunt Phoebe the while, before setting off again for Grove Street. But I forgot the quilt, had to go back for it, and naturally had another Bloody Mary while I was there. Then I got cold feet again (a kind of post-hot-flash cold spell). Deciding I must be drunk(!), I ducked into a grocery store to see if I could get some coffee.

I wasn't actually unraveling any faster than the quilt, which was beginning to curl hazardously out of its packaging. The store was crowded and people kept jolting me. I protested a bit. Half hatched from its cocoon, the quilt was beginning to reveal its most admirable qualities: its silky smoothness, and the dazzling colors. The perfect opportunity, I suddenly realized, to compare the thing to actual *Epicure* cans! So I went to see if they had any on the shelves. But on my way down the aisle some jerk jerked me, I backed into a whole row of Pepperidge Farm cookies, tripped over the loose corner of the quilt that was dragging on the ground, and ended up rolling across the floor! I came to a stop fully wrapped in the quilt.

A security guy peered down at me and said, "What's the story, Grandma Moses?"

Well, I paid for the cookies I crushed and got the hell out. That quilt had now cost me $48,028.56, and it had better work! But on closer inspection outside, by the light of the setting sun, I noticed my poignant offering appeared to have sustained some damage: a few faint stains, a rip or two. QUILT GUILT. Now Mimi would *never* forgive me! I'd not only wrecked her life, but her aunt's masterpiece too. $48,028.56 down, and no closer to rolling in my sweet baby's arms! If I didn't want to be alone with my expensive new bedspread for the rest of my life, I would have to put it in the hands of the dry cleaners and invisible menders around the corner from me on 8th Avenue. So I cabbed it uptown and relinquished my Mimi-bait into their, I hoped, capable hands.

Keenly disappointed by this delay in the resumption of romance,

I rode the elevator glumly up to my apartment, intending to drown myself yet again in the *Tempest*. But when I got in, my phone was blinking. A message from Mimi? *Mimi! Mimi!* She had relented, she couldn't stay mad at me forever. I leapt to the phone, *crazy 'bout my baby...*

But the message wasn't from Mimi. It was from an English policeman, telling me Bee was dead.

SARABANDE

CATASTROBURY

I WAS MET at the station in Canterbury, the *West* Station (the one that's further *East*), by the same cop who'd left the message on my answering machine the day before. He apologized for that now, but I was in no mood for a discussion of police etiquette. What would be a GOOD way to hear your sister's dead? Sherry on the veranda, moats, deer, skylarks, ha-has, and him whispering in my ear, "I'm afraid I have something a little awkward to tell you"?

He asked me if I wanted to go to my hotel first, but I wanted to see Bee, so he took me to the half-assed English morgue they'd set up in a hurry at the hospital, to cater for all the bodies. For Bee was among many—you can really kill a lot of people if you put your mind to it. We wove our way through a crush of journalists, who stuck their long-lens cameras right in my face. (As James Joyce said, all journalists are heartless.)

The *gunman* liked shooting people in the face too. The cop warned me of this as we approached Bee on her stretcher. Then the sheet was pulled back so that I could formally identify her. They hadn't even bothered to wipe the blood off! Maybe it was "evidence" or something. She was all messed up, but it was Bee.

All the way over I'd clung to the idea that they were wrong. Not my sister. Not *that* sculptress. Please, SOMEONE ELSE. That ignoble hope gone, I searched her face for an explanation. What did she *think* when he came running at her with a gun? Did she have a *chance* to think? I pulled Bee to me and hugged her for a long time.

When I first got the news, I assumed she'd been run over on that stupid bike of hers, or stabbed trying to intervene in another street fight. Unbearable, but at least an *accident*. How was I supposed to come to terms with the fact that some creep had spotted my sister across a field by chance, and (whether with nonchalance or insane glee) gone out of his way to shoot her?

I must have signed some forms, but all I remember is wandering the hospital corridors, pestered by policewomen trying to give me sandwiches and cups of tea. Tea: the English answer to all emergencies. They really seem to think it helps! But this tea had *scum* floating on the top, the scum Bee told me about.

My personal, po-faced policeman asked me periodically if I had any questions. Yeah! What'll I do without her? But I said nothing. When he tired of this, he offered a change of scene: would I like to see the place where Bee had died? But I'd had enough by then and asked to be taken to the hotel.

It was one of the tiniest hotel rooms I've ever seen, with a toilet that didn't flush. I tried calling Mimi but got no answer, then attempted to achieve temporary oblivion with the help of airline miniatures, and tranquilizers provided by the hospital. I fell asleep staring at the green shiny curtain cords that held the ugly curtains apart: yet another futile fabric fiasco. Why must we have all this disgusting decor? I was perturbed by how tightly wound those cords were. What angry twisted mind had created these angry twisted ropes? They didn't even go with the stupid curtains, which were yellow, with a kindergartenish peach pattern. It's all so *arbitrary*, our decor. We decide a million things arbitrarily. But arbitrariness would never seem innocent to me again: people get MURDERED arbitrarily.

I woke to the smell of air freshener used in accusatory quantities. And on every surface, frantic laminated signs:

TURN OFF THE LIGHTS

BEFORE YOU LEAVE

TURN OFF THE TV

TURN OFF THE HEATING

DON'T TOUCH

VERY HOT!

ARE YOU SURE YOU

NEED A FRESH TOWEL?

DO NOT OPEN THE WINDOW

TEMPERATURE AND PRESSURE

MAY CHANGE

PLEASE BE CAREFUL

PHONE CHARGERS ONLY

There were guilt trips everywhere you looked, telling you every-thing you could and couldn't do in that impossible room. All this attention to *safety*, in a city where people get gunned down willy-nilly! And still the toilet wouldn't flush.

I assumed I was too late for the hotel breakfast, and would get my ass kicked for *that* as well (or my bottom belabored). But no, a whole sorry bunch of breakfasters were there, squeezed into what seemed to be the *hallway*, munching cold toast while being lectured by the hotel manager who claimed Conrad had lived in Canterbury at some point. I was hungry, but not this hungry. As I left, I heard one of the guests remark, "You never see pictures of Joseph Conrad smiling."

I glimpsed the top of the cathedral. Assuming it to be in the center of town, I headed that way, trusting some bearable break-fast might eventually be found. Illogically or not, I wished Bee was there to show me around. The sidewalk was narrow, and ran right beside a busy two-way street full of assholes speeding by in cars, blasting me with their ignoramus pop music and calling out "Cunt!" as they passed. I may be a cunt, man, but you're the one who has to be *sung to* all day by sissies on the radio.

As soon as possible, I took a quieter path beside a shallow river, and had to squeeze past a student with her parents. They were all looking down at the water and she was telling them, "It's really clear. You can see all the traffic bollards and supermarket trolleys."

What a dump. I got to the main street, but the only forms of food offered were "chips," "burgers," and something called "bacon butties." I walked into some kind of café, but the frail girl sweeping the floor sent me away, on the grounds that it was "too oily" (which I could well believe). I found a small grocery store instead, and bought a load of English newspapers, all of which were bursting with gun massacre stats and stories: I felt I owed it to Bee to check what they were saying about her in there.

Canterbury really *stank*, whether it was from the oniony food outlets or the digestive gases farted out by the people who ate at them. The local populace certainly *looked* abdominally uncomfortable. As a plastic surgeon who thought he'd seen it all, I was left aghast by the medieval physiognomies of the townsfolk, a pasty race, vicious, gnarled, gnawed, and bloodthirsty. They liked a good massacre. There they were, milling around the main street to stare at spots where people had been murdered a few days before. These had been helpfully designated by police tape: "SCENE CRIME SCENE CRIME"—as if a crime had been committed against the *picturesque*, not people. Canterbury's about as picturesque as my ass, unless you care about cathedrals. But this one's a hell of a thing, a MONSTROSITY.

How does a place like Canterbury recover from a tragedy? By shopping! Everybody there seemed to get a big bang out of carrying a big bag. But what was in those bags? Guns? Ammo? Souvenir mugs of the massacre?

Everything I saw confirmed the necessity of the American

Revolution. How could Bee have lived here for a *day*, much less a *year*, a nice New York gal like her? But she'd never *wanted* to come. She hated the place! How she wailed about the weather, the water, the weariness and wariness. All that trouble with her stingy patrons. Jerks! The English are not a friendly people. She'd come all this way just to make a little money, and they let her down. And when that wasn't enough, they OBLITERATED her!

I found a little café called Saint something or other. Everything in Canterbury's called Saint something. But this place was at least trying to be French in the manner to which I'm accustomed (coffee and croissants, though minus the Gauloises and Gallic charm). There I sat, reading the paper like I was some normal man, but the more I read, the more furious I got—with *Bee*, for getting herself into this! Couldn't she have ducked? NO. Just a few minutes either way, and it might never have happened. Why'd she have to go out on her bike that particular day, why *that field*?

The facts were these: Gareth Lode, a British soldier, had returned from Afghanistan to find that his ex-wife was refusing him access to their joint progeny, because of his violent outbursts in the past. Old girlfriends confirmed that he was violent—they'd reported him to the police years before. Lode was in trouble with the Army as well: he'd tortured too many prisoners, even by their standards, and his superiors considered him volatile and unpredictable. They'd warned the Canterbury police about him, saying that he was "nervy" and might do something weird. The police did nothing (of course).

Everybody was tiring of this asshole, in other words, but *he* wasn't tired of *being* an asshole. So he stabbed and strangled his ex-wife in front of their children. The kids were next—neighbors heard them screaming and begging for mercy as he smothered them. Then he armed himself with a gun and went over to his mother's house, somewhere in Canterbury, and shot *her*. A murderous tour around town followed, with Lode randomly shooting dozens of women in the street, mostly middle-aged women, always aiming for the face.

I knew from gun rampages in America that if a guy wants to do this, there's no stopping him: you pretty much hand him the keys to the city and the Colonel Gaddafi Certificate of Permission to Wreak Mayhem. But it was still hard to believe that one guy had gotten away with this much death—"three years' worth of murder in a single day," as one paper put it. Afterwards, Lode hid in the woods, where he demonstrated several survival skills he'd learned in the Army before blowing his own brains out, surrounded by trigger-happy cops.

His last stand in the woods, along with his apparent hatred of women, had earned him his own little fan club, many of whom had raced to place garish bouquets and controversial condolence messages outside Lode's Canterbury barracks, saying, "RIP Gareth," and, "Gareth, you wuz wronged." One guy traveled down from the North of England somewhere with his three sons to lay a wreath at the Lode shrine. He described it as a good day out for the kids, and educational! In his opinion, Lode had done what any man would do when pushed too far: *explode*.

But it was the newspapers' exultation in the story that really got me. I wasn't used to it: in America, this kind of crime gets one day of front-page coverage, *tops*, then it's as if it never happened. It was now two days since the Canterbury event, and the papers were still slobbering over every detail, tracking the guy's every move from birth to death, offering blow-by-blow, bullet-by-bullet chronologies of his progress, maps charting his route, "interactive graphics" (whatever *they* were), diagrams, satellite photos, and full-color pull-out sections to keep for posterity. Now and then, an editorial in which some lone fool asserted that there was no reason to tighten England's already tight gun laws. No, of course not. Why deprive everybody of another massacre? The Queen's beleaguered subjects need their entertainment.

The papers were thrilled with the death rate: they could barely contain their glee. "Savage" Lode had outdone many mass murderers of the past. By killing twenty people, twenty-one if you counted Lode himself, he "beat" all their previous gun massacres, "leaving the charming streets of Canterbury stained with blood." The what? And the death rate might rise yet, they cheerily warned, given all the injured now screaming for their lives in a variety of charming hospitals.

They made a killing spree sound like a shopping spree! In fact, Lode himself had paused to pick up a new pair of trainers in the middle of it, while sales staff cowered in a corner.

Now came the tales of lucky escapes—people who'd sensibly hidden as Lode passed them on the street, people who'd been perilously close to the areas he covered, people who'd merely *thought* of going to Canterbury that day, and various characters who'd known Lode at some earlier point in his life. There were pictures of him as a baby, as a boy, and talk of his fixed stare, his many grievances, his money worries. What about *my* grief, *my* grievances, *my* fixed stare?

Lode's brother had been unearthed and interviewed: he insisted Lode was one of the nicest "blokes" you could ever meet, who'd fought for his country while the divorce lawyers were giving away his visiting rights. It was all their mother's fault, the brother said, for being severely depressed when they were young. He didn't like Lode being described as "violent and controlling" either—to him Lode had been "sweet." But isn't beating up all your girlfriends, stabbing your wife, smothering your children, and shooting dozens of women in the face about as violent and controlling as a man can get?

With espresso-fueled nausea, I waded through these outlandish documents, not even sure what I was looking for. There was hardly a single reference to Bee individually. Compared to their exhaustive treatment of Lode, the description of his victims was perfunctory. They were defined by their ages and occupations: barmaid, housewife, hairdresser, Health Visitor, university lecturer, receptionist, waitress, sculptress. . . A treatment that seemed to reduce them to almost *nothing*—when they were PEOPLE for godsake, people on whom other people counted! It really doesn't matter if they were bookish or banal. They meant something to somebody, and to *themselves*. (Maybe even to a few pets, who'd now have to be rehomed or put down.)

EVERYBODY MEANS SOMETHING.

But at least we were spared all the claptrap American gun outrages inspire, with the candlelight vigils, extremist defenses of gun ownership (as if owning lethal weapons were a *good* thing, rather than an incontrovertible sign of barbarism), and mawkish talk of god. After the Tucson murders, Obama had to lay it on thick, with "Scripture tells us this" and "Scripture tells us that." Everybody said it was his best speech ever! Come to think of it, there probably *was* some dumb religious rigmarole going on in that hokey cathedral of theirs—but I wouldn't be going.

A young guy with long black hair and a face like the Mona Lisa sat down at an upright piano, in the corner of the café, that I hadn't even noticed, and started playing 1960s tunes with some panache. The joint was jumpin', in an English kind of way. Customers became more animated, clapping politely between numbers... and I felt myself relax for the first time since I heard of Bee's death. Not because music is some goddam *relaxant*, but because it gave me another metaphysical plane to be on. I needed that more than coffee.

Any music was a help, but what I really wanted was Bach. So I struggled to my feet, went over and put a bit of money in the guy's tips teacup on top of the piano. All I said was, "Bach," and then sat down. But he didn't play me any Bach. Maybe he didn't do classical music, or he hadn't heard me, or he never played requests. Whether I'd blundered into another faux pas was of little concern to me anymore, since I'd now spotted on the front of one of the papers a reference to an obituary of Bee. I turned to the appropriate page, trembling.

The American sculptor, Bridget Hanafan, who has died age 53 as a result of the mass killing in Canterbury on 23 May, produced some of the most appealing public sculptures of recent years.

Born in the American Midwest in 1958, Hanafan studied at the Rhode Island School of Design, where she gained a reputation early on as one of the foremost sculptors of her generation.

After a hiatus caused by an unhappy marriage,

Hanafan started producing works in clay, culminating in her first one-woman show in 1994. Commissions for installations and public projects soon followed, along with a number of prestigious awards and fellowships.

Recently, Hanafan had relocated to Canterbury, in order to take up a post of artist-in-residence. There she enlarged on a series of assemblages begun in New York, which she dubbed Coziness Sculptures, life-size re-creations of domestic and rural scenes intended as "a glimpse of something good". Hanafan was exploring sculpture as a means of contributing to a sense of well-being in the spectator.

By including lighting and audio elements as well as family heirlooms and other found materials, Hanafan combined an awareness of personal struggle with a delight in the textures of everyday life. In touching works that are autobiographical in nature, she promoted the pleasure principle, revealing a newly humane approach in contemporary art.

She continued to expand her range of techniques. Two carved stone figures by Hanafan were recently installed in an underwater setting in Canterbury's River Stour. The grace and ingenuity of these pieces demonstrate an artist of burgeoning power, ambition and imagination, whose work was about to take off in a wholly new direction.

Hanafan was Gareth Lode's final victim. She leaves a brother.

My sister, "humane"—I liked that. But I never knew she could carve stone! And what was with all these awards she never told me about? I folded the newspaper and tried to swallow some more coffee—but at that moment the pianist started playing Bach (a bit of *Goldberg*), and I had to hold the paper up to hide the tears streaming down my face.

Back in the hotel, I tried phoning Mimi and flushing the toilet. No answer from either. It occurred to me now that Mimi probably knew nothing about what had happened to Bee, given her aversion to the News. American coverage of this English disaster was no doubt scanty: we like our gun crime *homegrown*. I hadn't even told Mimi Bee *lived* in Canterbury, as far as I could remember, just that she was in England somewhere.

I sank into a poky little armchair and watched the News myself, but it was all about the gunman and the government, and the way they pronounced "gunm'n" and "gubm'nt" sounded exactly the same, to surreal effect. I gave up, stuck a piece of Wrigley's Dubm'nt in my mouth, and fell asleep.

Later, my cop picked me up and took me to Bee's apartment (there was her studio at the art school to deal with too, when I was ready). Her home was on the first floor (*ground* floor) of a small row house in a grim part of town, but Bee had done her usual number on it. She was always amassing stuff from junk shops, or the gutter, I don't know which, and the place was one big altar to ephemera—though, I admit, it was kind of cozy.

This was what Bee worshipped: shells, coins, leaves, flowers, champagne corks, here a doll's arm, there a small chipped china dog on a velvet cushion, and a colorful African basket. A lot of old dark-blue medicine bottles decorated the window sills. And on a table, a tiny clay man was selling clay sausages on strings from a tiny stall. Bee's collages and photographs adorned the walls. The smell of Bee was there too. I had to sit down for quite a while.

But what was I going to do with it all? Bee's obituary-writer might have appreciated her taste for "heirlooms" and domesticity—but I was the guy who'd have to *pack* it all up, or give it away! The sadness of her medicine cabinet, or her fridge, equipped with coffee beans, and bread and cheese for grilled cheese sandwiches; the pile of dirty laundry. The innocent signs of someone in the midst of life, who didn't expect to die. Depressingly, I found several *fleece* garments. I couldn't imagine Bee ever wearing them! But that's what poverty and a cold damp climate can do to a nice Manhattan chick. She was so cold. She once told me she had to wear her *winter coat* just to cook in that tiny kitchen.

I was cold too, and didn't know how to work the heating system (if there *was* one). I also had a sense of shame, in invading my sister's privacy. I needed air. I felt like I was being buried alive in there! I reeled out of the building, gasping, and walked around the block. At least it wasn't raining. Instead, they were having what they deemed a "heat wave" (a few sunny days); this fine weather was often mentioned in the massacre reports. Much was made of the paradoxical(?) fact that dreadful things sometimes happen during clement weather. "The sun was shining. It was a beautiful day. . ." Were they all insane? Would the massacre be more comprehensible conducted in sleet? Or were they suggesting Lode had been maddened by the heat? (Another fine excuse.)

Bee had described to me the way they all rush outside whenever the sun comes out, drop everything for twenty minutes' sunbathing, and turn bright pink. For Bee it explained all of England's problems. "No concentration skills!" Ah, Bee.

I turned a corner—and came upon the martyrs' memorial that had so rattled her. It wasn't grand or very antique, just a small concrete obelisk with a Maltese cross on top, plonked on a mound of jagged stones in the middle of a miniature triangular park.

Everything in Canterbury's tiny—except the murder rate. The place was made for midgets and maniacs!

The names of the forty-one martyrs were carved into the sides of the monument but, sure enough, two were listed merely as "Bradbridge's widow" and "Wilson's wife," showing the disrespect that had infuriated Bee. To me, their anonymity gave these two women a kind of confederacy the other martyrs lacked. But they did seem somehow forlorn.

I walked on, past Fryer Tuck's Fish & Chips (shut) and into a leafy lane that seemed almost bucolic in the sun, full of bumblebees and purple stinging nettles. I avoided getting stung by either and continued down the alley. It reminded me of one of Bee's graveyard inscriptions I'd found among her papers:

WHEN YOU WALK THROUGH
PEACEFUL LANES SO GREEN
REMEMBER US AND THINK
WHAT MIGHT HAVE BEEN

I did.

*   *   *

They were speeding up the preliminary inquest and Bee's autopsy for *my* benefit, so that I could take her ashes home with me. But it would be a few days yet. Meanwhile, I sorted through her stuff, arranged for it to be packed and shipped to my apartment, and settled her bills. Her landlady offered to give me back Bee's deposit on the apartment, but I told her to keep it. This couldn't be easy for her either, having a tenant get slaughtered.

Finally I went to the art school, explained who I was to a frightened secretary, and asked for access to Bee's studio. Nobody knew what to say to me, nobody knew what to *do* with me in Canterbury (apart from the guy who played me Bach). It's frightfully ticklish to have the brother of a murder victim hanging about. But after a long wait, they showed me into Bee's studio and left me there.

My first tired reaction was one of *horror*, at the abundance of junk in there: I'd just have to get somebody to take it all straight to the city dump! There were stacks of wood, Perspex, corrugated iron, cardboard, and other materials. Bags of plaster, piles of cloth, lace, kelims, and other fancy items that might have belonged to one of Bee's aborted Coziness Sculptures...

There was such a weight of work in there—it was like coming across Schubert's unfinished symphony and wondering, What the hell? There were clay maquettes of sculptures Bee must have been planning to make, and many drawings and sketchbooks that I wanted to look at (later). And then, something I truly loved, positioned atop a grandiose plinth: the neat nest of some tiny bird, labeled with the words, "How cosy they must be." This was something Auden had said, in response to seeing birds in a nest, and *I'd* told Bee about it (knowing how much she liked to be kept informed of all references to "coziness"). *This* heirloom I wrapped carefully in a lot of paper, to take home with me.

Then I made a list of what, as far as I could tell, needed to be done in there, and was about to go when I noticed something soft and white peeking out from behind a partition. I scrambled over some boxes and peered through a gap—and there was my mother's bed!

Not the real one, no, that was long gone. This wasn't life-size either, but *bigger*, so big that when I twisted my way through the gap in the partition and stood beside it, the bed was shoulder-height— just as Mom's bed used to be when we were kids. Kind of spooky to find yourself suddenly dwarfed by your mother's bed, *forty years later*. But it wasn't icky, it was cozy! The bed was covered in the same kind of soft white knitted bedspread Mom always had but bigger, with the same kind of corny bobbles all over it. I was tempted to bury my face in it, it looked so warm, so *real*.

I patted it to see if it really was as soft as it looked, and all I could think about was the *crap* Mom went through on that bed of hers, something only Bee and I could know; our kind mom who *saw us through*, for what good it did her. Her sad end came to mind, and her funeral. When I started wondering what Mom would have said, if she'd lived to know what happened to Bee... I laid my head against my mother's bed and bawled like a baby.

I was accompanied to the inquest by my faithful policeman, who helped me push past the reporters at the door. "Keep those report- ers away from me or I'll kill them," I told him.

The inquest was handled with unexpected kindness, but they

couldn't save me from the results of the autopsy. Even though I'm a doctor, I'd never expected to have my sister's entrails described—all to confirm that she had died instantly as the result of a bullet to the head, which had passed through both hemispheres of the brain, causing the inevitable series of organ shutdowns.

I left the courtroom barely conscious, shaking all over. It would have been a good time to shoot *me*: I couldn't have defended myself. It was then that an enterprising journalist sidled up and asked me if the inquest had proved conclusive or provided "closure". I pushed the bastard away.

"You want closure. I want my sister!"

I hoped I'd be all alone at the crematorium, but a few of Bee's *friends* turned up, whom she'd never told me about: three women who taught at Kent University and hated it, for reasons they were too furious to go into. They took me to a pub, where an unseen parrot squawked all evening; I could barely speak at all. They bought champagne and told me great stuff about Bee, fun stuff. We didn't talk about Lode.

I liked these gals, and was pleased for Bee that she'd known them: the Champagne Girls were truly nice to me, and saw me through that terrible night. In retrospect, I think they must have been driven to become exceptionally nice, to compensate for the exceptional nastiness of Canterbury: everything must have its opposite and antidote.

Hungry and hungover the next day, I went for a walk in what seemed to be Canterbury's only real park, the Westgate. It was full of winos and wedding parties, and featured the most unhealthy-looking tree

I'd ever seen. The trunk was squat and bulbous, and covered in carbuncles—its bark looked like bubbling lava, frozen mid-eruption into a pretense of wood. Branches stuck out above at odd angles in all directions, and from their tips hung a million little brown balls. What fresh hell was this?

A kid caught me staring at it and told me the tree had long ago eaten a bench that used to be at its base. In my present agitated state, I immediately imagined it consuming an old couple *sitting* on the bench as well, as they innocently marveled at its ugliness.

I went on beside the shallow meandering river until the path became muddy and sylvan. I had to duck under huge willows, their trunks twisted in ancient agony, like squeezed-out laundry. I was composing a Canterbury chant for myself as I trudged.

> *Who took the cunt out of*
> > *Canterbury Kent?*
> *Guys yell "Cunt!" from their cars in*
> > *Canterbury Kent.*
> *Count the corpses in*
> > *Canterbury Kent.*
> *They litter the countryside in*
> > *Canterbury Kent.*
> *It's all buns and guns and whoresons by the ton, in*
> > *Canterbury Kent.*
> *Christians concentrate on cant in*
> > *Canterbury Kent.*
> *The cuntstabulary can't cuntrol*
> > *Canterbury Kent.*

Men hunt women down without relent in
  Canterbury Kent.
So who took the cunt out of
  Canterbury Kent?
Who took the CUNT out of
  CANTerbury KENT?

The rugged path suddenly turned into a fancy new cycle route through semi-wilderness. It was dotted with fuzzy brown caterpillars that I tried to avoid stepping on. The sun was low and a bend of the river gleamed in the distance like a knife. There was no sound but birds, and my steps, and a dog barking at his own echo under a railway bridge. And then I could go no further, because the path was sealed off with twisting police tape: "ENTER CRIME SCENE DO NOT..."

I had hit upon it myself, by accident: the spot where Bee had died! No one could see or stop me, so I stepped inside the taped-off area and sank to my knees, searching for any trace of her, even blood—head wounds bleed—but they'd washed it away, or rain had. The thought of her lying there, in pain, completely maddened me—Bee, whose sculptures were devoted to pleasure! I looked around at what Bee must have seen last before she died—the field, the low line of trees around it, the river, the sun, the sky?—and I wondered again what she thought at the end. Did she just *give up*, deciding life isn't worth living, in a world in which such things happen?

But she was wrong, WRONG. Golden light was hitting the opposite riverbank, and the green and gold trees were doing their reflection trick in the river, as if to say: I can face up or down, in a world that is both this and that. The water was clean and clear enough for ducks, who tootled to and fro, the *Appassionata* was playing in my head, and I longed to tell Bee that there's Bach and Beethoven and birds and bees and MIMI, Bee, Mimi, the greatest thing.

Don't give up, Bee, don't give up! The world needs to be BETTER, not gone.

My feet dragged all the way back through the park. How was I going to go on without Bee? How was I even going to get past the Cankerberry Tree, or "Onion Corner," without *dying*?

The heat was getting to me. Them and their heat wave! I stood for a while by the entrance gate to catch my breath. Some people had gathered on the bridge and were pointing down at something in the water. Another ditched shopping cart or baby buggy? Once they'd gone, I went over to see what they were all so fascinated by, and found two small naked female figures, carved in stone. Lithe, young, smooth-skinned girls, less than life-size. They lay stretched out on their backs under the surface of the water, their heads resting on their raised arms, ankles crossed—and they looked *happy*, relaxed, as if they were enjoying the sensation of the water flowing down their bodies and the weeds slowly brushing against them. They looked content to stay there forever, unfazed by being underwater, unfazed even by death.

A plaque on the bridge confirmed the sculptor's name—Bridget Hanafan—and the title: *Bradbridge's Widow, Wilson's Wife*.

*   *   *

My last morning in Canterbury, I thought I'd do the hotel manager a favor by telling him about the failing toilet in my room—*sotto voce*, to save him and his breakfasters any embarrassment.

"YOUR TOILET?" he responded in mock surprise. "Your TOILET's not working?" I recognized that tone of disapproval tinged with hysteria, from all the laminated signs that lay in wait for you throughout the hotel. If it even *was* a hotel—seemed more like a boardinghouse to me.

The total silence among the hotel guests at their little tables suggested they were busily envisioning a nice English toilet bowl besmirched and clogged by my oafish American turds, while the manager kept tsk-tsking and banging stuff around irritably on his desk. "Your toilet... your toilet..." he grumbled. I just stood there, astounded. Surely other toilets had broken down at some point in this shithouse? Finally, he said he'd have a "look" at it later, sighing deeply—the horror, the horror. That's when I flipped.

"Look, it's not MY toilet, you ass, it's YOURS. And as far as I'm concerned you can shove that stupid head of yours right in it, or I'll do it for you, and then you can have a *really* good 'look at it,' what do you say?"

I slapped some money down on the reception desk, grabbed my suitcase and left, slamming the door behind me loud enough to shake those toast racks good. On my way out, I caught sight of one of the laminated signs and decided, for the benefit of others, to hang it on the front door of the hotel:

DO NOT DISTURB

On the sidewalk I nearly bumped into a strange young woman with two great big pink dots painted on her cheeks. She had quite an outlandish get-up on, involving several brightly colored dresses over a couple pairs of baggy pants, and she was wheeling a stroller full of empty plastic bags. She looked like Bette Davis in *What Ever Happened to Baby Jane?* And then I suddenly remembered Bee telling me about a sort of miswhelped Molly Malone who wandered the streets of Canterbury all day and was never seen without that stroller full of junk. Bee had seen her once in the public library, asking for a map: "Not a map of everything, just the universe we live in. Where would I find that?"

GOOD QUESTION.

GAVOTTE I

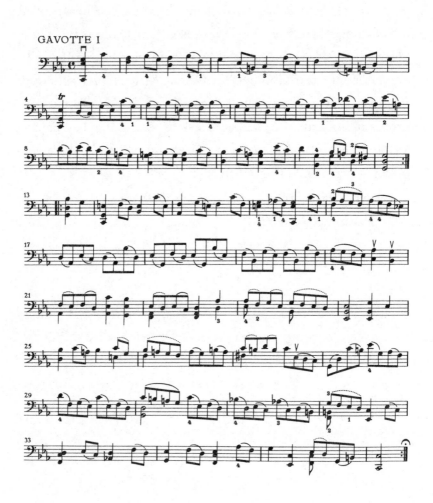

MEMORIAL DAY

SO I ESCAPED Angstland and the Anguish, and returned to New York with my sister's ashes, my cozy bird's nest, and one remaining hope: Mimi. I felt pretty confident about it. All I had to do was explain. Mimi wouldn't desert me now, just because she'd caught me squirming around on the floor with my ex (once!). No, my baby would rush to my side!

Mimì! Mimì! rang in my head now, even more than *Bee*. But I measured time by the hours (three hundred and eleven) and days (ten) since I'd last spoken to Bee, how long it was since she'd died (a week), and how long since I hugged her in the hospital (six days). It all went through my head on a continuous random loop, and I *still* thought Bee couldn't be dead. I had her ashes with me and I didn't think she was dead.

Bubbles greeted me joyfully. Deedee had kept her well fed. She was plumper than ever! And Gertrude too was "there for me." She seemed to view my sister's violent end as a chance for us to get back together. She'd besieged my answering machine with so many sickening messages of condolence, I had to call her just to get her to *quit it*.

"You can't help me," I told her.

"But did you see that fabulous obit in the *Times*?" She made an obituary sound like a rave review. "Bridget was such a wonderful artist, Harrison!"

HUH? If she'd thought that, why didn't she give her the grant she needed when Bee asked for one, thereby saving her from going to England at all? But there was no point in berating old Gertrude. SHE NEVER LISTENED. Even if I accused her of being the cause of all world suffering (which she probably was), she'd see it as some kind of sexual overture. Bee's death was a *foothold* for Gertrude. But anyone who saw my sister's death as a foothold was an oaf, and I'd had enough of Gertrude's oafishness *and* her overtures. Life is short.

Next I had to go meet Bee's dealer at the 2nd Avenue Deli (which was now on 3rd because the owner was shot by some bastard, on his way to the bank with the deli takings some years before). Bee's dealer was arranging a memorial for Bee in his gallery. He wanted to talk about that and also a major retrospective of Bee's work that he was planning. He needed the keys to her studio in Queens quick, and wanted to see all the stuff she'd been doing in "Can't-Bury," as he pronounced it, as soon as it arrived.

"There's quite a buzz, uh, right now," he told me, cramming a whole pastrami on rye into his face, mit pickle.

I hadn't met the guy before but had never liked the sound of him. He'd once passed Bee over when he had a big commission to hand out, dropped her in favor of some jerk who did big geometric constructions in welded metal. It's no fun being forgotten by your dealer (nor having to hear Bee cry about it over the phone). But now was not the time to berate *him* either. It was good of him to handle the memorial thing, and he'd be better at it than I. What was Bee's favorite *drink*, he wanted to know. Champagne cocktail, I told him, remembering her socking them back like there was no tomorrow, whenever she got the chance. He'd also hired a string quartet and asked me what I'd like them to play. I suggested Bach solo violin partitas, and Schubert's "Death and the Maiden"—just to make sure the whole occasion finished me off.

Then I went home to hide from the disaster area my life had become: Gertrude and her mania for me; the imminent arrival of a million boxes of Bee's stuff from Can't-Bury; the imponderable problem of my joyless job (which could only be put on hold for so long, without some bozo beefing about it); and the débâcle with Mimi.

I will arise and go now, and go to Innisfree

Deedee could handle the boxes, I realized, Deedee of the true compassion, and I could take a few weeks off. I would go to Sagaponack and take fresh breaths whenever opportunity allowed.

And I shall have some peace there, for peace comes dropping slow.

A different metaphysical plane, different "pace o' life". A different pace! What does that *mean*? Everybody on Long Island was always burbling about the "pace o' life". It drove me crazy! For me,

Sagaponack was just a place to hide for a while, me and my cat. No TV News (no TV!), no Gertrusions (once I'd unplugged the phone), no responsibilities, no friends, no nothing. It's an evolutionary achievement in animals to know when to flee. I fled.

> *Nine bean rows will I have there, a hive for the honey bee,*
> *And live alone in the bee-loud glade.*

INNISFREE

BUBBLES AND I arrived under cover of darkness, so as to avoid the curiosity and coffee cake of neighbors. I brought my own supplies, saving me from the general store: everybody's so palsy-walsy in there it makes you sick. Once a year these millionaires turn up and go feral in the countryside, getting in tune with nature. Most people can't get *away* from nature fast enough—this is why we built *cities*, for chrissake—but these guys with their brand-new jogging shorts, and the women with their bijou, flower-printed wheelbarrows, think they have an in with the elements. Aw, get your asses back to New York before you do something unecological you'll regret!

A woman came from Cold Spring Harbor once a month to keep an eye on the place, so the house was in good shape, and there was plenty of dry firewood on the porch. I set Bubbles up with a cushion in front of the woodstove in the living room, and she licked herself happily there, so plump now that her backside was half on, half off the cushion. I buried my face in her fur for a while.

I'd never intended to have a house on Long Island. Gertrude convinced me, and then dolled it up in so many rag rugs, colonial curios and free-floating hunks of fabric, I couldn't bring myself to enter the place until I got the Cold Spring Harbor woman to come take it all away. Gertrude had even managed to give the kitchen table a paunch, shrouding it in a stiff shiny tablecloth that draped to the floor. Gertrude's idea of decor is that if you can make it from one side of the room to the other without falling over, something's wrong. Her and her sarongs and her stupid baskets of shells and $300 beach towels, on which she lay in torpor for hours and wanted me to do the same! I'd finish the *New York Times* and want to go home, but by then Gertrude would have oiled herself up for a day's broiling and be too slippery to move. Her approximations of seaside contentment were truly dispiriting.

Now alone in the house, I was free to lie in bed all day if I wanted to. But Ant wasn't happy in his bed. Is it good for a fitted sheet to be so tight that every stitch of the seams stretches and strains around you all night, begging for mercy? Insomnia and its attendant hypochondria ensued, including heart fluttering, abdominal pain, sore throat and general malaise. I thought I had prostate cancer for about an hour there, followed by the usual tinnitus scare. Me on my taut bed! Who'd I think I was, PROUST?

And still to me at twilight came horizontal thoughts leading nowhere. *Mimì! Mimì!* I wanted to call her, but as time went on it was getting harder and harder to imagine explaining things. And now I couldn't eat or sleep or think (and was probably getting a cold). Why bother her? Mimi no longer trusted me, and I felt in no condition to assure anybody of my innate goodness: I was just a zhlub who let my sister languish and die (on foreign soil!), a work-shirking saw-bones, held in contempt by his colleagues. Some lover-boy.

The next morning, I stood in bare feet on my bare floorboards, and stared out at the windswept trees. I tried listening to Heifetz play the Bach solo partitas, but the music skinned me alive. It felt like BEE in the raw, pleading for help! I hid from Bee, hid from everything. Even the sun seemed threatening. It skulked around outside, sneaking peeks at me from behind bushes, then would pop out unexpectedly and blind me. If I didn't let it in the front, it crept around the side. *Leave me alone, wouldja?*

Just walk, I told myself, try to take in one sound, one color, before you go in. But all I heard were rabid gulls squabbling over some unspeakable delicacy, and all I saw was what I *thought* was a shark—it turned out to be a leaf fragment on my sunglasses. The ocean was a barroom brawl, with waves tripping over themselves to get in on the action. The shoreline was a series of mini-Niagaras. You'd think water would have worn away all opposition by now, but it seemed to *like* being thwarted, turning white with delight when it hit anything unerodible.

The wingnut waterfalls of the world.

Long tubular waves rolled in. The rhythm of it, the *drama*, as those tunnels curled, crested, and crashed. Hard to believe the sea wasn't trying to tell me something, each wave like a line of words or music.

I searched the beach for a message in a bottle, something, anything! And did find a few geological wonders: tough blades of grass growing through sand and, in a secluded spot sheltered from millionaires, a Zen garden of evenly spaced round stones, all the same size and each sitting snugly in its own wind-worn cleft, with a miniature peak of sand behind: my melancholy meadow.

I puzzled over the *colors* of the Sound. They kept changing for no perceptible reason, from turquoise to gray to Venetian green. It didn't seem to relate directly to the color of the sky; unpredictable factors were at play. But why should some schmuck, some schlemiel from the city be able to "predict" anything out here?

I didn't know the names of most of the birds I saw, I couldn't tell what the clouds were up to, or remember which kind they were. It was all a *big mystery* to me. I wasn't even completely sure if there was quicksand on Long Island or not. But what's a walk without a little danger?

Home to Bubbles and Glenn Gould. I once told Bee I thought Gould was playing one passage of *The Well-Tempered Clavier* too fast.

"Aw, leave him alone. The guy's a genius! He can do what he wants," she'd answered.

"Even the humming?"

"Even the humming."

And she was right. I made him play *The Well-Tempered Clavier* to me again and again, until all I could hear were the harmonics.

I get up in the morning and think of women. Not about *sex* (that was very far from my mind) but about the many breakfasts women have made me, starting with my mom and moving through just about every female acquaintance I ever had. They all want to feed you! Bee used to make me the best scrambled eggs when we were kids, and she didn't even like eggs.

I go downstairs and think of women, the many women I've drunk coffee with—and the many mornings I've drunk coffee alone, *thinking about* women.

I make toast for myself and think of women, in particular the problematic properties of my mother's toastings. She never distributed the butter evenly, so you'd get this big glop of half-melted butter in the first bite, then none the next! She also cut my toast into squares, when all the cool moms were doing triangles. But then there was her jam, which none of the other moms could offer. Peach, plum, strawberry, rhubarb, strawberry-rhubarb, blueberry, blackberry, boysenberry, pear and cinnamon, apricot and almond, plum and cardamom, sweet cherry, sour cherry, dense dark marmalade, even tomato jam, green *and* red. (Mom and her 'maters!) And dilly beans. Nevermore, nevermore.

I do some laundry and think of women, my mom again, who did the laundry for fifty years until it finally *killed* her—falling down the stairs on her way to transfer stuff to the dryer. But how vigorous she was, plowing on all those years with my father panting and ranting at her heels, working his way through a million temper tantrums he always considered legitimate.

What was he so angry *about?* And where does all the *female* anger go? "Underground," said Mimi once, "into all the slicing and sluicing and sieving and mashing." (And of course the stitching.) There are also a lot of opportunities for destructiveness offered by gardening: digging, pruning, weeding, burning stuff, poisoning stuff, trimming stuff, tugging at stuff, hacking away for *years* at tree stumps. My mother's anger went into the shaking-out of dishtowels. Seemingly peaceful mornings echoed with the slap and crackle of them, and then you knew not to go near Mom for a while.

I lounge on the porch and think of women, MY woman: sitting canoe-style in my arms on the couch in my apartment, just before everything blew up in our faces. . .

Bubbles startled me out of my reverie by jumping vertically into a pine tree, six feet in the air! She was putting on a show for me, acting crazy, and I liked it—I even laughed, though my laughter sounded odd to me and out of place. I went to stand below her, in case she needed help getting down, and then I remembered my rowboat in the shed. I'd bought it when I got the house, to make up for that old canoe Dad preserved in amber in the garage at home.

So I dragged my boat down to the marshy pond behind the house and, with Bubbles in the bow, rowed towards the middle of the lake, where there's an impenetrable little island. Then I just lay back and let the boat drift, with Bubbles walking back and forth on top of me, checking both sides for ducks. I closed my eyes and instantly remembered one of Bee's Coziness Sculptures, called *Creaky Boat in Maine*. This consisted of the bare skeleton of an old wooden boat, lit by watery flashes of light, with a soundtrack of boat creaking, water lapping, breezes blowing, frogs croaking, birds chirping. . . Now *I* was free to listen to the gentle sounds of real breezes and real waves lapping against my fiberglass boat, and Bee wasn't.

Not so gentle if you were a *duck* though. I gradually became aware of a big hullabaloo going on on the other side of the island. We rowed over to see what was happening, and it was duck rape on a grand scale! The drakes were chasing the females on land, on water, and in the air (a Churchillian assault). They fought with growing strength on the banks of the island. Whatever the cost may be, they would *never* surrender... When a male caught a female, he'd grab her by the neck with his beak and pin her down, practically drowning her during the actual coupling. It didn't look very consensual to me. The females, if they were lucky, just had time to get their feathers back in order before another aggressor crash-landed and started chasing them. Sometimes the males worked as a part of a gang, *tag-teaming*. They raped them on the beaches, they raped them on the landing grounds, they raped them in the dunes and in the reeds, they raped them on the hillocks...

"Boys, BOYS! I came here to relax!" I said.

Who knew? Ducks must be an exception to Mimi's rule— their main courtship tactic is brute force! But I really couldn't see the evolutionary advantage in the males' willingness to frighten, exhaust, and possibly *injure* the Egg-Layer. Such sharp dressers too, with that debonair white collar, the metallic blue or green or purple head, and the curlicues on the tail (all a bit undermined though by the joke-shop quack).

One female, who'd just endured a three-duck gang bang, seemed to have a broken wing. It looked awry: she kept flexing it, trying to stretch it out to get it working again, but it wasn't helping. There was a big gap in that pretty bit of striping the females have on their wings, their one major embellishment. She must have been hurt during all this antagonistic mating, and now her disability made her the classic "sitting duck"! She couldn't fly away from her pursuers, and didn't seem able or willing to swim either. She was just stuck, barefoot and pregnant, on her little island.

As I watched, four more male ducks paddled over to her at top speed. She squawked frantically when she saw them, and ran this way and that, but there was nowhere to hide. I couldn't reach her in time but yelled and clapped my hands and banged the oars together to try to scare the drakes off. They paid me no heed—I only succeeded in startling Bubbles. The drakes carried on marauding until another male duck turned up and grabbed one of the rapists by *his* neck, which worked: it drove him away. Then he saw the rest of them off the scene. This defender seemed to be the female duck's real mate: he was the only male who companionably stuck around anyway, and she seemed calm with him. But by now, she was *limping* as well as dragging her wing.

I went home to get some bread for her, then rowed right out again. She was still there—no place else to go—and she ate hungrily. She seemed desperate for food. So they'd not only raped her but managed to starve her by their terror campaign: because of the broken wing, she couldn't find food. I decided to feed her, to give her at least a fighting chance. With time, her wing might heal.

As I rowed away, one of the drakes who'd just molested her headed over to my boat, hoping for some bread for *himself*, and I felt like *killing* him—or throwing a stone at him anyway, to drive him away from her section of the pond. But what was I becoming? A guy who throws stones at ducks?! Bee had cured me early on of any interest in torturing animals, when she found me once trying to swing a neighbor's cat around by its tail. It wasn't what she said, it was her *inability* to speak that had quelled me.

I was losing my impartiality here—we're all supposed to let nature take its course, red in tooth and claw (and beak and wing). I was like a reporter in the field, who stops writing and starts *helping*, changing from heartless bastard to mensch. But was it good to get so personally involved, with *ducks*? Aw, who was I kidding? Interfering with nature is my business!

I worried all night about my duck, out there alone and in pain. First thing in the morning, Bubbles and I were in the boat again. The duck seemed to recognize us and came right over for her breakfast. She seemed alert, which was a good sign, and had a good appetite. She wasn't declining. But the wing was no better, and she was still being molested by every guy in town because she couldn't get away. Sheesh!

In an effort to thwart one of the rapists, I lunged forward at one point, waving my hat (not my sickbed hat, my Sagaponack baseball cap), and accidentally stepped on a Coke can in the bottom of the boat. That's how I discovered how much drakes hate the sound of a Coke can crumpling—it really messes with their heads. They lost concentration, allowing the injured female to flee into the reeds. There she was often safe, since the drakes couldn't be bothered searching too hard for her when there were plenty of other females to plague. From then on I brought all the empty cans I could find whenever I went to feed her, which was several times a day. But, like her partner, I couldn't be there all the time—I had to go indoors sometimes and eat *roast chicken* with Bubbles (the paradox be damned).

A few nights later, lying sleepless on my taut bed, I decided I could at least get the poor duck some real duck food. Superior nutrition might just give her the edge over the drakes. Ducks weren't supposed to eat bread all day. But I couldn't remember where a pet store was. And was a wild duck a "pet"? In disobedience to Bee and her abhorrence for my perusal of phonebooks, I found an old Yellow Pages downstairs and spent the rest of the night searching through it for duck fodder.

This is when you realize how homocentric we all are. There was hardly a mention of anything for animals in there, or anything *non-human*. It's as if the whole world is about us. It's all zinc, zodiacs, yachts and yoga, xylophones, windows and wills, vacuum cleaners, ventriloquists, upholsterers, underwater ballet, timber merchants, tailors, surgical supplies, surfing, silicone implants, salsa, rubber, rope, restaurants, rehab, quilting bees, pianos, personal injury lawyers, perfume, pearls and passports, orchestras and obstetricians, nurses, notary publics, noodles, nail bars, motels, morticians, mannequins, log cabins, locksmiths, liquor stores, kites, kitchens, kiss-o-grams, karaoke, jukeboxes, jack-o'-lanterns, Italian lessons, ice skates, hydraulics, hypnotists, gyms, geriatrics and gemstones, fire alarms, fertility clinics, electrolysis, drainage consultants, chapels of rest, cane furniture, Botox, antiques, advertising, and ambulances. Animals might take more of an interest if we included them more! (Not big spenders though.)

I finally located an animal feed merchant (maybe I should have started with the *A*s) in Sag Harbor, and drove straight over there. I'd only been a recluse for a few days but already felt like a wild man from the woods. Any minute now I'd get out the faded overalls and start constructing microscopic sailboats inside light bulbs. I'd forgotten that women wear earrings, for chrissake! I'd forgotten the effort they put into their skin and their hair and their nails, and *why*.

I walked down the street behind a "waif wife," as Mimi would have called her, a frail, drained gal bobbing along in six-inch heels beside a repellent fellow who seemed to be still in his *pj's* and talking on his cell phone, ignoring her entirely. How much had the poor duck blown on that fancy blouse, the tight skirt, and the tiny shiny red purse to go with the shiny red shoes, all to hang out with old PJ there?! The woman was dressed for a *cocktail party*, and it wasn't even noon. Later, I saw them buying potatoes.

The feed store only had a small sample bag of duck pellets, but they promised to get some more in. I also bought a book on duck care, with surprising information on the duck's alimentary canal: they've got no teeth, so they grind grain with these rock-like structures in their gullet. The book also said broken wings *don't* heal without human intervention. I could have done a splint myself, but she wouldn't let me catch her! Even if I invented the perfect trap, it would probably only frighten her off, or injure her more.

I reached the car just before a storm hit. The whole town turned a gloomy yellow, and the sunlit trees waving against black clouds looked *electric*, as if they were about to blast off. In that low light, the scene seemed staged for an opera.

OVERTURE
Every sound magnified.
Bikes rattle by.
Lawnmower moans.
Trees sizzle.
Birdsong.
Airplane.

ACT ONE

Soprano raindrops on water.

People start to walk faster, crouching over, adjusting clothing to
form makeshift hats.

Tenor (a cop) strikes nonchalant pose, as if ready for worse threats
than rain.

Alto and contralto chorus of umbrellas blossoms.

Amusing variety, no two the same.

Black common, polka dots popular.

But shapes differ, and the number of spokes.

Some are classical, with spikes on the end.

Others fold; these are never fully erect.

Like dogs meeting, a small black-and-white umbrella encounters a
big yellow one: they circle around each other.

Renoir poppy-field umbrella arrives, unfurling.

Coloratura star of the show: red umbrella, under which shelters
a woman in a pale pink dress and dusty-brown short jacket
(unexpectedly good color combo).

People calling out, "We're almost there!"

ACT TWO

Children fill the stage (nothing better in an opera, unless you've
got a donkey).

Kids don't carry umbrellas—that would impede play and eating
ice cream.

They don't mind the rain, don't cease to function when they get
wet.

They stamp in puddles.

They slip and slide.

They sail trash in the gutter.

Scene ends with bass baritone rain, now falling fast and noisily on
boats in the harbor.

ACT THREE

Driving home, I stop at a flower-stand on the highway that I
disdained earlier, coldly depriving myself of lilies of the valley
(my mother's favorite flower).

Now I buy bundle after bundle of them: I keep wanting more
than I picked up already.

Chorus of wide dark-green leaves and tiny cupped white flowers.

My duck liked the fancy duck pellets, as did her husband (though
he tended to eat too many at once and then choke). I continued
to row out and feed her several times a day. I loved that duck! Her
dark head, encircled by that black band that ran right across the eyes
and all the way around the back of the head—her wild streak. I'd
never noticed before how beautiful female ducks are. Her face was a
perfect Serpentine Line, that matched the intertwining reeds around
her. Her tawny breast gleamed in the sun when she took a nap.

What I really wanted to do was capture her, fix the wing, and
keep her safe and cozy in my yard. Maybe get her a big washtub
to swim in. Returning her later to the wild in some complicated,
disinterested way. But it was not to be. Any extreme efforts to help
her would only freak her out. So I contented myself with feeding
her, and foiling the plans of some of her stalkers when I could, by
crumpling Coke cans.

FINALE

Bubbles and me in a boat.

Sample bag of duck pellets.

Five empty Coke cans.

Five-pound note.

MIMI DREAM: Long Island. Twilight. I'm running through shallow water, trying to catch up with Mimi, who's a bit ahead of me. The sky is turquoise. We're about to board a boat lying further out to sea but I'm dawdling on this sandbar, because there are some little silver fish wriggling there, caught by the outgoing tide, and I want to show them to Mimi. Lights sparkle all around us from small boats and houses near the shore, sending wavy snakes of light towards me across the water, and I feel utterly happy, following in Mimi's wake.

Oh, Mimi, come! We will step nimbly through the sedge grass and never grow old!

"For those of you having trouble waking up this morning, here's some Brahms for you," says the radio announcer. BRAHMS? Brahms was a sweetheart, but he had trouble tying his own shoelaces! Next, some Wolfgang They-Can't-All-Be-Gems Mozart (would he get outta here with that glass armonica of his?). I usually seemed to tune in just in time for a big dose of Berlioz or Mahler, or *Wagner* for godsake, "Now that your ears are attuned to the key of C major." My ears aren't attuned to anything but *Bach*, you idiot!

Then the piquant biographical details would start to flow, all that fake poignancy of chronology. Before I can reach the radio, I know all about César Franck's love affair with some chick in his fifties, that pissed off his wife and Saint-Saëns. How is this my business? The news grates throughout Franck's *Reflections on Love*, ruining any romance and eroticism the announcer had promised.

How about Satie? Satie was a saddo. Thanks. Finally they play some more Mozart—it's *fantastic*—and they interrupt it! "Well, we've had about as much Mozart as time will allow," says the announcer—so *slowly* he could have fit a few more bars of Mozart in if he'd just shut up! Any classical station worth its interminable fund-raising drives would have *allowed* time for Mozart. But even when they do, they wreck it by talking about his debts and his early demise—until you're too upset to listen to the music! Mozart's "debts" indeed. What about what we owe *him*?

I turn the radio off and go downstairs to play some Bach for *myself*: his second *French Suite* in C minor is like watching the planes of a landscape unfurl as you walk. An avenue opens up, a valley, the ridge of a hill, something always emerging before you.

Later, I go for a walk in the dunes, where more paths unfurl, winds whirl, clouds form and deform, and sunlight lands on the earth like a bomb. Gulls sleepily patrol the shoreline. Life and death are allowed to pursue their modest course in the country. In cities you're at the mercy of everybody's ego, and that gets *tiring*. We create criminality wherever we go. Birds just do their job, uncomplaining, content merely to survive (ducks excepted).

But I am not a bird.

I go feed my duck but she isn't there. Drowned by rapist

ducks while I was off duty? Or just eaten by some predator? Nature ain't pretty, it's just the only game in town. I watch some ducklings instead. They're trying to catch bugs by parachuting off rocks. "Ee-ee-ee-ee!" they cry. A mother duck is trying to organize her brood to sleep under her, enclosing them in her wings. How cosy they must be! But one of the ducklings doesn't want a nap and won't stay put. All he wants to do is nuzzle his mother's soft brown neck. So do I. I thought of Bee's theory that pleasure is the purpose of existence. She was right. Animals aren't in pain all the time. Pain is an *aberration*, a sign of trouble. There's nothing irresponsible or dishonorable about seeking pleasure. It's what we're *here* for! Even bees look like they're having a ball.

Later, I searched for my absent duck again. I kept thinking I saw her lifeless carcass just beneath the surface of the pond, but it turned out to be water weeds. I would never know if she survived and escaped or, more likely, got eaten by some creature because she couldn't fly away. Had she hoped I might come help her? The recurrent idea chilled me.

I headed home, luckless and duckless, climbed the porch steps and there was a letter from Chevron High, forwarded by Deedee. A fearful woman with the letters, that Deedee. Chevron wanted confirmation that I was doing the speech on June 15th, now only a few weeks away—but I wanted confirmation from Mimi that she was going to help me!

Speech panic descends, excuses form—excuses I'm pretty sure I already used in high school:

sunburn

spontaneous combustion

anaphylactic shock

TB

cholera

stubbed my toe

under arrest

Pavarotti's final concert

busy making bouillabaisse

jury duty

tomato harvest time

dry cleaning mix-up

volcanic ash problem

under-reported military skirmish in my area

just lazy

deer tick

enslavement to dominatrix

got a duck to take care of

Foreign Accent syndrome

so depressed about Mimi I can't eat or think. . .

Oh, for godsake, I'd do it. I'd already bought the tickets. Bee's memorial party at the gallery was the day before the speech, so I'd have to go back to New York by then anyway. I could pick up my notes (for various half-begun speeches) at my apartment, and go straight to the airport from the memorial. What the hell, I'd give them a speech if it killed me. I owed it to Mimi.

That night I dreamed my duck got very big and vanquished all her assailants. She was about the size of an elephant! But when she still hadn't appeared the next day, I called the Sag Harbor store to cancel my order for more duck pellets. They didn't seem to care—they hadn't been impressed with my order in the first place—and their indifference hurt.

When I got home, I took Bee's book on Matisse out onto the porch, the only thing I'd brought back with me from England (besides Bee's ashes and the bird's nest). I'd intended to read it on the plane but some kid behind me kept saying "Ronaldo" and I couldn't concentrate. But that was no place to think about Matisse anyway. It wasn't a *metaphysical* plane.

Bubbles immediately claimed my lap and started licking herself, and then my hand, in an overspill of affection. She had a way of look-ing at me with such love it made me want to laugh—or cry. Bubbles was *good* at love, good at being happy; these are creditable skills.

As for Matisse—now there's a guy who liked his pajamas! *He's* in his pj's, the models are in pantaloons, and he tries to share in their *joie de vivre* by painting them. These women aren't overly concerned about how they look to him—they're in their own world, a zone of pleasure that Matisse envies. The perpetually anxious, heat-seeking, peace-loving Matisse longed to please with those odalisques of his, to please himself and us. Like Puccini, Matisse really came to terms with the fact that women EXIST. Matisse looks at women the way a lover does, not like a dad. Fathers only disapprove of their wives and daughters. The role of the lover is to approve and applaud them, appease them, *please* them. Even idealize them a bit, what the hell?

What have most men done for women's *joie de vivre*? All we've done is *bore* women to death, *bore* them into compliance with our idiocies. When we aren't beating them up, or burning them as witches, we deafen them with our noise—VROOM VROOM, BANG BANG, POW-WOW, RAT-A-TAT-TAT! We've filled the earth with radioactive waste. And all our kvetching, our pontificating, the prevaricating, the listless, unimaginative fornicating. No wonder women always seem on the verge of insanity!

I thought of what Bee went through, yelled at by our imperious (murderous) dad, battered by that lawman of a husband, and finally extinguished, brutally and for no reason, by a dope with a gripe against women. I lay on that porch and thought of the whole world of women wronged, burned, beaten, badgered, and bereft; ignored from birth. They trailed past me in a half-sleep. Was there a single woman alive who hadn't been mistreated by some maniac, simply because he knew he could get away with it? Was there a single woman who hadn't suffered injustices because she was a woman, *a single one*? For many it was worse than that: stoned to death in the street, beheaded in a grocery store, thrown overboard off a yacht. We all look the other way, we've seen it all before, yeah, yeah, you can't change human nature. . .

Half the women I knew were scared to walk through the countryside alone (and the other half probably should have been). Half the women I knew had been bashed up by some worthless guy. They'd all had to watch a million disrespectful movies about blonde bombshells, and then there was all the porn; and the News, the daily briefings on the ways in which women's lives can be scuppered by rapists, serial killers, or guys like Tiger Woods who can't keep his putz in his pants. They'd all watched a million male maestri conduct a million all-male orchestras, playing pieces only by men (okay, there's a little Clara Schumann once in a while—big deal). And all the women I knew (and *treated*) tried too hard to be good, to look good, be nice, be sweet, be patient—tried so hard, when they were all fine in the first place!

I looked down at the sage plant I'd saved. I'd bought it in Sag Harbor, outside the animal feed store, bought it because it was dying, and planted it at the bottom of the porch steps, and now it was thriving, twice the size. The unvoiced sufferings of plants could make you a nervous wreck! I looked at that sage I'd saved with the contentment that comes from freeing something that needs freeing.

Far away across the lawn, my neighbor was hanging up wet clothes on the line, with the thwacks and wallops that procedure always seems to entail. Yes, those wrinkles had to go! She arranged her wash in strict order: paired socks, pants, shirts, towels, pillow-cases—how big *was* this washing machine? Finally, out came an old patchwork quilt, and this too she carefully spread out on the line to dry. Was it because it was wet that it looked so great, or because I was seeing it against the sun? The battered old thing glowed like a stained-glass window! *This* was the way museums should show off their quilts (I had to tell Mimi some time): get them *wet* and light them from *behind*.

I lay on my lounger on the porch and thought about women, all the crazy stuff they do. The painted bowls of Brittany, plaited Russian loaves, all the knitted baby jackets, flower-embroidered handkerchiefs and pillowcases, the smocking, the snacking, the puddings and baked goods and preserves. The freezing and the thawing too, the wrapping and unwrapping, the cleaning and sorting and folding and smoothing—all the pooh-poohed peaceful arts of women, of ODALISQUES. Women *invented* coziness! They could see humanity was never going to get very far without some comfort, some sense of stability. People don't thrive on harshness and indifference. I thought of my own lunging odalisque, who'd come to me distrustful but then miraculously blossomed. Blood and bone, blood and bone, that's what women are. They're REAL.

The laundress had gone inside. I was all alone out there and everything was quiet. I moved the lounger onto the grass but the sun was so blinding, I shut my eyes and just listened to the swaying, swishing trees for a while—and when I opened my eyes, everything was *aglow*. Not just the sky and the clouds: every blade of grass, every different type of leaf, every petal glowed. The white shirts on the line were dazzling, soaking up the ultraviolet. Stones were sparkling. The whole world seemed devoted to the sun, *begging* for it and basking in it. Whether absorbing light (the dirt) or reflecting it (a puddle), everything was responding to light in some way. The thinnest leaves no longer seemed flimsy and vulnerable but intentionally diaphanous, so as to be filled with LIGHT. Everything out there wanted light and needed to glow. Bubbles too! Fur, hair, and feathers glow. Water glows, collecting and transmitting, no, *playing* with light. Everything seeks and leaks LIGHT.

This is what Matisse discovered in the South of France, eyeing up those odalisques. ALL artists know this (Bee was always talking about light but I never knew why until now). For a long time I'd had it in for fire, I didn't think we really needed it. Only earth, air, and water interested me. But that day I accepted that *the sun wins*. I was finally reconciled to fire.

The earth is pretty flat, just a bas-relief—you see this on Long Island. To get three-dimensional, you have to look up: at the clouds, the sky. Only the sky is really 3-D—that's *all* it is! Air, space, and *light*. A skein of geese flew overhead, not in a *V*-shape, but in the shape of a breast, with a nipple. The shape changed and several different types of breast were offered. But all of them were good.

Bubs and I took the boat out for one last voyage on the pond that evening, and scattered Bee's ashes there: my sage sister, goddess of rivers and springs, who loved Bach, Dickens, and Matisse, loved *me* (and hated *Ant and Bee*), and thought Ben Jonson much better than Shakespeare.

It is not growing like a tree
In bulke, doth make man better bee;
Or, standing long an Oake, three hundred yeare,
To fall a logge, at last, dry, bald, and seare:
A Lillie of a Day
Is fairer farre, in May,
Although it fall, and die that night;
It was the Plant, and flowre of light.
In small proportions, we just beauties see:
And in short measures, life may perfect bee.

With one day left, I went to the beach. I didn't want to leave Sagaponack, I didn't want to go to Bee's memorial, I didn't even want to go to the beach. In despair, I stumped along. The water wasn't moving: it looked weird, like ice, or the desert. Everything was so quiet I could hear my shirtsleeves rustle against my ribcage as I walked, and it irritated me. I could hear my breath. And then, in quick succession, A BOAT, A CAR, A MOTORBIKE, A PLANE. Only one of each, but still annoying. Every bird call grated, every mild wave bubbling against the shore gave me a start.

It reminded me of summer days when you're a kid, and you just don't know if you're going to make it through three months of this. When the sight of a cloud, or the Good Humor Man, is a major event—even though he came every day and handed me an ice-cream sandwich, and a popsicle for Bee. Our biggest hope was that a tornado would hit, blowing the roof of our house off, the sky suddenly darkening and your bed twirling up and up. Apocalypse fantasies.

I searched for my melancholy meadow of rounded stones, but couldn't find it. So I sat down and made my own sculpture, a miniature barbecue, with jagged little red rocks for steaks, and yellow oval pebbles for baked potatoes. Inside some tiny open clam shells I put lentil-like orange pebbles = scallops! Must have been hungry. An ant marched by carrying a huge seed. Never eat anything bigger than your head, man.

Then I headed home to find that Bubbles, who never bit or scratched or stole food, but instead licked me with love, Bubbles, who would stand outside on the porch and look at me so hopefully, waiting to be let in, Bubbles, who followed me around the house and the yard, and had come with me in the boat every time to feed the duck, Bubbles, who sat on my lap at the piano, at the kitchen table, on the lounger, in the car, Bubbles, who warmed herself so happily by the woodstove, and drank the milk I gave her and ate too much Fancy Feast (my fault, not hers), Bubbles, who knew and tolerated with true aplomb my every mood, Bubbles, who had found her way into my bedroom that first night in New York and poked her head around the door so inquiringly, so comically, Bubbles, who *definitely* had a sense of humor, Bubbles, who greeted me gently whenever I struggled downstairs all wrung out and hungover, Bubbles, who did stretches and jumps just as good as Kit Smart's cat Jeoffry, Bubbles, who could leap vertically, six feet in one bound, Bubbles, who, when lying on her side on a chair, could twist herself backward in a complete circle so you saw both her face and her ass at the same time, Bubbles, who played exuberantly with string (whenever I remembered that's what cats like and dangled some for her), Bubbles, with her inquisitiveness about all things, especially cupboards and boxes, Bubbles, with her great concentration powers, staring at stuff for minutes at a time, displaying greater intelligence and gifts of perception than any other cat (and some people) I'd known, Bubbles, who had spread herself out on my bed every night, wherever we were, taking up as much room as Gertrude ever had, but much more invitingly, Bubbles, who was also more fun as a movie companion, Bubbles, who *hated* Gertrude but took to Mimi instantly, Bubbles, who, when first released from her igloo death-trap on New Year's Eve, had gratefully rubbed against my leg and settled herself on my shoulder without a moment's hesitation, Bubbles, who loved me, yes, *loved* me, and *looked* at me with love, Bubbles, so beautiful, so warm and soft and funny, with her white, orange and black coloring like Hallowe'en candy, Bubbles, so full of beans, so appreciative of anything I did for her, Bubbles, with her supreme knack for coziness and contentment, flopping half off her cushion by the woodstove like the odalisque she was, Bubbles, who could intone, who had rhetoric. . . Bubbles got run over.

I heard miaowing coming from the shed as soon as I got near the house, and hoped, not so much selfishly as instinctively, that it was some other cat. But when I peered in, there she was, crouching in the darkest corner, among all the spiderwebs and snail shells and chipmunk shit. I couldn't reach her very easily, so I tried to lure her out with some Fancy Feast, but she wouldn't come. Then I knew something was up. So I slid over to her and gently pulled her poor crushed body to me, got her wrapped in a towel, and rushed her to the vet on Goodfriend Road in Easthampton. Once she was in the car, she was ominously silent.

They put her on a drip to get her temperature up before they could x-ray her—she was in shock. The x-rays confirmed that she'd been run over: the injuries couldn't have happened any other way. Somebody had run her over and left her to die. But the prognosis was good. The great Bubbles! She'd have to stay at the animal hospital for a few weeks to have surgery on her back leg, and a paw, but they thought she would walk normally again in the end.

"And jump?" I asked.

"And jump," the vet said.

"And no pain? She'll be pain-free?"

"Well, it's always hard to tell with animals. You know. They're good at resignation. They often don't show pain. But there's no reason that she should be in pain once we've fixed her up, Dr. Hanafan. Don't worry, she's going to be fine."

Bubbles, who'd been hit by some asshole of a millionaire and left to crawl away and die, crawl away and *die*, would be *fine*. She would be fine.

*   *   *

I went home and finished all the booze in the house. Then I went out on the porch and looked at the sage I'd saved.

Sunset in Sagaponack is when nature begins to regain some control and us homocentric humans don't seem so such much. Things settle and dampen. The dim blue sky still glows but night is forming in the shadows. I wanted to freeze time, hold on to that sky, that color. And then the smell of the moist earth hit me, the best smell in the world! I realized this was the smell I should have been smelling all my life—I should go out at dawn and dusk to smell it.

I watched as a lone bug rose up toward the sky. Nobody has ever helped her, I thought, she has always been alone. But that wasn't true. The *sun* had helped her. She flew toward it now.

Huge flocks of starlings molded and remolded themselves into one big undulating cloud, as if to celebrate surviving another day. We are free! they squealed. Free to live and mate and feed our young, and all is forgiven (the day's squabbling over food, the day's dangers). A grace of starlings, a murmuration? I once heard it's called a wedding.

The moon hovered low in the sky, not a perfect circle yet but big and sassy, friendly-looking, reflected brokenly in puddles—doing that staring act she's done a million times. She's been taking a very good look at us for years, the earth's long-suffering waif wife.

> *Saftly, saftly, through the mirk*
> *The müne walks a' hersel':*
> *Ayont the brae; abüne the kirk;*
> *And owre the dunnlin bell.*
> *I wudna be the müne at nicht*
> *For a' her gowd and a' her licht.*

GAVOTTE II

Gavotte I da Capo

FLAG DAY

I DIDN'T WANT to linger in my apartment any longer than necessary—without Mimi or Bubbles, the whole place *stank*. I checked my answering machine (condolences, but nothing from Mimi), put on a suit, threw some overnight stuff in my briefcase for the trip to Virtue and Chewing Gum later on, and set off for the gallery.

Feeling pretty monosyllabic after my fourteen days in the wilderness, I was hoping the memorial would be a quiet affair in a back room. But Bee's dealer had cleared the whole joint to accommodate several Coziness Sculptures (no small matter). The walls were covered in Bee's drawings, and (laminated) articles on Bee, not just obituaries but practically every review she'd ever received and a whole lot of letters and notes and other memorabilia I'd never seen. Hundreds of people were rushing from one wall to another in an orgy of appreciation and grief, some crying, some just nodding and smiling. I headed over to the violinist, who was playing the Bach partitas I'd asked for. Bach knew about death—half his children died. He would see me through, if anybody could, his worldliness and depth. Cleave to *that*. As Claude Rains says in *Deception*, it's extraordinary "that music can exist in the same world as the basest treachery."

Gertrude caught my eye. Of course she would be there, but who was that, draped all over her? It seemed to be *Gus!* Was she trying to stir my jealousy—at my sister's memorial? I wouldn't put it past her. Gus was very smiley (especially for a guy at a memorial), and kept a proprietary arm around Gertrude's shoulders at all times. Bee and I had once joked what a perfect pair these two narcissistic monsters would make, but I never expected it to happen! I could see their future, the arts administrator attending openings with triplets strapped to her waist like a suicide bomb, Gus bringing up the rear with a dead rabbit slung over his shoulder: the Bonnie and Clyde of Central Park East.

They'd met recently, it emerged, due to Gus's assiduous efforts to get hold of *me*. He'd claimed to be an old pal of mine. What else had he told her? I felt it my duty to draw her aside for a moment.

"You do realize the guy has criminal convictions, right?" I asked her, once we were out of earshot.

"I thought he was a friend of yours!"

"Gertrude, just because I hung out with him as a kid doesn't mean he's a nice guy. It just means I was too big a coward to get rid of him."

"Don't be down on yourself, Harrison."

"Has he given you the tragic tale of his girlfriend yet—the one who fell down the elevator shaft and is now paralyzed for life?" I could tell that he had. "Very touching, huh? The bit he always leaves out is that *he* pushed her into it! It was probably an accident, but still."

She didn't have a chance to reply—speeches began. Bee's dealer was up on the platform, telling everybody what he thought of Bee, in hindsight. He seemed to have hopes of turning her into a pillar of the art establishment. In aid of this, he portentously listed her various artistic stages: the interlocking cardboard stage, the clay monster stage, the assemblages, the installations, the Coziness Sculptures, and the recent ecstatic aquatic figures in stone, which he (predictably) considered a "culmination" of something or other. He made her sound like Picasso! He also viewed Bee's time in Can't-Bury as hugely productive (not exactly how I saw it). I was getting a bit sick of him, and was pleased when a woman who'd been at RISD with Bee objected to the dealer's use of the word, "subversive," in connection with the Coziness Sculptures.

"Subversive of what?" she asked. "The only thing they subvert is our downgrading of pleasure, and the dismissal of anything female and domestic as childish, trivial and unpatriotic. They're not!" Cheers from the crowd.

Bee, "childish"? The idea had never occurred to me. *I* was the child! Watching my cartoons, reading my children's books, coveting new gadgets, wearing sneakers to work, succoring myself on oceans of SOUP, and being taken care of by millions of women. I was just a big kid before Bee died! Not anymore though, not anymore.

Another fellow student from RISD, a man this time, got up on the platform and talked about a teacher of theirs who'd told Bee to go big, go big. "He told *everybody* to 'go big'—the men, so we wouldn't seem effeminate, and the women, well, for the same reason!" he said. "Whenever you see a male artist praised for 'playing with scale,' you can be pretty sure he went big, probably *too* big!

Bridget never made that mistake. Her stuff was always on a human scale. That's what I loved about it."

Someone else piped up from the floor, reading from an index card she'd brought along (this event was anything but formal). I felt like an outsider at my own sister's memorial! But I was pleased when somebody mentioned Bee's *Primordial Egg*, an installation of hers I liked but had almost forgotten about. It had filled a whole room in some gallery. Bee had hung about a zillion little objects from the ceiling, all dunked in white paint: doorknobs, light bulbs, wooden spoons, cups, sunglasses, pencils, forks, scissors, bottles, bric-a-brac, baby shoes, and other crazy shit. They hovered, at about head height, on strings attached to pulleys, and when someone pulled on one of the white objects (spectator participation was encouraged), another white object somewhere else in the room would rise up: each item had its partner, and that partner was an egg, a white "primordial" egg. It was both funny and beautiful. Lit from above, it looked like a cherry orchard in full bloom. The guy at the memorial said he used to think Bee's *Primordial Egg* was about death, but now thought it was about birth, the birth of the *universe*—before color got added.

Someone else stepped up to the platform and declared that Bee was a composer as well as a visual artist, because so many of her Coziness Sculptures included sound: children at play, crackling fires, creaking boats, croaking frogs, chack-chacking crickets. I'd never thought of it as music, just part of the nutty shit she came up with. I was always *scared* for Bee, scared that nobody else would get why she did those things. These people seemed to get it. They couldn't get enough of it! I'd wasted a hell of a lot of time being protective of her, instead of just appreciating her. But now I was proud: Bee was a real HERO to these people. The wrong person in our family was pushed, the wrong kind of success valued. I'd made money, while Bee just needed money. I should have given her my apartment—it was wasted on me, I was never home! It would have suited an artist too, all that light and space, and a whole roof to spread out on.

I remembered buying a small Coziness Sculpture that had an audio element. That was what made it interesting. Visually, it was very plain. All you saw was this bare wooden window frame, and behind it, a painted backdrop of red and yellow autumn foliage. But what you *heard* was the sound of rain falling lightly on wood. And I'd bought it and put it straight into storage. What a lousy brother.

Needing to share out some of the guilt, I glared at Bee's dealer for giving that commission long ago to one of those jagged metal guys who work big. Then I turned my ire toward that big patootie Gertrude, because she hadn't helped Bee when she could have. (Bee always loved the word, "patootie.") But the truth was, with or without our help, Bee had accomplished more than most. While I'd regarded her as hapless, aimless, deluded and doomed, she'd been pumping out one much-loved sculpture after another! She *had* "done well," if doing well wasn't only about making money— she'd done all this for chrissake! She hadn't waited for approval or permission from us patooties, she'd just plowed on. And all I could do for her now was not abandon her. I vowed I wouldn't ban the thought of her from my mind to save myself pain — as I had when my parents died (in my father's case, *before* he died). No, I wouldn't kill Bee a second time. If I could be Mimi's attorney, I could be my sister's advocate.

Next up on the platform was Bee's ex-husband, Hunter (the biggest kid that ever was). Get a load of this guy, hopping around, hopping on the old *bandwagon*. His personal connection to a victim in an international news story was just too good an opportunity to miss. Towering over us all, with his chest puffed out, at first flexing his hands like he was about to write us a ticket, then lowering them to his groin (the "fig leaf" position!), he announced, "I was married to Bridge." (I'd forgotten Bee was his Bridge for three years.) "We were very much in love. She made herself a real part of the family. We just liked hanging out. Bridge was on a break from art at that time, she didn't really care about all that stuff, she just wanted to have fun—"

I couldn't stomach any more of this. "She was on a break from *civilization*, pal!" I yelled from the floor. "She wasn't doing any art because you didn't let her, you jerk."

Was it the cop in Hunter, or the wife-beater, that led him to take a swipe at me over the heads of the crowd? He missed by a mile.

"Can't push *her* around anymore, I guess, so it'll have to be me," I taunted. I was longing to get my hands on him too. I'd never stopped wanting to tear the guy limb from limb (and I'm a surgeon, I know how to do it!).

But nobody else seemed to want to watch us punch each other's lights out, so Hunter was escorted to the exit, and I was allowed to remain, Hanafan's brother taking precedence over Hanafan's self-appointed widower. The speeches were over now anyway. While we toasted Bridget with champagne cocktails, the quartet started up with "Death and the Maiden."

"You always were a goofball, Hanafan."

I knew that tone. Who else would insult me at my sister's memorial? Gus and Gertrude had made their way through the throng to bully me. But that wasn't his only motive. He also wanted a favor. This was why he'd been trying to get in touch with me for months, bombarding me by letter, phone, and email. What Gus wanted, it turned out, wasn't just a freebie, but some *sub rosa* surgery done on his face. For *Gertrude's* benefit, he claimed (yet I knew his recent pestering of me *pre-dated* his dating her). It was all because of an ancient broken nose, he said, and... he didn't want to get into the precise details right now, but he was hoping for some alterations to his hairline and ears, to fob off the cops in his furtive future. (Cops identify people by their ears more often than you might think.)

"So how about it, old buddy?" he asked.

"Sorry, Gus. No can do."

"Aw, come on. Old times' sake."

"Nope."

"Well, why the hell not?"

"Well, Gus... because I'm no longer a plastic surgeon."

"Huh?"

"I quit!"

Gertrude's hand leapt to her throat; and her mind to the issue of moola. "But, Harrison! How will you make a living?"

"Call this living?"

The quartet was in full flight as I left. The scratch of the pen, flick of the brush, scrape of the bow—this is when things start to happen.

* * *

I had lusted after quitting in my heart. I had dangled it like a carrot before my own nose whenever the going got tough. But it wasn't until Gus requested my services that I knew my nascent love affair with quitting must finally be consummated. The prospect of remodeling that guy's head for old times' sake wasn't my only reason—but it sure was a good one!

I still had an hour or two before I had to head for the airport, so I acquired some placatory gladioli for the nurses and receptionists, and headed on over to the office. Cheryl's face fell as I explained my position. I refused to reconsider though, despite all her tears and entreaties, and was on my way out when I met Henry in the waiting room. There sat the classic assortment of potential victims, abjectly hoping to be augmented or whittled down, *perfected* by us in some way.

"Ah, Harrison. You're here, are you?" old Henry asked me jovially.

"No, I'm not really here, Henry. I quit."

"Ha ha ha. We were wondering when you'd deign to—"

"No, I mean it, Henry. I just quit. Ask Cheryl!"

"WHAT?"

"This is me quitting, Henry. I quit!" I began to wonder if I would have to repeat the word "quit" seven times, as some presentation coaches recommend, before he'd take it in. I turned to our little audience and added, "I advise you all to do the same, folks. Get out while the going's good!"

"Uh, Harrison, would you mind coming into my office—"

"Your office stinks, Henry. It gives me the heebie-jeebies! Think of all the pointless painful procedures people have endured in there! Life-endangering stuff, and all for what?! Nope, I've duped my last dope, Henry, you do what you want," I said. And to the crowd, "You too!"

Henry spluttered, "For your information, this fellow, this fellow's had a rough few weeks—"

I interrupted, to tell the baffled little crowd, "For your information, you're *all* fuckworthy!—" I felt Henry's hand like a big mitt coming over my mouth, but struggled free. "Yes, there's nothing actually wrong with you people. Now, scat!" They stared. "Are you coming?" A few did rise to follow me, the Pissed Piper of plastic surgery, but I was too fast for them. I ran, RAN out of that building. Free at last, free as a bird! I did feel like I was flying.

I'd never quit a job before, and had no idea how great it feels. Quitting is FABULOUS. I recommend it to everyone. I walked down the street and could *smell* things again, for the first time in years. The car fumes, the hot-dog stands, sweaty men in suits (or was that me?), flowers, perfume, dog shit, french fries. Jobs are all very well, but quitting feels soooo GOOOOD.

Enough guff, enough rebuff. "To Grove Street, between Bedford and Bleecker, and step on it!"

I rang Mimi's bell about a billion times, and howled up at her window, "Man *my* barricades! Or better yet, bare my manni-cades!" But it was no good. No Mimi.

Mimì! Mimì!

At the airport, awaiting my flight, I sat at a bar, eating nuts and *going* nuts. Since Bee had died, I'd felt like a guy clinging to the wreckage in a hurricane. And they expected me to do my *job* at the same time! They wanted me to play the ready, steady doc, while the palm trees all around me were *bent sideways*, cars sailing past, people floating by on the roofs of their houses... I was pleased with myself for finally recognizing the practical impossibility of all this. But, fearing any second thoughts, some failure of resolve, some unforeseen requirement to do the exact opposite, I jotted down on a napkin my reasons for quitting:

- the pole-dancing kid I couldn't help
- Mimi's disdain for what I do (it's not that I can't *take* her to a medical conference—she wouldn't go!)
- medical conferences
- the sadomasochistic mauling of healthy flesh, old or young. Leave 'em alone!
- "First, do no harm"—but we harmed people every day, flagrantly, for money
- the woman who died to save her son from having a fat mom (moms are *supposed* to be fat!)
- the women who want their labia trimmed (to match their inner emptiness)
- the man who dreamed he could have a penis the size of a horse's, and asked *me* to do it for him
- the creepy requests to re-virginify Arab brides
- the veiled requests for female circumcision
- the suspicion that, by working as a plastic surgeon, I have personally contributed to the current epidemic of female self-hate and self-harm
- patients who come spinning in like a tornado, flinging sad tales in all directions

– the shame of working with Henry. Some beauty expert! He once
  gave a woman a *monster eye* (she'd asked for two)
– reading and writing medical papers
– speaking at clinical meetings and scold-fests
– energy-saving bulbs in the office
– Cheryl's melancholy plight
– the noose of email
– the noise of lawyers
– trying to avoid garlic and onions before appointments
– being away from Bubbles all day!
– the diner near the office: matzo ball soup never hot enough
– I don't really know what a good nose *is* anymore

Sure, I'd miss surgery itself—it's a craft and I'd gotten good at it. But I could turn my hand–eye coordination to better things, like playing the piano, and working on my inventions. After all, I had enough money in the bank to live for the rest of my life ("as long as I die by 4:00 today," as Henny Youngman would say).

It was only as the plane for home juddered down the runway for take-off that I realized that, during that pit stop at my apartment, I'd managed to grab a change of underwear but forgot my notes for my speech! (Such as they were—I'd never even settled on a definite subject.) What we had here was a real Grandma-died-and-her-dog-ate-my-speech situation, and an extra pair of underpants wasn't going to help.

I could still cancel. (*Could* I still cancel?)

FULL MOON, JUNE 15TH

THE THING BEE and I always liked about the Chewing Gum Plaza Hotel when we were kids was the modernistic indoor waterfall and fishpond in the lobby. This had now been replaced by a muggy rainforest of rubber plants and a dozy cockatoo chained to a log. The Ritz it wasn't. Not that I noticed much when I got there: I was too busy trying to scrabble a speech together on hotel notepads, too nervous to resurrect any of my possible topics. Three chunks, I reminded myself hysterically, three ideas, three ideas per chunk, three chunks per idea, nine ideas per speech… Nothing but a few lousy phrases came to mind (and Mimi's just dismissal of them). The last thing I wrote before falling asleep was an execrable thing about the ironies of plastic surgery, based on my trusty airport napkin.

I walked out of that hotel the next morning with what bravado I could muster and pockets stuffed with little pieces of paper (as well as a letter of apology, in case I chickened out), and took a tour around town just to re-familiarize myself with *its* execrableness.

The last time I was there was for my mother's funeral—but then, *Bee* was with me. Now I was alone: jobless, sister-less, Mimi-less, mindless, pointless, speechless. *Mimì! Mimì!*

Walk. Take in one color, one sound.

Nothing was left of Bee's graffiti now—the very buildings she'd daubed were gone. But some things remain the same. I first discovered SKY in Virtue and Chewing Gum, the sky and then the rest of it, from the ground up: twigs, grass that could cut you (glass too), pebbles, puddles, pencils, much prized popsicle sticks, sewer drains, cigarette stubs, dog do, asphalt, oak leaves, cracks in the sidewalk that would break your mother's back (and in my case, did!), tree roots, buttercups, sprinklers, hoses, inflatable pools, fire hydrants, trash, rose thorns, favorite tricycles, and little red wagons. It was the look of the sidewalks that got me most, the actual squares of cement under my feet: they were the same. The tree-lined playground with the tallest swings, and bark shavings to soften your fall. The ice-skating hut where Bee and I put on our skates every winter, and the field on which we skated and lost a few baby teeth: it was all there but so tiny!

But it was *lush*, my hometown—all the trees had grown. And there was the bakery that used to sell cherry cobbler pie, and still did. The river too was still rushing by of course—but no little red truck. The smoldering remains of what was once my childhood: earth, air, water, fire. Born twixt pee hole and shit hole, the brown and the yellow ale, east and west, north and south, spring and fall, black and white, Virtue and Chewing Gum, I was back in the land of contrasts: home. But *I* now inhabited a gray area, where Ant's got no Bee, and Rodolfo needs his Mimì.

*   *   *

Big black beetles had gathered on the high-school lawn in their carapaces, the black gowns of bamboozlement. Parents were taking photographs. My audience: just kids, soon to be locked into mortgages and marriages. Don't graduate, you fools, *individuate!*

I wandered into the Principal's office. Why was I surprised he was younger than me, and too busy to talk? He sat me down in the corridor with a copy of the high-school yearbook, and I flicked through headshots as if tasked with identifying a murderer. I didn't even glance at my notes, though I fingered my letter of apology off and on. It's no big deal, I kept telling myself. Humans make speeches: I am human, therefore I can make one too. People make speeches all over this goddam country every day! Really *stupid* people. (I ran rings around myself, logically.)

Once positioned amongst the School Board on stage, I had to resort to fantasizing about Mimi to calm myself, picturing her hands all over me and her lips on mine, throughout the Principal's platitudinous oration, and then the militaristic handing-out of diplomas. The thought of Mimi was the only thing that stopped the shakes!

Bee-oh-double-you-el, I-en-gee,
Let's go bowling, bowling, bowling,
My baby and me!
Bee-oh-double-you-el, I-en-gee,
Let's go bowling, bowling, bowling,
For the whole fam-i-lee!

For "bowling," read... But now I had to snap out of it. The Chairman of the School Board seemed to have finished his generous, as of yesterday wholly erroneous, characterization of me as a successful doctor (he made me sound like Ant and Bee's doctor: *huge*), and was handing me the floor. It seemed a little late to deliver my letter. I stood, knees wobbly, stomach tensing up, palpitations starting, mouth dry: I needed Meno-Balls! But then I remembered Mimi's injunction to look directly at my audience... and they were a sad sight, all those awkward girls, dolled up and smiling—my future patients perhaps, if I hadn't quit, with their wonky noses, plump thighs, and blemishes. Poor ducks, I'd give my speech for THEM.

"Yeah, thanks. Thanks. Yes, it's true, I did go to this school," I began. *Isolated cheers.* "Yeah, hey, it wasn't *that* good!" *Laughter.* "In fact, I came here to tell you how *awful* it was, and give you a few of my most bitter memories of the place." *Whoops of delight; a few boos.* "But... that can wait." *More laughter.*

"While you guys were finishing your Senior Year, taking SATs, and getting laid..." *Chortles; coughs.* "Ripping up your prom gowns, or mending them with safety pins..." *Laughter.* "My sister..." Throat threatening to seize up. "My sister Bee, Bridget Hanafan, a sculptor, *also* a former student here..." *Deep breath.* "Maybe you heard about it on the News. A guy in England went berserk and started shooting people, complete strangers mostly, and... my sister was one of them." *Gasps; women fanning themselves with programs.* "After he'd killed twenty people, he came up with a better idea and killed himself." *Vast, attentive silence.*

"What this event has left me with is: *one*, no sister... and *two*, a sense of how badly we treat women in general. We treat 'em like shit, my friends!" *Harrumphs from the School Board behind me.*

"Like SHIT, I tell you. Every single day, the girls in this very hall have to hear about women being beaten, stoned, raped, and murdered. Every day of their *lives* they hear this stuff!

"And we just throw up our hands in surprise at the latest male atrocity and say, Yeah, it's a pity, but there's nothing I can do about it. Right?. . . " *Murmurs.* "RIGHT?" *Vague assent.* "Nothing we can do, nothing we can do. . . " *Inaudible heckle.*

"All my life this has been going on and I thought there was nothing I could do: some men are idiots, some are scary bastards, just forget about it. . . But now my sister's dead and I *can't* forget about it!" *Silence.*

"I have a confession to make." Butterflies in stomach; take fresh breaths whenever opportunity allows. "Yes, a confession." Pause.

"I am a terrorist." *Gasps.* "*I AM A TERRORIST!*" *Pause.* "ALL men are terrorists!" *A few feeble boos.* "We may not be active members of the terrorist movement, not knowingly anyway, but we all have *links* with terrorism, with fellow terrorists, and with terrorist organizations.

"The whole world is run by terrorists. And those terrorists are MEN. The fathers, brothers, uncles, and grandfathers who've gathered here today are terrorists." *Muffled sighs and growls.* "We're *all* terrorists!" *Giggles and throwing of programs.* I pace the stage thinking, whatever you do, don't jingle the change in your pocket!

"We are all part of a war against women. Women are on the front line, getting beaten, raped, murdered. They try to work their way *around* it, they try to *avoid* such fates, while fearing for their lives every day.

"EVERY DAY. This is the society we live in! America is not a safe place for a woman. The enemy is all around her: in the bushes, in the bedroom, in the boardroom and on the boob tube." *Giggles.* "TV provides our daily dose of propaganda, it's like a kind of night school for violence against women. And then there's pop music, advertising, fashion demands, the so-called Beauty Industry, and porn. Is this all we can think up? A nonstop diet of disrespect?" *Isolated claps; wolf whistles.* "Because, you know? Disrespect paves the *way* for violence—they're old pals!

"The war against women isn't fought in the open. It hasn't been officially declared by Congress. (Or not *that* kind of congress anyway.) No, we fight *dirty!* Most of the hostilities are conducted underground. We try to keep it quiet, keep it subtle, keep things private. . . We *isolate* women so we can grouse at them. We get them on their own and undermine them." *Snickers; an idiotic clap; some distant heckle involving "underpants."*

"Yep, we're pretty clever about it. But it's a fight to the death— and the dead lie all around us!" *Silence. More fanning with programs.*

"We terrorize women through violence, always the threat of physical attack. But we back it up with ideology, literature, history, religion, tradition, a whole way of life. We intentionally misunderstand women. We ignore them—don't tell me you never tried that trick! We misrepresent them. We mislead them. We silence them. We refuse to give them what they ask for. And we criticize them—god, do we criticize! We never let them do or be or say or have what they want." *Clapping from some girls.*

"We will not leave women BE. Be whatever they want to be. No, they gotta be *this*, they gotta be *that*. They gotta be fun, they gotta be sexy, gotta be thin, be glamorous, be cheerful and good-looking and tolerant of *us*. They gotta cook, they gotta clean. *And* they gotta work! Yeah—women now have to bring home the bacon, and COOK it as well!" *Cheers from the girls; claps from mothers. But a heckler yells, "Hey, men cook too!"* Always acknowledge what's going on in the audience, Mimi said. Anticipate criticism.

"I know a lot of men cook these days," I replied. "But it's usually *voluntary*. That's the difference. Or they're making money at it, as TV chefs." *Laughter.*

"The point is that through our constant sniping, griping, and mockery, we keep women down. Through plastic surgery too! Yeah, I never had to actually *hit* women: cutting them up was good enough for me!" *Claps; laughter.*

"As a result, women aren't having a very good time... And they're so *tense!*" *Big laugh.* "As someone said to me recently, we don't even know what women *are* yet, they've been repressed for so long." *A few isolated claps.* "Well, AREN'TCHA CURIOUS?" *Nervous laughter.*

"Oh, we pat ourselves on the back in this country because we don't stone women in the street, or stop them becoming doctors. Sure, we let girls go to school... for what good it does them!" I gesture at the audience. *Cheers; whistles.*

"But do we honor and esteem women in America? Oh, sorry. I meant to say, do we honor and esteem our bitches?" *Big laugh.*

"What's going to happen to the women graduating today? These beautiful, hopeful, vulnerable young women, who've probably already encountered all kinds of sexual discrimination from their friends, their boyfriends, their fathers..." *Grumblings and mumblings.* "The school system, college application system, the softball coach, the job market, strange men who follow them down the street...

"Lambs to the slaughter, lambs to the slaughter...These women sitting here today have already been *hammered* by sexism. Their lives have been *hampered* by it, as their mothers' lives were hampered before them.

"Debased and wasted women are all around us. I've *seen* what happens to women in this world, while men roam free, wreaking havoc. Not just with my sister, but my patients and my friends... My own mother was tormented for decades by my nutso father, who once tried to kill us all by setting fire to the house!" *Coughs.* "Yes, in pretty little Virtue and Chewing Gum. Fathers are the worst!" *A few mild boos.* "No, mothers!" *cries another heckler. Laughter.*

"And what I want to know is, when did men get the idea the world is just about *them*? Who gave us permission to go messing with things? The *UN*? Messing women around. Messing children around. Messing up the house and the yard." *Laughter.* "Messing with guns, messing with the environment, messing with animals, the economy, plutonium, messing with the Gulf of Mexico! We're talking about the future of life on earth here!...The air, the water! Who gave us the right to ruin it for everybody?

"Filling the globe with our porn and our violence and our radio-active waste, and our corporations... Who decided *that* was a good idea? And—WHY... WEREN'T... WOMEN... ASKED?" *Wild applause.* This public-speaking jazz is a breeze! Keep your head though: reel 'em in, reel 'em in.

"Are we going to let men obliterate the whole world, like that guy obliterated my sister, just for the hell of it?" *Clapping.* "Just because that's the way things have always been done around here?

Do we really crave catastrophe that much? I'm sick of these people who say you can't change human nature, that pollution and poverty and starvation and nuclear war are inevitable, so there's no point in worrying about it.

"START WORRYING, PAL! *Do* something! Isn't it at least worth a try? Do you really want to give up on the whole of human civilization *without a fight?* What, are you NUTS?" *Cheering.*

"So, let's say that everyone in this room agrees that, in an ideal world, women would be respected. Assume we can all agree on that." Inclusiveness: Mimi would be proud! "That, in an ideal world, women would be *respected* instead of mutilated.

"Well, let me ask you this: what bestows status in our society?. . . What ensures you get respect?" *"An SUV!" "Naw, Cadillac!" "Porsche!" "Tattoos!" "Home runs!" "AK-47!" "Ivy League."*

"Good suggestions, but what I think it boils down to is MONEY. Money is power, money is privilege. Money buys you clothes and food and shelter. Money buys you security, *and* that car, or the hotshot education. Money is your *ticket to ride* in the Western world. Money buys you *respect.* I'm not saying I agree with it. I don't, as a matter of fact." *Right-wingers shake their fists; someone yells, "Commie!"*

"Yes," I said, "I'd rather see a dead capitalist than a dead peasant any day!" *Cheers in acknowledgment of Michael Moore reference; boos likewise.*

"But, given the current political climate, money is still the surest route to gaining respect and safety. So what I want to say to you today is: GIVE 'EM THE MONEY!

"Make women rich! All of 'em! Give women power, so that nobody dares mess with them anymore. Never mind a 'room of her own,' give her DOUGH of her own! It's payback time!" *Cheers and stomping from girls; boos from boys. I get out my wallet and aim some dollar bills at girls in the front row, eliciting shrieks of delight and some scuffles. Pockets of applause elsewhere, pockets of matriarchy.* "Hey, can'tcha throw it a bit farther?" "Guy's a sissy." "Send some our way, dude!". . . Once it dies down a bit, I continue.

"We *had* our chance, guys, and we blew it! Men had the run of the whole show for the last five thousand years and look what we did with it. So do something *right* for a change: hand over the dough!" *Girls applauding.*

"What we need is a simple redistribution of assets, from men to women." "Redistribute my ass!"

"I realize of course that many of you are just starting out and probably don't *have* much money. So start small: give her a dime!" I fling my pocket change into the aisles, causing another scramble; it's a relief to be rid of it. I also float some more bills, folding them in half this time, lengthwise, and shooting them like paper airplanes so they go further.

"Give *something* to a woman or women of your choice—or a charity that helps women. Anything you can afford. Just get into the habit of·handing it over, and encourage all the guys you know to do the same. No, don't just encourage, *persuade* them to help women instead of hassling them, to *endorse* women instead of diss-ing them." "Yeah, Karl," *jibes some kid at another.* "Fuck off!" *his pal replies.*

"Tell your father, tell your friends!. . . I *would* say, tell the *women* you know to help other women too. . . but you know what women are like when you try to tell them what to do!" Cheap joke but effective: *laughter; applause.* I'm a natural!

"By the way, this is not an *exchange*, guys, it's not a trade-off. Giving women money doesn't entitle you to guilt-trip the recipient into sleeping with you or doing your laundry for the rest of her life." *"Aw, shit!" from the floor.*

"Nope. This is a no-strings-attached deal. It's. . . a *gift*. A revolutionary one. Just give them the money, no questions asked. Because, once women are in charge of all the money, all the land, all the property. . . we can RELAX, guys! No more male work ethic, no more murders, no more war—I hope. No more *violence,* if women are in charge, since all violence hurts women. Even if it's not directed at them, they are the mothers, sisters, wives, and girlfriends of the dead and injured.

"Oh, I know there are some women you wouldn't trust with a wooden nickel." *"Yeah, my mom!" "My gramma." "Mrs. Topola!" "Jane!" "Tamsin!" "That girl's a witch!" "Slut!". . .*

"Yes, there are some mean women out there, *scary* women, *crazy* women. But they'd probably all be a lot less cranky if the world was their oyster!" *Laughter; a few claps.* "Anyway, it's completely up to you who you choose to give your money to, just as long as you give it to a woman." *"I know who I'd like to give it to!" and other bawdy remarks follow. Small scuffle somewhere near the back.*

"No fighting now!" *Laughter.* "The beauty of my scheme is that this will be a nonviolent, gradual, *peaceful* form of revolution, achieved behind the scenes, without chaos and bloodshed. After all, nobody can stop you giving away your dough if you want to.

"And what's the worst possible outcome?" *A heckler calls out, "No money!" Pause; breathe; let the audience start to wonder if I have an answer to my own question.* "That women are *happy*. Would that be so bad? Are we so attached to self-destruction, misogyny, and the vainglory of killing, that we can't even consider a change?" I'm losing them—time for a slam-bam finish. "And here's what's in it for *you*, guys. . . " *"TV dinners!" "More chores."* *"Chick flicks!"*

"Nope. . . " Dramatic pause. "SEX. Sensational sex!" *Gasps and coughs behind me; exclamations from parents.*

"The fact is, our whole society's got things ass-backward. We've got Chewing Gum where Virtue should be!" *Laughter.* ". . . And men where women should be.

"Men are confused about what sex is for, because nobody ever told us the truth:. . . SEX IS FOR WOMEN!" *Giggles; boos; a few claps.*

"Men are always talking about their own sexual needs. Our movies, our books, are all about *men's* needs. This is *beside the point!* Because, here's the dope, kids: women are not here to please men, men are here to please *women*. That's how it works in nature! Males court the females, they protect them—and they try to please them." *More boos from the back; cheers from the front. Somebody groans, "Aw, come off it!"*

"This is what men are physically and biologically designed to do: give pleasure to women. . . And we'd better start soon!" *Laughter; cheers.* "*Men* should be the sex slaves! They'd LOVE it!" *Stomping; cheering; wolf whistles. "Woo-hooo!" "Yeah, baby!" Standing ovation among some of the girls.*

"The female orgasm is one of evolution's greatest achievements! Male orgasms are *nothing* by comparison." *"Ew!" "Oh my god!"* "Yes, I said it. I said it!" *Laughter in appreciation of Chris Rock echo.*

"Nurture the female orgasm, guys!" *Hilarity; stamping of feet.*

"In other words, ladies and gentlemen, we could all be having a great time in the sack!" *Cries of moral outrage from the School Board.*

"So let's stop bullying, bludgeoning and boring women to death. Let's bed them instead!" *"You said it, man!" "Yes, sir!"* "Pleasuring women is your new job. OURS NOT TO REASON WHY, OURS BUT TO DO HER OR DIE!" *Uproar.*

"Change the world! Give women your spare change!. . . Thank you."

Pandemonium. The Principal and his acolytes probably would have slept through any amount of bombast, nostalgia, vitriol, and racing tips—but one mention of orgasms and all hell broke loose. I was dragged away, still speaking, like some washed-up vaudevillian getting the hook. One at each elbow, others prodding me from behind, gowned geezers jostled me toward the steps at the side of the stage.

"This is just what I was talking about!" I yelled to my beaming, screaming supporters below. "Physical force! That's their answer to everything. . . "

I could see young men rolling in the aisles—not from amusement but because they'd gotten tangled up in their gowns on their way to *pulverize* me. They needn't have bothered: the School Board was handling the matter personally. I tried to cling onto the Principal's neck—if I was going down, I'd take him with me. But I lost my grip and found myself on the floor, enclosed by a fence of old farts' legs and asses. Threats of lawsuits and civil action were mooted on both sides.

And then I had the most astonishing feeling of being lifted up like a newborn babe, torn from my strange man-cave and lovingly—if kind of hurriedly—jolted toward the light. A wave of women had snatched me away from my enemies, and now triumphantly bore me on their shoulders out of the building!

Once deposited on the front lawn, I was showered with praise, beers, hugs, kisses, veneration, and raunchy propositions. People wanted me to sign their programs, and the back of their hands, their legs... Hot dogs arrived from somewhere, and I think somebody started playing the guitar. It was wild, wild stuff.

Then, faintly, over the tumult, came a high clear note like a duckling's call—"Ee-ee-ee-ee!"—only longer. A very high-pitched sound, like a whistle... *Mimi's* kind of whistle! She'd come after all, to hear me speak! And now I could see her making her way to me through the crowd, her face pink from crying. I grabbed her by the hand, and then the waist, and held her close to me, while the friendly crowd continued to besiege us.

"Can I have your autograph?" asked a stray adherent of mine, offering me her high-school diploma to sign.

"Sure," I said, without letting go of Mimi for a second.

After I'd signed it for her, the girl just stood there gaping at me. Finally she asked, "What's your revolution called?"

On impulse, I answered, "The Odalisque Revolution."

"The Ode o' what...?!"

"Odalisque," I said, with growing certainty, clasping Mimi to my side. The girl rushed off to spread the word—giving me a chance to ask Mimi what she thought of my speech.

"It was okay, I guess," she said, smiling. "Bit too much jargon." (A mischievous reference to my criticisms of her book at Kelley & Ping, all those months, or moons, ago.) "I told you you could do it!" she added.

"Ah, Mimi. . ."

She stopped smiling, drew back a bit, and said, "I'm so sorry about Bee. I didn't know!"

I nodded. And then she put her arms around me and planted a *big hot one* on my lips, in front of THE WHOLE SCHOOL!

"Wooo-hooooooo!"

The place erupted. People were spraying beer in the air and throwing their graduation gowns into the trees. And chants of "The Odalisque Revolution! The Odalisque Revolution!" rang out across the lawn.

GIGUE

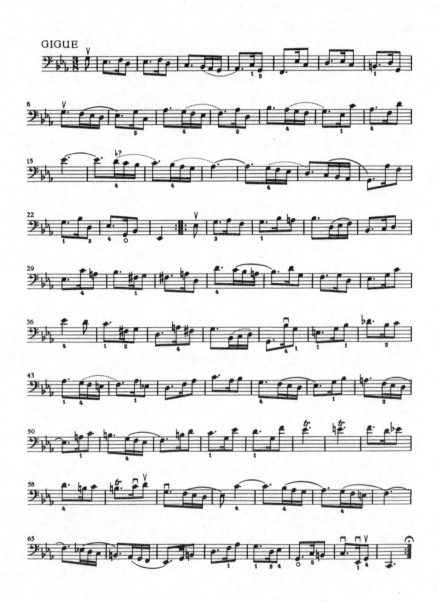

LABOR DAY

"THERE'S NOTHING IN the whole world except us," says Bette Davis to Paul Henreid in *Deception*. "Nothing."

"Nothing," Paul agrees.

The nutshell ending? Benchmarks? We were together, we got married, we were in love—so shoot me! A lot of people did want to shoot me. My Homeland Insurrection was Yahooed, YouTubed, Tweeted and Facebooked all over the world, and discussed on the News. Hunter got himself a talk-show slot and called me a traitor to my sex. *Time*, the *Herald Tribune*, the *New York Times*, *Esquire* and the *National Enquirer* all wanted to interview me... But I only wanted to be with Mimi. *Mimì! Mimì!* Crab lunches, oysters at the Grand Central Oyster Bar, now and then a little soup, and orgasms, *odalisque* orgasms.

Being with Mimi was everything to me. I was only sad that we had ever been apart. It felt like we'd been in a terrible car crash, but survived. (Like Bubbles!)

"Where *were* you, Mimi?" I asked on our way back to New York after my speech. "Why wouldn't you answer my calls?"

"I was mad at you. I was hurt!"

"I know. I'm so sorry about all that, Mimi. . . But thanks for the bagels!"

"I had to get away for a while. I went to the Bronx."

"Home to Mommy?"

"Yup. And then, when I tried to get you, you didn't answer. I thought you were avoiding me, that you. . . that you didn't want to see me anymore."

"Never! Never," I said (privately excising all memory of my craven jerkball *attempt* to reject her on the grounds of big feet and bra-straps).

This is the one problem with New York: too little protection from your enemies, and too much from your odalisque! You can lose each other, confuse each other, in a big city. But Mimi wasn't giving up so easy: she'd decided to surprise me at the graduation ceremony. She couldn't miss my maiden speech!

There were two attempts to tear us asunder, and not by lone right-wing Christian snipers but by people I *knew*. First came Gus, who wormed his way into my apartment and started flashing a knife around, rambling about my personal betrayal of *him* as well as my more general betrayal of all men. . . until Mimi whopped him with one of her shoes, and the knife fell (her big feet saved my life!).

We'd just succeeded in bustling Gus out onto the street when we were accosted by the pole-dancer's father, who must have been skulking there for days, waiting for an opportunity to take a punch at me. He too felt I'd ruined life as we know it for all hot-blooded American males (which was and still is my intention). I'd ruined *his* life in particular, since his kids had gone into hiding with their mother, following the inconclusive police investigation.

"You shouldn't have done that, you asshole!" he yelled at me. "You don't come between a man and his family."

"I'm no family man, I'm afraid," I replied. "And yours *needed* dispersal."

"Why I oughta..." The pole-dancer's father started pawing at a suspicious black trash bag he had under his arm.

"Yeah, go for it," Gus chimed in, standing back from the fray but egging him on.

At last wrenching his rifle free of the bag, the guy aimed it at me. But again, Mimi had the effrontery to nudge the guy's arm just as he inexpertly pulled the trigger. The gun went off but didn't hit anything.

"Women!" he moaned, collapsing on the ground.

Mimi later claimed she'd assumed it wasn't loaded, but I think she just likes saving my life. Brave Mimi!

So we sought safety in sea and sand in Sagaponack, where each day is an event of a gentler nature. Yesterday at sunset the cresting waves were pink-tipped like opals; today, more like a crowd of white mice, leaping. Bubbles follows us around, a real beach bum: she can leap again.

And Claude visits. After Gus tried to kill me, Gertrude had second thoughts about him as a paramour: she wasn't up for a prison romance, with no beau to attend her soirées or share the *amuse-gueules* of life. She and I are civil to each other now, and have worked out an arrangement whereby Claude can spend time with Mimi and me, since no woman should have to bring up a kid all on her own (and no kid should be all on his own with Gertrude!).

The first night he stayed with us, I dreamed we all went swimming in a big wide greenish river, much slower and safer than the Chevron, and only about five feet deep. It was early morning, the sky just starting to turn that poignant shade of blue. Mimi and Claude were near me, and we all swam easily through the water, zooming around as fast as we liked. I realized I didn't even need to swim, but could just lie back and let the river carry me where it would, while I looked up through the trees at that beautiful sky. The sensation of being held by the water this way felt very like love.

My Manifesto for the Odalisque Revolution©, or rather, my *womanifesto*, hit the streets on the Fourth of July, all proceeds going to the Bee Hanafan Foundation, which offers microloans (and megaloans) to women who want to make art. My sage sister. Her own art sales go into it too. The Champagne Girls keep in touch, and will be coming over for the Retrospective. Bee's dealer is fully engrossed in the preparations for it, hoping to cash in on what he calls "renewed interest" in Bee's work (post-massacre). I still have my doubts about that guy, but liked seeing him on his knees among her valentines.

All my worldly goods are Mimi's now, with any income from inventions going into our joint account. As for Pocket Change™ (formerly known as Meno-Balls™), a few technical hitches still need to be cleared up, but then we're going into production. Mimi has chosen all the shapes, based on prehistoric patterns and artifacts, mostly goddess or vulva imagery, I gather: eggs, spirals, chevrons, fish, frogs, butterflies, and rings. ("Hey, what's this bagel shape doing here?" I asked her, but got no answer.) We were going to charge $39.99 for the basic "balls" (I have *got* to stop calling them that), and $249.99 for the "Precious Jewel of Nature Collectible Robin's Egg" version covered in Swarovski crystals—in this you might correctly divine the hand of our publicist and marketing advisor, Andy, whom I poached from my old practice. But there are ongoing arguments between him and Mimi about the money. She'd like the balls [*sic*] to be FREE. "They are meant to free women," she says. "Free to the free!"

"But I thought you said thar was gold in them thar hills!" I pointed out to her. "Or maybe you meant thar were *hills* in that thar *gold*, as Hitchcock said when Grace Kelly wore a gold dress and falsies."

"You can charge for the Swarovski ones," Mimi conceded. And who am I to say no to freebies, *or* to Mimi?

As for the quilt, Deedee got it back for me from the dry cleaners, good as new. It is, I now fully acknowledge, a work of art. It *is* somehow Rothko, it is Leonardo. I presented it to Mimi as a wedding gift, and did she cry when she saw it? Did she ever! It's now in the living room at 36th Street, hanging in front of the internal window between living room and dining room so you can see it against the light.

Mimi's wedding gift to *me* was an Alisa Weilerstein recital, playing Bach solo cello suites, and Kodály. This woman makes the cello sound like it's every instrument in the orchestra—you don't *need* any of them anymore, she's *it*. She can make the cello sound like a drum, like a recorder, she can make it sound like whirling water and water weeds, like a breeze, like flashing lights, stained glass, compassion, consumption, eighteenth-century cellars full of dirt, reflections, rocky places, animals of every sort, fire, and leaves blowing in the wind.

The aim of a musical instrument isn't to imitate the human voice, as everyone's always saying, but to be EVERYTHING.

Walking near the house in Sagaponack one day, Mimi and I came upon a field of poppies. The man in me just stared, thinking about the power of numbers. *Rebel! Arise and rebel, you fools, against the tyranny of work and war!* The kid in me took Mimi by the hand and walked right into the field, to *be* a field of poppies, be JOY.

What more can a man want than to please one gorgeous gal, a clever cat, and an amiable boy?

"By the way," Mimi blurted out this morning before Claude was up, when we were eating peaches and cream out on the porch. "*I* tripped you over on Christmas Eve. You didn't just fall."

I dropped my spoon. "What?! *Why?*"

"I dunno. Just liked the look of ya, I guess!" she said cheerily.

Baba Yagas all!

Any zhlub can kill, but he wouldn't if he'd ever seen the moon all bent out of shape in a puddle, or noticed the courage of grass growing through sand, or come upon a group of rounded stones on a beach, each in its own wind crevice—when all you want to do with the world is grab and adore it!

Don't give up on life, life in the ascendant and descendant, crescendoing and decrescendoing, male and female, hot and cold, dark, bright, beautiful or ugly: it's yours and mine. Don't cherry-pick the bits you like, you've got to cleave to the whole ball game!

It ain't all bad. Seeds still germinate, bees pollinate, birds migrate, caterpillars mutate, kangaroos gestate (externally!), beluga whales are born and somehow cared for, home runs are hit, snow falls, wine ferments, cork trees helpfully grow bark, spiders spin their own real estate, ivy winds lovingly around tree trunks, parrots preen, asparagus aspires, cats leap vertically six feet into the air... and somewhere, *somebody* gets a good haircut!

There are runnels of water gurgling through meadows, the smell of moist earth at dusk and dawn, streams and archipelagos and warm seas, waves like cozy canopied caves, and water weed that waves like hair in the current. There are quilts and carpets, and odalisques to lie on them. There are zebras, giraffes, okapi, aardvarks, and elephants. There are even still some bears and bison. And sex.

There's light, shadow, color, the dank smells of women and cigars, the babbling of children, buzzings of insects, popcorn popping, drunken guffaws. Wild garlic, coffee, basil, mimosa, moldy autumn leaves, and the brand-new air of winter.

There are little girls who skip fearlessly down hospital corridors to unknown fates, wearing their favorite sandals (I've seen them!). There are porches and rocking chairs, figs and fig leaves and lilies of the valley. Come on, life is worth living just because there are *cardinals.* What could be better than a red bird?

It's worth living just because there are horses' manes, and clouds. Bach, Beethoven, Mozart, Puccini, Verdi, and Casals. Mist, mint, honey, and bourbon. Saffron and sage. Eggs and nests. Hooves and paws. Snouts, tails, wings, feathers. Swimming and fucking and eating and drinking and just lying down. Pomegranates, monkeys, movies, cilantro, and jam! Matzo ball soup, pastrami, and Amatriciana. Clothes hanging on a line. Giotto, Giorgione, Masaccio, Rembrandt, Matisse, and Bee Hanafan. Starlings forming one big melting thrilling trilling ball at the end of each day. And all the other rustlings and scamperings and flutterings and weeping in the night. And all delight.

Cleave, you jerk! CLEAVE.

Love is a fact, neither tenuous nor debatable. You can hold yourself back from a woman and never be possessed. But if she can't possess you, she'll never be happy. And the world has got to start making women happy.

It saddens me sometimes that we met so late. And we both mourn our painful period apart. Mimi also wishes she'd met Bee. But what's love without a little melancholy?

What I like most in *Deception* is that there's never any question that they'll shack up together, once they find each other again at the Haydn concert. What's hers is his—Bette even carries his cello for him. She takes him straight home to her apartment, where the closet is instantly shared with him (the truest test of love: is there closet space?). She finds him a huge armchair by the fireplace, promises to get him a big cup for his coffee tomorrow, does the whole housewife act (with ironic sophistication), mopping his brow, bringing him a sandwich, kneeling at his feet. Come on, it's the sexiest reunion in the movies!

But what is with that priest-like collar she's got on, its prim white trim soon to be crushed by Paul's mighty cellist's hands when he tries to strangle her? Not his most heroic moment, but the guy's confused. It's not easy adjusting to all this love and comfort, all this *coziness,* after years in a concentration camp. It's not easy adjusting to BETTE DAVIS, even if she *can* play the *Appassionata.* And she keeps changing her story about Claude Rains.

Oh, for god's sake, man, why do you think she's got that gold telephone? She ain't no priest. She's a ho!

THE END

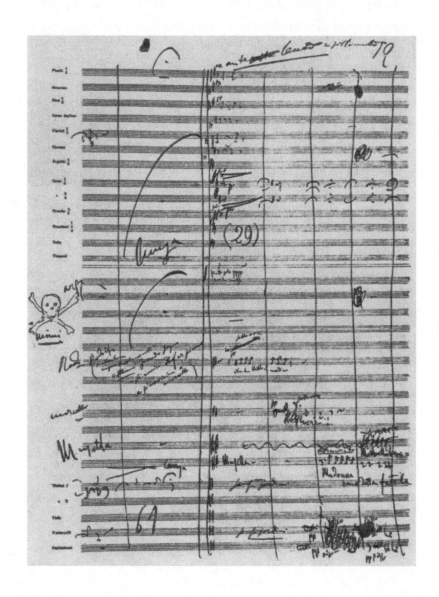

APPENDIX

ATTACKS ON ODALISQUE MAN

Two men were apprehended in midtown Manhattan yesterday on suspicion of attempted assassination. Both are alleged to have threatened or attacked the outspoken Harrison Hanafan, a notable plastic surgeon who recently excited comment with his controversial views on the emancipation of women.

In two apparently separate incidents, Hanafan was first confronted by a man armed with a knife, whom he had admitted to his apartment. No one was hurt. Not long afterward, Hanafan was approached outside the building by a man with a gun. One shot was fired. No injuries have been reported. Both assailants are now in police custody.

Harrison Hanafan, 51, is best known for his far-fetched plans for the redistribution of wealth. He has suggested, in many public forums and online, that men should gradually transfer all cash, property, and other financial assets to women. Hanafan appears to believe that this would somehow reduce violent crimes against women, and lead to other benefits for society at large. Most bizarrely, he has also suggested that the scheme would enhance sexual satisfaction for both sexes, though especially for women.

His most vociferous opponents include Dick Cheney, Donald Trump, Vladimir Putin, and O. J. Simpson. The machismo expert and cult philosopher, Richard Sly, has publicly challenged Hanafan to

a duel, calling him "a lily-livered mommy's boy
who has failed to grasp the real meaning of
masculinity."

Hanafan's sister, the sculptor Bridget Hanafan, was
fatally injured in May, a victim of a gun rampage in
England. Since then, Harrison Hanafan has become
a familiar figure, expounding his outlandish views at
numerous small gatherings. A video clip on YouTube
shows him inciting a riot at a high-school graduation
in June.

Nationwide outrage grew in response to the publi-
cation on Independence Day of Harrison Hanafan's
political pamphlet, the "Manifesto of the Odalisque
Revolution," a confused and eccentric document that
has sold well worldwide.

Along with numerous death threats, Hanafan has
been the subject of an FBI investigation, in accordance
with Homeland Security measures. His notorious asser-
tion that "All men are terrorists" has been denounced by
Dick Cheney as a violation of the Patriot Act. Hanafan's
female supporters, however, are said to be growing in
number.

RECIPES

MY EGGNOG

- 1 whole entire lb. confectioner's sugar (always Gertrude's "last box")
- 1 whole doz. eggs (big deal!)
- 40 fl. oz. booze or more (depending on your level of festive dismay): brandy and/or Scotch
- 3 quarts heavy cream
- nutmeg

Day One: Amass your ingredients (this may involve a trip or two to a town at least twenty-five miles away).

Day Two: Beat the sugar into the liquor. (Zone out on the smell.) Leave mixture overnight.

Day Three: Separate the eggs, saving the yolks of our oppression. (Permit the egg whites to be assigned some much more noble function.) Beat the liquor mixture into the egg yolks (zoning out again). Leave overnight.

Day Four: Beat cream until stiff. Fold cream into egg-and-liquor mixture. Taste frequently for flavor. Relish these moments of privacy! Honor the opportunity to get soused! Then spoon the Eggnog into wine glasses, sprinkle nutmeg on top and serve to the cognoscenti.

Repeat whole process in time for New Year's Eve.

MOM'S JAM

Equal amounts sugar and fruit. Cook to thick stage. (Or, extract fruit after initial boiling stage and continue boiling juice until ball stage. Useful trick with pears and plums.) Pour boiling water in jars and swish around. Cool jam slightly. Fill jars. Pour melted beeswax on top, to seal. Apricots—leave whole. Strawberries—break up a bit. And other long lost secrets.

MIMI'S AMATRICIANA

Kiss me. Chop two-inch hunk of guanciale (smoked) into large half-inch-thick pieces. Kiss me again. Put chopped guanciale and good amount of diced chili into frying pan with plenty of olive oil. Fry until almost burning. Don't distract me. Throw whole glass white wine into pan, and let it bubble away. Now kiss me! Strain big can tomatoes through sieve (optional step). When guanciale's almost dry again, add tomatoes. Leave to simmer for twenty mins., until smooth and velvety. Kiss me. Cook fusilli, spiraled in honor of serpentine energy (the spiral is a goddess-cult symbol). Grate fine one cup pecorino cheese, and kiss me.

Five mins. before pasta is done, add the cheese to the tomato sauce, along with some black pepper. Stir until smooth. Strain pasta and add it to the sauce in the frying pan. Stir thoroughly. Cook further five mins. Kiss and eat.

Weekly Specials

MONDAY

Soups

Vegetable, Mushroom barley, potato.......cup/bowl
Split pea, hotborscht, cabbage $4.00/4.50

Specials

Macaroni and cheese & cup of soup $8.00
Salmon croquettes & cup of soup $9.00
Stuffed cabbage & cup of soup $10.50
Veggie balls w/spaghetti & cup soup $9.00
Knish & cup of soup.....................$6.50

TUESDAY

Soups

Mushroom barley, vegetable, lentil.....cup/bowl
Split pea, hot borscht.................$4.00/4.50

Specials

Tuna fish sandwich.....................$8.00
& cup of soup
Potato pancakes & cup of soup $8.00
Poerogi or blintzes & cup of soup......$8.50
Fish cakes w/spaghetti & cup of soup ...$9.00
Stuffed cabbage & cup of soup..........$10.50

WEDNESDAY

Soups

Musroom barley, vegetable, potato.......cup/bowl
Split pea, hot borscht, Yankee bean $4.00/4.50

Specials

Vegetarian chili over brown rice $8.50
& cup of soup
Lasagna & cup of soup $8.50
Grilled cheese sandwich $7.25
& cup of soup
Fried or broiled fish $10.50
(Salmon or Flounder) & cup of soup
Tuna melt & cup of soup $8.50
Macaroni and cheese & cup of soup......$8.00

THURSDAY

Soups

Musroom barley, hot borscht, vegetable ....cup/bowl
Split pea, cabbage yankee bean $4.00/4.50

Specials

Stuffed , cabbage & cup of soup.........$10.50
Veggie burger & cup of soup $7.25
Tuna fish sandwich $8.00
& cup of soup
Pierogi or blintzes & cup of soup $8.50

FRIDAY

Soups

Musroom barley, matzo ball, vegetable ....cup/bowl
Hot borscht, split pea, lima bean $4.00/4.50

Specials

Vegetable cutletw/rice & cup of soup ...$9.00
A la parmesan.........................$9.25
Potato pancakes & cup of soup $8.00
Grilled cheese sandwich & cup of soup ...$7.25
Smoked white fish sandwich $8.50
& cup of soup
Vegetarian chili over brown rice $8.50
& cup of soup

SATURDAY

Soups

Mushroom barley, vegetable, lima bean,....cup/bowl
hot borscht,split pea, matzo ball $4.00/4.50

Specials

Veggie burger & cup of soup $7.25
Macaroni and cheese & cup of soup $8.00
Tuna melt & cup of soup $8.50
Lasagna & cup of soup $8.50
Egg sandwich & cup of soup $7.50
Stuffed cabbage & cup of soup $10.50

SUNDAY

Soups

Mushroom barley, vegetable, Lima bean ....cup/bowl
hot borscht, split pea $4.00/4.50

Specials

Smoked white fish sandwich $8.50
& cup of soup
Vegetarian chili over brown rice $8.50
& cup of soup
Pierogi or blintzes & cup of soup $8.50
Salmon croquettes & cup of soup $9.00
Knish & cup of soup....................$6.50
Fish cakes w/spaghetti & cup of soup ...$9.50

B & H
Vegetarian Restaurant
127 Second Avenue
☎ 212-505-8065
Fax: 212-673-4025

Kosher

Free Delivery
($10 Minimum)
Tax Included

BREAKFAST

Two eggs any style, home fries $4.25
Homemade challah bread
Egg sandwich on homemade bread: one/two
Challah bread....................$2.00/2.25
With cheese......................$2.75/3.25

OMLETTES

Lox and Onions $8.00
B&H Special...........................$6.25
(Onion, pepper, tomato, mushroom)
Cheddar cheese and apples $5.25
Spinach $5.50
Cheese $5.00
(Cheddar, American, Swiss, farmer, feta)
Green pepper..........................$5.50
Mushrooms............................$5.50
Tomato $5.50
Onion $5.50
Extra items add ....75¢
omelets served with home fries
& home made challah bread
Substitute with bialy/bagel/kasha add .. 75¢

FROM THE GRIDDLE

Famous challah French toast $5.00
Buttermilk pancakes $5.00
Blueberry pancakes w/syrup.............$5.00
Fresh fruit pancakes $5.00
Choice: Strawberry, banana, apple
Matzo brie............................$5.50
Potato pancakes $5.50
Served w/apple sauce or sour cream.
75¢ extra if served w/both

BAKERY

Our own muffins: $1.50
Corn, raisin bran, blueberry, banana walnut
Our own challah bread:
W/butter or jam, 20¢ extra if w/both .. $1.00
W/shmear $2.00
Bagel or bialy w/butter or jam $1.00
75¢ extra if served w/both

OUR SPECIALS

Potato knish w/gravy...................$3.25
Blintzes:.........................2pcs/3pcs
Cheese, blueberry, cherry $6.75/8.50
Pierogis:.........................4pcs/8pcs
Cheese, potato, sauerkraft-mushrooms $6.00/8.50
Served w/sour cream or onions 75¢ extra if served w/both

OUR FAMOUS SOUPS

Vegetable, mushrooms barley, lentil ....Cup/bowl
Split peas, cabbage, potato, lima bean.......$4.00/4.50
Hot borscht, matzo ball, yankee bean
For season: cold borscht, cucumber, gazpacho

HOT AND HEARTY

Sautéed or steamed vegetables $7.20
over brown rice
Kasha varniskas w/vegetables............$7.50
Vegetable cutlet w/rice w/kasha 50¢ extra ...$6.50
a la parmesan.......................$7.75
Vegetarian chili over brown rice..........$7.00
Macaroni and cheese $5.00
Vegetarian lasagna $6.50
Vegetarian stuffed cabbage $8.75
w/kasha, brown rice or steamed vegetable
Veggie balls with spaghetti $7.50
Veggie burger $5.00
with cheese........................$5.50
Salmon Croquettes....................$7.25
Fried or broiled fish with rice, potato,
kasha or steamed vegetables.........$8.75
Fish cake and spaghetti $7.75
Spaghetti with tomato sauce $5.00

OVERSTUFFED SANDWICHS

Chream cheese and nova lox $7.50
Individual tuna........................$5.50
Tuna salad $5.50
Tuna melt $6.50
chopped egg salad.....................$4.50
Cream cheese with vegetable...........$4.75
Swiss cheese $4.00
American cheese.......................$3.50
Grilled cheese.........................$4.25
Fried fish $6.75
Smoked white fish.....................$6.00
Salmon croquettes $4.75
Whole sandwich plus tomato 50¢ extra

SALAD PLATTERS

Chef's salad platter $6.00
Nova lox platter $8.75
Tuna salad platter $7.75
Egg salad platter $6.25
Individual tuna platter..................$7.50
Smoked white fish platter...............$8.00

SIDE DISHES

Sautéed or steamed vegetables $4.75
Fresh garden salad.....................$4.00
Kasha varniskas.......................$4.00
Kasha with mushroom gravy $3.75
Home fries $2.50
Fresh fruit salad.......................$4.00

DESSERTS

Rice pudding $2.50
Chocolate cake $2.50
Carrot cake $2.50
Chocolate chip cookie $1.25

BEVERAGES

Freshly squeezed juices
Fruit or Vegetable sm. $3.00 / md. $3.50 / lg. $4.25
Apple, cranberry, grapefruit, tomato, V-8 ... $1.00
Iced tea or iced coffee ......sm. $2.00 / lg. $2.50
Egg cream $2.50
Hot chocolate..........................$1.25
Coffee or tea $0.80
Herbal tea or soda $1.25

SONGS

THE YELLOW ALE

As I was going the road one fine day,
O the brown and the yellow ale!
I met with a man that was no right man.
O love of my heart!

He asked was the woman with me my daughter
O the brown and the yellow ale!
And I said she was my married wife
O love of my heart!

He asked would I lend her for an hour and a day
O the brown and the yellow ale!
And I said I would do anything that was fair.
O love of my heart!

So let you take the upper road and I'll take the lower
O the brown and the yellow ale!
And we'll meet again at the ford in the river.
O love of my heart!

I was walking that way for one hour and three-quarters
O the brown and the yellow ale!
When she came to me without shame.
O love of my heart!

When I heard her news I lay down and I died
O the brown and the yellow ale!
And they sent two men to the wood for timber.
O love of my heart!

A board of holly and a board of alder
O the brown and the yellow ale!
And two great yards of sack about me.
O love of my heart!

And but that my own little mother was a woman
O the brown and the yellow ale!
I could tell you another pretty story about women.
O love of my heart!

SHE'LL BE COMIN' ROUND THE MOUNTAIN

She'll be comin' round the mountain when she comes.
She'll be comin' round the mountain when she comes.
She'll be comin' round the mountain

She'll be comin' round the mountain
She'll be comin' round the mountain when she comes.

We'll all have chicken 'n dumplings when she comes
We'll all have chicken 'n dumplings when she comes. . .

SPARKLING BROWN EYES

There's a ramshackle shack
Down in ol' Caroline
That's calling me back
To that ol' gal o' mine.

Those two brown eyes
I long to see
For the girl of my dreams
She'll always be.

Those two brown eyes
That sparkle with love
Sent down to me
From Heav'n above.

If I had the wings
Of a beautiful dove
I'd fly to the arms
Of the girl that I love.

OLD DAN TUCKER

Old Dan Tucker was a fine old man
He washed his face in the frying pan.
He combed his hair with a wagon wheel
And died of the toothache in his heel.
Git out of the way for old Dan Tucker
He's too late to get his supper
Supper's over and the dishes washed
Nothing left but a piece of squash.

TURKEY IN THE STRAW

There was a little hen
And she had a wooden foot,
Made her nest
In the mulberry root.
She laid more eggs
Than any hern on the farm,
Another wooden foot
Wouldn't do her any harm.

Did you ever go fishin'
On a warm summer day
When all the fish
Were swimmin' in the bay?
With their hands in their pockets
And their pockets in their pants

Did you ever see fishie

Do the Hootchy-Kootchy Dance?

Turkey in the straw

Turkey in the hay...

JOE HILL

I dreamed I got the rights to *Joe Hill* last night,

But then he invoiced me!

I said, "Whoa, Joe, this sure is a lot—"

He said, "It's called a Royalty..."

BRIDGET HANAFAN:
THE RETROSPECTIVE

(EXHIBITION & SALE)

VALENTINES (PRICES VARY)

1. 1979: cardboard and pencil (5" × 3")
2. 1980: metal (key) and paper (2" × 1")
3. 1981: chalk on paper (9" × 4")
4. 1982: tinfoil and card (4" × 4")
5. 1983: paper and ink (3" × 4")
6. 1984: wood (clothes peg) (4" × ½")
7. 1985: paper and ink (5" × 4")
8. 1986: paper packet containing botanical specimen (seeds) (3" × 2")
9. 1987: fabric and safety pin (6" × 5")
10. 1988: breakfast cereal (Cheerios), flour glue, paper (approx. 30½" units; 2" × 8")

11. 1989: paper and tinsel (7" × 5")

12. 1990: dried flowers (daisies) and paper (approx. 5, 2" diameter; 3" × 3")

13. 1991: (no trace)

14. 1992: (no trace)

15. 1993: (no trace)

16. 1994: watercolor on paper (4" × 2½")

17. 1995: cellophane packet containing spice (ground cumin) (2" × 3")

18. 1996: metal (bottle top) (1" diameter)

19. 1997: paper and ink (bus ticket) (2" × 1½")

20. 1998: plastic roundel (sink plug) (2¾" diameter)

21. 1999: sheep's wool (carded), button, ink, and card (1 oz.; 1" diameter; 2" × 2")

22. 2000: paper, Saran Wrap, and pencil (4" × 3")

23. 2001: color Xerox (A4)

24. 2002: candy (jelly beans), paper and ink (approx. 6; 3" × 4")

25. 2003: breadcrumbs, cardboard, and acrylic (approx. 1 tsp.; 7" × 6")

26. 2004: papier mâché (heart shape) (3" × 4½")

27. 2005: paper collage (including recipe card) (6" × 7")

28. 2006: frottage on paper, crayon (3" × 6")

29. 2007: metal (chicken wire) and paper, pencil marks (4" × 4")

30. 2008: cotton (name tag) (1" × ½")

31. 2009: paper and ink, wax (vampire teeth) (2" × 3"; 2½" diameter)

32. 2010: plastic medallion (4" diameter)

33. 2011: paper and ink, and tea bag (3" × 4"; 2½" × 2½")

*

WORKS IN CLAY (PRICES VARY)

1. 1994: *Mojave Desert footsteps*—series of 24 fired clay disks. From Hanafan's first solo show (approx. 19" diameter)
2. *circa* 2011: 9 maquettes for sculptures in stone (approx. 12" × 16½"; 17" × 37"; 62" × 18"; 25½" × 23"; 36" × 19"; 23" × 8"; 2" × 5½"; 4¾" × 8"; 9" × 10")

*

WORKS IN CARDBOARD (DATES UNKNOWN; PRICES VARY)

1. Three-dimensional human torso—interlocking grid form (19" × 60" × 10½")
2. Reconstruction of children's playpen—cardboard and poster paint (52" × 46" × 34")
3. Large bas-relief triptych with acrylic—still life (72¾" × 140" × 4")
4. Self-portrait: three-dimensional face—grid form (approx. 10" diameter × 6¼")

*

WORKS ON PAPER (DATES UNKNOWN; PRICES VARY)

1. *Still Life with Cat*—oil pastel (8" × 12")
2. *Cat and Indian Bedspread*—oil pastel (8" × 12")
3. *Fern and Bottle*—watercolor (8" × 12")
4. *People Pile*—ink (13" × 11")
5. ditto (18" × 12")
6. ditto (14" × 10")
7. ditto (13" × 10")
8. ditto (12" × 10")

9. ditto (9" × 6"—vertical).

10. *Personal Space*—ink (7" × 5")

11. *Odalisque (after Matisse)*—watercolor (10" × 12")

12. ditto

13. ditto

14. ditto

15. ditto

16. *Hunter—Mr. Marriage*—oil bar (8" × 10¼")

17. Drawing for sculpture—charcoal (10" × 12")

18. ditto

19. ditto

20. ditto

21. ditto

22. ditto

23. ditto

24. ditto

25. ditto

26. ditto

27. ditto

28. ditto

29. *Monster Eye*—ink (6" × 8")

30. *Self-portrait*—oil pastel (9" × 10")

*

INSTALLATION

1997: *Primordial Egg*—ready-made and found materials, white emulsion paint, string, metal pulleys (264" × 349" × 349")

*

COZINESS SCULPTURES (A SELECTION)

1. 2001: *Creaky Boat in Maine*—found materials: wooden boat remnants, card, stones, artificial foliage, lighting effects, audio element (approx. 98" × 66" × 53")

2. 2002: *Twilight Snow*—wooden window-frame, oil paint on canvas, lighting effects, audio element (48" × 30" × 6")

3. 2003: *Paris café*—found materials: round metal table and chair, china ashtray, small glass tumbler, audio element (28¾" diameter; 14" diameter; × 38")

4. 2004: *Fall Rain*—wooden window-frame, painted backdrop (acrylic), audio element. (50" × 34" × 9")

5. 2005: *Infant Coziness*—found materials: conglomeration of knit-wear (baby garments), child's building blocks, buttons, plastic toys, wooden spoon, cardboard box (approx. 27" × 29" × 20")

6. 2005: *Period Coziness*—found materials: antique candlestick, clock, inkwell, footstool, doily, teacup and saucer, stuffed cat, chaise longue, paisley shawl, frayed carpet (approx. 86" × 49" × 36")

7. 2005: *Vacation Coziness*—Sand pile, artificial sedge grass, stones, shells, towel, wine bottle, two wine glasses, lighting effects, audio element (240" × 230" × 17")

8. 2007: *Log Cabin in Wisconsin*—found materials: eiderdown quilt, feather mattress and pillows, camp bed, partial banister or balcony, lighting effects, audio element (40" × 48" × 67")

9. 2009: *Spring*—found materials: wood planks suggesting porch, banister portion, rocking chair and cushion, lighting effects, audio element (120" × 65" × 60")

10. 2010: *Fireside*—found materials: table, lamp, chair, book (by Dickens), sherry glass, lace tablecloth, mantelpiece (with imitation fire in fireplace), lighting effects (67" × 72" × 59")

11. 2011: *Mom's Bed*—some found materials: cotton stuffing, woolen bedspread, pillows, oversize wooden bed frame, audio element (96½" × 89½" × 60½")

*

WORKS IN STONE (PRICES VARY)

1. 2011: *Bradbridge's Widow, Wilson's Wife*—plaster reproduction of the original two figures carved in white sandstone (46¾" × 11" × 5"; ditto) (originals not available)

2. 2011: Five untitled works in sandstone (48" × 18" × 12"; 6" × 5" × 5"; 39" × 9" × 5"; 66" × 48" × 17"; 2" × 2" × 4")

All proceeds, minus commission, go to the Bee Hanafan Foundation, which helps women artists by offering them loans and other forms of support.

CACOPHONY

THE MAN OF FEELING:

[Did] you know by what complicated misfortunes she had fallen to that miserable state in which you now behold her, I should have no need of words to excite your compassion. Think, Sir, of what once she was! Would you abandon her to the insults of an unfeeling world…?

The Man of Feeling, by Henry Mackenzie

MELANCHOLY:

I have always carried a large load of melancholy [*un gran sacco di melanconia*] with me. I have no reason for it, but so I am made and so are made all men who feel and who are not altogether stupid.

Giacomo Puccini

What we think is secondhand, what we experience is chaotic, what we are is unclear. We don't have to be ashamed, but we are nothing, and we earn nothing but chaos.

My Prizes, by Thomas Bernhard

COZINESS:

Think how cosy it must be in its nest.

W. H. Auden

HEROES:

This is your farewell kiss, you dog. This is for the widows and children of Iraq!

Muntadhar al-Zaidi

Not like the brazen giant of Greek fame,

With conquering limbs astride from land to land;

Here at our sea-washed, sunset gates shall stand

A mighty woman with a torch, whose flame

Is the imprisoned lightning, and her name

Mother of Exiles. From her beacon-hand

Glows world-wide welcome; her mild eyes command

The air-bridged harbor that twin cities frame.

"Keep, ancient lands, your storied pomp!" cries she

With silent lips. "Give me your tired, your poor,

Your huddled masses yearning to breathe free,

The wretched refuse of your teeming shore,

Send these, the homeless, tempest-tost to me,

I lift my lamp beside the golden door!"

The New Colossus, by Emma Lazarus

But only be good, dear, only be brave, only be kind and true always, and then you will never hurt anyone as long as you live, and you may help many, and the big world may be better because my little

child was born. And that is the best of all... it is better than everything else, that the world should be a little better because one man
has lived—even ever so little better, dearest.

Little Lord Fauntleroy, by Frances Hodgson Burnett

[Each] month the ovum undertakes an extraordinary expedition
through the Fallopian tubes to the uterus, an unseen equivalent of
going down the Mississippi on a raft or over Niagara Falls in a barrel.
Ordinarily too, the ovum travels singly, like Lewis or Clark, in [a]
kind of existential loneliness... One might say that the activity of ova
involves a daring and independence absent, in fact, from the activity
of spermatozoa, which move in jostling masses, swarming out on
signal like a crowd of commuters from the 5:15.

Thinking About Women, by Mary Ellmann

"Business!" cried the Ghost, wringing its hands again. "Mankind
was my business. The common welfare was my business; charity,
mercy, forbearance, and benevolence were, all, my business. The
dealings of my trade were but a drop of water in the comprehensive
ocean of my business!"

A Christmas Carol, by Charles Dickens

I'll just say that I believe—not empirically, alas, but only theoretically—that, for someone who has read a lot of Dickens, to shoot his
like in the name of some idea is more problematic than for someone who has read no Dickens. And I am speaking precisely about
reading Dickens, Sterne, Stendhal, Dostoevsky, Flaubert, Balzac,
Melville, Proust, Musil, and so forth; that is, about literature, not

literacy or education. A literate, educated person, to be sure, is fully capable, after reading this or that political treatise or tract, of killing his like, and even of experiencing, in so doing, a rapture of conviction. Lenin was literate, Stalin was literate, so was Hitler; as for Mao Zedong, he even wrote verse. What all these men had in common, though, was that their hit list was longer than their reading list.

Nobel Lecture, by Joseph Brodsky

MUSIC:

I consider that music is, by its very nature, essentially powerless to *express* anything at all, whether a feeling, an attitude of mind, a psychological mood, a phenomenon of nature, etc. . . . *Expression* has never been an inherent property of music. That is by no means the purpose of its existence.

An Autobiography, by Igor Stravinsky

PUBLIC SPEAKING:

There can be few honours more pleasing to an old boy than to be called upon to speak at his old school. . . [Face] the audience squarely and then commence the peroration.

Speeches and Toasts, by Leslie F. Stemp and Frank Shackleton

Avoid distracting gestures. . .

- *The commander* places her hands on her hips.
- *The chilly presenter* crosses his arms over his chest.
- *The gun-shot victim* clings to her upper arm with one hand.
- *The armless presenter* leaves his hands behind his back.

- *The pocket jingler* puts a hand in her pocket, shaking keys and coins.
- *The clutcher* grasps a pen or pointer and never puts the object down.
- *The slapper* makes noise as he hits his palms against his thighs.
- *The exposed presenter* clasps her hands in front of her, where a "fig leaf" would be.

> *Guide to Presentations*, by Lynn Russell and Mary Munter

DUALISM:

[It] is characteristic of men-values that they set the world apart in sharply divided pairs of opposites, one of which is favoured, and the other not... [This] is like a solar mythic view, since all shadows flee from the sun.... [In] the lunar mythic view, however, which is the more naturally feminine one,... the interplay of the opposites creates wholeness.

> *The Wise Wound*, by Penelope Shuttle and Peter Redgrove

FEMALE PLEASURE:

[The] important question for a male is not: Can I place my sperm inside this female? Rather the crucial question is: Can I persuade this female to use my sperm instead of some other male's?... [The] primary role of the penis is none other than to act as an internal courting device—shaped to provide the vagina with the best possible and reproductively successful stimulation.

> *The Story of V*, by Catherine Blackledge

THE COLONIZATION OF WOMEN:

I don't think about men. I really don't care about them. I'm concerned with women's capacities, which have been infinitely diminished under patriarchy.

Mary Daly

While European cultures continued a peaceful existence and reached a true florescence and sophistication of art and architecture in the 5th millennium B.C., a very different Neolithic culture... emerged in the Volga basin of South Russia... This new force inevitably changed the course of European prehistory. [Its] basic features [included] patriarchy; patrilineality; small-scale agriculture and animal husbandry... the eminent place of the horse in cult; and, of great importance, armaments—bow and arrow, spear, and dagger. These characteristics... stand in opposition to the Old European... peaceful, sedentary culture with highly developed agriculture and with great architectural, sculptural and ceramic traditions.

The Language of the Goddess, by Marija Gimbutas

[Political myths] codify men's consciousness of and violent maintenance of their own sexual-political supremacy which can be sustained only through an endless process of vigilant suppression, exploitation and *ideological deception* of the female sex.

Blood Relations, by Chris Knight

[The] more warlike and authoritarian a society is, the stronger its menstrual taboo... Warlike, aggressive male societies are in rivalry with women over which sex sheds the most sacred blood.

Margaret Mead

[Only] the bad effects of the menstrual cycle have ever been system-atically described.

The Wise Wound, by Penelope Shuttle and Peter Redgrove

I'm convinced that accounts are kept somewhere, that everything is entered on the record somewhere... and the bill will have to be paid. Sooner or later, the time will come. So let us imagine women (that hardly negligible half of humankind, after all), those Baba Yagas... sallying forth to settle the accounts?! For every smack in the face, every rape, every affront, every hurt... widows rising from the ashes where they were burned alive... homeless women, beggar women... women with faces scorched by acid... hundreds of thousands of girls destroyed by AIDs, victims of insane men, paedophiles... the circum-cised women with their vaginas sewn up... the women with silicone breasts and lips, botoxed faces and cloned smiles... the millions of famished women who give birth to famished children...

Baba Yaga Laid an Egg, by Dubravka Ugrešić

MALE NUTTINESS:

People would sooner watch the natural environment collapse than transfer the responsibility of governance from men to women.

Antony Hegarty

[S]ooner or later... we will use up energy supplies, minerals and resources. Current green thinking will just delay the inevitable. Getting off the earth is the only way to make us truly sustainable. Our heavy industries could be moved to the moon, or just put into orbit...

Letter to the paper

Technical in the social situation, sociable in the technical situation? That's the hallmark of a nerd.

Charlie Brooker

WAR:

Politicians who took us to war should have been given the guns and told to settle their differences themselves, instead of organising nothing better than legalised mass murder.

The Last Fighting Tommy, by Harry Patch

This memorial commemorates the 48,000 members of the Commonwealth who died in the campaign in Italy which commenced in June 1943. All these battles were fought at great cost and the total casualties, killed, wounded and missing were 300,000. There are 50 Commonwealth cemeteries in Italy. We of the Italy Star Association do not forget our gallant American, French and Polish comrades, who with other nationalities... fought and died alongside us.

WHEN YOU WALK
THROUGH PEACEFUL
LANES SO GREEN

REMEMBER US AND
THINK WHAT MIGHT
HAVE BEEN

WE DO REMEMBER THEM
Memorial in the Westgate Gardens, Canterbury, Kent

ITEMS FROM THE NEWS:

A single scream, a brutal end: police work to uncover murdered woman's secret
fears

DNA match leads to life sentence for man who raped and strangled girl 26
years ago

Boy, 14, in court over murder of schoolgirl

Gunman shoots girlfriend, then kills four more, in Helsinki attack

Ex-employee arrested for Orlando office shooting

Mother and daughter found murdered

Twelve children die in rampage by gunman

Stalker who killed woman with bolt gun is jailed

Man arrested over woman's murder 14 years after her death

Body of 11-year-old girl found after kidnapping

Killer who murdered woman dog-walker was in "bad mood"

11 bodies and counting... angry families in Cleveland ask why police ignored
their pleas

Dad is guilty of daughter stab murder

Plea to killer to reveal where he hid woman's body

8 years for drunk driver who killed two women

Man murdered partner after argument about Facebook

Girl murdered by her father had hoped to be a doctor

Newlywed admits oar attack

Driver who killed six at Dutch Queen's parade had lost his home in the recession

Husband arrested after car bomb killing

Man crashes plane into US tax office after angry online rant

Millionaire facing ruin shot wife and daughter then killed himself

Yorkshire Ripper asks for limit on sentence

Children filmed before murders: father arrested

Anguish over murder girl

Jilted men behind spate of killings in Italy

Killer of widow gets life

Father who killed son in hotel plunge is cleared by Greek court

Student sportsman accused after ex-girlfriend found dead

Life for killer who battered grandmother to death

Post Office killing—husband arrested

Freed mental patient killed woman in random attack

Father who kicked and punched baby to death gets life

Jilted schoolboy jailed for killing two girls in house fire

"I'm the crossbow cannibal," oddball PhD student tells court

Horror house of death for mother and baby: police name man who killed them

Man linked to missing girl and murder victim

Chef who hid wife's body in trash found guilty of murder

Man in family killing had been arrested over death threats

Ex-boyfriend held after nurse is stabbed to death

"They want it really"—review of police attitudes to rape

Decades of police blunders in murder case: killer could have been stopped

Four killed in China care home attack

Campaign for mother facing death by stoning

Bouncer accused of shooting three people told police, "You aren't taking me seriously"

Bodies of sisters lay by mother: family deep in debt: father killed wife and girls
    and then himself

New Orleans shooting spree—officers charged

Driver shoots 8 dead after being fired

Murder victim had reported her ex-husband to the police four times

Husband killed wife 5 months after wedding

Man kills seven in Bratislava shooting spree

Husband is jailed for ordering machete murder

Murder case jury sees video of attack on baby

Teenager in court over rape of woman found dead

"How could they dump our daughter like trash by the side of the road?"

Youngest Tucson victim laid to rest

Jail for man who strangled wife in front of sons

Officers "too busy" to visit murder scene

Father faces life for murder of daughter, 5

Murders of partners by men rise steeply

Carpenter convicted of gruesome canal murders as police warn of more victims

Family grief over girl whipped to death

Women left widowed by violence

Secret video shows US air crew gunning down Iraqi citizens

Five campaigners for female MP killed in run-up to Afghan polls

Teenager raped five-year-old after being spared jail term

Man pleads guilt for locking nurse in trunk of his car for 10 days

Teenager who attacked woman with bleach gets detention

Football star jailed for sex assault

Pedophile ringleaders get jail for appalling attacks

Teenager remanded over schoolgirl rape on video

Hanged girl bullied for being "too pretty"

Family's fury after daughter murdered by ex-partner who had repeatedly raped her

US death rate for women giving birth declared "scandalous" by Amnesty

Father allowed to rape daughters for 33 years

Fashion under fire as leading photographer is accused of sexually exploiting models

Police officers jailed for being cruel to woman in custody

Landmark US ruling to grant asylum to victims of severe domestic abuse

Stepfather guilty of raping two-year-old girl

School attack motive was "hatred of humanity"

Earthquakes blamed on "immodest" women

Sisters sprayed with acid by men on motorbike

Women's hearts at risk from stress, study shows

Actor advises fan to "cut" ex-girlfriend

BP Deepwater slick now worst oil disaster in US history

Ordeal of Austrian cellar girl to be filmed

Female circumcision continues worldwide

Police hunt after rapist escapes from courtroom

Woman jailed for not testifying against rapist husband

Increases in eating disorders in women over thirty

Reluctance of women to ask for salary increases

Single mother and child, stabbed by ex—child died later

Drama in court as felon shoots woman judge

Woman accused of having "rebellious streak" ate at McDonald's

Speeding police car kills girl, 16

Man battered twin babies to death: "They cried like sheep."

Woman shot in the head for an affair

Man who killed wife and daughter then hanged himself had financial problems

Mel Gibson investigated for domestic violence against former partner

Police officer raped vulnerable women

Man who killed wife with hammer claims "momentary aberration"

Woman spent eighteen years in captivity

Jimmy Carter severs ties with Southern Baptist Convention over misogyny

Police find more bodies in search for serial killer stalking Long Island

TV sets girls up for lifetime of objectification

The gender pay gap starts with allowances: parents give girls less cash to spend
    than boys

Aung San Suu Kyi praised more for beauty than her politics

Police hunt father as bodies discovered in garden

"I feel buried alive," says woman blinded by partner

Female crickets select which sperm fertilizes eggs

MANIFESTO OF THE ODALISQUE REVOLUTION

by
Harrison Hanafan

Table of Contents

1. VIRTUE AND CHEWING GUM

My first rejection of a woman came at birth, when, in a tsunami of bodily fluids, my own and hers, I slid through my mother's brutal confines, folds, and egress. Malehood had begun, and with it, my right to everything in the world:

Apocalypse, assassination, apathy, arson, type A personalities, Asperger's, Adonis, Attila the Hun, athlete's foot, architecture, the Army, the Air Force, the air itself, the alphabet, almanacs, Woody Allen, Aristotle, and the atom bomb.

Bach, Beethoven, Berlioz, boners, barbecues, Bluegrass, business, brothels, bills, bachelor pads, the Boston Strangler, baseball, belching, bestiality, and bubblegum.

Capitalism, computers, confusion, Confucius, currency markets, castration complexes, cars, cheeseburgers, child custody conflicts, charisma, cuckoldry, catastrophe, and the cosmos.

Decisions, diplomas, discord, debate, disapproval, Dickens, Dohnányi, daggers, debt, deception, Dietrich Fischer-Dieskau, duty, deities, duels, dairymaids, drones, and dynamite.

Employment, eminence, edifices, enterprises, euphoniums, Einstein, ethics, entropy, extinctions, economics, equipment, enlistment, executions, education, excellence, and exactitude.

Feasts, fellowship, fraternities, Freud, fraud, firsts, fisticuffs, flatulence, fury, fireworks, flashing, fumbling with your fly, fatherhood, fame, force, fortunes, folly, fantasy, and the future.

Guns, guts, gals, gum, games, god, gall, gallantry, governments, granite, glockenspiels, the Gettysburg Address, gambling, global warming, gynecology, Gershwin, Guantánamo, geometry, Genesis, Giotto, and genocide.

Horror, homicide, heroism, Hitler, harlotry, hostility, hiking, ham sandwiches, hard-ons, hound-dogs, hangovers, hunting, Hemingway, Hollywood, highways, hypochondria, hors d'oeuvres, and heraldry.

Irritation, impotence, the internet, the Ivy League, the Industrial Revolution, ice cubes, ice hockey, institutions, the Infantry, importance, and irresponsibility.

Jesus, jism, Joyce, jail, jests, jealousy, jerking off, Jung, juntas, jalapeños, Jekyll and Hyde, Andrew Jackson, joyriding, jostling for position, jurisprudence, jilting, and self-justification.

Knowledge, know-how, knives, knots, knuckle-dusters, knighthoods, kinky stuff, go-karts, kites, karate, kick-boxing, Kennedy, Buster Keaton, Keats, King Kong, Kierkegaard, and killing.

Law, land, language, life, liberty, liquid lunches, license, luxury, lounge lizardry, logic, laurels, Lancelot, Lolita, learning, leering, Leonardo, Tom Lehrer, and getting laid.

Might, merit, muscles, medals, marching, manliness, appliance manuals, mystery, Marilyn Monroe, Melville, Machiavelli, metallurgy, machines, mountaineering, mischief, monuments, masterpieces, Molotov cocktails, museums, myths, monsters, mothers, mistresses, megalomaniacs, and the Marx Brothers.

Napalm, nations, nightclubs, nightcaps, naughty nurses, nautical talk, nuclear energy, Napoleon, Nabokov, necrophilia, neuroses, thick necks, nonsense, nerdism, and noise.

Oil, ore, onanism, 007, obedience, obligations, opinions, objections, sex objects, oysters, oligarchies, obfuscation, ophthalmology, Old Boy networks, offices, obituaries, and obliteration.

Power, pride, purpose, planets, pricks, prizes, prestige, priapism, pussy, profanity, polygamy, pedagogy, Proust, Puccini, Picasso, pianos, propofol, pulpits, parades, processions, possessions, *Playboy*, the police, policies, police policies, pedantry, pickup trucks, particle physics, poetry, and pointlessness.

Quotations, quotas, quips, quagmires, quandaries, quarterlies, Quasimodo, quarrels, quizzes, quests, string quartets, quarks, and quirks.

Rape, rights, reason, respect, revenge, rules, regulations, Claude Rains, rhetoric, rockets, rifles, razor blades, rumpus rooms, anything risqué, rodeos, rascals, rain checks, ridicule, retaliation, Reagan, rudeness, recollections in tranquility, riots, and radiation.

Superman, Stalin, spunk, smart bombs, sports, statistics, statues, squish mittens, solemnity, stilettos, the Stock Exchange, sadomasochism, soppiness, sloppiness, spy stuff, the space race, science, systems, soapboxes, strategies, satellites, stalagmites, stalactites, success, supremacy, snoring, simultaneous orgasms, and steak.

Terror, torture, trumpet fanfares, tyranny, technology, travel, transvestites, travesties, tragedies, Tolstoy, thrusting, threesomes, theology, *The Thinker*, tomes, toys, the telephone, and tinkering in the basement.

Unlimited mileage, uniforms, the universe, ugliness, underlings, untidiness, unctuousness, *Übermenschen*, underdogs, untold wealth, understanding, uselessness, and uxoriousness.

Vice, virtue, value, VD, vistas, visas, vivas, the vote, verandas, vacations, vessels, valet parking, vapor trails, ventriloquy, Vivaldi, Verdi, Valentino, violin virtuosi, vanity, veneration, vacillation, vixens, victims, vas deferens, and VROOM-VROOM.

War, the world, world wars, wine, women, witches, wealth, worth, winking, wanking, whaling, whittling, whistling, wrestling, weightlifting, wrong, Westerns, Whoppers, Fats Waller, wheat, *Webster's* dictionary, whips, work ethic, arrest warrants, whoring, Walt Whitman, Walt Disney, and free will.

X-rays, ex-girlfriends, exoneration, Xerox machines, Malcolm X, X chromosomes, and xylophones.

Yawning, yearning, yodeling, Yeats, yachts, yawls, Yes men, yens, Ysaÿe, yuck, yellow fever, the Yellow Pages, and yo-yos.

Zippers, zithers, Zen, zirconium oxide, zoning out, zoos, zoom lenses, zucchini and zoot suits.

And I, a trusting little baby!

All my life I have been fed by women, loved by women. They have offered gifts, attention, sincerity—and in return I have ignored, pitied, and patronized them, avoided and forgotten them. I have rejected, neglected, denied, and deprived women. I have lied to them (lied to myself most of all!). I have used women for sex, and recoiled from their corresponding demands on me, which I saw as infringements of my liberty. I have dumped girlfriends without regret, showing no concern whatsoever for their future welfare—not even making sure they got home safely!

And yet, I've always thought of myself as A PRETTY GOOD GUY.

Falling for the notion that you must at all costs Keep The Supremacy, I perfected the ancient habits of malehood: the ability not to listen to women or understand them; the custom of mocking them; the indifference to their problems; and the assumption that women are here to do the shit jobs, and to serve us. Almost unconsciously (I *have* been almost unconscious all my life), I grew to inhabit a position of unspoken authority and superiority over women. And all this, while trying to be "fair" to them.

In my professional life, I have milked my patients' insecurities, encouraging women to focus negatively on their appearance, and misled others into undue preoccupation with "beauty." I have allowed my patients to embark on painful, expensive, and sometimes life-threatening procedures in order, supposedly, to improve their looks. And I have profited financially from this. I made a living out of preop and postop female distress and discontent. Just by participating in the beauty industry, I have pressured women from *afar*. What women need is *less* scrutiny of how they look, not more nose-jobs.

I've contributed to female tensions and difficulties in my personal life too. Yet, until my own sister was *killed* by misogyny, I was convinced there was nothing wrong with our society that couldn't be cured or at least ameliorated by a more socialist democracy, redistribution of wealth through tax cuts for the poor, free health care for all, better laws to protect the environment, universal contraception, and stringent birth control.

Thus, I was a typical American man-child, barely able to wipe my own ass; and behaved as if I was wholly innocent of, rather than wholly complicit in, the violent and degenerate acts of a sexist society.

All my life, there has been a war conducted against women. All my life, I have inadvertently conspired in this war. I admired my arse of an arsonist dad over my splendid, loyal, resourceful, and kindly mama. I felt embarrassed by my sister, merely because she was female, while I condoned and participated in the sexual antics of my friends, merely because they were male.

All my life I have been a witness to a war against women and did nothing about it. This war takes many forms, from direct action like rape, wife-beating and strangling, to the more subtle kinds of attack: plastic surgery, discrimination at work, and a constant barrage of misogynist jibes. All of these tactics are direct and indirect assaults on women, in an ongoing terrorist offensive.

2. ALL MEN ARE TERRORISTS

I am a terrorist. ALL MEN ARE TERRORISTS. The world is run by and for terrorists, in a perpetual atmosphere of male coercion of women through psychological and physical means. It is largely a guerrilla fight, with occasional public skirmishes. Men don't fight out in the open—we fight *dirty*.

The terror and damage inflicted on women by male violence and misogynistic injustice are incalculable. THEY AREN'T SAFE. No woman is safe. The enemy is all around her: in the bedroom, in the boardroom, and on the boob tube. Exultation in terror is reflected in the male propaganda war, a diet of horror movies, thrillers, and crime novels, rap music, porn, and the nonchalant attitude to crimes against women displayed by the news media. These terrorist tactics leave women tainted with disdain, ridicule, and despair; and their doom-ridden position in society is enforced and regularly renewed through physical violence.

WE ALREADY OWN THE WHOLE WORLD, but can't resist kicking the enemy when she's down.

We carry out authorized and unauthorized attacks. Ignoring women is easy, erasing their contributions to the arts, to philosophy, to medicine, science, business and commerce, to history—these are all effortlessly accomplished in an atmosphere already rife with contempt. Through concerted, I would say *Hitlerian,* effort—no stone left unturned, no cruelty shunned—women's place, in culture and in society, has been meticulously obliterated.

The terror campaign is fueled by tradition, religion, misogyny, and mild grievances: women nag, we claim, they stink, they suck, they're nuts, they're sluts, they're always late, they menstruate, they fail, they succeed, they refuse our advances, they *accept* our advances, they swell up with babies for no reason, they can't throw a ball, they let us down. We twist the truth, turn the tables, try to make black white, night day! What wrongs have women possibly done to men that haven't been infinitely exceeded by men in their treatment of women?

We've gone to a lot of trouble to characterize women (mothers and life-givers) as reprehensible, and men (deadbeat dads and death-wielders) as right, or at least forgivable: men smart, women dumb; men creative, women destructive; men artistic geniuses, women lazy and uninspired. A total reversal of the truth! We denigrate women, and besmirch them; and when we can't deny our culpability any longer, we make bad seem good, and blame the victim for the crime. We run rings around them, logically.

It *costs* to be a woman in this society. Financially, emotionally, physically, socially, politically, and *erotically,* they've had to pay up. And boy, have they been nice about it!

Women are killed every day by some man or another, while we yawn and turn to the sports page, telling ourselves it's none of our business. Every day, another rapist gets acquitted, another stalker or wife-beater or child-molester gets off. But these rapes and murders *are* our business! Rapists work for US.

Newspapers use the more sensational cases to sell copies, while the rest get forgotten. But a world in which such crimes come with their own inbuilt triviality is no world for women. A world in which women are disrespected, discounted, and disheartened is also no world for women. In fact, it's no world for anybody!

The terrorist threat to women is severe, CODE RED. It's all around us in this woman-dissing, woman-dismissing world. What woman has not had to hear, almost daily, of violent crimes committed against women? This is terror.

- ☞ Pimps are terrorists.
- ☞ Priests are terrorists.
- ☞ Fashion designers and beauty-mongers are terrorists.
- ☞ Plastic surgeons are terrorists.
- ☞ Employers who underpay women are terrorists.
- ☞ Men who criticize women are terrorists.
- ☞ Men who ignore women are terrorists.
- ☞ Men who get in women's way are terrorists.
- ☞ Men who "innocently" follow women on the street (and terrify them) are terrorists.
- ☞ Men who take up more than their fair share of space in public places are terrorists.
- ☞ Husbands who make unilateral decisions without consulting their wives are terrorists.
- ☞ Male religions are terror tracts.
- ☞ Every teacher who hits a pupil is a terrorist.
- ☞ Every man who rapes a child is a terrorist.
- ☞ Every ass who takes revenge on his wife by killing their kids,

or revenge on his girlfriend by killing her whole family, is a terrorist.

☞ Anybody who takes a gun onto the streets and conducts a murderous rampage is terrorizing *women*—since every single person is born of a woman and probably loved by one.

☞ What woman has not feared for her life at some point when walking alone at night? This is terror.

☞ What woman isn't frightened in general of going out alone? This is terror.

☞ What woman's life has not been sullied, possibly even short-ened, by the unwelcome attentions of egotistical men? This is terror.

☞ What woman has not been *unjustly* deprived of opportunity, approval, appreciation, understanding, peace, quiet, safety, pride, power, wealth, health, and respect? This is terror.

☞ How is the rape of the earth itself, the ignorant and destruc-tive capitalistic exploitation of nature (our air, our water), not part of the terrorist project? All forms of annihilation are ultimately aimed at *women* (as the life-givers). This is terror.

LOOK at the wasted women, LOOK at the wasted earth! We have lauded the male and belittled the female, to our own cost and calamity. Through male greed, cruelty, sadism, insanity, and insouciance, as if in service of some long-forgotten gripe or decree, we have plundered and squandered the earth until there's almost nothing left! We behave as if men *must* rule—but men have proved themselves unfit to do so. ONLY THE DEAD KILL.

The success of male propaganda against women, against life itself, is reflected in our complacency about humanity's imminent disappearance. It's now considered fashionable and sophisticated to be entertained by visions of apocalypse. People behave as if there's some kind of *virtue* in apathy. They resign themselves to radiation leaks, irreversible climate change, bee diseases, nuclear weaponry, and late capitalism's perpetual war... without a qualm! They've hypnotized themselves into believing that the end of the world is not only nigh, but maybe even *bearable*.

Now wait a minute!

Nobody who cares what human beings *are*, what we've *made*, what we've *loved* and striven for, nobody who cares about human thought and art (as well as the arts and loves of *animals*, what about them??), nobody who has noticed how intricate and beautiful the world is, nobody who has studied the wide dark-green leaves and tiny, white, cupped, jiggling, bell-shaped flowers of lilies of the valley... nobody who knows what's REAL and gives a damn what women and children feel, would be content to let the whole damn enterprise—nature, a habitable, inheritable planet, and all of human culture, history, and civilization—go down without a fight! Nobody who gave a damn would let bankers, arms dealers, nuclear industry proponents, oil merchants, and oligarchs—the biggest liars, losers, and crackpots in the world!— nobody who gave a damn would let MEN decide our future.

3. FREE THE ODALISQUES!

Imagine a world where women aren't badgered or beleaguered, a world in which women have what they want and need, and are free to go about their business unmolested. A world in which you don't have to watch your mother, sister, daughter, wife, or girlfriend get stalked and stabbed and shot and swindled and sneered at, you don't have to watch them lose out, run adrift, go nuts.

This would be a better place for *everybody*.

We got it all wrong! The secret of life isn't POWER, it's PLEASURE. *Arbeit* doesn't make us *frei*, pleasure does. The pursuit of pleasure isn't irresponsible, immoral, dishonorable, or self-indulgent. It is a *fact*, and deep in our make-up. It's not a frivolous choice but an inalienable right. Pleasure-seeking is what we're born for, and all the rest— the corporate life, the capitalist life, the misogynist life, the sadistic life, the ignoble self-destructive life of men with their guns and their tanks and their poison gas and their goddam leaf-blowing machines (what a racket we men make!)—all of this is a mistake, a distraction from the pleasure, ease, and comfort we all really want.

The secret of life is life, *not* death, and life at its fullest expression is pleasurable, not painful. Most animals aren't in pain all the time. Even bees seem bent on being happy. The natural state of things is not suffering and mayhem, but peace and contentment. *This* is how you get things done!

Would it be so hard to be fair to women? Would it be so hard to admit that, rather than witches and bitches, women are actually pretty handy members of society, a society that, it just so happens, *belongs* to them as well as us? Would it KILL us to admit that?

After all, their worst ethos is *coziness*. Women want roses and chocolates and puppies and cushions everywhere. So what? They want pleasure: aesthetic, sensual, sexual, and cultural pleasure. Well, they invented these things! Women were the first farmers, the first artists, the first astronomers, the first botanists, the first doctors, the first philosophers, the first parents, the first cooks, the first CIVILIZERS.

It's women who did the cave paintings! Women invented the wheel! (Men reinvented it.) Women needed the wheel to help them push around their cartloads of babies and radishes. Women were the first to harness *fire*. They like to keep warm—is that so bad? It's healthy. It's COZY. And now look at them, careworn and poverty-stricken, trailing home with their bags of groceries beneath the gigantic nuclear power plants men built *without their permission*.

Men just sat on their asses or went hunting for the first two hundred thousand years or more of human history. The only things *we* harnessed were belching, ball games, and bubblegum. And women: that was our breakthrough.

Patriarchy wasn't necessary, inevitable, or desirable, it just happened. Men have conspired ever since in the erasure of prehistory, because it was matriarchal and it makes MEN look bad. Humanity would never have *survived* two hundred thousand years of patriarchy—look at us now, after only *five* thousand years of it. Patriarchy's not a viable long-term option: our devotion to the male death wish has brought us all to our knees.

Women are now slaves (they make quilts!). Until relatively recently, they weren't even allowed to vote. They are still wasting their lives trying to please, posing for us in their bikinis and high heels and doing all the housework. They push strollers uphill like Sisyphus. They bake lasagne, make jam, get their eyebrows threaded, their pubic hair shaped and shifted. Them and their little savings accounts, making do, dying from neglect, winning praise only for pliancy and self-abnegation!

It wasn't always so. Women once ran the show. And life was easy, and fair, and artistic! There was plenty of leisure time for art, music, dance, and other cultural activities. Neolithic people had a four-hour working day! Women, as childbearers, were recognized and valued in a society concerned with life, art, and knowledge, *not* ignorance, *not* beauty contests, bombast, and death. Women's *bodies* and bodily *processes* were valued too.

Then men, bored, restless—envious after thousands of years of menstruation festivities—rose up and insisted on playing things *their* way: war, rape, despotism, empire, carnage, genocide, racism and class divides, pollution, and energy-saving light bulbs. Okay, they also caught fish, built some stuff, created the occasional public park or nature reserve, and developed a few ideas of jurisprudence, but at what cost? The desecration of the air, land, and sea, the ruin of happiness, the ruin of intimacy, the ruin of *sex*.

In a mere five thousand years, men have wrecked life on earth. Thanatossers! Power meant more to them than survival itself. Only the dead kill.

Equality no longer seems enough. What we need is matriarchy.

IT'S ODALISQUE TIME!

4. WE'LL ALL HAVE CHICKEN AND DUMPLINGS WHEN SHE COMES

The odalisques Henri Matisse painted in the 1920s *aren't* slaves. They feel swell, lying around topless in harem pants, taking it easy, basking in the breezes of the South of France: these are post-orgasmic women delighting in sunshine, serenity, and safety. Matisse was a guy with coziness on the brain. His odalisques, as an expression of coziness, are the designated emblems of the Odalisque Revolution.

Ever wondered why women go to such lengths to be attractive?

They want what Matisse's odalisques are having! Joy, comfort, kindness, color, and light. They just want their DUE.

Men have been missing the point about sex for thousands of years. Though obviously necessary and exciting for both genders, sex is not primarily about male pleasure, but female. Biologically speaking, the male animal exists to please the female. The penis is shaped specifically to enhance *female*, not male, orgasms—because pleasing the female is the best way for a male to help ensure his genes get carried on. Rape is rare in nature. Instead, much attention is given by most species (excepting *ducks*, maybe) to courtship, and to the female orgasm. Nature is very keen on female pleasure.

Men have thwarted women's pleasures as a psychological means of hanging onto male power. And, in doing so, we've depressed everybody! Instead of hassling women, we should be humoring them, instead of boring everybody to death with our dreary male desires, fetishes, and fantasies, we should be finding out what *women* want. *Men* should be the sex slaves—they'd love it!

Because, if men are here to please women, we've wasted a lot of time. What a drag, when we could all have been getting laid!

Enough guff, enough rebuff. Enough of feminism and its backlashes. Enough tweaking of the patriarchal setup here and there. It's time to concentrate on making things *monumentally* better for women. We don't *have* to deprive and displease them: it would be more fun to *please* them. A world in which the female orgasm isn't nurtured, celebrated, applauded, and generously sought, is no world for women *or* men.

We don't even know what women are yet—that's lost in the mists and myths of patriarchy. We've been so busy bossing, badmouthing, begrudging, and bullying women, and boosting ourselves, we missed out on buddying up! Missed out on a *lot* of stuff. . .

Imagine a world of proud, content, amorous, sexually satisfied women. No more bored housewives descending into hypochondria, no more irate teachers and belligerent waitresses, inconsolable single moms, hopelessly infatuated secretaries. Ever wonder why teenage girls are (statistically speaking) the most troubled people on the planet? Because they know they are about to have to engage with all this bullshit! They already know they will never be loved, honored, and obeyed enough, they will never even be humored, hugged, and *kissed* enough—and it's *getting them down.*

Enough of men's free-floating contempt for all forms of life. HAIL the much-maligned uxorious man! He had it right all along. This is a man's natural role: devotion! *Not* disdain, *not* disapproval, *not* violence and subjugation. We got everything mixed up and turned around, upside-down, topsy-turvy, back-assward. For centuries we've treated uxoriousness as an oddity, a minority aberration—when in fact it's what men are made for!

5. THE STATUE OF LIBERTY IS A WOMAN

The Statue of Liberty is a woman. Okay! But men can be liberators too. After all, women have done enough. It's time for all good men to come to the aid of the people, time for them to get up off their lazy-boys, and all those fences they've been sitting on, and start reversing some of the damage men before them have done. In Delacroix's *Liberty Leading the People*, there are lots of men lying around at Liberty's feet. Rise up, comrades, and lend a hand with those barricades!

Hand over the power *and* the privilege. Give women respect.

But what bestows respect in our society, besides youth, beauty, street cred, up-to-date computer technology, a talent for learning languages, an in with royalty, and frankincense and myrrh? MONEY. At this point in human interaction, money really counts. Men base their lives, their whole sense of self, on how much dough they make— and they base their contempt for women on how little *they* make, these low-status appendages of ours.

So here's the plan, guys: GIVE WOMEN THE MOOLA.

Next time you're revolted by the bombing of innocent civilians or the torture of prisoners, *give money to women*. Next time you're heartbroken about nuclear plant meltdowns, *give money to women*. Next time you hear about violence against little girls, or the raping of babies, *give money to women*. Turn the tide, man! Give women the freedom to act, and they just might save us. GIVE THEM THE MONEY.

A lot of us don't want to be terrorists, we had terrorism thrust upon us (by our fathers, teachers, priests, and peers). REBEL. Stop degrading women—parade them! Stop demoting them: promote them. Honor and obey, praise, pamper, and pleasure them. THIS IS YOUR NEW JOB (forget the old one!).

We don't even know how much the guilt over our complicity in their suppression has grated on us. But divesting ourselves of power might be a big relief. Then we can get on with helping women repair society. They shouldn't have to do it all alone: they're odalisques! They should take things easy.

So no more pleas of innocence whenever another woman gets garroted and dumped in a trash can, or a girl gets acid thrown in her face by an indignant boyfriend. "What the hell can I do about it?" is no longer an excuse. You *know* what you can do about it: GIVE WOMEN THE MONEY.

Give a woman or women, of your choice, your checkbook, your stocks and shares, your credit cards, your spare change. Give them the land. Give them the parks and the buildings. Give them *the power*. They couldn't do a worse job than we have.

Sure, there are madwomen out there (not just in the attic either, though our literature is full of those!). Women who kill, women who go along with murder, or give their lovers HIV. There was at least one woman who stopped her husband seeing his mother on her death-bed. There are unfair women, unpleasant and conservative women. Let's face it, they're nuts! But *you'd* have a screw loose too if you'd been harassed and disrespected from birth. Women might be a lot less cranky if the world was their oyster.

You get to choose which woman to give your money to; but if each man, throughout his life, transferred the majority of his assets, earnings, property, and wealth to one or more women (or a charity run by and for women), wealth and power would soon be in women's hands. In such an atmosphere of respect, a diminution of violent crimes against women is likely to follow. Eventually, it should become *taboo* to bother a woman. So let's do something right for once: GIVE WOMEN THE MONEY.

This is not a bribe or bargaining ploy —no, the hand-over of money to women entitles you to *nothing* in return. It must be given freely, no strings attached, in acknowledgment of, and recompense for, your voluntary or involuntary participation in the campaign of terror against all women that has gone on for thousands of years. This is one way you can start to make amends.

Enough lip service to women's freedom and equality—just go ahead and empower them! Don't creep up behind them on the street. *Help* them. Give women priority, give them a fair chance, give them the benefit of the doubt. Stop stereotyping them from birth to death. Stop criticizing and complaining about them. Stop glorifying that minute proportion of women chosen to act as examples of womanly perfection to beat other women with. Just *enrich* them all.

And stop taking up all the room on the couch! That couch was made for ODALISQUES.

Enough mother-in-law jokes too, and all the jovial sneers at women. These are the condescending chortles of the slave-owner. Enough fatherly disapproval of daughters. ENOUGH. Dad, you've had your day. Show them you regret their being terrorized, *show* that you don't condone the massacre of women all around us. Show them some *respect*. Stop sitting on your slave-owner ass talking the talk, and put your money where your mouth is: start freeing those slaves, man! GIVE WOMEN THE MOOLA.

I used to scorn the ancient womanly pursuits, like my mother's bottling and baking. A cake, or a jar of jam, seemed feeble and futile efforts to me (compared to my father's hotshot job at a *gum* factory!). I scorned domestic comforts like quilting and cleaning and childcare. I scorned cushions! But I was really just scorning *femaleness*, that half-buried force for good in the world, and those lowly female concerns like life, pleasure, and well-being. I had no respect for them (but I ate the jam!).

GIVE WOMEN THE MONEY. Respect will follow.

During and after the revolution there will no doubt be "pockets of patriarchy" (male tyranny): bankers banking on their banks, toy-boys toying with their toys, farmers who won't hand over the deeds to the land. Vulnerable women, targeted by resentful men, may be persuaded to divert their newfound wealth to them. Don't let this deter you. As with speed limits, you only need the *majority* of people to go along with the idea for it to work. Women will gradually get braver about keeping the cash.

Mayhem isn't amusing anymore; we're all sick of slaughter. The Odalisque Revolution is a last heroic stand against the male death wish. Therefore, its aim is an unobtrusive, undisruptive, nonviolent handover of power. The beauty of the Odalisque Revolution is its gentleness, and its voluntary nature. Giving your money away can be an entirely intimate, intuitive, personal, private, even clandestine, process.

In time, the Odalisque Revolution may be refined to become a truly cooperative redistribution of wealth—not communism perhaps, but *commonism*. Once capitalism, patriarchy, and war have been superseded, women will be free to rethink the entire monetary culture that has ruined life for everybody, and new designs for human happiness may be instigated. *But that's up to them*, not us. All we have to do is clear the way for women to act, and assist them in carrying through their wishes.

Puccini's Rodolfo would have given Mimì all his money (if he'd had any) but in the end, it's *Musetta* who buys Mimì her muff. Let's do something *right* for a change:

GIVE WOMEN THE DOUGH!

6. INSTRUCTIONS TO MEN OF FEELING*

$ GIVE women a chance: *first* chance. Never mind maintaining the "Supremacy."

$ RELINQUISH any lingering sense of superiority over women. It is wholly erroneous.

$ ALLOW women to decide the future.

$ SCORN the mockery of women, the denial of women, the judging of women, and discrimination against them.

$ PRIORITIZE women's welfare, women's concerns, and women's interests.

$ HAND OVER the dough (but without fanfare or self-aggrandizement). Regularly transfer any funds you can muster to a woman or women of your choice, and help any woman you can to acquire *more* money, so as to improve her social status and the status of women generally—any increase in women's status will lead to greater safety for us all.

$ END all war, which has always been used to oppress women.

$ RESIST all impulse to bully, baffle, belittle, and buffalo women.

$ NOMINATE yourself to redress the injustices done to women and all the errors, misconceptions, crimes, and outrages committed in the name of your terrorist organization (patriarchy).

$ OBJECT to being a terrorist and belonging to a terrorist group (men). Your organization has pestered half the human race for thousands of years through violence, coercion, exploitation, and selfishness, helped along by financial, political, religious,

---

* WHEN COMBINED, IN ORDER OF APPEARANCE, THE FIRST LETTERS OF EACH ITEM ABOVE FORM AN APT FINAL INSTRUCTION, DEPENDENT OF COURSE ON THE WOMAN'S CONSENT. (H.H.)

medical, and psychological pressure. It has denied women rights, opportunities, respect, sex, peace, and pleasure. It has even denied them pie!

$ WITHHOLD your critical assessments of women's looks, clothes, plans, aims, snacks, foibles, fripperies, and book choices. THEY ARE NONE OF YOUR BUSINESS.

WARNING: For formal deeds and transfers of assets in the USA you will have to go to the County Clerk's office. Retirement and insurance policies can be transferred only by written arrangement. Gift Tax is an impediment if you are handing money over to your wife. This will be taxable.

The OR (Odalisque Revolution©) takes no responsibility for individual consequences resulting from the policies proposed above such as outrage, affront, altercations, disinheritance, blackmail, family jokes, and jealousies which may result from your reallocation of private funds to a woman or women of your choice. It is up to each man individually to decide how best to accomplish this financial readjustment. Be tactful, and good luck!

ADDITIONAL SUGGESTIONS (TO BE DECIDED UPON BY WOMEN ONLY):

1. The immediate confiscation of all firearms and other assorted weaponry.

2. The automatic confiscation of the financial assets of any man convicted of committing any crime against a woman, women, or children, or violent crime against anyone. (Proceeds to go to women's charities, such as the Bee Hanafan Foundation.)

3. Legal redress in a case of violent attack will no longer

depend on the victim's willingness or ability to press charges. All violence is a crime against *society* as well as the individual: the society can take the perpetrator to court on behalf of the victim.

4. Public and private disparagement of women to be made a crime subject to automatic fines. Likewise, incitement of violence against any person.

5. Reclassification of *all* violence, including war, as a crime against humanity.

6. Reclassification of the nuclear power industry as a crime against humanity.

7. The UN to be made the only body entitled to use force, and *then* only in direct relation to the procurement of peace. (A system of checks (or chicks) would have to be put in place to ensure the UN itself did not become a tyrannical military force set on global tyranny and Esperanto exams.)

8. All investment in defense programs, space programs, genetically modified food, oil exploration and drilling, fracking, strip-mining, and other polluting processes to be diverted to social improvement projects, health care, education, the arts, and environmental repair.

9. Encouragement of childlessness, through government incentives, so as to reverse population growth.

10. Education in female sexuality, and the place of women in history and prehistory, for all! Also, a working knowledge of gardening, first aid, midwifery, weaving, ceramics, painting, sculpture, music, literature, cooking, brewing, and contraception.

11. Non-compulsory sex camp for teenagers.

12. Car manufacture to be phased out. Cars eventually to be banned. Public transport and bicycles to be free. Emergency initiatives to save the environment to be set up.

13. The natural world to be placed under protective orders of all kinds.

14. Donkeys never to have to work again.

15. Everything essential to human health and happiness to be free: air, water, basic foodstuffs, energy, medical care, contraceptives, tampons, Band-Aids, aspirin, etc.

16. A cap on all income, with all further earnings above that level to be diverted to women's charities (such as the Bee Hanafan Foundation).

17. Gradual abolition of TV, porn, pop music, computers, the internet, and other forms of mass hypnosis and enslavement. Also, energy-saving light bulbs.

18. Revision of the calendar to incorporate the lunar month: thirteen months in a year.

19. The abandonment of nations and borders: we are all citizens of the world.

20. Membership of the Odalisque Revolution eventually to be made a compulsory requirement of world citizenship.

* * * * * * * * *

So ends The Manifesto of the Odalisque Revolution.

* * * * * * * * *

O.R. CERTIFICATE
OF MEMBERSHIP

ISSUED BY HARRISON HANAFAN, TEMPORARY ACTING HEAD

THE MEA CULPA DECLARATION

I, the undersigned, confess to having, consciously or not, overtly or not, been part of a worldwide terrorist conspiracy that has constrained women's lives through centuries of violence, repression, distress, and discouragement.

I recognize that this treatment of women has been a ploy in a power game—the result of male cowardice, stupidity, perversity, and corruption—and that the status of men has been artificially exalted by it.

I acknowledge that vast numbers of women have been unfairly treated throughout the period of male rule. I therefore apologize for any tyrannical behavior of my own, and that of other men, and pledge to do my utmost to prevent such injuries, insults, and injustices from occurring ever again.

I apologize for stubborn male resistance over the centuries to women's ideas, thoughts, decisions, and remarks—in the home, at work, in business, in the arts, in education, and in government. In light of this loss of female input over centuries, I now agree to abide by the decisions women make, without resorting to mindless criticisms or meaningless reflex contradictions and derision, no matter how wacko or whimsical the ideas expressed by women may seem to me to be.

I renounce male power and privilege, on the grounds that they were unsportingly won. I wish to relinquish all remaining economic, social, and political advantages I may have obtained, either as a mere consequence of being male, or because of my active participation (now regretted) in misogynist acts of terror, either overt or underground.

In aid of this, I have transferred and/or will transfer, and will continue to transfer, my financial resources to a woman or women, with no strings attached.

By such means, I hope to foster a more humane environment, in which women are less likely to be mistreated and maligned.

It is my hope that the hand-over of power and property to women will ultimately lead to a transformation of society, benefiting people, animals, and the natural world, as well as ensuring a future for human culture, and the preservation and continuation of artistic endeavors.

I believe in the pleasure principle, and therefore renounce the male work ethic as an indecency imposed by men who wished to profit from enslavement and subjugation. I hereby attest the inalienable right of *all* creatures to life, liberty, and the pursuit of happiness.

NAME:

DATE:

NB. To apply for membership, please sign the Mea Culpa Declaration and send it to me, Harrison Hanafan, care of the Publisher, accompanied by a letter of no more than two hundred (200) words, detailing the way or ways in which you have shared your wealth with women. If your letter is deemed satisfactory the certificate will be given the official Odalisque Revolution stamp of approval and returned to you. Please enclose a stamped, self-addressed envelope, and $5.00 (or the equivalent in other currency) to cover costs.*

Display your O.R. Certificate on the wall of your office, or over the fireplace at home! Expensive mugs and T-shirts available (front: "WHAT ARE WE WAITING FOR?" back: "THE ODALISQUE REVOLUTION!" or vice versa). Bumper stickers also (profits to go towards the O.R. cause):

ODALISQUE REVOLUTION
HONK IF YOU'RE IN!

WE'LL ALL HAVE CHICKEN AND DUMPLINGS
WHEN SHE COMES!

(Thank you for your support—H.H.)

---

* if in doubt, just send all your spare cash to Lucy Ellmann, care of the publisher.

Ich habe genung

BWV 82

Fassung in c-Moll für Baß nach der autographen Partitur

ACKNOWLEDGMENTS

The following people have helped me, whether knowingly or not:

John Aberdein, Leila Aboulela, Arlene Addison, Dawn Ades, Pierre-Laurent Aimard, Jason Alexander, Woody Allen, Martin Amis, Malcolm Andrews, Sarah Anthony, Andrew Appleby, Sigrid Appleby, Edward Ardizzone, Michael Aris, Claire Armitstead, Caitrin Armstrong, Andrea Arnold, Aaron Asher, Linda Asher, W. H. Auden, Jane Austen, Johann Sebastian Bach, Emma Bainbridge, Karin Bamborough, Joann Baney, Angela Banner, Sarah Barlow, Roseanne Barr, Cecilia Bartoli, Jayne Baum, Alida Becker, Samuel Beckett, Ludwig van Beethoven, Kathy Belden, Steve Bell, Ludwig Bemelmans, Marina Benjamin, Lauren Berlant, Silvio Berlusconi, Thomas Bernhard, Harriet Bernstein, Leonard Bernstein, Quilly Bevan, Arwen Bird, Catherine Blackledge, Tom Boncza-Tomaszewski, Julia Borossa, Louise Bourgeois, Seàn Bradley, Johannes Brahms, Beth Brandes, Blake Brandes, Rand Brandes, Alfred Brendel, Joseph Brodsky, Maria Brodsky, Charlotte Brontë, Charlie Brooker, Jean de Brunhoff, Bérangère Bruno, Thomas Bruno, Frances Hodgson Burnett, Peter Burnett, Christy Turlington Burns, John Burnside, Jonathan Burt, Neil Butler, Al Byrnes, Katty Byrnes, Lydia Cacho, Brian Cain, Alexander Calder, Chris Calhoun, Joseph Campbell, Rosy Canale, Frank Capra, Sorcha Carey, Mosco Carner, Ruby Carnivale, Catherine Carver, Pablo Casals, Johnny Cash, Brian Catling, Jean-Baptiste-Siméon Chardin, Nick Child, Alistair Chisholm, Winston Churchill, Susannah Clapp, Tom Clark, Barbara Clarke, Jeanne Clegg, Ethan Coen, Joel Coen, Connie Cohen, George Cohen, Paul Cohen, John Collier, Billy Collins, Andrew Conn, Joseph

Conrad, Steve Cook, Geraldine Cooke, J. California Cooper, John Cruikshank, Billy Crystal, Barry Cuda, Effie Currell, Anita Cutting, Mary Daly, Larry David, Bette Davis, Elizabeth Gould Davis, Judy Davis, Sue Deakin, Patrick Deare, Patricia Debney, Arthur DeBoer, Eugène Delacroix, Teresa Delcorso, Sarindar Dhaliwal, Janet Dick, Charles Dickens, Eric John Dingwall, Ernst von Dohnányi, Robert Donat, David Downie, Jelto Drenth, Isla Drever, Jane Drouot, Lindsay Duguid, Carol Dunbar, Grace Durham, Aida Edemariam, Barbara Ehrenreich, John Elderfield, Barbara Ellmann, Carol Ellmann, Claudia Ellmann, Doug Ellmann, Erwin Ellmann, Mary Ellmann, Maud Ellmann, Mike Ellmann, Richard Ellmann, Steff Ellmann, Steve Ellmann, Nora Ephron, Barbara Epstein, Ralph Evans, Susan Evans, Carel Fabritius, Wuzzy Fawdry, W. C. Fields, Craig Fitt, John Fitzpatrick, Carol Flett, Caroline Forbes, Becky Ford, Harrison Ford, Tom Ford, Pat Fox, Rob Fox, César Franck, Helen Frankenthaler, Rena Fredman, Maureen Freely, Christine Froula, Sue Fyvel, Muammar Gaddafi, Nancy Gaffield, Chris Gaggero, Janine Garofola, Emily Gasquoine, Felice Gasquoine, Simon Gasquoine, Marion Gatherer, Giuseppe Giacosa, Paul Giamatti, Sara Gilbert, Marija Gimbutas, Lesley Glaister, Amy Goad, David Godwin, John Golding, Benny Goodman, John Goodman, Dolly Gordon, Rosemary Goring, Steve Gough, Gerard Gould, Glenn Gould, Lawrence Gowing, Francisco Goya, Cary Grant, Kylie Grant, Richard E. Grant, Yvonne Gray, Andrew Greig, Dorothee Grisebach, Simon Groom, Abdulrazak Gurnah, Lucile Hadžihalilović, Ellen Hair, Elizabeth Hardwick, Barbara Hardy, Bridget Harris, Graham Harris, Anjum Hasan, Franz Joseph Haydn, Alfred Hayes, Alethea Hayter, Iris Hayter, Teresa Hayter, William Hayter, Antony Hegarty, Jascha Heifetz, Drue Heinz, Libby Henderson, Paul Henderson, Tilly Henderson, Paul Henreid, Katharine Hepburn, Barbara Hepworth, Billy Higgins, Daniel Hilton, Tim Hilton, Alexa von Hirschberg, Alfred Hitchcock, Jim Hobley, Julia Hobsbaum, Anat Hoffman, Alan Hollinghurst, Bill Hook, Margot Hook, Christine Hooper, Polly Hope, Bob Hughes, Ishtiaq Hussain, Sara Hussain, Leslie Hyde, Luigi Illica, Caithin Ingham, Lyn Innes, Daniel Irvine, Edith Irwin, Michael Jackson, Waldemar Januszczak, Elfriede Jelinek, Derek Johns, Kate Jones, Justine Jordan, James Joyce, Sebastian Junger, Maira Kalman, Ellen Kameny, Fred Kameny, Sasha Katsnelson, Molly Keane, John Keay, Grace Kelly, Samantha Kelly, Stuart Kelly, Andrew Kemp, John F. Kennedy, Leslie Kenton, Graham Keppie, Ian Kerr, Nikita Khrushchev, Phil Kiggell, Ralph Kiggell, Tim Kiggell, Mick Kilgos, Martin Luther King Jr., Richard King, Naomi Klein, Chris Knight, Eric Korn, Peter Kravitz, Stanley Kunitz, Patrick Kurp, Aung San Suu Kyi, Donna Landry, Giles Large, Stephen Large, Philip Larkin, Alan Lash, Emma Lazarus, Louise Leach, Mike Leigh, Chris Lehmann, Jack Lemmon, Leonardo da Vinci, Elizabet Leonskaya, Jon Levi, Stephanie Levi, Alan Linsley, Michelle Lloyd, Julia Louis-Dreyfus, Kristen Lowman, Philippa Lowthorpe, Molly Ludlum, Rod Lurie, Wendy Mack, Henry Mackenzie, Shirley MacLaine, Tam MacPhail, Guy Maddin, Katharina Malecki, Nelson Mandela, Ruth Marcus, Filippo Marinetti, Robin Marsack, Masaccio, Georges Matisse, Henri Matisse, Mio Matsumoto, Walter Matthau, Pam Matthews, Tom Matthews, Ann McClintock, John McClintock, Boone McElroy, Joe McElroy, Dick McEwen, Kirsty McEwen, Patty McEwen, Todd McEwen, Kirsty McLachlan, Catriona McLean, Duncan McLean, Fiona McMorrow, Maureen McWilliams, Margaret Mead, Marion Meade, Herman Melville, Alan Michelson, Peter Mickleburgh, Patrick Millard, Margot Miller, Lionel Miskin, Prue Miskin, Kenji Mizoguchi, Gunnie Moberg, Alfred Molina, Marilyn Monroe, Michael Moore, Barbara Mor, Heather Morgan, Wolfgang Amadeus Mozart, Hugo Muir, Mary Munter, Arunachalam Muruganantham, Vladimir Nabokov, Denise deCaires Narain, R. K. Narayan, Anna Netrebko, Mary Newcomb, Randy Newman, Oscar Niemeyer, Ethan Nosowsky, Clarissa Notley, Barack Obama, Scott O'Dell, Claes Oldenburg, Irene Oppenheim, Jack Oppenheim, Alice Oswald, W. Benton Overstreet, Zac O'Yeah, Anna Pacheco, Kate Parkinson, Li Pasternak Slater, Harry Patch, Luciano Pavarotti, Chris Pavely, Rose Payne, Alistair Peebles, Jacquie Perryman, Makeda Peter, Darryl Pinckney, Ainhoa Pinero, Michael Podro, Mira Pospisil, Kyrill Potapov, Alexandra Pringle, Giacomo Puccini, Kate Pullinger, Sue Purdie, Thomas Puttfarken, Craig Raine, Claude Rains, Sajjad Raza, Peter Redgrove, Christopher Reid, John C. Reilly, Rob Reiner, Rembrandt van Rijn, Auguste Renoir, Jean Renoir, Yasmina Reza, Adrienne Rich, Catherine Richardson, Thelma Ritter, Robin Robertson, Earl Robinson, Chris Rock, Derek Rodger, Jane Rogers, Irma Rombauer, Maurog Romer, Michael Romer, Caroline Rooney, Anya Rosenberg, Catherine Rosenthal, Philip Roth, John Rothery, Lynn Russell, Paul Rust, Meg Ryan, J. D. Salinger, Eric Satie, Wendy Savage, Mark Scearce, Simon Schama, Irv Schenkler, Richard Schiff, Michael Schmidt, Franz Schubert, E. F. Schumacher, Clara Schumann, Robert Schumann, Martin Scofield, Janet Scott, Elzie Segar, Jerry Seinfeld, Richard Selzer, Frank Shackleton, William Shakespeare, Susan Shatto, Sue Shephard, Kate Shiner, Mark Shiner, Raj Shrivastava, Penelope Shuttle, Simone Signoret, Astrid Silins, Neil Simon, Monica Sjöö, Christopher Smart, Fraser Smith, Graham Smith, Luke Smith, Margaret Smith, Rupert Smith, Valerie Solanas, William Soutar, Mike Spells, Alan Spence, Art Spiegelman, Hilary Spurling, Lorin Stein, Leslie F. Stemp, Alan Stewart, Jimmy Stewart, Igor Stravinsky, Meryl Streep, Rick Stroud, Carmel Sunley, David Swinburne, Ingrid Tait, Alan Taylor, Jason deCaires Taylor, Joseph Than, Franny Tietov, Titian,

Leo Tolstoy, Marisa Tomei, Mary Tomlinson, Paul Tortelier, Barbara Trapido, Jeremy Treglown, Saskia Tsushima, Michiko Uchida, Dubravka Ugrešić, Jean Uppman, Ted Uppman, Joe Val, Lindeth Vasey, Giuseppe Verdi, Johannes Vermeer, Louis Verneuil, Rolando Villazon, Paul Violi, Richard Wagner, Fats Waller, Wendy Waller, Sue Walsh, Janet Ware, Jeff Ware, Mary Warnock, Colin Waters, Roderick Watkins, Doc Watson, Alisa Weilerstein, Mae West, Chris White, Peter Wilby, Laura Ingalls Wilder, John Wilkinson, Sara Wilkinson, Nik Williams, Patrick Williams, Helen Wilson, Shena Winter, Glen Wisdom, Joyce Wisdom, Pieter Wispelwey, Tara Womersley, Sarah Wood, Joyce Wray, James Wright, W. B. Yeats, Emily Yoffe, Henny Youngman, Farhan Younis, Harris Yulin, Muhammad Yunus, Muntadhar al-Zaidi, Nicky Zeeman, Kairen Zonena, and others.

The following institutions have also helped me:

archive.org; B & H Dairy, New York; Bärenreiter Kassel, Basel; "Dear Prudence", slate.com; the *East Hampton Star*; Edinburgh Central Library; Edinburgh Royal Infirmary; the farmers' markets of Chicago; Folk Arts Museum, New York; The French Fancies, Edinburgh; the *Guardian*; The Hallmark, New York; Historic Scotland, Orkney; Japonica, New York; John's Pizza, New York; Kelley & Ping, New York; Kent and Canterbury Hospital, Canterbury; literature.org; The Little Owl, New York; The Lyric Diner, New York; Louvre, Paris; luminarium.org; Metropolitan Museum, New York; Metropolitan Opera, New York; Museum of Modern Art, New York; Milady's, New York; National Maritime Museum, Greenwich; the *New York Times*; Nobel Media Archive; the *Orcadian*; The Patio, Edinburgh; The Royal Literary Fund; The Scottish Poetry Library, Edinburgh; The 2nd Avenue Deli, New York; Sinclair Office Supplies, Stromness, Orkney; slate.com; Stromness Books and Prints, Orkney; Stromness Public Library, Orkney; Tankerness House, Kirkwall, Orkney; Thirsty Books; Union Square Market, New York; Victoria and Albert Museum, London; Western General Hospital, Edinburgh; Wikipedia; William Harvey Hospital, Ashford.

People and institutions that have hindered me:

It would be churlish to say.

Cats that have helped me:

Bartholomew, Bathsheba, Beanie, Bubbles (the original), Chuffy, Clodie, Delilah, Equal, Martini, Patch, Piccadilly, Ptolemy, Sam, Mr. Spock, Sushi, Tigger, Trilby.

ACKNOWLEDGMENTS

Dogs that have helped me:

Pierre, Pepito, Taxi, Klara, Poppy, and Dan.

Other pets that have helped me:

Edward, Sesame, Ipsy-pee-dwain.

Stuff I stole:

References to "valentines" reflect the author's own impressions and fantasies based on original works of art by Barbara Ellmann.

The source for the fictional sculpture (called here *Bradbridge's Widow, Wilson's Wife*) is a sculpture called *Alluvia* by Jason deCaires Taylor, positioned, as suggested in this novel, underwater in the River Stour, Canterbury.

Irv Schenkler was the originator of the "sex camp" idea.

Tam MacPhail said, "Don't graduate. Individuate!".

The recipe for Eggnog is based on Irma Rombauer's in *The Joy of Cooking*, with modifications; and the recipe for Amatriciana is based on David Downie's in *Cooking the Roman Way*.

No artist was harmed in the making of this book, but flagrant annexing of J. S. Bach, Giacomo Puccini, Eugène Delacroix, Emma Lazarus, W. B. Yeats, W. H. Auden, Ben Jonson, William Soutar, and various songs, did occur. War memorials, gravestones, newspapers, and films were also quoted.

The depiction of the "museum of folksiness" is not based on any actual folk arts museum in New York or elsewhere; it reflects the characters' skepticism about crafts and textile arts, *not* the author's.

And Matisse really did paint odalisques.

Finally, with love to Todd McEwen, a heroic man. "*We take all the room we need in the sky.*"

L.E., 11/11/11

The author and publishers express their thanks for permission to use images and excerpts from the following copyrighted material:

pp. viii, 19, 57, 183, 206, 237, 264: Suite V—BWV 1011, from Johann Sebastian Bach—Six Suites for violoncello solo. Edited by August Wenzinger, BA 320, pages 42–51. Scores reproduced by kind permission of © Bärenreiter-Verlag Karl Vötterle GmbH & Co. KG, Kassel.

pp. 37 and (in full) pp. 283–284: *The Yellow Ale* from *James Joyce* by Richard Ellmann, 1959. Quoted by kind permission of Oxford University Press, Inc.

pp. 131 and 140: original artwork © Lucy Ellmann.

pp. 209–210: *The Lake Isle of Innisfree* by W. B. Yeats. Quoted by kind permission of A P Watt Ltd on behalf of Gráinne Yeats.

p. 236: *The Lanely Müne* by William Soutar. Quoted by kind permission of the National Library of Scotland and The Soutar Fund (the copyright holders), from: *Into a Room: Selected Poems of William Soutar*, 2000, Argyll Publishing.

p. 281: The B & H restaurant menu is reprinted here by kind permission of Fawzy Abdelwahed.

p. 293: *My Prizes* by Thomas Bernhard, 2010. Quoted by kind permission of Random House, Inc.

p. 294: W. H. Auden quote from *W. H. Auden: A Tribute*, Oliver Sacks (author), Stephen Spender (editor), 1974, 1975. Quoted by kind permission of The Orion Publishing Group, London. © George Weidenfeld and Nicolson Ltd.

p. 295: *Thinking About Women* by © Mary Ellmann, 1968. Quoted by kind permission of Houghton Mifflin Harcourt Publishing Company. All rights reserved.

pp. 295–296: Joseph Brodsky's Nobel Lecture, 1987. Quoted by kind permission of © The Nobel Foundation. Source: nobelprize.org.

p. 296: *An Autobiography* by Igor Stravinsky, 1936. Quoted by kind permission of Oneworld Classics Ltd.

pp. 296–297: *Guide to Presentations*, 3rd Edition, by © Lynn Russell and Mary M. Munter, 2011. Quoted by kind permission of Pearson Education, Inc., Upper Saddle River, New Jersey.

pp. 297 and 299: *The Wise Wound* by Penelope Shuttle and Peter Redgrove, 1978. Quoted by kind permission of David Higham Associates/Marion Boyars, Victor Gollancz.

p. 297: *The Story of V* by © Catherine Blackledge, 2003. Quoted by kind permission of Weidenfeld & Nicolson, a division of the Orion Publishing Group, London.

ACKNOWLEDGMENTS

pp. 298–300: Quotations from Mary Daly, Antony Hegarty and Charlie Brooker were taken, with kind permission, from the *Guardian* newspaper, Guardian News & Media (2011). References to well-known speeches were inspired by Tom Clark's series, 'Great Speeches of the 20th Century', *Guardian,* 2007.

p. 298: *The Language of the Goddess: Unearthing the Hidden Symbols of Western Civilization* by © Marija Gimbutas, 1989. Quoted by kind permission of Thames & Hudson Ltd., London, and HarperCollins Publishers.

p. 298: *Blood Relations* by Chris Knight, 1991. Quoted by kind permission of the author and Yale University Press.

p. 299: *Baba Yaga Laid an Egg* by © Dubravka Ugrešić, 2007. English translation of Part III copyright © 2009 by Mark Thompson. First published in Great Britain by Canongate Books Ltd, 14 High Street, Edinburgh, EH1 1TE. Quoted by kind permission of Canongate and Grove/Atlantic, Inc.

p. 300: *The Last Fighting Tommy* by © Harry Patch, 2007. Quoted by kind permission of Bloomsbury Publishing plc.

p. 305: *Reclining Odalisque* by Henri Matisse, 1923. Museum of Modern Art, New York, © Succession H. Matisse / DACS 2012.

p. 334: *Ich Habe Genug.* Johann Sebastian Bach—Kantaten zu Marienfesten I—BWV 83, 82, 125, 200—Kantaten zu Mariae Reinigung—NBA, Serie I, Band 28, 1, BA 5084, page 77. Edited by Matthias Wendt and Uwe Wolf. Score reproduced by kind permission of © Bärenreiter-Verlag Karl Vötterle GmbH & Co. KG, Kassel.

p. 339: *Away from the Telephone* by © Todd McEwen, *Deliberately Thirsty*, Issue 7, August 2000, and Argyll Publishing. Todd McEwen granted permission to use his poem while he was in the shower.

p. 342: *Rubini in His Great Feat, Beheading a Lady!* (1869.) © The British Library Board.

EGYPTIAN HALL
PICCADILLY.

RUBINI

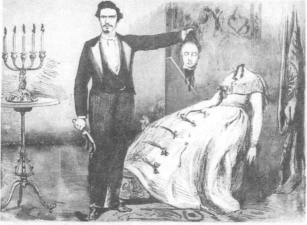

IN HIS GREAT FEAT,

BEHEADING
A LADY!

EVERY EVENING AT 8
WEDNESDAY & SATURDAY at 3 & 8.

ADMISSION, ONE SHILLING

Stalls (numbered and reserved), THREE SHILLINGS.   Balcony, TWO SHILLINGS.

A NOTE ON THE AUTHOR

Born in Illinois, Lucy Ellmann was dragged to England as a teenager. Her first novel, *Sweet Desserts*, won the *Guardian* Fiction Prize. It was followed by *Varying Degrees of Hopelessness, Man or Mango? A Lament, Dot in the Universe* and *Doctors & Nurses*. She now lives in Edinburgh.